Elusive

Kay Hooper

BERKLEY SENSATION, NEW YORK

B

A Berkley Sensation Book
Published by The Berkley Publishing Group
A division of Penguin Group (USA) Inc.
375 Hudson Street
New York, New York 10014

Book design by Kristin del Rosario
Cover design by Rita Frangie
Cover photograph by Marty Heitner

PRINTING HISTORY
Berkley Sensation trade paperback one-volume edition: March 2004
Elusive Dawn: published 1983 by Second Chance at Love; 1993 by Jove Books
On Her Doorstep: published 1986 by Second Chance at Love; 1994 by Jove Books
Return Engagement: published 1982 by Second Chance at Love; 1995 by Jove Books

Library of Congress Cataloging-in-Publication Data

Hooper, Kay.
Elusive / Kay Hooper.
p. cm.
Contents: Elusive dawn—On her doorstep—Return engagement.
ISBN 0-425-19415-9
1. Love stories, American. I. Title.

PS 3558.O587A6 2004
813'.54—dc22   2003067224

Printed in the United States of America

10 9 8 7 6 5 4 3 2 1

Contents

Elusive
Dawn

For Beth . . .
the niece born while
this book was being written.

Chapter One

The party had been going on for nearly an hour, and Robyn was numb from the music and laughter. Vaguely, she wondered where Kris was, and wondered again why she had allowed her cousin to talk her into coming. She had never been very good at parties anyway, and the past year had quite effectively destroyed her ability to laugh.

She was looking around, trying to find her cousin, when a face across the room suddenly caught her attention. It was a hard face in many ways, the planes and angles of it strong and proud, the features roughly hewn and magnetically attractive. And there was something familiar about that face . . . something hauntingly familiar.

The man looked up and saw her just then, his eyes first widening and then narrowing as they took in her slender figure poised as if for flight. Without so much as a word to the other man at his side, he crossed the room in a few long strides, halting before her to stare down into her dazed eyes.

"Hello," he murmured, a peculiar huskiness in his deep voice.

Robyn stared up at him, only dimly realizing that he was taller than she had first supposed, topping her by a head in spite of her high heels. "Hello," she whispered, barely conscious of the people and noise now, feeling that she was drowning in the darkening green pools of his eyes.

"Dance with me."

It wasn't a request, and Robyn didn't even question her own desire to be in this man's arms. The music had changed to a slow, sensuous beat, and she felt it entering her body, keeping pace with her heart and the blood rushing through her veins as he led her out onto the cleared space reserved for dancing. With no attempt to be coy, she drifted into his arms naturally, eagerly, feeling his hands at her waist, his breath stirring the hair piled loosely on top of her head. Their steps matched perfectly.

"You're a little thing," he murmured, his large hands easily spanning her waist. "I could almost put you in my pocket and steal you away from whoever brought you tonight." His voice was still husky, low, and intimate.

Silently, dreamily, Robyn allowed her body to mold itself pliantly to his, her hands moving naturally to his shoulders. Her trembling fingers began to stroke the dark hair on the nape of his neck. She was aware of his hands moving slowly over her back, which was left bare by her shimmering aqua dress. She rested her forehead against his crisp white shirt, feeling a pulse pounding and not sure whether it was hers or his.

"You're not real!" he breathed suddenly, pulling her lower body against him fiercely. Their steps were so slow they were very nearly dancing in place. "I dreamed you. I've always dreamed you."

She wished vaguely that he wouldn't talk, would leave her alone to live in her own dream. She felt so safe, so content in a world where pain and tragedy were unheard of.

"Tell me your name," he commanded softly, and when she didn't respond, one of his hands slid down her arm to the delicate silver identification bracelet on her slender wrist, his thumb toying with the tiny charms and then brushing across the name engraved in flowing script. "Robyn?"

She lifted her head at last, nodding slightly as her eyes met his. The music had changed again to a faster beat, but they continued to dance slowly, completely wrapped up in each other and totally oblivious to anything else.

"Robyn," he murmured, the deep voice turning her name into a caress. "It suits you—something small and fragile." He brushed his lips across her forehead and added, "My name's Shane."

Robyn pushed the information aside. It didn't belong in her dream. But his desire did. She could feel his urgency in the tightening muscles of his strong body, could feel the need he made no effort to hide, and it matched her own need. There was an ache in her body which, she somehow knew, could only be assuaged by this man's touch.

She would lose herself in the dream. For this one night, she would forget everything that had gone before.

She looked up at him through long, thick lashes, and her lips parted in instant response as he bent his head to kiss her. She held nothing back, made no attempt to insist on the slow building of passion that was an ages-old rule in the mating game. She felt his lips moving on hers, at first gentle and then demanding.

He made a soft but rough sound deep in his throat, his eyes gleaming with the hard shine of raw emeralds as he drew back far enough to gaze down at her. "Let's get out of here," he muttered hoarsely. "I want to do more than just hold you in my arms."

Robyn followed as he led her from the room, barely noticing the startled faces of the other guests. She had forgotten her cousin, her eyes fixed intently on the man whose hand she held tightly.

He turned in the entrance hall of the apartment, looking down at her almost impatiently. "Did you have a wrap?"

"No," she murmured. "But my purse . . ." She left him standing there while she went into a small room off the hall and located her handbag. Stepping back into the hall, she suddenly heard her cousin's worried voice.

"Robyn?"

She half pivoted, staring toward the doorway of the den where her cousin stood. Kris's eyes were concerned, a faintly shocked expression gripping her Florida-golden features.

For a moment, a tiny split second, the dream cracked and allowed reality to seep in. But Robyn knew just how brutal reality could be, and she preferred her dream. Waving good-bye and turning her back on her worried cousin, she walked steadily across the hall and put her hand with absolute trust into Shane's.

His eyes flared oddly, and he made another one of those strange, rough sounds under his breath, carrying her hand to his lips briefly before leading her from the apartment.

He put his arm around her in the elevator, holding her close to his side, and Robyn cuddled up to him like a sleepy kitten. She felt safe, at home; nothing else mattered. She only dimly noticed the luxury of the black Porsche he tucked her into a few moments later.

The Miami night was hot, still, almost waiting, just as she waited for them to reach their destination. She half turned on the seat, watching Shane's profile, bemused and bewildered by the strength of her own need. She didn't remember that; it wasn't part of the dream. But then, it had been so long.

He handled the powerful car easily as they crossed the bay into Miami Beach, weaving it among the late-night traffic common in this tourist city of hotels and night spots. At last the car drew to a stop in front of one of the more luxurious hotels, and he got out and came around to open her door even before the doorman could reach them. Again, Robyn put her hand in his with complete trust and assurance, silently following him into the building.

Five minutes later he was closing the door of the penthouse suite, leaning back against it and watching as she wandered into the sunken living room. She looked at the ultra-modern furnishings, the abstracts on the walls, the ocean view from a row of floor-to-ceiling windows. None of it really registered. Only the man did.

She turned to look at him. What was he waiting for? Did he think she expected the ritual drink, casual conversation? That would be a waste of precious time; they had only tonight. With simple directness, she asked, "Do you want me?"

He slowly pushed himself away from the door, walking toward her as if in a daze, the emerald eyes glowing. "Oh, yes," he breathed, halting before her. "I want you very much."

Robyn dropped her purse onto a chair and stepped closer to him, her arms slipping up around his neck. "Then what are you waiting for?" she asked softly.

He caught his breath sharply, bending to swing her into his arms and striding down the short, carpeted hallway to the bedroom. The room was lit only by moonlight when he carried her in, but after setting her gently on her feet, he reached to turn on a lamp on the night table, casting a soft glow over them and the huge bed.

"Do you mind?" he asked huskily. "I want to look at you."

"No," she murmured, surprising herself by adding honestly, "I want to look at you, too."

His eyes darkened to a mysterious shade that Robyn found completely fascinating, and she could only gaze into those pools, lose herself in them, as his head bent slowly toward her.

His lips touched hers lightly, teasingly, feathering gentle kisses from one corner of her mouth to the other. His hands were expertly unfastening the clasp of her dress, sliding the zipper down. The dress slid to the floor with a mere whisper of sound, and

Robyn stood before him clad only in the skimpiest of bras and delicate white panties.

The strange rumble came again from the depths of his chest, and she tried vaguely to identify it as she stared up into his brilliant eyes. The sound reminded her of something, but what? And then she had it: the curious sound was very like the throaty, rumbling purr of a contented lion.

"Undress me," he whispered hoarsely, guiding her hands to the buttons of his shirt. He shrugged from the casual jacket as she willingly complied with the request, her slender fingers moving nimbly from one button to another, her eyes still fixed with almost painful intensity on his face. She pushed the shirt from his broad, tanned shoulders, her fingers lingering for a moment to explore the corded strength of his neck and then sliding slowly down the hair-roughened chest to find the belt riding low on his hips. With unconscious familiarity, she unfastened the belt and then the zipper, pushing the pants down over his narrow hips.

Obviously losing patience with the time-consuming task, he groaned softly and brushed her hands aside, rapidly removing the remainder of his garments. Robyn watched unself-consciously, stepping out of her high-heeled sandals and kicking them aside.

She was astonished at the beauty of his lean body, oddly moved by the tremor of his hands and the naked longing in his eyes. He looked at her the way a starving man might gaze at a feast, she mused to herself, and she was dimly troubled by that. But then he reached out for her again, and she forgot the disturbing image.

His large hands smoothed away her delicate underthings with gentle roughness until at last she stood as nude as he. With a strange catch in his voice, he groaned, "God, but you're beautiful!" One hand rose to cup a small, full breast, his thumb teasing until a nipple rose to taut awareness.

Robyn gasped, her arms sliding up around his neck and her fingers thrusting fiercely into his thick black hair. She needed him so desperately. She rose on tiptoe to fit herself more firmly against the hard length of him. He crushed her to him for a moment, then swept her up and placed her gently on the bed, apparently too impatient to strip away the plush velvet spread.

Robyn didn't mind; she scarcely even noticed. She held out her arms to him as he lowered his weight beside her, and the green eyes flared again with some fleeting emotion she didn't try to identify. Green . . . his eyes were green. It was a jarring note in her dream. She closed her own eyes and made his blue.

She felt his fingers in her hair, releasing the pins and smoothing the waist-length silky mass over the velvet-covered pillows.

"A siren," he rasped, a peculiar shivering moan in his deep voice. "A raven-haired witch." His lips lowered to drop hot kisses on first one breast and then the other, teasing and tormenting each throbbing nipple in turn. "Such a tiny witch to possess such power . . ."

"Power?" she asked throatily, her fingers kneading his muscle-padded shoulders, her eyes flickering open in curiosity.

He laughed huskily, lifting his head to stare down at her with green flames in his eyes. "Power," he confirmed softly. "Don't you know, sweet witch, what you do to me? Can't you feel the fire in me—the fire you started? The fire only you can extinguish?"

Robyn trailed one hand down his back, letting him feel the gentle scratch of her long nails, and experiencing, indeed, a strange sense of power when he shuddered and groaned. "Am I putting out the fire?" she teased softly, watching the flames in his green eyes leap even higher.

"No!" he grated, lowering his face to her throat and pressing feverish kisses on the soft, scented flesh there. His hands moved over her body urgently, possessively. "Oh, Robyn, love, I need you so badly! Go on touching me, sweetheart—don't ever stop!"

Robyn wondered briefly at the endearments, then decided that they fit her dream very well. Eagerly, she explored his body, entranced by the strength and heat of his desire. She moaned raggedly as his own fingers searched and probed, finding at last the heart of her quivering need and causing her body to arch almost convulsively against him.

She gasped aloud, dizzily aware of his erotic touch, of the exquisite tension filling her body, her consciousness. "Oh, please, Sh–Shane!" The name rose to her lips uncertainly, her voice trembling with intolerable desire.

With a low growl of answering male need, Shane rose above her, slipping between her trembling thighs and allowing her to feel his heavy weight for the first time. He came to her then. Came to her as though he intended to make her his for all time.

Robyn clung to him, moving with him, staggered by the feelings ripping through her body. The tension built higher and higher, an avid, primitive craving for satisfaction. She was keenly aware of his taut face above her, of digging her nails into his shoulders, and of pleading with him in an unfamiliar, drugged voice.

Then there was an eternal moment of shattering rapture, and she heard him groan her name hoarsely even as she cried out with the force of her release.

Silence reigned in the room for a long time as they lay in an exhausted tangle of arms and legs, hearts gradually returning to normal and breathing losing its ragged edge. It was Shane who finally broke the silence, and there was an unexpected spark of humor in his deep voice.

"Shall we get under the covers, or would you rather freeze in the air-conditioning?"

Robyn giggled sleepily. She was still firmly enmeshed in her dream, and she welcomed the humor that allowed her to resist reality a while longer.

"I gather that means you're leaving it up to me!" He gave a smothered laugh and then went through a series of complicated maneuvers designed to get them both under the covers without his losing his possessive hold on her.

By the time the feat was accomplished, Robyn was giggling even more. Shane drew her firmly into his arms, pulling the covers up around them and then reaching to turn off the lamp. "Don't laugh, witch—next time, I'll make *you* get the covers!" he warned with a deep chuckle.

Robyn snuggled up to him contentedly, feeling his hands stroking her long hair gently, his arms holding her tightly. Oh, God, it had been so long since she'd gone to sleep in a man's arms! If she pushed the dream a bit farther, she could almost believe . . .

"Robyn?"

"Ummm?" she murmured, her voice muffled against the warm flesh of his throat.

"We've skipped a few stops along the way; you realize that, don't you? We're going to have to talk in the morning."

"Ummm," she responded, determined to keep reality at bay just a bit longer.

He laughed softly and drew her even closer. "Go to sleep, honey," he murmured.

Robyn did just that, lulled by the steady sound of his heart beating, the curiously familiar warmth of his hard body against the softness of hers.

She woke in the gray morning hours, immediately aware of what had happened the night before and still reluctant to end her dream. But she had no choice. If she remained with this man . . . She moved cautiously to free herself from his loosened embrace, holding her breath when he muttered something and then turned his face into her pillow. Still cautious, she eased from the bed and dressed quickly in the aqua dress, her gaze turning again and again to the man sleeping in the huge bed.

Dressed, and aware of the lightening sky over the ocean, she still hesitated, staring at Shane. "Thank you," she breathed to the sleeping man. "You made me feel alive again. But I can't stay. It's better this way . . . a beautiful night to remember."

She didn't feel the least bit odd in standing there speaking softly to a sleeping man in a room filling with dawn light. She felt that she had to voice her thoughts. It seemed a fitting ending, somehow, to her dream.

"I only wish . . ."

The wistful whisper died away before she could form the thought fully in her own mind, and she was glad. Wishes too often didn't come true, and she wanted nothing to spoil the memory of her dream.

She slipped silently from the bedroom after a last, lingering glance at the man in the bed, retrieved her purse from the living room, and then left the suite. Her dress whispered softly around her ankles as she walked briskly to the elevator.

She found a cab outside the hotel and climbed in, giving the driver her address and then sitting back for the long ride across the bay. She realized absently that her hair was still loose, mussed from Shane's fingers, but she didn't bother doing anything about it.

The sun was hanging low in the eastern sky when her cab at last drew into the drive of her secluded home a few miles south of Miami. She paid the driver and watched him leave, then turned her gaze to the sprawling, Spanish-style house with its tile roof and mellow, sand-colored stucco finish. High hedges provided privacy, and tropical plants gave the place the look of someone's idea of paradise.

Abruptly, Robyn realized that the place was far too large for just one person—well, two, counting Marty. And, really, it wasn't as if it contained a lot of memories. She and Brian had traveled so much during that year; they had rarely been home, and never for very long.

She slowly moved up the walk, fishing her keys from her purse and silently questioning her decision to keep the house. Why not sell it and move somewhere else? Somewhere with definite seasons—snow up to her eyebrows in the winter! If it weren't for her store . . . Well, she could have another store, couldn't she?

Still arguing with herself, Robyn aimed the key at the lock, but it never quite connected. The door was pulled open suddenly, and a middle-aged woman with graying hair and a fierce frown on her face regarded Robyn sternly.

"So, you're finally home," she announced with awful politeness. "And just where have you *been* all night, Miss Robyn? Miss Kristina came by after that party last night and waited here for three hours; she was very upset with you!"

"And you aren't?" Robyn murmured dryly, stepping inside and closing the door firmly behind herself.

The older woman gave a sniff of disdain as she stared at Robyn's rumpled dress and loose hair. "Coming in with the sun and looking like something the cat dragged in!"

"That's enough, Marty," Robyn said mildly.

She was ignored. The older woman followed her into the bright, sunny den, still scolding. "Leaving the party like that and causing poor Miss Kristina to worry! Not to mention me!"

"Let's do mention you!" Robyn dropped her purse onto the couch and turned with a militant lift of her chin. "I seem to remember someone pestering me to get out of this house once in a while. I even remember at least one distinctly pious wish that I *would* come in with the morning sun!" She glared at the woman who had practically raised her, a challenge in her stance.

Marty maintained her affronted expression for a full minute, then smiled suddenly, her face assuming its usual cheerful look. "So I did," she chuckled. "And it's about time, too! You've been brooding too long, Miss Robyn. There's a time when grieving has to stop. You're too young to bury yourself with Mr. Brian."

Robyn smiled slightly. "I finally let him go, Marty," she confided quietly. "Last night. Even the guilt is gone."

Marty shook her head. "You should never have felt guilt, anyway! You couldn't have stopped Mr. Brian—that day or any other. He was a reckless man; you knew that when you married him."

Robyn shrugged vaguely. "I knew. But . . . Oh, never mind! If you're through fussing, I'd like to have breakfast. I'm starving!"

Her housekeeper and general mother-hen opened her mouth to comment, then apparently thought better of it. Muttering to herself, Marty headed for the kitchen.

Two hours later, refreshed by a shower and breakfast, Robyn lounged by her pool in a brief bikini and blinked like a contented cat at the shimmering blue water. Her thoughts turned to the night before, and she wondered dimly if Shane would be disappointed to wake and find her gone. Probably not. From the look of him, he could certainly have any woman he wanted—and he probably had! One more or less wouldn't matter to him.

Oddly enough, that thought hurt.

"Robyn!"

She turned her head, staring at her cousin who was approaching with a strange look on her face. Robyn felt a flicker of amusement at that look, wondering if Kris would scold her or commend her.

"I nearly died!" Kris exclaimed, her long, graceful body collapsing onto the twin lounge beside Robyn's. "For you to just leave like that—and with Shane Justice, of all people!"

Something tapped at the back of Robyn's mind when she heard his last name, but she ignored it. "Something special about Shane Justice?" she inquired, putting on her sunglasses to hide the intense curiosity she felt. "What . . . is he married?" Sudden dread gripped her even as she haltingly voiced the thought.

"Not that I know of." Kris waved a hand in a vague, bewildered gesture. "But, Robyn—*Shane Justice!*"

Robyn pulled the sunglasses down her nose and peered at her cousin over the top of them. "So?" she questioned blankly.

"You really don't know, do you?" Kris took a deep breath, then said carefully, "Robyn . . . Shane Justice races. Stock cars. Like Brian did."

Chapter Two

For an eternal moment, *Robyn continued to stare blankly at her cousin.* Then she laughed, a strained laugh, just a whisper away from hysteria. "Isn't that ironic," she said very quietly, a statement rather than a question.

"You really didn't know." It wasn't a question either.

"Do you think I would have left with him if I had?" Robyn tossed the sunglasses onto a table between the lounges. "I swore— *swore*—after Brian was killed that I'd never have anything to do with a man who raced! I must have built-in radar where they're concerned," she went on bitterly. "I'll bet he was the only man there who raced, so of course I had to pick him to—"

"To?" Kris prompted when her cousin broke off abruptly. "Robyn . . . did you . . . ?"

"I did," Robyn confirmed dully, her earlier contentment vanishing as though it had never been. "There was just something about him. I guess he reminded me of Brian, and I thought . . . oh, hell, I don't know what I thought! Nothing intelligent, obviously."

Kris smiled suddenly, her blue eyes showing an unexpected flash of humor. "Oh, I don't know about that! You're certainly looking better than you did this time yesterday. It was just an . . . unusual thing for you to do. Going off with a virtual stranger, I mean. Why, Brian courted you for six months before you were engaged, and I'm willing to bet you didn't sleep with him the whole time!"

Accustomed to her cousin's cheerfully blunt manner, Robyn only smiled wryly. "Maybe I'd had too much to drink," she murmured, trying to rationalize her behavior of the night before.

"Not a chance! You had one drink—a screwdriver, if I remember correctly—and nursed it for nearly an hour. You'll have to come up with a better excuse than that!" She lifted a questioning brow. "Couldn't be love at first sight, could it? It's hardly in character for you to tumble after a single glance!"

"Hardly," Robyn agreed, staring out over the water. "I don't want to fall in love, Kris!" she blurted. "Especially not with a man who races. Life's too short to watch someone you love risk death on a whim."

Kris was silent for a moment, then said dryly, "My feminist friends would kill me for saying this, but you need a man, Robyn. You're the type of woman who'll never be happy living alone. You should have a husband. And kids."

"Maybe I will one day." Determined to change the subject, Robyn spoke in a light voice. "But that husband definitely will *not* be Shane Justice, or anyone like him! He'll be a comfortable, sedate man, with a nine-to-five job and a safe hobby—collecting stamps or something."

Kris gave a crow of laughter. "You'd be bored to tears in a month!" she announced. "Robyn, sweetie, you're just not a comfortable sort of woman!"

"Thanks!" Robyn muttered tartly.

"Well, it's true. You've been in limbo for the past year, ever since Brian was killed. And heaven knows you were nearly out of your mind with terror for him during the year you were married. But your personality is a far cry from 'sedate and comfortable'! You have a temper, for one thing, and you're too damn impulsive for your own good!"

"I am *not* too impulsive!" Robyn defended herself irritably.

"Oh, no?" Kris lifted a mocking brow. "And I suppose last night's decision to leave a party with a man you'd just met, and subsequently spend the night with him, was a carefully thought-out plan?"

A flush crept up into Robyn's cheeks. "I'm twenty-seven years old," she snapped, "and certainly entitled to do whatever I like! If I wanted to spend the night with Shane Justice, then it's my own business."

"Sweetie, I'm not arguing with that." Kris's lovely face brightened suddenly. "In fact, I'm glad you met him! You need the strong, masterful type, and, from what I hear, he's certainly that! But if you're going to see him again—"

"I'm not," Robyn interrupted firmly. She thought again of the night before and shivered slightly. "I'll admit to a certain amount of . . . attraction, but I'm not about to get involved with a man who's so utterly careless with his own life that he looks for ways to risk it! Shane doesn't even know my last name, so—"

"Maybe not," Kris interjected, a certain satisfaction in her voice, "but he's trying his best to find out."

"What?" Robyn asked uneasily.

Kris grinned and settled back in her lounge. "The phone caught me just as I was leaving my place," she explained cheerfully. "It was Tony—the host of last night's party, remember? Anyway, he sounded very rattled, and he demanded to know my cousin's last name. He complained that I'd introduced you simply as 'my cousin Robyn.' Naturally, I wanted to know *why* he wanted your last name."

"And?" Robyn prompted.

"And," Kris continued obligingly, "he told me that he'd been disturbed at the crack of dawn by a call from Shane Justice, who demanded to know your last name. Tony was so unwise as to ask why Shane hadn't gotten it last night after he left the party with you; he practically got his head bitten off. I gather that Shane can be quite intimidating when he chooses. Anyway, Tony promised to make a few calls and then get back to him. He called me."

"You didn't tell him, did you?" Robyn asked, horrified.

"No, of course not," Kris said soothingly. "I promised to get back to him after I talked to you. I figured that if Shane didn't know your name, you might not want him to know."

"I don't!"

"Then I won't tell Tony. But I have to warn you, sweetie—if Shane is as determined as I think he is, he'll get everything he can out of Tony. And that means *my* name. What am I supposed to say if he comes knocking at my door?"

Robyn chewed on her thumbnail for a moment. "Tell him—tell him that I was just visiting, and that I've gone home. And make *home* as far away as you can."

Kris giggled. "You know, you're displaying an unholy amount of panic, Robyn. Why? You can always say no if he asks you out! You're not afraid of him, are you?" she asked solicitously.

"Don't be ridiculous; of course I'm not afraid of him." Robyn wasn't about to confess that what she was afraid of were her own feelings. She wanted to see Shane Justice again, and that realization scared her to death. "He'll forget about me soon and race on to whatever's next on the circuit!" she finished bitterly.

"Daytona," Kris murmured soberly. "Tony mentioned that Shane was in Florida for the race. Apparently, he had some business to take care of here in Miami first."

Robyn tried to ignore the information, but her mental calendar automatically registered that the Daytona race was only two weeks away. "There should be no problem; I can avoid him until then," she said calmly.

"I don't know." Her cousin looked at her a little doubtfully. "I've known Tony for five years, and I've never heard him so completely flustered. And it wasn't just a case of morning-after-the-night-before, either. Shane really shook him up. He wants to find you, sweetie—and very badly, I should think. What did you do—put a spell on him?"

Unwillingly, Robyn remembered a deep, husky voice calling her "sweet witch." And "honey," and "sweetheart." Fiercely, she shoved the recollection aside. "He'll forget about me," she repeated stubbornly.

"And what about you?" Kris smiled faintly. "Will you forget about him?"

"He's forgotten," Robyn replied lightly, lying and knowing it. She hopped up from the lounge, determined to change the subject. "I'm going to get dressed and go shopping. Are you game?"

"When have I ever refused shopping?" Kris laughed and rose also, apparently realizing that the subject was closed.

It remained closed for the rest of the weekend. Robyn refused to allow herself to brood about Shane Justice, and she busied herself almost frantically in order to avoid it.

After shopping, she and Kris went horseback riding and then ended up teaching two beginners' classes as a favor to the stable owner, who was a friend of theirs. Although her cousin's students seemed to have grasped the basics, Robyn had to spend over an hour showing her small group the correct way to fall off a horse. One six-year-old in particular won her heart with his fierce determination to master the art, keeping the rest of the pupils in stitches as he gently slid beneath the patient horse's belly again and again.

Sunday was traditionally Robyn's day to help with the housework and washing. Because that didn't keep her as busy as she wanted to be, she also rearranged her bedroom and re-lined the kitchen cabinets.

If Marty thought the unusual burst of energy odd, she said nothing about it. Robyn was too tired on Saturday and Sunday nights to do more than tumble into bed in exhaustion. But she dreamed of eyes of green flame, and a deep, husky voice . . .

Kris called early Monday morning, waking Robyn from her dream-haunted sleep. Robyn rolled over in bed and fumbled for the receiver, mumbling, "What?" when she managed to get it to her ear.

"He came. Last night."

"Who came?" Robyn forced her reluctant eyes open.

"Shane Justice." Kris sounded disgustingly bright-eyed and bushy-tailed. "He offered me everything but an illegal bribe to tell him your last name."

Sitting bolt upright in bed, Robyn awoke with a vengeance. "You didn't tell him?" she wailed.

"Of course not," Kris laughed. "But the man could probably charm a rattlesnake. As it was, I had to keep repeating the multiplication tables in my head in order to maintain control over my own mind."

"Funny," Robyn muttered.

"I thought so." Kris laughed again, cheerfully wished her cousin a good day, and hung up.

Dragging herself from bed, Robyn thoughtfully dressed for work, wondering when Shane would lose patience and give up. Soon, she hoped. She reached into her jewelry box, removed her plain gold wedding band, and slipped it onto her finger. At Marty's insistence she'd finally stopped wearing it to social events, but she was grateful for its repressive effect on her store's male customers.

Moments later, she was driving her small economy car toward the city, wryly remembering Marty's stern command to eat something filling for lunch. She hadn't had much of an appetite during the past year, but then she'd never really been a big eater. She never, much to Kris's loud envy, gained an ounce.

Arriving at her bookstore, she parked her car and went inside, discovering that her assistant, Janie, had already opened up and was busy with several early customers. Placing her purse behind the counter, she began her own work, putting everything else out of her mind.

The morning was hectic, and it was well after noon when things finally quieted down. Glancing sympathetically at her flushed and weary-looking assistant, Robyn grinned. "Okay, Janie, go ahead to lunch. But don't go too far; if I scream hysterically, you have to be near enough to come running!"

"What is it with today?" Janie demanded, leaning against the counter for a moment to recoup her strength. "Is there a blizzard forecast, or what? I've never seen so many people desperately in need of something to read!"

"Beats me, but don't knock it. And get going, before I change my mind and—" Her blonde assistant snatched up her purse and made a mad dash for the door, in so much of a hurry that she nearly collided with the tall red-baked man who was just then coming in.

Holding several books in her arms, Robyn started toward the new customer, feeling a fleeting sense of where-have-I-seen-you-before. "Good afternoon," she said pleasantly. "May I help you?"

His light blue eyes held a peculiar expression as they swept from the smooth coronet of raven hair braided atop her head down over her entire figure, clothed in a casual sundress.

Irritated, Robyn repeated a bit dryly, "May I help you?"

"Um, I'm looking for a book," he announced.

Robyn glanced around at her large store, filled wall-to-wall and floor-to-ceiling with books, and then looked back at the customer. "Well, you've come to the right place," she said, and she watched the tips of his ears redden.

"A book about, uh, about witchcraft!" he elaborated almost defiantly.

Choking back a giggle, Robyn pointed toward a corner of the store. "The occult books are in that section." Odd, she thought, he didn't look the type to be interested in the occult. Well, you never knew these days.

The customer wandered toward the section she'd indicated, and Robyn went back to work, sensing his eyes on her occasionally but ignoring him. He came over to the desk a few minutes later and placed a book on the wooden surface. Scanning the title as she picked up the volume, Robyn shot a faintly amused glance at the man.

"Do you participate in seances?" she asked politely.

He started visibly, confirming her suspicion that he'd simply selected a book at random. "Oh, uh, a friend of mine is. The book's a gift," he explained rather lamely.

Still amused, Robyn rang up the purchase and gave him his change and the book. "Hope your friend enjoys the book."

"I'm sure she will. Thank you, Miss—?" He lifted an eyebrow inquiringly.

"Lee," Robyn supplied calmly, pointedly placing her left hand on the countertop. "Robyn Lee."

His eyes dropped to her hand and widened in surprise. Without another word, he turned on his heel and left the store.

Robyn wondered about his abrupt departure but shrugged it off. When Janie returned, Robyn took a break herself, ducking around the corner to a small Italian restaurant she favored. After a quiet lunch, she returned to find the store fairly calm, so she went into the back room to review the account books.

Janie poked her head in a few minutes later. "Robyn, someone to see you."

Robyn look up, frowning. "Who is it?"

"Never seen him before." Janie grinned. "But if I weren't married . . . !"

Robyn rose from her small desk, groaning, "It's probably a salesman. They're always good-looking. And that radio station's been pestering me to advertise."

"Well, this guy could sell rocks!" Janie grinned again and headed back into the store.

Sighing, Robyn stepped out of the office and looked toward the front counter. And froze. Of all the thoughts tumbling through her head right then, the only clear one was a panicked, *How did he find me?*

Shane spotted her immediately and began crossing the room toward her. That he was upset was obvious; there was a curious tautness about his lean body, and his face was masklike in its total lack of expression. He halted barely an arm's reach away from her and stood there, staring. She thought she saw relief shine briefly in the emerald eyes—relief and something else, something she couldn't read—but the fleeting expression was quickly gone, leaving only the reflective glow of cut emeralds.

"Hello, Robyn," he greeted quietly.

She felt again that instant attraction, the magnetic pull stronger than anything she had ever known. The sensation frightened her; it was too intense to be real. "H–hello, Shane," she got out weakly.

"You left without saying good-bye."

Robyn gazed up at him uncertainly, puzzled by his voice. He almost sounded as if he were in pain. Nervously clasping her fingers together in front of her, she murmured, "I thought it would be best."

"Why?"

The one word was stark, oddly raw. She had the sudden, insane impression that he was struggling against reaching out and touching her. The impression was so unreasonably strong that she took an instinctive step backward, blinking in bewilderment. Almost immediately, though, she took a firm grip on her imagination.

"Because . . ." Her voice trailed away as she tried to come up with a logical reason for leaving him without a word. The truth? That she didn't believe in magic, or in anything that was too perfect to be real? That fairy tales happened in fiction but not in fact?

"Dammit, why didn't you tell me?" he rasped suddenly, barely louder than a whisper. "I would have understood, Robyn. People make mistakes. You aren't the type to hop into bed with a stranger just because your marriage went sour; I would have known that. You didn't have to creep away as if you were ashamed of what happened between us! It was special—"

"It wasn't real!" she blurted out suddenly, looking down at the gleaming gold band on her left hand.

Surprisingly, Shane seemed to understand at least a part of what she meant. "It *was* like a dream," he agreed huskily, a faintly twisted smile softening the tautness of his face as she looked up at him. "And we both felt that. But it was right, Robyn, and you know that as well as I do." He hesitated, then began slowly, "Your husband—"

"Is dead," she interrupted, unable to allow him to go on thinking she had broken her marriage vows. "I'm a widow."

"Then . . ." He stepped toward her quickly, unhidden eagerness leaping into his eyes.

Startled, she said hurriedly, "But I don't want to get involved with you, Shane!" She watched the flame in his eyes die and a baffled expression replace it.

"Why not?" he asked very quietly.

Robyn bit her lip and again sought reasons. Very conscious of customers moving about in the store, and unwilling to go into a long explanation of her fear of racing, she avoided the subject entirely. "Just let it end, Shane, please," she murmured.

"After a night of heaven? I'm a lot of things, honey, but a fool isn't one of them." His voice was steady.

Desperately, she tried to explain a situation that made no sense, even to herself. "It wasn't *me*; don't you understand? Something happened and—and I don't know what it was! I'm not used to drinking; maybe that was it."

"No." His voice remained steady, the emerald eyes searching her face intently. "You weren't drunk. Robyn, what does it matter *why* it happened? We looked at each other and—"

"It matters!" she cut him off abruptly, afraid of what he might have said. "I've never done anything like that before."

"You don't have to tell me that," he said softly.

"You can't know," she managed unsteadily.

"Can't I?" He smiled slowly, something she didn't understand flaring in his eyes.

For a moment, she felt an almost overpowering impulse to give herself to the magic and let it take her where it would, as it had on Friday night. But she mastered the reckless desire, firmly reminding herself of Shane's racing.

"I don't want to get involved with you," she said flatly.

His smile faded. With obviously forced lightness, he asked, "Is it my breath, or what?"

"Don't be ridiculous." To her astonishment, Robyn found herself choking back a laugh.

"That's better." Clearly approving of the airier atmosphere, he smiled again. "If it isn't my breath," he went on solemnly, "it must be something worse. You don't like the way I dress?"

Beginning to enjoy the exchange, despite the inner voice warning her that every passing moment was involving her more and more with this man, she eyed him consideringly. "You look very nice," she said politely after looking over his slacks and sport shirt.

"Thank you." He inclined his head gravely. "Let's see . . . Green eyes bother you? I'm told mine are a bit startling."

"To say the least," she murmured, thinking of the curious vividness of his eyes. "No, green eyes don't bother me."

"Not that either, huh? Well . . . You don't like my hair?"

"It's a bit shaggy," she pointed out.

"I'll get it cut," he promptly offered.

An uncomfortably clear vision of herself twining her fingers in that dark, slightly shaggy hair flashed through her mind. "No," she muttered. "No, don't get it cut."

"Whatever the lady wants."

The vision had drained her amusement. "What the lady wants," she said quietly, "is for you to leave her alone."

He reached out suddenly, one hand cupping her cheek warmly, and she was surprised to feel a faint tremor in his fingers.

"I can't do that." The words were carefully spaced, emphasized with soft fierceness. "I can't walk away from you, Robyn. And I won't give up what we found together the other night. I don't know what you're afraid of, but I'm not going to give you up. I'll just go on asking until I find out what's wrong."

Bemused by the tingling shock of his touch as well as by his words, Robyn stared up at him for a long moment. She wasn't quite sure how to deal with this man. His determination to go on seeing her in the face of her refusal seemed unshaken. He hadn't even been angry at finding out—how had he found out?—that she was married; he had seemed more hurt because she hadn't told him herself. How strange. In Shane's place, Brian would have been furious.

She swallowed hard. "This is the twentieth century, Shane. I don't have to see anyone I don't want to see."

"Then tell me that." His voice was still softly insistent. "Tell me that you never want to see me again. Truthfully."

Robyn dropped her gaze. "I—"

"Look at me!" His fingers tightened slightly against her skin. "Look me in the eye, Robyn. I have to know that you're telling me the truth."

"You're not being fair," she accused him unsteadily, looking up once more. His emerald eyes allowed her no escape, holding her own with an intensity that bewildered her. "Shane, please . . ."

He swore softly beneath his breath and glanced around at the busy store. "This is no place for us to talk. What time does the store close, Robyn?"

"Shane—"

"What time?" He shook his head slowly as he met the appeal in her eyes. "I can't let it end like this, honey. I can't."

Robyn felt her resolve weakening, something in the emerald eyes draining her willpower. "Five," she murmured at last. "The store closes at five."

"I'll pick you up out front," he said.

Robyn again thought she saw relief flicker in his eyes, but she simply nodded weakly. Her nerve endings tingled again as he softly brushed his fingers against her cheek. Then he was striding from the store.

She stared after him for an eternal moment. Catching Janie's questioning glance, she smiled—reassuringly, she hoped. Automatically looking around to make sure she wasn't needed at the moment, she turned and hurried back to her tiny office.

Sitting behind her desk, she watched her hands shake for a good ten minutes.

"Idiot," she muttered, addressing the boxes of books stacked all around her. "Damned fool. He races. *Races*. You can't take that again. You know you can't."

Thoughts of racing inevitably brought Brian to mind, and she wondered again at Shane's lack of temper. He hadn't raised his voice once, she remembered. A man worth knowing . . .

"No," she told the boxes again. "You just miss Brian, that's all."

In spite of herself, she remembered Friday night. She had never felt such grinding need with Brian. She had never felt such a fierce desire, a primitive yearning, to join herself to him body and soul. He had never roused in her the feelings she remembered so clearly from her magical night with Shane.

A little desperately, Robyn pushed the thoughts away. She had imagined the depths of those feelings, she told herself firmly. It was only because she'd been so long without Brian.

It was nothing more than that. Never mind the strange shock of recognition she'd felt in that first moment. Never mind the staggering bolt of electricity arcing between green eyes and gold across a crowded room. Never mind the dazed, churning thoughts that had filled her mind, thoughts of fate and destiny and sheer luck. Never mind the sense of utter belonging she'd felt in his arms . . .

A t five o'clock, determinedly hiding her nervousness, she waved good-bye to Janie and locked up the store, realizing even before she looked that Shane was standing behind her. Dropping her keys into her purse, she turned slowly and stared up at him.

"Ready?" he asked, taking her arm and beginning to lead her toward the black Porsche parked by the curb.

"Would it matter if I said no?" she muttered.

"Not a bit," he told her cheerfully, guiding her around to the passenger side of the gleaming car and opening the door for her.

Robyn sighed as she took her place inside and watched him close her door and walk around the car again. His first words when he got into the car caught her off guard.

"How long have you been a widow?"

She found her fingers twining together nervously in her lap. "A little more than a year."

"And how long have you owned that store?"

"What is this—twenty questions?"

"If you like."

She watched his profile as he started the car and pulled out into the stream of rush-hour traffic. "I've owned the store for about three months," she answered finally.

"Did you work while your husband was alive?"

"No," she replied stiffly. She didn't know why, but she felt very uneasy talking to Shane about her marriage.

He shot a glance at her, and his barrage of questions ceased. She was relieved when he began speaking in a casual, friendly tone. "My family owns a wine business in California. My parents began it more than thirty years ago, and Mother still keeps a firm hand on the reins." He chuckled softly. "She keeps threatening to retire and shove everything onto my shoulders, but I don't think it's very likely. Especially since she violently disapproves of my 'hobby'."

Her relief evaporated. "Your hobby?" she asked politely, already knowing the answer.

"I race stock cars."

"Oh." For the life of her, she couldn't think of anything else to say. Not wanting him to know about her reluctant involvement in racing, she thought it best to betray no knowledge of the sport. He had probably met Brian, and would certainly recognize her married name if she revealed it.

"That's one of the reasons I'm in Florida," he continued cheerfully. "I intend to qualify for Daytona."

Robyn had to change the subject; she couldn't bear to think about racing, let alone talk about it. "Where are we going?" she asked.

He glanced at her again and replied softly, "I know a quiet restaurant nearby. It's a little early for dinner, but we need somewhere to talk. Somewhere public, I think." He seemed to hesitate, then added with outrageous calm, "With other people around, I might—possibly—be able to keep my hands off you."

She felt a flush coat her cheeks in scarlet, and her mind spun crazily. Good Lord, but he didn't pull his punches! Never in her life had she met a man like him. Desire, she had been taught, was a very private thing. Abruptly, she remembered her own behavior of Friday night, and her flush deepened. Well, maybe he had good reason to speak so bluntly!

He was laughing softly. "After Friday night, you surely can't doubt that I want you?" That peculiar huskiness was suddenly back in his voice, turning the soft question into a caress.

Robyn shifted uneasily on the narrow bucket seat. "I don't want to get involved with you, Shane," she repeated for what felt like the hundredth time.

"Too late now," he responded lightly.

She stared at him, her mind working with the grinding slowness of dry gears. No, it wasn't too late. There was only one reasonable explanation for what had happened on Friday night. The magic, the dreamlike feeling . . . She had pretended Shane was Brian.

It was the only thing that made sense. Hadn't she failed to ask his name because that would have ruined her dream? Hadn't she wished his green eyes blue?

Almost blindly, she watched Shane pull the powerful little car into a parking place in front of an elegant-looking restaurant.

No, it wasn't too late. All she had to do was tell Shane the truth. He had been a stand-in for a ghost. That should quite effectively destroy his hopes for a relationship between them. She wouldn't have to live in fear again . . .

Shane switched off the ignition, smiled suddenly, and reached out to cup her cheek in one large, warm hand. "Why so worried?" he asked softly. "It can't be as bad as that, surely!"

Robyn felt his thumb move lightly across her lips, and she fought back a shiver as her body responded wildly to the tiny caress. *It shouldn't be this way!* a panicked voice inside her head screamed.

Before she could begin to think clearly, he groaned deep in his chest and abruptly leaned across the console, his green eyes gleaming like gems.

"Just let me kiss you," he breathed.

Robyn made no effort to stop him, although the little voice continued to scream warnings. His lips touched hers gently, and a sigh seemed to rise from deep inside her.

With his familiar lion's growl, Shane deepened the kiss, his hand sliding down to encircle her throat. His tongue explored her mouth, taking full advantage of her lack of resistance. His free hand moved suddenly, slipping around her waist and then sliding up to draw her upper body firmly against his across the console.

Robyn lost herself in the warm, drugging feel of his embrace, telling herself silently that there was no danger here—not in a car parked at a restaurant. But she knew there was danger. The problem was that the danger was inside her. She couldn't seem to fight the flood of sensations elicited by his touch.

Her hand lifted of its own volition to touch his lean cheek, needing the fleeting contact for some reason her mind didn't begin to understand.

With an obvious effort, he tore his lips from hers at last, muttering a violent, "*Damn* sports cars!" He drew slowly away from her, the tautness of his body betraying an impatient restlessness. "Next time I'll drive something without a gear console!"

Coming abruptly to her senses, Robyn stared at him with a surge of panic. What was wrong with her? With every moment that passed, she was becoming more drawn into this man, and it would only hurt more when . . .

"Don't worry, little witch." He was laughing. "We'll talk first. But you're going to have a hard time keeping me at bay!"

Feeling a sudden, aching sadness mixed with weary relief, she watched him slide out of the car and come around to open her door. She would not, she knew, have to keep him at bay. Once he found out why she'd gone with him that night, he would want to have nothing more to do with her.

He would quite probably hate her.

He helped her from the car, and they silently entered the restaurant. The place was dim and shadowy and nearly deserted at that time of the day. They were led to a corner table, and Shane looked inquiringly at Robyn when a waiter approached.

"A drink for now? We can order later."

She nodded and murmured, "White wine," then watched as Shane relayed their order to the waiter.

As the waiter left, Shane reached across the table to cover her hands with one of his. His smile suddenly faded. He lifted her left hand, frowning. "Take it off," he ordered.

"What?" She stared at him blankly, not understanding.

"When you're with me, you won't wear another man's ring," he told her tautly. "Take it off, Robyn . . . please."

She hesitated for a moment, then removed the ring and placed it in her purse. She knew the meek obedience was uncharacteristic, but she didn't feel up to making a stand on the subject of her ring—especially as she was already dreading the anger her confession would certainly provoke.

Still holding her left hand with his right, Shane leaned back in his chair and smiled. "That ring threw poor Eric for a loop," he murmured almost to himself.

"Eric?"

He nodded. "Eric. A friend of mine. He knew that I was tearing Miami apart to find a raven-haired, golden-eyed witch named Robyn, he just happened to stumble into your bookstore, and you were wearing a wedding ring. He didn't know whether to call me or just to hope I never found you."

"The man with the red hair," she murmured, suddenly realizing why the customer had looked so familiar. "He was with you at the party." She flushed as his comment about tearing apart Miami sunk in, and dropped her gaze to the cream-colored tablecloth.

The waiter approached with their wine, and Robyn tried to pull her hand away from Shane's. She was suddenly aware that they must look like new lovers, and the image disturbed her.

But he wouldn't release her hand, holding it firmly as he smiled absently at the waiter. One of his fingers trailed across her palm in a strangely intimate little caress, and Robyn shivered, feeling nerves all through her body prickle to awareness.

After the waiter had deposited their glasses and left, Shane turned his full attention back to her, his green eyes warming almost as though the sight of her delighted him. "You look very beautiful today," he said softly. "Cool and calm—except for the slight trace of panic in your eyes."

Hastily, Robyn lifted her glass and took a sip of wine. She didn't want him to talk like that, flattering though it was. "Don't you want to know why I don't want to get involved with you?" she asked uneasily.

"Later," he answered easily. "You and I are going to have dinner and talk, get to know each other. Then we'll go back to my place, or yours, if you prefer. That'll be soon enough for explanations."

Somewhat to her surprise, Robyn found herself relaxing as the time passed. Shane, she found, was an interesting conversationalist, and he possessed a sinful amount of charm. He never once broached the subject of her marriage, but his casual questions covered practically every other phase of her life.

Astonished, she found herself telling him about her rootless childhood: about her mother, who'd died when Robyn was three; about her career-army father, whom she'd followed from base to base; and about Marty, who had raised her. Shane told her bits and pieces of his childhood in turn, confessing a love for animals and a powerful affection for his strong-willed mother.

It was a peculiar interlude, Robyn realized. Having leaped headfirst into the most intimate of relationships, they were now backtracking slowly, almost feeling their way.

She wanted to keep the conversation away from racing, but since that was a large part of Shane's life, the subject inevitably came up.

"My family wants me to settle down," he was saying now, casually. "I'm usually on the road from January through September, following the circuit."

"And the rest of the time?" she asked, toying with her wine glass.

"Wine." He smiled slowly at her puzzled expression. "The vineyards," he clarified. "Of course, I take care of a lot of the business even when I'm on the road. But I really get into the thick of things when I'm back home."

"Do you enjoy the wine business?" she asked curiously.

"Sure. I've grown up in it. I helped harvest the grapes when I was just a kid. As a matter of fact, my father used to say that I was always underfoot—and making a nuisance of myself."

Robyn tried to picture an eager, black-haired little boy with bright green eyes, but the grown man across the table from her kept getting in the way. Her awareness of him was so powerful it felt almost like a fixation.

And that was scary. It didn't fit in with her neat little explanation for Friday night. But if Shane hadn't been just a reminder of Brian, then why had she . . . ?

Robyn thrust the half-formed question from her mind. Of course he had been; there was no other possible explanation.

She would tell Shane the truth. He would be angry. Angry and probably disgusted. He would leave her life as abruptly as he had entered it. And he would leave hating her.

But it had to be that way. Involvement with him would only plunge her back into the strangling web of worry and terror that her marriage to Brian had woven around her. She wouldn't let that happen; her confession would drive him away from her.

Now . . . before it was too late.

Chapter Three

Hours later, Shane pulled the Porsche to a stop in the driveway of Robyn's home. She had chosen her own place rather than his hotel mainly because she had a feeling that she just might need moral support once Shane knew the truth. At least here she had Marty, although, judging by the darkened house, Marty was already in bed.

It was late. They had stayed in the restaurant for hours, then simply driven around Miami, still talking. Weary with pondering her emotions, Robyn had allowed herself—or, rather, forced herself—to think of the meeting as just another date, one that would be ending any time now.

"Nice place." Shane got out of the car and came around to open her door. "A little big, though."

Robyn waited until they were standing beneath the front porch light before responding to his comment, and when she did speak it was in a very deliberate tone. "Brian bought it shortly after we were married. We both wanted a large family." She sensed him tensing beside her, but she continued to pay careful attention to locating the keys in her purse.

Once they were found, she unlocked the door and silently moved ahead of him into the house, leading the way to the den, where a lamp burned. She turned on another lamp and dropped her purse into a chair, trying to fight the cravenness inside her that wanted to avoid this confrontation at all costs.

"Robyn—"

"There's the bar," she said quickly, pointing to one corner of the large room. "Help yourself."

Shane stared at her for a moment, obviously puzzled by her nervousness, then strode across the room and splashed some brandy into a snifter. He looked over his shoulder at her. "What will you have?"

"Nothing." Robyn had never in her life wanted a drink as badly as she did right then, but she knew Dutch courage wouldn't help her. She sank down onto the couch and watched as he came over to lower his weight beside her. When he put his arm around her, she straightened tensely.

"Robyn . . ." There was a curiously bleak tone to his voice. "Honey, don't pull away from me."

She glanced at him, then rose to her feet, turning to face him and feeling a little less intimidated because he was still seated. Her mind kept repeating *Get it over with* as though it were a litany.

Steadily, she said, "Friday night was a mistake, Shane. What you think is between us—it isn't real."

He sipped his brandy slowly, watching her through hooded green eyes. "It felt real enough to me," he objected quietly.

"That's because you don't know why—why I left with you. Why it all happened."

"Then tell me." He continued to watch her steadily. "Why did it all happen?"

Almost inaudibly, she whispered, "You reminded me of—of Brian."

For a long moment, she thought he hadn't heard her, or hadn't understood. Then, with unnatural care, he reached out to set his glass on an end table, his eyes never leaving her face. And suddenly those emerald eyes were the only splash of color in his whitened face.

"What?" His voice was quiet, as unnaturally calm as his movements of a moment before.

A flashing memory of some of Brian's rages made Robyn take an instinctive step backward, but even as she did so she realized that Shane wasn't angry. Instead, he seemed stunned. Would the rage come later?

"You . . . you reminded me of my husband, and I wanted to . . . spend one last night with him. It was a dream! It wasn't real!" she defended herself shakily.

Shane abruptly rose to his feet, as though he couldn't be still any longer, as though he desperately needed to move. "You pretended I was your dead husband?" he asked in a curiously dazed voice.

"I'm sorry," she whispered, wanting suddenly to unsay the words, to wipe away the horrible stricken look on his face.

"Sorry," he repeated dully. "You're sorry." He turned away from her and walked jerkily to the window, standing with his back to her and staring out the window into darkness. "Too perfect to be real," he murmured, as if to himself.

Robyn wrapped her arms around herself, trying in vain to ward off the chill invading her. She didn't know how to cope with this; the intensity of his emotions unnerved her. Anger she had been prepared for, but this strange, quiet agony was totally unexpected. It was somehow more upsetting than rage would have been.

"You should have just let it end, Shane," she said huskily. "You shouldn't have made me tell you." He swung around abruptly and came toward her, and she involuntarily shrank back.

But the large hands that grasped her shoulders were as gentle as though they held a fragile, frightened bird. Though the green eyes were fierce, there was no anger in them. Only disbelief.

"Tell me you lied, Robyn," he said hoarsely, the words a plea rather than a command. "Tell me there was no ghost in my bed that night!"

She shook her head silently, not trusting herself to speak.

"I don't believe you," he grated softly. "No, I don't believe you." His head swooped suddenly, taking her completely by surprise.

As his lips captured hers, his hands sliding down her back to pull her slender body almost roughly against the hardness of his, Robyn found herself totally unable to struggle. She told herself vaguely that it was the abruptness of his attack, the strength of his embrace, that had drained her resistance.

Except that it wasn't an attack.

His lips moved on hers with gentle, insidious persuasion, pleading for rather than demanding a response. Of their own volition Robyn's arms slid around his neck, her lips parting instinctively beneath his. She felt the now familiar flood of wild emotion sweep her body, and she gave herself up totally to the joy of the feelings he aroused in her.

He slid the zipper of her strapless sundress down, and the colorful material fell in a heap around her feet. The cool air on her skin seemed to intensify the raging sensations in her body, bringing a vivid, almost painful awareness to her fogged senses.

She felt his tongue moving in a possessive invasion of her mouth, and she found herself mindlessly responding, her own tongue joining his in a passionate duel. A sudden feeling of vertigo told her that he had lifted her into his arms, and then she felt the softness of the plush couch beneath her back.

Tearing his lips from hers, Shane pressed hot kisses down her throat to the pulse beating madly in the hollow of her shoulder. Robyn bit her lip with a soft moan as he expertly unfastened the front clasp of her strapless bra and smoothed the lacy material aside.

"Tell me you lied," he whispered raggedly, sensually abrasive fingers tracing the curve of her full breast, thumb and forefinger tugging gently at the hardening nipple. "Dammit, tell me you lied!"

His harsh, cracked voice and the demand he made vibrated against her flesh, somehow making its way through the veils of need and desire. Realizing that her lips had parted to tell him just what he wanted to hear, she felt panic sweep over her.

"No," she moaned desperately, her arms falling away from him as she tried to gain control over her scattered senses.

"You lied," he grated roughly, his fingers locking in her hair as he raised his head and stared down at her. "You lied to me, didn't you?"

Robyn saw something terrible happening in his eyes, on his face. She had never before seen such sheer primitive emotion in a man, such naked hunger, and it awed her as rage never could have.

"No," she repeated in a whisper, trying to shrink away from him. "I told you the truth."

He stared down at her, breathing raspily, for a long moment. Then, as though it were torture for him, he pulled himself away from her to sit on the edge of the couch. "You're afraid of me," he muttered in obvious disbelief, shock adding to the whirlpool of emotion in his eyes. "My God, you're afraid of me!"

Robyn's fear drained away as she realized finally, completely, that Shane wouldn't hurt her. As obviously upset as he was—had been, from the moment of her confession—he was in complete control of whatever disturbing emotions he felt. But before she could say anything, he had risen to his feet, still gazing down at her.

"Dammit to hell, Robyn—" He broke off abruptly and strode to the door, looking back over his shoulder only once, his face taut and masklike. And then he was gone.

Automatically, Robyn fastened her bra and dragged herself from the couch to find and put on her dress. Listening to the violent roar of the Porsche as it pulled out of her drive, she murmured very softly to the empty room, "Liar."

She had lied to him, told him something no one should ever have to hear—that he had been a stand-in for another man.

She knew then that she hadn't pretended Shane was her husband on Friday night. Not even in the beginning. Even when she had wished his green eyes blue, there had been no ghost between them. She had only been trying to find some reasonable, rational explanation for what had been happening between them—for her own irrational, uncharacteristic behavior. And she'd latched on to pretending that a stranger was her husband. It was not an impossible fantasy. Contemptible, perhaps—certainly pathetic. But not impossible.

Love at first sight was impossible. Not reasonable or rational. Not *real*. A dream. Two people finding one another by chance, by fate, sharing a dream.

But the dream had shattered the moment she'd found out that Shane Justice raced. Like Brian had.

Feeling a misery such as she had never known, Robyn silently turned off the lamps and made her way from the den, heading for the wing of the house that contained its five spacious bedrooms. The hall light came on as she was crossing the foyer, and Marty came forward, wearing a battered robe over her nightgown.

"Robyn?" Dispensing with the half-teasing formality she normally assumed, the older woman sounded concerned. "Are you all right? I thought I heard—" She broke off abruptly as Robyn came fully into the light.

"I'm fine," Robyn answered quietly. Noticing Marty's stare, she put up a hand to find that her cheeks were wet. Odd, she hadn't even realized she was crying.

In a strange tone, Marty said, "I haven't seen you cry since you were a little girl. Not even when your father died. Not even when Brian was killed. What's happened, Robyn?"

Not sure herself, Robyn could only shrug wearily.

Marty glanced toward the front door. "I heard a car leave. Was it the man from Friday night, Robyn?" She had wormed the bare facts from Robyn and Kris and, while not condemning Robyn's behavior, she clearly hadn't entirely approved, either.

"Yes." Robyn tried a smile and knew from Marty's expression that it hadn't come off. "He won't be back, though."

"Why not?"

Almost whispering, Robyn replied, "Because I sent him away, Marty. I sent him away hating me."

Despite the fact that Marty knew who—and what—Shane Justice was, and that she probably had a good idea why Robyn had "sent him away," she asked the question anyway. In the quiet, motherly tone that had pulled Robyn through both childhood disasters and adult tragedies, she urged, "Why, honey?"

Robyn felt fresh tears spill from her eyes; it was beyond her ability to halt them. "Because I'm a coward," she said starkly.

Robyn went to work the next morning at her normal time, and, between the heavier-than-usual makeup and her rigid control, neither Janie nor any of the customers noticed anything out of the ordinary.

Her night had been tormented and sleepless, filled with painful thoughts on the ironies of love. What punishing Fate had decreed that she was to fall in love with two men in her life—both of them obsessed with a dangerous sport that terrified her?

Kris had been right in her speculation, and Robyn no longer

fought the knowledge that she had fallen in love with Shane that first night. With that first glance, in fact.

She should have realized from the very beginning. Her own response to Shane should have told her the truth. Sex and love had always been inextricably tied together in her mind. If she didn't feel love, she didn't make love . . . and she had made love with Shane.

It had taken months for her to be certain of her love for Brian. And even then she had hesitated, torn by her fear of his racing. But her feelings for Shane had overpowered hesitation. She had loved him, and, loving him, had wanted only to be with him.

But Shane raced, and it would have torn her apart to watch him risk his life over and over again.

With Brian, she had been able to stand it for nearly a year. But, although it shocked her to admit it even silently, her love for her husband had been tame compared to the wild, desperate yearning of her love for Shane. What would it have done to her to love him with her entire being—perhaps even to be loved in return—and then lose him?

It would kill her, her heart answered.

So she had driven him away. Before she could commit herself to that love. Before she could—

"Excuse me?"

Robyn looked up hastily, the familiar surroundings of her store—and the red-haired, blue-eyed man staring at her across the desk—coming into focus. Shane's friend. Eric?

"Excuse me, Mrs. Lee—"

"Ms.," she corrected calmly, not wanting to explain that Lee was her maiden name.

"Ms. Lee." He looked a bit uncertain. "I'm looking for Shane. I was wondering if you might know where he is."

Robyn frowned at him, pushing her disturbed thoughts away. "No. Why would I know?"

"He was with you last night . . ."

She stiffened and then relaxed suddenly, telling herself wryly that she was going to explode one day if she kept letting tension get to her this way. "He left my place sometime around midnight," she told Shane's friend quietly. "I haven't seen him since."

It was Eric's turn to frown. "He hasn't been back to his hotel. It isn't like him to just disappear—"

"I told you years ago not to worry about me, friend."

It was Shane, and Robyn didn't know whether to kiss him or throw a book at him. She did neither. What she did do was stare at him with wide eyes.

Eric, too, turned to stare at his friend, one rusty eyebrow rising. "Well, you're certainly looking chipper," he grumbled in mock disgust.

Not having given Robyn a single direct look, Shane responded calmly. "Why shouldn't I? I had a shave and a shower—at the hotel, by the way. The desk clerk told me I'd just missed you."

Robyn searched his appearance guardedly, noting the still-damp hair, the casual slacks, and the fresh pullover knit shirt. He didn't look as if *his* night had been filled with violent emotions, but something in his eyes told Robyn that he had slept no better than she. Why was he here?

Eric was speaking in a faintly harassed tone. "Well, next time, how about giving me notice if you plan to stay out all night? I got a call late last night from Sonny. He said the truck broke down in some little town in Georgia, and it'll take a couple of days to find the parts they need. The car won't be in Daytona until the weekend."

Shane frowned and then shrugged. "Soon enough. That'll give me a week before the trials. How about the pit crew?"

"On their way." Eric grinned. "Sonny had to bail three of them out of jail in South Carolina. A brawl in a bar, I think he said."

Shane laughed, but before he could respond, Robyn, tired of

being virtually ignored, broke in irritably, "If you gentlemen wouldn't mind very much, I'd appreciate it if you took your business somewhere else. This is a bookstore, not a racetrack!"

As if he hadn't heard her, Shane said calmly, "Robyn, this is the friend I was telling you about. You two haven't been properly introduced. Robyn Lee—Eric Michaels."

"Ms. Lee." Eric was smiling in a friendly manner.

Inwardly sighing, she murmured, "Robyn—please." She leaned an elbow on the high counter and propped her chin in her hand, one part of her ruefully appreciative of the moment. Each time she'd thought herself free of Shane's presence, he'd somehow reappeared. Worse than a boomerang, she silently groused, wishing that her eyes would quit sneaking glances at his face.

Incredibly, her sense of humor had reasserted itself, and she didn't bother to wonder why. She was tired of brooding, tired of worrying about things that hadn't happened yet. One day at a time—that was the ticket. For now, she was just glad that Shane had come back—for whatever reason.

"Robyn it is, then." His smile turning into a cheerful grin, Eric added conversationally, "You know, I meant to tell you yesterday how glad I am that Shane met you. I've been warning him for years that one day he'd join the human race and take his fall just like the rest of us poor mortals. Trouble was, he never believed me. I'm sure he does now, though."

"That's enough, Eric," Shane said mildly.

Robyn looked from one to the other of them, more than a little puzzled. "Clue me in?" she requested politely.

"Eric never makes sense," Shane told her easily, casting a sidelong glance at his friend.

As if that look had been a signal, Eric immediately began making getting-ready-to-leave noises. "Yes. Well. It was nice seeing you again, Robyn. I, uh, I'm having a little party at my place tomorrow night; I'd like for you to come."

"She'll be there," Shane responded before Robyn could even open her mouth. "And, if you ask her nicely, she might even bring her cousin along."

Eric cocked a quizzical brow at his friend. "You mean the leggy blonde I somehow missed at the party Friday night? The one you said was a knockout?"

"The very same."

With a purely masculine gleam in his blue eyes, Eric smiled charmingly at Robyn. "By all means, bring her along!"

"I'll pass along the invitation," Robyn replied, not committing herself one way or the other. No matter what Shane said.

"Good enough." Eric waved cheerfully at them both and left the store.

Robyn watched him go, avoiding Shane's gaze as long as possible. Tuesday was a slow day for the store; at the moment, the place was empty. Janie had gone to lunch, so they were alone.

She finally looked at Shane as he leaned against the counter, very much aware of their solitude. Trying to think of something casual to say, she murmured, "He's more than a friend, isn't he? He has something to do with your . . . hobby."

Shane nodded, watching her with curious, inscrutable intensity. "He generally takes care of details for me. Deals with the sponsors, makes sure the car and the pit crew are where they're supposed to be. Since I travel so much, Mother saddles me with the family business, and it's a little hectic to take care of both. Eric has a house here in Florida, though. North Miami."

Suddenly determined, Robyn met his gaze squarely. "I didn't expect to see you again."

He shook his head slowly, still watching her intently. "After what happened last night, I'm not surprised."

Robyn made a vague gesture with one hand. "Then why are you here Shane? Last night—"

"Last night I was upset, and not thinking too clearly," he interrupted flatly. "You threw me a curve, and it wasn't the easiest thing in the world to accept." He sighed softly. "I spent most of the night walking along the beach and thinking. Somewhere around dawn, I finally realized that there was something off-center about your explanation."

"Off-center?" Surely he hadn't discovered the truth!

"Yes. You might very well have . . . pretended that I was your husband on Friday night." His face tightened on the last words, and there was a brief flash of something uncomfortably grim in his eyes, then he went on softly. "But you weren't pretending last night. You knew damn well who was making love to you. There was no ghost between us. And you wanted me. *Me,* Robyn."

Robyn hastily picked up a pencil on the desk and began toying with it, watching her fingers. "So?"

"So . . . despite whatever you still feel for your husband, you want me. You feel the same desire that I feel for you."

"Desire isn't exactly uncommon." She forced an uncaring lightness into her voice. "If you believe movies and television, it's practically epidemic."

"Not the kind we have." He leaned forward slightly, his green eyes darkening. "I'm thirty-four years old, Robyn. I've felt desire for a woman. I've felt desire *in* a woman. But not like what we have. And I'm not willing to throw that away."

She watched one of his hands reach out to cover her restless ones, and she instinctively looked up to meet his intent gaze. "What are you saying, Shane?" she whispered, her heart clenching in a sudden combination of pain and hope.

Slowly, as if he were uncertain about how to word it, Shane answered, "We owe each other something. We owe each other an opportunity to find out if this desire we feel is real, if it can grow into something more. Our first night together, you may or may not have thought of me as someone else. Last night, I walked out on you. We haven't given ourselves a chance, Robyn."

She felt the hand covering hers tighten, and she sensed a strange tension in him as he waited for her response. Did it matter so much to him, she wondered dimly. "Are you suggesting an affair?" she asked slowly.

Immediately, he shook his head. "No. The opposite of an affair, Robyn. I'm suggesting a friendship."

"Do you think that's possible, Shane?" she murmured.

"Yes," he responded firmly. "It's possible. We started out all wrong. Instead of first becoming friends, we became lovers . . . for whatever reasons." A hint of grimness crept into his tone and then disappeared as he went on. "We broke all the rules by starting out that way—and probably short-circuited all our instincts as well. What we need is a little time to get to know each other, uncomplicated by a physical relationship."

"And—and if we find that we can't be friends?"

"Then we won't have lost anything, will we?" He sighed, the emerald eyes rueful. "I don't expect it to be easy, Robyn—for me, at least. I expect a lot of sleepless nights and more than one cold shower." Robyn felt herself flush at his bluntness, and his voice was amused when he continued, "But I'm willing to try."

Robyn told herself that she'd be an idiot to agree to anything this man asked of her. She told herself that familiarity would only deepen the emotions that already had the power to make her doubt her own sanity. And then where would she be? But she wasn't very surprised to hear herself agreeing to his suggestion.

"All right, Shane."

His hand tightened almost painfully over hers for a moment and then relaxed. "Terrific. Now, I have a question . . . friend."

Robyn felt a smile tugging at her lips as she stared into the laughing emerald eyes. "And what's that . . . friend?"

"Do you think your assistant could run the store for you for a few days?"

"Why?"

"Because, in the interest of getting to know one another, I propose that we spend some time alone together. I have a little trip in mind."

Robyn thought of Daytona and felt her face stiffen. "A trip?" she asked unevenly.

"That's right. Eric has a sailboat he's offered to lend me. I thought we could take a few days and sail down along the keys." He grinned. "Swim, fish, cultivate an indecent tan. What do you think?"

Robyn was so relieved to avoid the possibility of going near a racetrack that for a moment she couldn't say anything. Shane obviously misunderstood her silence.

"Robyn? Will you trust me to keep to our bargain? We'll have separate cabins on the boat."

"It's not that, Shane. It's just . . ."

"Just what?"

She paused, uncertain how to object. Suddenly laughing, she challenged: "Who's going to do the cooking?"

With a startled chuckle, he responded, "We'll share the galley duty—how's that?"

"Well, all right. But I have to warn you; the only thing I know about sailboats is to duck when the boom swings across!" She stared at him with mock sternness. "I hope you know more than that, or heaven only knows where we'll end up."

"I know enough to keep us off reefs and sandbars, and to get us there and back in one piece," he said huffily. "It's been a few years, but I've sailed the keys."

Robyn glanced at the door as a customer came in, then looked back at Shane. "Can you afford to take the time? I mean, with the race coming up . . . ?"

"We should be back by Monday, which will give me plenty of time." He smiled at her. "We'll start out early tomorrow morning, okay? I'll check out the boat and stock the galley this afternoon."

"Fine. What time tomorrow?" Robyn was astonished at her easy acceptance.

"I'll pick you up at eight." He waited for her nod and then turned away, only to turn back. "Uh oh, I just remembered something."

"What?"

"Eric will kill me if your cousin doesn't show up at his party tomorrow night!"

Robyn laughed. "Give him Kris's number and tell him to call her tomorrow. Once I describe him, she'll go to the party!"

He lifted an eyebrow. "I'd like to hear that description."

She smiled sweetly. "See you tomorrow . . . friend."

Chapter Four

"You're going where? With who?"

"Whom," Robyn corrected in a deliberately offhand voice, frowning down at the selection of clothing laid out on her bed. She was trying to think of a reasonable answer to the question she knew her cousin was on the point of asking.

Kris made a rude noise and ignored the correction of her bad grammar. "You're really going sailing with Shane Justice?" She looked over at Marty. "Is she crazy?"

"She says not." Marty's voice was as grim as her face. "I'll take leave to doubt that, though."

Her gaze swinging back to Robyn, Kris said carefully, "You're jumping into this—this relationship with Shane awfully quickly, sweetie. Are you sure, you're not—"

"Rushing things?" Robyn looked up at last, a faint smile lifting her lips. "That's what this trip is for—to make sure we . . . get off on the right foot." Her smile faded but didn't entirely disappear.

She added quietly, "Brian's dead, Kris. And he wouldn't have wanted me to grieve forever."

Kris made another rude noise. "He wouldn't have grieved this long. For you, I mean." She hesitated when Robyn frowned at her, then went on coolly, "He wasn't a very deep person emotionally, you know. I'm not saying he didn't love you; he loved you as much as he could, being Brian." When Robyn made no response, Kris sighed and ruthlessly returned to the original topic. "Why go with Shane? He races, Robyn, and you can't take that. You know you can't!"

Robyn rolled up a colorful T-shirt and stuffed it into the duffel bag at her feet. "We're going sailing, Kris, not getting married."

Kris sank down onto the opposite side of the bed and gazed at Robyn with transparent concern. "You're getting involved with him, Robyn. You got involved with him that first night. I don't want to see you terrified out of your mind like you were with Brian. It'd kill you this time."

Hearing Kris echo her own earlier thoughts, Robyn absently stuffed a bikini into the bag, then looked across the bed levelly. "Would it? I don't know. But I know one thing, Kris." She included Marty in her level stare. "I can't walk away from Shane just because I'm afraid. And I can't go through life being afraid of things I can't change. If I do, I'll become an emotional cripple."

Kris was frowning now as she stared at her cousin; Marty looked thoughtful, her face unreadable. Robyn continued calmly.

"I may live to regret it, I know. The thought of going through what I went through with Brian makes me sick to my stomach. But I won't walk away from Shane without giving myself a chance." She hesitated, then finished almost in a whisper, "Love's so rare. I owe it to myself to see if I can find it again. A stronger love. A mutual love."

"Something tells me," Kris said very quietly, "that you've already found it. That's why you're going with Shane, isn't it?"

Robyn abandoned pretense. "It's another chance, Kris. And I can't throw that away."

R*obyn thought about her own words as she lay in bed that night,* wondering if she were only fooling herself. She turned restlessly and pounded her pillow in irritation. It was useless, this soul-searching. Utterly useless. She and Shane would have a nice little trip, and that would be the end of it. Maybe.

She was still trying to convince herself that that was what she wanted when she entered the den the next morning, dragging the heavy duffel bag behind her. Shane had already arrived. He was standing facing Marty, smiling slightly. Marty, Robyn noted, wore a defiant, minatory frown.

Abandoning the bag in the doorway, Robyn walked into the room, saying immediately, "Marty, take that frown off your face. What have you been saying to Shane?"

Before Marty could answer, Shane turned to face Robyn, his warm green eyes sweeping her faded jeans and full-sleeved pirate blouse. "She was warning me to take good care of you," he replied. "I told her that the warning was completely unnecessary." The look in those emerald eyes brought a flush to Robyn's face.

Trying to ignore her response to that slumbering green passion, Robyn glanced at Marty. "There was no need for that," she said uncomfortably. "He isn't kidnapping me, Marty, and I'm not a child!"

"She was worried about you." Shane strode across the room to her side, casually catching her hand in his. "And I don't blame her. You and I haven't known each other very long, after all."

Robyn sneaked a glance at his face but said nothing more as he led her to the door, pausing only long enough to pick up her duffel bag. Marty spoke to Robyn at last, and her voice was perfectly calm. "You two have fun."

Shane smiled winningly at her. "We'll let you know if something delays us. Otherwise, expect Robyn home by Monday."

Robyn barely had time to wave before Shane was tucking her into the black Porsche and stowing her bag in the trunk. Silently, she watched him handle the powerful car for a few moments, then she spoke wryly. "Why do I get the feeling that you tried to charm Marty?"

He grinned unrepentantly, confessing with a theatrical sigh, "It didn't work. She doesn't trust me."

Smiling in spite of herself, Robyn murmured, "I wonder why?"

Wounded, Shane protested, "I'm a prince among men!"

"Put not your trust in princes," she intoned meaningfully.

Shane started laughing, and Robyn reflected briefly that it was good to laugh with someone, good to share a joke or an understanding remark. She felt close to Shane in that moment, and she had to squash her instinctive alarm and remind herself that she was going to have this chance.

Even if it scared her half to death.

When they reached the marina, Shane helped her from the car, cheerfully reporting that the galley was stocked and everything ready for them. He retrieved her bag from the trunk and carried it for her as they threaded their way through the bewildering maze of boats of every size and description. He finally stopped beside a boat that looked, to Robyn's inexperienced eye, like a battleship. The thing was huge.

Perhaps reading the anxiety in her gaze, Shane assured her, "Don't worry—two can handle it."

"But I don't know anything about sailing," she protested hesitantly, watching him toss her bag aboard and then step neatly onto the deck.

"I'll teach you." Shane appeared unconcerned.

She stared at the hand he held out to her, then mentally burned her bridges. Taking the hand, she made use of the one bit of nautical protocol she'd culled from movies and television. "Permission to come aboard?"

"Granted." He grinned at her, his emerald eyes incredibly bright in the early morning sunlight. He helped her over the side, steadying her as the boat shifted slightly. Robyn suddenly had a horrid thought.

"Oh, no! What if I get seasick?"

He chuckled softly. "I thought of that. There're some pills for motion sickness in the galley. You can take one now, if you like. They really do the trick."

"I think I will," she murmured, releasing her death grip on his hand and bending carefully to pick up her bag. The thought of getting sick drove other thoughts from her mind. She looked toward a doorway and then lifted a quizzical brow at Shane. "Down there?"

"Down there," he confirmed, seemingly amused by her uncertainty. "The galley's to the left when you reach the bottom of the steps. Your cabin's to the right. The galley, by the way, is the kitchen."

Robyn swung the duffel bag over her shoulder and staggered under the weight of it. Glaring up into his amused eyes, she stated with offended dignity, "I'm not that dumb. I *know* the galley's the kitchen."

She got a firmer grip on her bag and stalked—carefully— toward the doorway. "Are we going to float here all day like a lily pad, or are we going somewhere?" she questioned huffily over her unburdened shoulder.

"We're going somewhere," he assured her, laughing. "You put your stuff away and take a pill, then come back up here and give me a hand and we'll get underway."

Robyn went down the steps carefully, leaving her bag in the cubbyhole of a hallway while she explored the galley. The cramped room hardly seemed large enough to store anything in, but she soon discovered that quite a large amount of supplies and food-stuffs had been neatly placed in the cabinets and drawers. She puzzled for a moment over the somewhat elaborate latches that secured doors and drawers, then realized that such precautions would be necessary in rough seas.

Her already nervous stomach tightened at the reminder, and she hastily began looking for the motion-sickness pills. She located them in a cabinet over the postage-stamp sized sink. Moments later she had washed down the required number of pills with some orange juice she found in the small refrigerator.

Making sure that everything was again fastened securely, she left the galley. She looked in briefly at the tiny bathroom complete with a narrow shower stall, then opened the remaining door in the hall.

The tiny cubicle, which bore the glorified name of "cabin," was only slightly larger than her closet at home. Two bunk beds took up most of the available room. The remaining space was merely a narrow walkway, lined by the beds on one side and two small chests on the other. Above the chests was a small mirror carefully secured to the wall. Directly opposite the door was a large porthole.

Electing to put her things away later, Robyn lifted her bag to the bottom bunk and then went back out into the hall, shutting the cabin door behind her. She stood there for a moment, knowing there was something bothering her but unable to figure out just what it was. And then she had it.

Separate cabins. He'd said that they would have separate cabins on the trip.

She stared carefully at the three doorways, looked in each room a second time, and then stood in the hall frowning at the steps. Granted, the cabin had two beds. But two beds did not separate cab-ins make. And Robyn had a feeling that Shane had known exactly how many cabins the boat had before he'd invited her.

Oddly enough, she was more curious to hear his explanation

than angry. Climbing to the deck, she blinked in the bright sun-light and briefly took note of the activity going on around them in the marina. Shading her eyes with one hand, she finally located Shane near the front—was that port or starboard, or bow or stern?—of the boat. He'd shed his slacks and stood clothed in a pair of white swim trunks. He was busily engaged in untangling a pile of ropes.

Robyn picked her way carefully along the deck toward him, avoiding more tangles of rope. Reaching his side, she inquired with deliberately deceptive calm, "Weren't we going to try to be friends?"

"Sure." He cast a sidelong look at her, and Robyn had no trouble reading the mischief in his eyes.

"Then tell me something—friend. Why did you lie about there being two cabins on this boat?"

"I didn't exactly lie." He threw her another glance, then bent his attention back to the rope in his hands. "I said we'd have separate cabins. My cabin's out here; I'll sleep on deck."

"On deck?" she exclaimed as though he'd just proposed sleeping in the ocean. "You can't do that!"

"Why not? The weather's supposed to be fine, and I've certainly slept in worse places."

"But—"

"As a matter of fact, I'll probably be more comfortable than you. The cabin tends to get stuffy at night."

"But—"

Cutting her off smoothly, he murmured, "And you wouldn't want to share the cabin, now, would you?"

Robyn opened her mouth to suggest just that, and then suddenly acquired the suspicion that she was being neatly maneuvered. Beginning to be able to read his expression and subtle body-language, she studied his faint smile and the almost imperceptible tension in his lean body. So he was plotting, was he?

Smiling sweetly, she folded her arms, careful to keep her feet solidly apart on the shifting deck. "I wouldn't think of it," she returned politely. "Why would I deprive you of the pleasure of sleeping out under the stars?"

He turned to look at her, and she nearly giggled at the look of almost comic dismay on his face. "You're not going to let me get away with much, are you?" he murmured wryly.

"Not if I can help it. But don't worry—when this trip's over, you'll be stronger in character." She reached up to give his cheek a friendly pat, and she nearly gasped at the almost electrifying sensation of flesh on flesh. Hurriedly drawing back her hand, she feigned interest in what he was doing with the ropes. "Can I help?" she asked brightly.

He stared at her for a moment, the green eyes strangely dark, then flexed his shoulders abruptly as if throwing off an unwelcome hand . . . or thought. "No," he muttered, clearing his throat. "No, not right now. We won't be able to raise the sails until we clear the marina. Have a seat in the stern until we're ready to cast off."

Since the only seat she could see—an L-shaped bench—was in the back of the boat, Robyn assumed that that was the stern. Her nerves jumping after the unexpectedly stimulating sensation of touching him, she wasn't about to protest his order. A little shakily, she made her way to the stern and sank down onto the padded bench.

Good Lord, what was wrong with her? She was about to spend several days alone on a boat with a man, and she couldn't even touch him casually without experiencing a heart-stopping shock! She had a funny feeling that their undemanding "friendship" wasn't going to last very long. Her only hope was to keep things light and humorous—and to avoid touching him as much as possible.

Shane had been right—in her case, anyway. Her instincts were in turmoil. After a year of terror for her husband and a year of grief after his death, she had come alive again—extremely so. And she was all too aware of Shane's magnetic, sensual appeal.

Wide-eyed, she watched him moving about the boat, taking note of his catlike grace and sure motions. She remembered his lion's growl, shivering as her nerve endings responded even to the memory, and directed her gaze out over the water.

"Robyn?"

She blinked and jumped in surprise to find Shane standing directly in front of her. "I'm ready," she muttered with clenched-teeth determination, feeling as cheerful as if he'd just announced that the dentist would see her now.

Shane laughed, but his eyes were intent on her face. "Regretting the trip so soon?" he asked softly.

Robyn stood up slowly, all at once aware of the heat of the morning sun, the salty sea breeze, and the curiously vivid green of his eyes. And she wondered why she was wasting time with stupid, useless fears. "No," she responded just as softly. "Not regretting."

A muscle leaped in his lean jaw, and one hand jerked up as though pulled by strings. His fingers hesitated just before touching her cheek, then the hand fell heavily to his side. "Don't look at me like that," he warned roughly. "It plays havoc with all my good intentions!"

"Good intentions?" A smile hovered around the corners of her mouth. "I'll bet this is the first time you've ever denied yourself something you wanted."

He gave her a lopsided grin. "Don't rub it in. And stop smiling at me, you little witch! You have no idea what it does to my blood pressure."

Robyn experienced a sense of wonder at the desire he made no effort to hide, realizing that she'd never in her life met a man who spoke so openly about how he felt.

He reached up to rub his knuckles down her cheek with gentle roughness, then turned her around briskly and gave her a firm swat on the bottom. "Grab that line and cast off when I tell you to!"

Rubbing the abused portion of her anatomy, Robyn threw a half-laughing glare at him over her shoulder and stalked away to take the line he'd indicated. "Aye, aye," she said resentfully. "But please don't ask me to do anything desperately important, skipper, or we'll both end up in the drink!"

Within half an hour, they had left the marina behind. Shane had used the small engine to propel the boat until they were well out, and then cut its power and commanded Robyn to take the wheel while he showed her how to raise the sails.

A bit gingerly, she stood behind the big brass wheel and held it firmly, resisting her desire to watch the colorful sails of other boats heading out to sea. Dutifully, she watched Shane at work, trying to make sense of his movements and not having very much success. She nearly lost him once, swinging the wheel instinctively when a large motorized boat came a bit too close for her peace of mind.

Having regained his balance swiftly, Shane gave her a short lecture on maritime law, which inexplicably proclaimed that the smaller boat had the right of way. Robyn listened meekly.

She felt like a fool until he winked solemnly at her, and she realized that he wasn't at all dismayed by her ignorance. After that, it was easier to absorb his instructions.

"Swing it a bit to port," he called back to her, busily tying off one of the innumerable ropes.

Barely able to hear him over the snapping and cracking of the wind-filled sails, she responded hastily, "You're talking to a land-lubber, remember! Is port left or right?"

He laughed. "Sorry! Port's left."

Wary after her near-catastrophe earlier, Robyn carefully turned the wheel to the left and felt rewarded when Shane gave her a thumbs-up signal. She swung her head to throw the single heavy braid back over her shoulder, and reflected that it was a good thing she'd decided on that style this morning. Her fine hair tangled easily, and, without the braid, she would have looked like a wild woman by now.

Apparently satisfied with the sails, Shane made his way back to her side. He moved deftly and easily about the heaving deck, and Robyn envied him his steady sea legs. She didn't feel sick—yet—but only her death grip on the brass wheel steadied her balance.

She watched him lean against the side of the boat, his arms folded casually across his chest, and she asked uneasily, "Aren't you going to take over now?"

"Why? You're doing fine." Before she could protest, he went on briskly, "We're going to drill a little nautical terminology into your head so you won't panic."

"I never panic," she informed him indignantly.

"Uh huh. Port's left."

Sighing, Robyn realized he wasn't going to let her get out of learning how to sail. Aware that they were far out to sea, and interested in spite of herself, she resolved to learn. "Port's left," she parroted faithfully.

"Starboard's right."

"Starboard's right."

"The front of the boat is the bow, and the rear is the stern. Or you can call it fore and aft—"

"Let's stick with bow and stern," she interrupted quickly, "There's no need to thoroughly confuse me our first day out."

Solemnly, he said, "You have to learn, Robyn. In case something happens to me."

"In case something—" The boat made a decidedly ungentle

lurch as her hands jerked on the wheel. "Shane! I can't sail this thing by myself! If you fall out, I'll never forgive you!"

"Overboard," he corrected, his lips twitching.

"What?"

"If I fall overboard. Not out."

She glared at him. "Now, look—"

"Starboard?"

"Right," she supplied irritably. "Shane—"

"Port?"

"Left. Will you—"

"Bow?"

"Front."

"Stern?"

"*Rear.*" Her voice held more than a suspicion of gritted teeth.

"Very good," he commended cheerfully. "Think you can remember that much?"

Robyn stared at him for a long moment, then spoke carefully. "Did I ever tell you that I know karate?"

"Nope." His lips twitched again.

"Well, I do. I'm probably a little rusty, but I'm sure I could manage a few lethal moves."

"Should I bear that in mind?"

"I would."

Shane grinned and then sobered abruptly. "I'm not trying to scare you, Robyn. I certainly don't expect any problems between now and Monday. But it's best that you be prepared for anything. You can never take the sea, or the weather, for granted. When we get a little farther out, I'll show you exactly how to raise and lower the sails and the anchor, how to read the compass and handle the radio, and what to do in an emergency." He hesitated and reached out to touch her cheek lightly. "Okay?"

Reassured more by the tingling touch than anything else, she nodded and smiled. "Okay. But don't go too fast!"

"Right." He laughed. "Port?"

"Right. I mean left! Dammit."

"Starboard? . . ."

wo hours later, Robyn had raised and lowered the sails twice by herself, had mastered the peculiar art of hoisting an anchor, was reasonably certain that she could handle the radio, and could make a stab at reading the compass.

She was also hot, tired, aching in more muscles than she'd known she had, and teetering on the brink of telling Shane to forget the whole damn thing.

She collapsed at last onto the cushions of the stern seat, glared at the rope burns on her hands and then at Shane, who was standing comfortably near the big wheel. In the tone of a litany, she recited, "The sails are down, the anchor's in place, we're heading south-by-southwest, and I'm catching the first shore-bound seagull."

He was laughing at her, dammit!

Trying to infuse her voice with hearty good cheer and succeeding only in sounding weary, she asked, "Anything else, skipper?"

"I think you've done enough, sailor. How about a break?"

Robyn peered at him uncertainly, then sighed with relief when she realized he was being serious. "Oh, thank you," she breathed. "I think I'm dead and you haven't bothered to tell me."

Shane grinned at her. "Don't be ridiculous. Think your stomach could stand some lunch?"

Surprised, Robyn realized that she had been too busy to worry about the possible revolt of her stomach. The gentle rocking motion of the boat wasn't bothering her in the least. "Was that the method to your madness?" she asked suspiciously.

Shane didn't misunderstand. "Partly," he confessed with a grin. "It's a question of mind over matter, if your mind's occupied, the matter generally remains stable. Lunch?"

"Lunch," she agreed. "But only if you fix it."

"That's mutiny!"

"Call it anything you like," she said with a sweet smile.

He sighed dramatically and headed below deck. "It's a good thing I'm a nice guy," he threw over his shoulder at her.

"Attila the Hun probably said the same thing!" she yelled with a final burst of energy. She smiled as she heard Shane's laugh. Glancing around, Robyn was surprised to find that there was no land in sight and the nearest of the colorful sails that had left the marina with them looked miles away. She sincerely hoped that Shane's navigational skills were in order. Her newly acquired compass-reading abilities notwithstanding, she had only the vaguest idea of how to get the boat back to dry land.

The subject of her thoughts came back on deck at that moment, carrying a blanket under one arm and a wicker basket in his free hand. He tossed the blanket at Robyn. "Spread this out on deck while I rig the sun shade. Your nose is getting pink."

"It is not," she automatically countered, spreading the blanket and watching while he stretched an awning over their heads. "I never burn."

"No?" He glanced back at her as he snapped the canvas into place, his green eyes glinting in a smile. "Wrinkle your nose."

She did as he ordered and nearly winced at the tight, prickly feeling of slightly scorched skin. "Well, not much," she amended.

He joined her on the blanket, bringing the hamper with him. "Don't worry, I have some first-aid cream that'll take care of it— and your hands as well. I have a feeling you have some rope burns."

Robyn flexed her hands slightly and smiled at him. "They're a little sore," she admitted, "but not bad."

Shane opened the hamper and began pulling forth goodies from within, a self-satisfied expression on his face that made Robyn instantly suspicious. "Wine, ham and cheese sandwiches, cheese and crackers, assorted fruit, potato salad," he enumerated solemnly.

"You didn't fix this stuff!" she exclaimed. "Where did it come from?"

He grinned at her. "Didn't you see it in the galley? I had the hotel fix it up this morning, and I stored it in the second refrigerator in the galley—where Eric normally keeps his beer."

"Oh." She stared at him, then began dividing the food onto two paper plates while he coped with a stubborn cork. By the time he had opened the wine and poured some of the ruby liquid into two plastic goblets, everything was ready.

Handing her a glass, he lifted his own in a toast. "To friendship," he murmured, a smile playing around the corners of his mouth.

She lifted her glass, softly echoing his words, then sipped carefully, grateful for the drink after her work. She watched him from beneath lowered lashes as they began to eat, wondering at his apparent ability to put the past behind him. Granted, it had been nearly two days since her confession, but he still seemed to have gotten over it awfully quickly. She again inwardly remarked on how little anger he had actually shown.

The only real experience Robyn had had with masculine anger had been with Brian. Her father had been a loving, even-tempered man, and she hadn't been close to any other man except Brian. Brian's reckless temper had been of the long-lasting variety—a deep-freeze of rage that lasted days after the initial explosion.

"You're thinking about him, aren't you?"

She quickly looked down at her wine glass, suddenly afraid that her wayward thoughts had spoiled their trip already. She didn't want Shane to be angry, and she was unable to explain that only the growing and striking contrast between Brian and him had brought her husband to mind.

"Can't you forget about him for a few lousy days?"

There was an odd note in Shane's voice that immediately brought her eyes back to his face. Not anger, but weariness and something that might have been pain quivered in his low tone. And his lean face was so somber that it gave her the courage to speak.

"Shane, the more I get to know you, the more I can't help . . . comparing you to Brian."

He stared down at his half-finished meal, his lips twisted. "Unfavorably?"

"No. Favorably." She smiled a little painfully as his gaze swiftly lifted to hers. "Shane, there were . . . problems in my marriage. Problems that ultimately would have torn it apart, I think. I'll never know for sure. But Brian's gone. He's not a part of my life anymore. Please believe that."

Green eyes now glowing, he stared into her eyes for a long moment, then reached out to clasp her free hand. "Just don't think about him too much, honey," he said softly. "It hurts."

Moved almost beyond bearing by the vulnerability he wasn't afraid to show her, Robyn felt the sting of tears in her eyes. He seemed to care so much, yet they had met less than a week ago.

What did he want from her, this green-eyed man of so many moods? What did he see in her that he was so determined to know her and to have her know him?

He lifted her hand suddenly, rubbing her fingers lightly against his cheek. "Tears?" he queried softly. "For me?" He shook his head slowly. "Don't cry for me. Not unless I don't get what I want, what I need. In that case, I may join you." Before she could respond, he quickly added, "I'll go get that cream for your burns."

He left her staring after him in wonder.

Chapter Five

Robyn slowly put the lunch things away, knowing that neither of them would finish the meal. She left out only the wine, sipping hers as she tried to understand what had just taken place between her and Shane.

She wasn't quite sure, but she felt that a turning point had somehow been reached and successfully weathered. She didn't think that Shane would be upset again over Brian or her thoughts of him. But Shane, she knew, still had questions about her marriage. And she wasn't certain how to answer the questions when the time came.

She had been honest with Shane—and with herself for the first time. Her marriage to Brian would have been torn apart, either by his eventual infidelity or by her terror of his racing. That didn't mean that she had stopped loving her husband. He would always hold a special place in her heart. He'd been her first love, her first lover; nothing would ever change that. But that was then.

Now she was facing a relationship that could possibly be

shadowed—just as her marriage had been—by racing. If she and Shane discovered that they had something special, something to build a future on, then she would have to either conquer her fears or allow them to ruin her life. She would never ask Shane to give up something he loved for her. No matter how dangerous that "something" was.

She would not try to change him.

That resolve had just filtered somewhat painfully into her mind when she heard Shane return and looked up to find him kneeling on the blanket in front of her. He was unscrewing the top of a small tube in his hand and looking at her with smiling eyes.

"The nose first, I think," he said judiciously, and he promptly began smearing some of the white cream across her nose.

Robyn giggled at the cool sensation, but her laughter died when the now-familiar shock tingled over her nerve endings. She stared up at him gravely.

Shane's fingers seemed to quiver slightly as he met her look, and his own emerald gaze became fathoms deep. Somewhat hastily, he finished with her nose and picked up one of her hands, using both of his to work the soothing cream into her reddened palm. He lowered his eyes to the task, and she could have sworn that he caught his breath.

The movements of his fingers over first one palm and then the other were strangely erotic, causing a trembling to start deep inside her, spreading outward until her fingers shook within his. She could feel her heart thudding against her rib cage and wondered dimly if he was aware of the pulse pounding in her wrist.

The cream disappeared into her skin, and still his fingers continued their gentle stroking, caressing. Without looking up at her, he said very quietly, "I had to touch you. You realize that, don't you?"

The soft statement made her thudding heart skip a beat. She tried to swallow the lump in her throat, her eyes searching his face as though it held the secrets of the universe. Still he refused to look at her. When he went on, his voice had deepened, hoarsened.

"I've tried to keep my hands off you all morning and haven't succeeded worth a damn. I *have* to touch you, Robyn. The same way I have to breathe. Don't hate me for that."

"I don't hate you, Shane."

He looked up at last as she whispered the denial, and his hands closed convulsively around hers with a gentle, savage strength. His eyes were nearly black. "Don't look at me like that, dammit," he swore softly. "Even when you don't mean to, you look at me with bedroom eyes!"

"Who says I don't mean to?" she managed shakily.

His eyes flared with emerald fire, and he released her hands to cradle her face with his large palms. "Honey, you don't know what you're saying. We're supposed to be getting to know each other as friends."

"I know." She reached up to grasp his wrists, suddenly understanding his statement about needing to touch her. She needed to touch him, desperately, almost painfully. It was like a hunger eating away at her soul. Bewildered by the strength of that need, the throbbing emptiness inside her, she pleaded huskily, "Please don't think I'm a tramp, Shane! I—I need you to touch me, I want you to! I can't help it . . ."

He abruptly rose on his knees, releasing her face to pull her up against his body, wrapping his arms around her firmly. "Of course I don't think you're a tramp!" he scolded unevenly. "You're confused, honey; everything's happened too fast. I just want you to be very, very sure of what you feel."

She intuitively sensed he was holding something back. What were the words he didn't speak, she wondered dimly, slipping her arms around his lean waist with a need beyond reason. Was he afraid that she still saw him as a replacement for Brian? Was he still thinking of another man's ghost?

Shane drew back far enough to gaze down at her face, his own very serious. "I want nothing less than a commitment from you, Robyn, and I don't think you're ready for that yet."

Unbidden, she thought of his racing, and a stab of fear shot through her. The fear must have been reflected in her eyes, and Shane obviously misinterpreted what he saw there.

He drew away suddenly, getting to his feet. "You see?" He smiled reassuringly, softening the blow of his taut voice. "You're scared to death of committing yourself to me, honey. You aren't ready for that yet."

Robyn wanted to voice another denial, but she couldn't work up the courage. Then the moment had passed, and it was too late.

"Give me a hand, and we'll get underway," he was saying lightly. "I'd like to reach Key Largo this afternoon."

Clamping a lid over the turmoil of her emotions, Robyn silently set about helping him to get the boat underway. Once they were skimming over the blue-green sea again, she left Shane at the wheel, gathered up the remains of their lunch, and went below.

She put everything in its place and then went into her cabin, emptied her duffel bag on the bottom bunk, and began putting her things away in one of the chests. The other chest, she noted, held Shane's clothing. She resisted an impulse to run her fingers through his things, telling herself firmly not to be an idiot.

And then, unable to delay the moment any longer, she changed into a pair of cut-off jeans and a very brief halter top and went back up on deck—to the man who would or would not become her future.

Shane was standing behind the wheel. He watched her until she sat down on the padded bench, a lambent flame flickering for a moment in the depths of his eyes. Then he was paying attention to their course again.

"Have you ever seen the living coral reef off Key Largo?" he asked casually.

Robyn drew one foot up on the bench and hugged her knee, watching him. "No. Will we see it?"

"If we get there in time today, we can tie up nearby and take a ride in a glass-bottomed boat. How does that sound?"

"Great." She frowned slightly. "Tie up? Won't we just drop the anchor?"

"We'll tie up in the marina tonight, since we'll be leaving the boat. And once we reach Key West, too. In between, we'll just drop anchor in some little cove."

"Swim and fish?" A smile played over her lips.

He sent her a quick, answering smile. "Sure. I wouldn't advise swimming out here in the open sea, but the coves should be safe enough. Have you ever fished?"

"Years ago, but never in the ocean. I'll just watch you."

"That won't be any fun."

Silently, she thought: That's what you think! Aloud, she murmured, "How long does it take to get to Key Largo?"

"A couple of hours, if the wind holds."

A companionable silence fell between them. She joined him in staring out to sea, wondering what he was thinking and trying to make sense of her own thoughts. When he finally spoke, she almost wished he hadn't.

"Do I really look so much like him?"

Robyn felt her fingernails biting into her arms and had to make a conscious effort to relax. "Not really. He was dark but blue-eyed. And you're taller." When Shane turned his head to meet her steady gaze, she repeated, "Not really."

"Tell me about him. How you met."

She hesitated, staring at him. "Shane—"

"I have to know, Robyn."

Robyn stared down at her knee for a moment, then told him what she could. "We met at a party . . ." She looked up quickly, wishing she could recall the words, but Shane showed no reaction other than a slight frown. Hastily, she went on.

"My father had died recently, and I wasn't really used to going out much. But I was attracted to Brian. He always seemed to be smiling. We dated for a few months. He traveled quite a bit in his . . . work." She took a breath and finished calmly, "He asked me to marry him and—and I accepted."

"You don't like talking to me about your husband, do you?" he asked quietly.

"No," she replied honestly.

"Why not?"

"Because I'm afraid." The stark words were out before she could halt them, and they had to be explained. "I'm afraid you believe that I'm seeing Brian whenever I look at you, and that's not true. And I don't want you to see Brian's ghost every time you look at me."

Staring straight ahead, Shane told her huskily, "When I look at you, honey, I see *you*. I see a beautiful woman whose life I very badly want to be a part of. If there were ten men in your past, a dozen ghosts at your side, it wouldn't matter."

Robyn took a deep, shaky breath. "Then can we put the subject behind us? At least during the trip?"

He nodded, automatically glancing down to check their direction by the compass and then swinging the brass wheel slightly to starboard. "We'll put it behind us," he agreed.

This time, the companionable silence stretched for nearly an hour, broken only by an occasional comment. Robyn was enjoying the sound of the wind snapping the sails, the steady slapping of water against the hull, and the feel of the salt spray in her face.

A pair of dolphins joined them as Key Largo came into sight, and Robyn was completely entranced by their antics. The beautiful mammals leaped in and out of the blue-green sea, bright black eyes seeming to invite the watching humans to join their game. Robyn laughed in delight as their friendly escorts stood up on their tails and chattered gaily, clearly wishing their observers a fond good-bye before heading rapidly back out to sea.

She stared after them, unaccountably wistful. "Oh, Shane, aren't they beautiful?" she marveled.

"Beautiful," he confirmed softly.

But she saw he wasn't looking at the dolphins.

They spent the remainder of the afternoon exploring, leaving the boat tied up in the marina. They put the past behind them and threw off the trappings of dignity and caution. Cheerfully, they became more and more childlike as the day wore on, each trying to top the other and stretching toward the heights of absurdity.

Shane solemnly told the other tourists on the glass-bottomed boat that his companion was his niece, home from school for the holidays, and he earned dubious looks from his listeners as they took in Robyn's somewhat revealing halter top and shorts. Robyn stared back at them, wide-eyed, and slowly blew a bubble with the gum Shane had bought her only moments before.

She got even with him sometime later, telling the owner of a small tourist shop they wandered into that she was being kidnapped and would shortly be sold into white slavery. The ploy wasn't very effective, however, since Shane was playfully leading her around by her braid.

The shopkeeper, with an expression that clearly said he'd heard it all, watched bemusedly as the "kidnapper" bought his "slave" a stuffed dolphin and a book on sailing. The odd couple was still arguing spiritedly over who needed a book on sailing as they wandered out.

They located a hot dog stand near the marina and elected to stop there for a casual supper after Robyn flatly refused to try cooking on the boat.

"I'm not even sure I can light that stove," she declared.

"We agreed to share the galley duty!"

"Well, you haven't done your share yet. You cheated with lunch."

"I never cheat—"

"So I'll cheat with supper," she interrupted firmly, sniffing at the delicious aroma of bubbling chili. She tucked her blue and white dolphin under one arm and smiled at Shane sunnily.

He gave her much-abused braid a tug. "You should be keel-hauled!"

"What's that mean? They're always threatening that in pirate movies."

"It means something terrible. Fatal, in fact."

"Then you can't keelhaul me. I'm your only crew."

Shane gave her a long-suffering look, tucked the small paperback on sailing into the waistband of his slacks, and reached for his wallet. "Uh huh. Tell the man what you want on your hot dog."

"What's he got? Let's see . . ."

Ten minutes later, they were seated on a bench near the hot dog stand finishing their supper. Robyn licked one finger clean and said thoughtfully. "Hot dogs are like pizza and spaghetti—impossible to eat with any dignity."

"To hell with dignity," Shane replied indistinctly, reaching for his soft drink to wash down the last bite.

"Dignity is important," she objected in the tone of one looking forward to a good argument.

"Only when meeting kings and presidents."

"And prospective in-laws." Robyn wished that she could call back the comment, and added hurriedly, "And policemen."

"Doctors, lawyers, Indian chiefs?" he murmured, casting her a sidelong smiling look.

Robyn pretended she hadn't said that about in-laws. She explained apologetically, "It probably comes of being raised by a career-army father. I have a phobia about authority figures."

Shane crumpled up his hot dog wrapper and shot it neatly into a nearby trash can. "Any other phobias I should know about?" he asked politely.

"Well . . . there's my fear of water—"

"*What?*"

"I'm kidding, I'm kidding!" She jumped up hastily, swinging her braid out of his reach. "Oh, no, you don't! If you pull on that braid one more time, I'll be bald!"

"Come here, you little witch!" He got to his feet, advancing toward her purposefully.

Robyn clutched her dolphin in front of her like a shield and cast harried, mock-fearful looks around her. But they were interrupted before Shane could wreak vengeance on her.

"Aren't you Shane Justice?"

Both of them turned instinctively as two teenaged girls approached them, beaming happily at Shane and totally ignoring Robyn. They wore cut-off jeans and T-shirts with NASCAR emblazoned in bold black print across jutting breasts. Robyn wasn't the slightest bit surprised to find racing fans here. She'd seen them in stranger places.

The girls were pelting Shane with questions about his racing, barely letting him get a word in and giving him no opportunity to introduce Robyn. More amused by Shane's embarrassment than irritated by the interruption, Robyn quietly gathered up the remains of their supper and made a short trip to the trash can. She returned to his side just as the girls were happily telling Shane that they were in Florida for the race and were heading toward Daytona the next day. Of course, they'd see him there.

Robyn took another good look at them and admitted to herself that she'd been wrong about their ages. The blonde was quite possibly her own age, and the brunette only slightly younger. And both were looking at Shane with eyes that ate him alive.

"Could we have your autograph?" the brunette asked, producing a felt-tipped pen and turning her back so that Shane could sign her T-shirt. He did so, politely.

The blonde was made of sterner stuff. When Shane turned to her she threw back her long hair and stuck out her chest with what appeared to Robyn to be excessive pride. "Over the 'a'," she murmured seductively, gazing into his startled eyes.

Robyn rested her chin on the nose of her dolphin and bit back a laugh as she watched the red creep up into Shane's cheeks. He obviously tried not to touch the blonde's ample gifts with anything but the pen. At the last possible moment, however, the blonde inhaled, and Shane's signature ended in a rather peculiar scrawl. He hastily returned the pen to the brunette.

The blonde finally looked at Robyn with speculative eyes. "Are you his sister?" she asked sweetly. "Or his maiden aunt?"

Robyn wasn't about to let her get away with that! She quickly grasped Shane's arm and rubbed her cheek against his shoulder adoringly. "Actually, I'm his mistress," she confided gently.

The brunette gasped as though her idol had just developed a bad case of clay feet. The blonde continued to smile, however forced it may have been. "Really?" she asked disbelievingly.

"Oh, yes." Robyn's voice was still soft and gentle, but her cool eyes met the narrowing blue gaze of the other with more than a hint of warning. "I practically never leave his side."

The dueling match of eyes continued for a long moment. Ultimately the blonde turned away, saying meaningfully over her shoulder, "See you in Daytona, Shane!" Her friend hurried after her.

Robyn released Shane's arm, acquiring a firmer grip on her slipping dolphin, and looked up at her silent companion. "Groupies?" she asked innocently.

"Sorry," he murmured, staring down at her with an odd expression. "Racing fans are . . . fans."

"Short for fanatic, I assume." She didn't like that considering look on his face. "Uh, the sun's going down. Shouldn't we head back toward the boat?"

He didn't move. "You were very convincing with that possessive act, Robyn."

She wasn't about to answer the question he hadn't asked. "Did it bother you?" she asked lightly.

He shook his head slowly. "I'm just wondering why you went to the trouble," he said very softly.

"No trouble at all," she responded flippantly, adding easily, "Isn't the marina this way?" Determinedly, she headed off. Within a few steps, Shane had silently joined her. He remained silent until they had nearly reached the already lighted marina.

Robyn was caught up in her own thoughts, emotions, and sensations. Both her hand and her cheek were still tingling from the brief contact with Shane, and she was belatedly astonished by the surge of possessive rage she had felt when that blonde had looked at Shane with proprietary eyes. She had wanted to do much more than sweetly warn away the other woman. What she had wanted to do was to drop her dolphin, launch herself at the blonde's throat, and engage in a grade-A, number-one catfight.

To a woman who had never lifted her hand against another person in anger, that desire was as shocking as it was totally unfamiliar.

"Penny for your thoughts."

Hastily dragging her mind from its contemplation of the latest in a series of unfamiliar sensations, Robyn responded briefly, "They're not worth that."

"Robyn, if those fans upset you—"

"No, of course not," she interrupted, resisting her impulse to look up at him. She knew that Shane was puzzled by her suddenly guarded mood, but she wasn't about to explain that she was disturbed by primitive emotions she had never experienced before. That confession would ultimately lead to the one she was as yet unprepared to make. She was not ready to tell Shane that she loved him.

He sighed. "You're baffling, do you know that? Every time I think I have you figured out, you change moods on me. Is it a game to you, Robyn?"

She stopped walking suddenly and looked up at him, able to see him clearly in the harsh light from the marina. "No. Shane . . . let's don't spoil the day. Please? With—with soul-searching, or whatever. It's been fun, and I . . . Don't spoil it."

He gazed down at her for a moment, and she saw a muscle tighten in his jaw. Then he was smiling. "Okay, witch," he said lightly. "We won't spoil anything."

Relieved, Robyn started toward the walkway leading down to the boats, but a sudden commotion halted her in her tracks. A royally groomed and beribboned poodle was dashing toward them, barking hysterically. In front of the poodle ran a scrawny black cat with wild yellow eyes and a crooked tail. The dog was gaining.

Robyn thrust the stuffed dolphin at Shane and, as the cat started to run between them, she snatched it up into her arms. The dog, dodging Shane's instinctive swipe with the dolphin, turned tail and ran.

Shane turned immediately to Robyn. "Honey, turn it loose—it looks as mad as a hatter! The dog's gone."

But his obvious fears that the cat would scratch or bite Robyn were completely misplaced. Thin sides heaving and tail twitching erratically, the animal made no move to struggle.

"The poor thing! Look, Shane, its ear's all torn." She gently fingered one tattered ear. "Its coat's all matted, and I can feel every rib—"

"Robyn," Shane broke in patiently, "we can't take a cat with us on the boat. We'll find someone—"

"It's hungry!"

"—to take care of it," he finished firmly.

"It might be sick!"

"All the more reason—"

"Every boat needs a mascot. And it doesn't have a home; I just know it doesn't. It wouldn't take up much room."

"Robyn—"

"I'll take care of it!"

"Robyn, you can't paper-train a cat!"

She looked up at him pleadingly. "We can work something out. Please, Shane?"

"Oh, hell," he muttered. "You're more trouble than you're worth, do you know that?"

"Am I?"

He stared at her, then gruffly answered, "No." He handed her the dolphin, turned her toward the walkway, and gave her a light swat on the bottom. "Go on to the boat. I'll see if I can rustle up a litter box and some cat food."

Robyn smiled at him over her shoulder as he strode off into the darkness, then made her way carefully to the boat. Luckily, the marina was somewhat thin of boats at the moment, so she had very little trouble finding theirs.

On board, she went below and turned on the battery-powered lights in the galley. She rummaged around until she located a can of tuna for her new pet. While the cat—a "he" she had discovered—was eating, she went into her cabin and left the dolphin on the bunk, then found her spare hairbrush, her shampoo, and a towel.

The cat didn't like the small galley sink. Nor did he enjoy having every inch of his emaciated self ruthlessly washed. He was, however, remarkably docile about the situation. He never once threatened to scratch or bite.

Robyn dried him carefully with the towel, talking to him all the while, and fed him another small meal of condensed milk. When Shane returned nearly an hour later, she was sitting cross-legged on the floor of the galley, gently applying peroxide to one battered ear of a hesitantly purring and much-improved-looking black cat.

"Got it tamed, I see." He set a plastic box and two bags on the tiny table. "It looks like you've made a friend for life."

"He doesn't look so bad now, does he?" Robyn inquired in a rewarded voice, putting the top back on the peroxide bottle. "In a week or so, he'll be a new cat!"

Shane sat down on the narrow bench by the table. "He, huh? Well, what are you going to name him?"

"I don't know. Suggestions?"

"Pyewacket," Shane supplied instantly.

Robyn started laughing. "Why that?"

"Because he's obviously going to be a witch's familiar."

"Funny, funny. Be serious!"

"King George, then."

Robyn cocked her head to one side. "Which King George?" she asked gravely.

"The one they had to lock up."

"George III?"

"If that's the one they had to lock up. He was mad as a hatter, too. Kept screaming 'Off with their heads!' "

Robyn frowned at him. "I think you're a little confused. The Queen of Hearts in *Alice in Wonderland* screamed that. King George III was just a little batty."

Shane's emerald eyes twinkled down at her. "If you say so. Anyway, that's a King George if ever I saw one."

"Have you?"

"Have I what?"

"Ever seen one?"

"Don't be so literal."

Robyn grinned at him, then sobered abruptly. "Thank you for letting me keep him, Shane." She looked down at the sleepy cat in her lap. "I've never been able to have a pet before."

"Why not?"

She waved a hand vaguely, still watching the cat. "Oh, Daddy traveled so much, from base to base. It just wasn't practical. And Brian had an allergy."

"So you compromised."

"I suppose." Robyn was dimly surprised that both she and Shane were beginning to take any mention of her husband so calmly. Shane no longer tensed whenever Brian was mentioned, and Robyn found herself a little less guarded.

"You've always compromised for the men in your life, haven't you, honey?" he suggested quietly.

Robyn looked up, startled. "I don't know what you mean," she said uncertainly.

"I think you do." Shane was watching her very intently. He shifted sideways on the bench, leaning forward and resting his elbows on his knees. "You traveled with your father, even though I'm willing to bet you never enjoyed it. You didn't have a pet because it would have been a problem for him."

"I traveled with Daddy because I wanted to be with him," Robyn insisted quietly. "My mother died when I was three; Daddy was all I had. And he never refused to get me a pet."

"Because you never asked."

More than a little startled by Shane's perception, Robyn could only stare at him mutely. He went on, his voice determined.

"Then there was your husband. I think you compromised a great deal with him. You said that he traveled a lot in his work—and you traveled with him. He had an allergy, so you didn't have a pet. And I'll bet you didn't work because he didn't want you to."

"I didn't have to work."

"But you wanted to. I'm sure you went to college. Business degree?"

She nodded slowly, her gaze dropping to the sleeping cat.

"You wanted to work, maybe start your own business. But your husband didn't want you to. So you didn't."

"Make your point, Shane," she said in a low voice, tacitly admitting that his guesses were on target.

"You're a very . . . selfless woman, Robyn. You always seem to be molding yourself to someone else's wishes. Even this trip. The thought of getting involved with me threw you into a panic, but you agreed rather than fight me."

"Would you rather I'd said no?" she snapped suddenly, looking up at him with stormy eyes.

"There it is," he said softly, as if to himself. "That spark of temper. How much you must have resented doing what was best for someone else instead of what was best for you."

"You didn't answer my question, Shane," she pointed out tightly.

He smiled slightly, his green eyes still thoughtful. "You know the answer. I'm very glad you said yes. But, Robyn, don't ever hesitate to get mad at me, or tell me what you really think. It's very important for you and me to be honest with each other. Agreed?"

Robyn got to her feet slowly, holding King George in her arms. Shane was so patient, she thought wonderingly, so determined to set their relationship on the right course. "It's been a long day. I think I'll take a shower and turn in. Good night, Shane."

"Agreed, Robyn?" he repeated firmly.

"Agreed," she murmured at last, heading toward her cabin.

She put King George on her bunk and watched the cat curl himself into a contented ball, then she gathered up some things and went into the tiny bathroom. She coped with the narrow shower stall almost automatically, her mind occupied with what Shane had said. Emerging from the bathroom minutes later, she found that he had fixed the litter box for George and left it in the hallway. She was at her cabin door, wearing her terry robe and carrying odds and ends, when Shane stuck his head out of the galley.

"I got my sleeping bag and some other stuff from the cabin, so I won't have to disturb you later. Good night, honey." The emerald eyes flared slightly as they took in the damp robe, but he said nothing more.

Robyn murmured a good night and went into her cabin, shutting the door quietly behind her. She sat on her bunk for a long time, watching George with eyes that never really saw him.

Shane was right: they had to be honest. In theory, that was fine. But in practice . . .

She could never be truly honest with Shane, she knew, until he was told who and what her husband had been. Until he knew how terrified she was of giving her heart to another reckless man . . .

Chapter Six

George claimed his new role of ship's cat with great gusto and rapidly learned certain key words of nautical terminology. Phrases such as "You damned cat!" irately bellowed at him by Shane while Robyn laughed obviously meant that sail-climbing wasn't encouraged.

Robyn tried her best to teach the seagoing cat a few manners, but he seemed obstinately determined to get on Shane's nerves. In fact, as Shane pointed out menacingly, he seemed to have a death wish. Robyn spent most of Thursday alternately yelling at the cat and warning Shane not to yell at the cat. She finally pointed out to George that swimming back to land wasn't something to look forward to, but since her pet chose to ignore the lecture in order to attack the end of a line Shane was tying off, she couldn't feel that she had done much good.

"Robyn!"

"I know, I know! George, don't do that! Maybe if I wrap you up in one of these ropes, you'll stop playing with them."

"I'm going to tie him to the anchor and drop him overboard!"

"You wouldn't do that to a defenseless creature—"

"Defenseless? He scratched the hell out of me not an hour ago!"

"You pulled his tail!"

"How else was I supposed to get him down from the sail? Now look at him, dammit! You stupid cat, that's a mast not a tree!"

"Shane, don't—" She listened to words of blue origin for a moment, then murmured, "—pull his tail."

"Robyn, I'm warning you—!"

"All right, all right! I'll get him down."

When she wasn't saving George from the jaws of death or becoming an accomplished sailor, Robyn spent most of her time trying to learn how to work the stove in the galley. Shane had fixed breakfast—and very well, too. Lunch had been sandwiches, but supper had to be cooked. Robyn was elected.

The stove was a gas model, and the pilot kept going out. Being just a bit wary of fires on boats at sea, Robyn kept yelling for Shane to come down and light it for her. After his fifth patient trip below deck, Robyn noticed a somewhat frantic gleam in his eyes, and she decided prudently to handle the stove by herself from then on.

She pulled out all the stops with supper, determined to give Shane the best meal he'd ever had on land *or* sea. The boat was anchored in a small cove near Long Key, and Shane was topside getting everything ready for night, so other than stepping over George every time she turned around, Robyn was able to work undisturbed.

She delved into her memory for Marty's cooking lessons and produced a meal that even that stern critic would have praised. Ruthlessly making use of all the fresh vegetables Shane had stocked, she fixed a savory stew, the heavenly aroma of which made her mouth water. She took advantage of the cook's privilege of "tasting" and managed to stave off starvation while completing the rest of the meal.

The stew was to be accompanied by creamed corn, a crisp green salad, and biscuits made from a special southern recipe. She also found a can of apples and managed to make an apple pie in spite of the oven's recalcitrance.

She was hot, tired, and smudged with flour by the time she yelled for Shane to come and get it. The expression of surprise on his face, however, made up for her weariness. But she became more than a little irritated by his unflattering astonishment when he tasted the first bite.

"My word. She can cook!"

"Well, you don't have to look so surprised."

"How was I to know? You seem to be a lily of the field when it comes to everything else."

Robyn picked up her fork and glared at him. "Can you walk on water?" she asked with deceptive mildness.

"No," he replied, eyeing her warily.

"Then you'd better quit while you've still got a boat under-foot."

"Sorry." Shane bent his attention to the meal and was silent for a few moments. Soon he began murmuring, "This is terrific . . . I haven't eaten a meal this good in years . . . spices and every-thing . . . Is that an apple pie I smell?"

Robyn finally looked up at him with laughing eyes. "All right, you can stop now! I've been suitably mollified. Besides, I didn't rave like that over your bacon and eggs."

"Those weren't worthy of raving. This is." He grinned at her, then stood to get himself another helping of stew.

After the pie, they shared the cleaning-up chores, which soon became a comical enterprise in the cramped quarters—particularly since George insisted on getting into the act. George retired to the cabin, however, after Shane stepped on his tail for the second time.

By the time the last dish was washed and put away, Robyn was beginning to feel more than a little breathless at Shane's nearness. Aloud, she blamed the stuffiness of the galley and quickly climbed the steps to the deck for some air.

She stared out over the sea, listening to the gentle slapping of water against the hull and the night sounds coming from the tiny island a few yards away. When Shane came up behind her and pulled her back against him in a gentle embrace, she didn't resist.

He rested his chin on the top of her head. "I've enjoyed today," he murmured softly, as though reluctant to disturb the peace all around them.

Robyn smiled into the darkness. "Even George?"

"Even George." He pulled her a bit closer, then added whimsically, "Do you know that you have a smudge of flour on your nose?"

"And you're just now telling me about it?"

"I think it's cute. Adds a certain something."

"I'm sure!" Robyn reached up to wipe the smudge away, but Shane turned her around to face him.

"No, let me."

Robyn looked up at him, able to see him now in the glow from the huge yellow moon rising over the horizon. She felt the tingling shock of his fingers softly brushing over her nose, and she became suddenly, painfully aware of a churning emptiness in the pit of her belly. Without conscious volition, her hand lifted to rest lightly on his chest, feeling the springy softness of curling hair exposed by the opening of his shirt.

Shane's brushing fingers began to caress, tracing the curve of her cheek, the trembling softness of her lips, finally cupping her face warmly. His free hand lifted to her hair, raking through it gently and freeing the heavy mass from the pins she had used to keep it out of her way.

"I want you so much," he breathed huskily.

Robyn was sure the fingers lightly touching her throat could feel her pounding pulse, but she didn't care. "You made up the rules," she whispered. "You have all the good intentions."

"Would you have come with me if I hadn't decided on the rules and the good intentions?" he asked roughly.

"I . . . don't know," Robyn answered honestly. "But I think I would have."

Shane's hand slid down her back abruptly, pulling her lower body against his and making her all too aware of his pulsing desire. "Robyn, you're driving me out of my mind!" he groaned hoarsely. "How can I keep my hands off you when you say things like that?"

Robyn was very tired of conversation. She slipped her arms up around his neck, standing on tiptoe to mold her body against his. "I don't know," she murmured. "Tell me."

"Robyn . . ." His mouth unerringly found hers in a fierce kiss of driving need. It was like that first night, when nothing seemed to matter but their mutual desire, their need to touch and go on touching because it was something they couldn't fight.

Along with the excitement fluttering through her veins, Robyn felt a sense of triumph and exhilaration. She was tired of playing by Shane's rules, and more than a little dissatisfied with the platonic relationship he had imposed on them. Unwilling to make a commitment, she was still fiercely determined to be in his arms, to feel his touch on her reawakened body. She wanted him.

Her fingers threaded through his hair, her mouth echoing his demand with a heat that matched his own. Shane's hands moved up and down her back unsteadily, shaping her willing flesh and pulling her closer until their hearts seemed to beat with a single pounding rhythm.

Robyn threw her head back, shivering, as his mouth finally left hers to press hot kisses against her throat. Through half-closed eyes, she stared up at the stars, thinking dimly that they had never seemed so close. She could almost reach out and touch them.

"Robyn, you're playing with fire," Shane warned hoarsely, his hands defying the protest with increasingly demanding caresses.

She gasped when one hand closed around a sensitized breast, forgetting the stars for more earthly things. She could feel his thumb probing through the material of her knit top, and she managed to say fiercely, breathlessly, "I hope I get burned!"

Quite suddenly, her upper arms were gripped in steely hands, and she was held nearly a foot away from the body she wanted so badly to touch. Shane was staring down at her, his jaw taut, his eyes a glittering neon green in the moonlight.

"But *I* don't want to be the one to burn you. Don't you understand that?" he asked hoarsely. "I don't want to wake up in the morning and find you gone because you only needed one night. I need *more* than one night, dammit! And until I'm sure—"

Robyn broke the grip of his hands and took a careful step backward. For the first time, she was furious with him. Utterly and completely furious. He was trying to back her into a corner, and she didn't like it one damn bit!

She was only dimly aware that there was a curious role reversal in the situation. She was taking the "traditional" male attitude, insisting on no strings and no complications. She wouldn't make a commitment while the threat of his hobby haunted her. But Shane wanted more.

Robyn didn't say a word as she turned and made her way to the top of the steps. There she spun about abruptly to face him. "Tell me something," she requested, her voice amazingly mild under the circumstances. "How many times do I have to throw myself at you before you catch me?"

With his back to the rising moon, she could make out nothing of his expression. But his silhouette was stiff with tension, and she could see that his hands were clenched into fists at his sides. When he answered her question, his voice was a hoarse rasp in the darkness.

"As many times as it takes. Until you get it right."

Robyn's smile showed most of her teeth but was not meant to be taken as amusement. "I'll keep that in mind."

She turned back to the steps, making her way down them to the hall. Going into her cabin, she flipped on the light, shut the door with unnatural care, and then looked around for something to throw across the tiny room. The only thing she found was her pillow, and that made a disappointingly quiet thump against the wall.

She ducked under the top bunk to sit on the lower one, leaning against the wall and staring with brooding eyes at the small chests containing her and Shane's clothing.

How, she wondered vaguely, did one go about seducing a man?

Oddly enough, she had never had the opportunity to employ such tactics, and she hadn't the faintest idea how to go about the thing. And there was no one to ask advice of. She couldn't very well radio the Coast Guard and ask them to find someone to give her a verbal crash course in the art of seduction.

She should have asked that blonde . . .

The thoughts and speculation that sailed lazily through Robyn's mind during the next hour surprised her. She was tired of playing Shane's games, but her determination to play a game of her own struck her as being not only odd but also potentially dangerous. It would be much simpler to just go up to Shane, announce that she was ready to make a commitment, and then attack him.

Robyn chuckled as that scene played out in her mind's eye, then she sobered. She couldn't do that. Maybe because she wanted to put off facing what had to be faced—his damned racing.

In the meantime, however, her nerve endings were shrieking at her, and she had a feeling she wouldn't sleep tonight. Her body cried out for Shane. Slightly less than a week before, he had shown her delights she didn't want to have to do without.

Yet for some reason, she was determined to have what she

wanted without having to commit herself. Perhaps it had something to do with Shane's calling her "selfless."

For once in her life, she was going to be selfish. So all right. She chewed on a knuckle thoughtfully. Intuition told her that if she wandered up on deck stark naked and started talking casually about the weather, she would probably accomplish what she wanted.

That, however, would hardly be subtle. In fact, it would be downright blatant. Even if she could find the nerve for it.

She slid from the bunk and stepped over to her chest, opening drawers and taking out an item now and then. Funny . . . she might almost have had seduction in mind when she'd packed for this nice platonic trip. And even if Shane suspected what she was up to, there wasn't very much he could do about it. So she had until Sunday night to accomplish her "task." By Monday afternoon, they'd be back in Miami, and Shane would be on his way to Daytona.

Three days . . .

When Robyn entered the galley on Friday morning, Shane was busily making pancakes and George was sitting beneath the tiny table with an aggrieved expression on his furry face.

"You've been stepping on George's tail again, haven't you?" Robyn demanded in lieu of a more traditional good morning.

"He got in my way." Shane cast an irritated glance at their feline mascot. "That's probably how his tail got to be crooked in the first place." He half turned to look at Robyn, and his eyes widened almost comically as they swept her petite figure, which was clad only—apparently—in a dark green button-up shirt that belonged to him.

"I borrowed a shirt of yours," she said casually. "Hope you don't mind." She could see his eyes speculating on whether or not she wore anything beneath the flimsy cotton.

"Not at all," he muttered, turning back to the stove.

Robyn smiled slightly as she gazed at his broad back. The smile was new to her, something that had surprised her only moments before while she'd looked into the mirror and brushed her hair. Her smile, she had realized, was feline in the extreme. The way she imagined women down through the ages must have smiled while busily plotting the downfall of a man . . .

"Can I help?" she asked brightly.

"Feed your cat," he grunted.

Robyn crossed to his side to open a cabinet door. "My, but we're surly this morning," she observed, getting out the cat food. "Didn't we sleep well?"

Shane neatly flipped a pancake out of the pan and onto a plate. "Since neither one of us is royalty," he said tersely, "you can dispense with the 'we.' *I* slept fine."

Since Robyn had heard him pacing the deck above her head long after she'd turned out her light, she knew that to be a barefaced lie. But she hid another smile and silently fed her cat.

She was encouraged rather than upset by his irritation. It showed her clearly that his good intentions were beginning to get a bit threadbare. And that was just fine with her.

They ate breakfast in something of a strained silence, then Shane went up on deck to get them underway while Robyn cleaned up the galley. By the time she mounted the steps, he was ready to raise the sails. Robyn took the wheel, watching him and humming to herself. Her hair, not braided or pinned up today, fanned out behind her in the breeze as the boat began moving in the brisk wind.

It was oppressively hot even with the wind, and the sky looked a bit hazy. Robyn saw Shane cast several thoughtful glances up while he worked, but he said nothing.

Shane shed his shirt and tossed it back to land at Robyn's feet, leaving him only in shorts and sneakers. She inhaled deeply at the magnificent spectacle. She saw him glance back at her more than once, but what was on his mind she couldn't tell. He came to take the wheel once they were well underway, and she stepped back with a smile.

He returned the smile—half forced and half wary, Robyn thought—but the expression died an almost ludicrous death when she calmly started unbuttoning her shirt.

"Robyn—"

"I think I'll get some sun," she said casually. "Is it too hazy, do you think?" She tossed the shirt onto the padded bench.

Shane's eyes swept her body, taking in the bathing suit that would have turned heads on the Riviera, and then skittered away hastily. "No," he rasped, and then cleared his throat. "No, I don't think it's too hazy. Watch out that you don't burn, though."

"I'll be careful," she promised, leaning against the side of the boat and reaching back to brace herself on the low chrome railing. The suit, she thought cheerfully, certainly had the effect the saleslady had promised.

It was black, one-pieced, and far from demure. Tying at the neck, two narrow strips came down to just barely cover the tips of her small full breasts before joining below her navel, becoming one strip that continued between her thighs and back up over the gentle swell of her bottom. Two skimpy strings anchored the bottom part of the suit by tying around her waist.

The strings were tied in a bow.

Robyn had bought the suit on a whim—mainly because Kris had been teasing her—and had never gotten up the nerve to wear it. Until now.

She was feeling reckless, and the feeling was wonderful. She felt marvelously free for the first time in literally years, pleasing herself by deciding to tempt the fates and do something out of character. If she had been playing with fire the night before, she was playing with dynamite now, and there was something wild and exhilarating about it.

In that moment, Robyn came closer than she ever had to understanding why men like Shane and Brian shared a love of danger. She was not, like them, risking her life on a dangerous impulse, but she began to understand how danger—any kind of danger—could hold a strange, addictive joy.

"Robyn?"

Emerging from her reflections, she turned her head to look at Shane. "Yes?" she responded, reaching up to brush back a strand of windblown hair and blinking at him in the still-hazy sunlight.

"Where did you get that?"

"What?"

"That suit you nearly have on."

"Why? Don't you like it?" she asked in injured innocence.

Shane very nearly glared at her. "If you're wearing it when we sail into Key West," he said flatly, ignoring her question, "you'll probably be arrested."

"Don't be ridiculous. Everything that should be covered is, so why worry?"

He looked as if he wanted to argue with her, but he said nothing more.

Robyn turned her face back up to the sun, feeling rewarded and wondering if her strategy was working as well as she hoped it was. She could feel Shane's eyes on her from time to time, and she discovered yet another unfamiliar sensation: a heady pleasure in the knowledge that he found her body beautiful. She felt a bit like an exhibitionist posing in her skimpy suit, but she told herself firmly that the cause was certainly worthwhile.

Shane's temper became more than a little frayed as the day wore on. He anchored the boat close to one of the small keys near Marathon at lunchtime and dove over the side without explanation. Robyn, whose suit really wasn't designed for swimming, calmly went below and fixed a lunch of sandwiches. A lunch Shane hardly did justice to when he emerged, dripping, from the sea.

Robyn kept her suit on until they got underway again, raising the sails herself this time. She was an old hand at it by now and didn't have to ask for instructions or help from her silently watching skipper.

Tying off the last sail, she started back toward Shane, wondering if she had imagined his low groan moments before. He certainly looked a bit odd, she thought, and she suffered a brief moment of compunction. But only a brief moment.

She wasn't *doing* anything, after all.

Robyn went down to her cabin and stared at herself for a long moment in the small mirror over the chests. She carefully brushed the tangles from her hair, then changed out of the suit and into a pair of very brief white shorts and a flimsy button-down shirt, the tails of which she tied in a knot beneath her breasts. No bra, and it was obvious. She stared into the mirror again, then turned away, muttering to herself, "I must make a lousy vamp."

The afternoon, however, progressed quite nicely—for her, anyway. Other sailboats were in strong evidence as they neared Key West, and Robyn enjoyed waving at anybody who waved at her. Most of the wavers, she noted, were men. Shane didn't seem to notice all the attention Robyn was drawing, but he did swear somewhat violently when one busily waving skipper nearly plowed his small sailboat into an even smaller catamaran.

"You," Shane declared flatly, "ought to be locked up!"

"Why?" She looked at him innocently.

"You're a hazard to navigation. And get that damned cat down off the sail!"

"Temper, temper," she chided as she hurried to foil George's attempt to see the world from the top of a mast.

Prudently, she held George in her lap during the rest of the trip into Key West. Nudging Shane was one thing, she decided, but there was no sense in shoving him. Coping with George was the straw he didn't need. There was a fine line between passion and anger.

They tied up the boat at a marina in Key West and went ashore for the few remaining hours of daylight. Shane kept Robyn close to his side while they visited the lighthouse, the Aquarium, and the Little White House. Drawing the inevitable masculine glances, Robyn looked up once to see Shane bestow a stony glare on one perfectly harmless-looking man. She hid a satisfied smile.

She wondered vaguely if falling in love with Shane had done this to her: made her a mass of contradictory impulses. She wanted him, but didn't want to make a commitment. She had been grateful for his platonic rules only days before, but now she wanted them broken.

She wanted him to carry her off to their boat and make love to her until she couldn't think straight, until questions of right and wrong and what was good for her no longer mattered.

Lying alone, but for George, on her bunk that night, Robyn suspected a little grimly that Shane had finally caught on to her game. She wondered what had taken him so long. Not that it mattered. He knew now; there had been speculation in his eyes as he'd wished her good night up on deck. Now that there were two in the game, what role would he play?

He had become a little thoughtful while they'd eaten supper at a hamburger place, narrowed eyes watching her intently. But he had continued to talk to her casually, certainly not demanding an explanation for her behavior.

He didn't ask for an explanation on Saturday, either.

Robyn wore a skimpy bikini during the morning, waving energetically at other boats as they left the marina and nearly hanging over the side in her enthusiasm.

Shane looked amused.

Robyn dug out her bottle of suntan lotion once they were well underway, and asked him to get her back for her since she couldn't reach it.

Shane complied with perfect calm.

Robyn found the remains of the first day's bottle of wine and toasted his health all through lunch.

Shane drank half the bottle and stayed sober as a judge while Robyn fell asleep on the padded bench.

Robyn woke up mid-afternoon, feeling cranky, and purposely let George finally succeed in climbing to the top of the mast.

Shane laughed.

By the time they dropped anchor off Long Key late that afternoon, Robyn was ready to consign man and cat to Davey Jones's Locker and sail home alone.

Banging pots and pans in the galley while Shane got everything ready for night, she was torn between irritation and amusement. Some vamp she was! She couldn't even get the man drunk and take advantage of him, for God's sake!

Damn that chameleon she'd idiotically fallen in love with! She needed a scorecard to keep up with his moods. Wonderfully tender on that first night; utterly stricken when she'd told him about Brian; calm and reasonable when he'd proposed this trip; charming the first couple of days; bad-tempered and brooding yesterday; and completely cheerful today.

It'd serve him right, she thought sulkily, if she made him fix his own damn supper!

Before she could do more than roughly plan a meal, Shane was yelling down at her from the deck, effectively wiping rebellious thoughts away.

"Better make it a cold supper, Robyn!"

Robyn braced herself automatically as the gentle rocking motion of the boat began to increase in intensity. Frowning, she stared out the tiny porthole above the sink, uneasily realizing that the setting sun was now hidden behind leaden clouds. She quickly put away the pots and pans, hanging on to the sink from time to time to brace herself.

Latching everything securely, she started up the steps to the deck, meeting a nervous George and watching him over her shoulder as he dashed into her cabin.

She found Shane carefully tying the sails down, and her uneasiness increased as she saw his serious face. "What's going on?" she asked, looking worriedly at the choppy water surrounding them.

"Storm," he replied briefly, double-checking the knot he'd just tied. "Coming out of the Gulf."

"How bad?"

Shane must have heard the anxiety in her voice, because he turned his head to smile reassuringly at her. "Shouldn't be too bad. These late afternoon storms usually blow over pretty quickly. And we're in the lee of the island, which helps. We'll probably feel quite a bit of motion, though, so if you're nervous, you'd better go take a pill."

"I've been all right so far," she defended hesitantly.

"Suit yourself." He shrugged.

Robyn decided to take a motion-sickness pill just to be safe.

She'd nearly reached the steps when Shane called out to her.

"Have you started supper yet?"

"No." She paused, looking inquiringly at him.

"Just as well. We probably won't feel like eating until this is over with."

Having completely abandoned her attempts in the art of vamping, Robyn silently went below and took a pill. Two, actually. Then she sat on the narrow bench by the table in the galley and stared at the porthole. It darkened rapidly, brightened from time to time by flashes of lightning. Thunder rumbled distantly, and then closer.

Robyn became aware of rain pattering on the deck above her head just as she heard Shane's feet on the steps. A moment later, he was sliding onto the bench beside her.

"That should do it," he said as if to himself, then sent a sidelong glance at her tense face. "Not worried, are you?"

"Me? Worried? Why should I be worried?"

"We'll be fine, Robyn."

"Right," she murmured. "Right, skipper."

"I promise."

"I'll hold you to that."

Shane smiled slightly and then suddenly asked for his explanation. "Mind telling me the rules for the little game you've been playing since yesterday?"

Robyn stared at him for a long moment, then asked wryly, "Is this what's known as 'getting her mind off things'?"

"Acquit me of any ulterior motives. I'm just curious, that's all."

Suddenly embarrassed by his perception and her own ridiculous games, Robyn stared down at the table top, flushing. "Well, find something else to be curious about, dammit," she mumbled.

In a thoughtful voice, for all the world as though he were talking about something inconsequential, Shane said, "I couldn't decide whether to take you up on your somewhat blatant offer, or throw you overboard."

"Thanks!" she snapped tartly.

"However, since I'd already decided to abide by my good intentions, there was only one thing to do."

Robyn gave him a speaking glare. "Which was?"

"Enjoy the show," he stated solemnly.

She decided very sanely that the first chance she got, she was going to brain him. Or hang him from the mast like a flag. Or—what was it?—keelhaul him. Or feed him to the sharks.

"So it was funny, huh?" she asked mildly.

"Not funny. Amusing."

"Some difference."

"A distinction, actually. A small distinction."

"Did you ever read that story 'Murder on the Boat'?"

"No." His lips were twitching.

"Stick around," she gritted.

The emerald eyes gleamed at her. "Actually, you make a pretty fair seductress," he commended judiciously.

Robyn's sense of humor suddenly began producing giggles. "Really? Then tell me, O knowing judge—what was wrong with my technique?"

"Wrong?" he asked innocently.

She watched as he rose from the bench and stepped over to the stove, expertly keeping his balance as he began to make a pot of coffee. "Yes, wrong. Obviously, I did something wrong."

"Well, there's one thing you didn't realize," he drawled, keeping one hand on the pot's handle as he held it over the burner.

"Which was?"

"All you had to do was ask," he explained gravely.

Robyn stared at him a bit wildly, totally oblivious now to the rocking of the boat.

"Coffee, Robyn? I think it's going to be a long night."

"You can say that again," she muttered.

Chapter Seven

As the night wore on, Robyn drank black coffee steadily, watched lightning flash outside the porthole, and listened to the heavy rain and booming thunder. The rough motion of the boat didn't bother her, but she didn't try to get up from the bench to test her sea legs.

She was obstinately determined not to ask Shane to explain his cute little remark.

Shane seemed content to sit in silence, occasionally getting up to fill their cups or make more coffee.

By the time midnight crept by, with the storm still raging outside, Robyn was too sleepy to care much about anything except her inviting bunk in the cabin across the hall. Making a fool of oneself, she decided wryly, was certainly tiring.

With a certain perverse pleasure, she jabbed Shane in the ribs with her elbow, and murmured, "Move, will you, please? You have to get out before I can, and I'm going to bed."

Shane slid out from the bench and got to his feet, rubbing his lean ribs and staring at her ruefully.

Robyn held on to the table until she found her balance, then looked up at him. "Since you obviously can't sleep on deck tonight, you're welcome to the other bunk."

"I can sleep in here."

She stared rather pointedly at his six-foot length and then at the miniscule floor space. "George couldn't stretch out in here, let alone you. Take the other bunk. I only hope you don't snore."

"You couldn't hear it even if I did," Shane retorted as another crash of thunder rattled the boat.

Not finding the remark worthy of response, Robyn carefully made her way out of the galley and into the cabin, grabbing an occasional doorframe or wall for support. Trusting that Shane would give her time enough to get ready for bed, she closed the cabin door, flipped on the light, and rapidly encountered problems.

For instance, it was damnably hard to balance on one foot with a boat heaving underneath that foot. And pulling off the knit top she had changed into after her nap gave her a giddy sense of vertigo and caused her to sit down rather abruptly on the floor.

Changing took much longer than usual, so that when Shane tapped on the door, she was just pulling her sleeping gear—a large white T-shirt—into place. "Come in," she muttered, her back to the door while she tried to pull her hair out from under the shirt.

"Need some help?" Shane asked in amusement when he opened the door and stepped into the cabin.

"Never." Robyn wasn't particularly in charity with him at the moment, and didn't care if he knew it. Having finally won the wrestling match with her hair, she picked up her brush from the chest she was hanging on to and then stepped rather carefully over to the bottom bunk. Pushing George off her pillow, she crawled under the light blanket, still pointedly ignoring Shane.

There was barely room enough for her to sit up without banging her head on the top bunk, so she had to bend her neck a little.

Brushing her long hair steadily, she murmured vaguely, "Get the light, will you?"

Leaning against the chest containing his clothes, Shane sighed. "Are you going to sulk all night?" he asked dryly.

"Probably," she reflected calmly, shooting him a guarded glance from the corner of her eyes. "By tomorrow, though, I'll probably be good and mad. Are you going to get the light?"

"In a minute. I think I should explain something first."

"Don't go to any trouble on my account," she advised politely.

He sighed again. "Robyn, before you waste a lot of energy getting mad at me—"

"I thought you wanted me to get mad. You told me not to be afraid to get mad at you."

"I meant for a good reason. This isn't."

"Funny, I thought it was."

"Dammit, are you going to listen to me?"

Robyn tossed her brush to the bottom of the bunk beside George, plumped up her pillow, and lay back. "What choice do I have? I can't walk on water, either."

Shane rested his weight on the low chest while he pulled off his sneakers, tossing them into a corner before beginning to unbutton his short-sleeved shirt. "I thought you might be curious," he said casually, "to know why I've apparently been cutting off my nose to spite my face these last few days."

Robyn linked her fingers together behind her neck and stared fixedly at the underside of the top bunk. "So you're going to enlighten me?" she asked just as casually, but with her entire attention riveted on him.

"I think it's time." The light went out, and Shane climbed easily into the top bunk, murmuring, "Some things are better said in the dark. Especially when they're being said to an indignant lady."

"Don't bother being polite. Actually, I'm mad as hell."

He chuckled softly above her. "I know. That's why I want to lay all my cards on the table and be completely honest."

Robyn felt more than a little nervous when he said that, but her voice was calm when she responded, "Shane, if this trip has showed you that you really don't want to get involved with me, just say so."

"You know better than that. Robyn, when we met that night, I thought you were something I'd dreamed up. And after we'd spent the night together, I wouldn't have willingly let you go for any reason I could think of."

A peculiar hot-cold sensation churned in Robyn's middle at the seriousness of his deep voice, and she felt a fleeting sense of panic. The entire situation was about to come to a head, she knew, and she still wasn't ready to confess her fear . . . or her love.

Shane continued quietly, and even though they weren't touching and couldn't see each other, Robyn was aware of a strange, almost painful intimacy between them in the darkness.

"When I believed that you had a husband lurking around somewhere, I wasn't sure what I felt. Rage, jealousy, even betrayal. But stronger than anything else was the desire to see you again, to find out if you'd been struck by lightning that night the way I had."

"Lightning?" Her voice was barely a whisper.

"Didn't you feel it, too?" He sighed roughly. "Songs and poems are written about it, psychologists try to analyze it, scientists try to explain it logically, skeptics say it doesn't exist." He paused for a moment, then went on huskily, "I was never in that last group, honey; I always believed in love. But I never expected to look across a crowded room and fall head over heels in love with a tiny, raven-haired, golden-eyed mystery lady."

"Love at first sight?" she asked unsteadily, a part of her wanting to see his face for the truth, and part already knowing that he was speaking it.

"Why do you think I've been chasing after you like a madman?" He swore softly, roughly, his voice half amused and half pained. "I wouldn't admit this to anyone except you, honey, but my dreams of romance were just that—dreams. Vague, impractical things. I never expected to have to deal with the memory of another man, or those fears of yours that are keeping us apart."

Robyn swallowed hard, her throat dry. "Fears?"

"We both know you're afraid. I was hoping this trip . . ." His voice trailed away, and he cleared his throat. "I don't know what you're afraid of, Robyn, or whether something about your marriage has you afraid of a commitment, or whether it's me—"

"Not you," she interrupted quickly. "Never you."

"Well, that's something." He shifted restlessly on his bunk. "I hope you'll tell me what you're afraid of when you're ready to. All along, I've felt as though I were . . . fighting something in the dark. It seems best to just take things one day at a time, to give you time to get to know me. I didn't think I was getting anywhere until you started your seduction act on Friday."

The amusement in that last sentence brought a flush to Robyn's face, but she was curious. "You knew . . . that I wanted you before that. You knew the first day on the boat. Why did yesterday make a difference?"

Shane answered slowly, as though he were working it out in his own mind. "The first couple of days on the boat, you were . . . aware of me. The electricity, or whatever it is, between us wouldn't let it be any other way. But you were still running scared. Then something changed. You admitted that you wanted to touch me, needed to, and instead of taking the decision out of your hands and making love to you, I told you that I wanted you to be sure."

He chuckled suddenly. "I'm just guessing, honey, but I think that's what made you mad. You stopped running long enough to turn around and fight. But you still wanted me to make the decision, so you started pushing me."

Listening, open-mouthed, in the bunk below, Robyn realized

abruptly just how childishly she'd been acting. Shane was right, damn him! She'd wanted to be absolved of the responsibility, swept off her feet and able to make only a token protest.

"Are you psychic?" she mumbled.

"I'm right, then?"

"Bull's-eye."

His voice was warm with amusement. "That's when I realized I was getting someplace. Even though you didn't want to commit yourself, you still wanted me badly enough to be a bit reckless."

"Oh, God, I feel like a fool!" she moaned, grateful for the sheltering darkness.

"That wasn't my intention, honey," he murmured, his voice becoming serious. "But I wasn't kidding when I said you only had to ask. I'm not trying to punish you for anything, and I hope to God you don't think that! I just believe that you should be sure enough about what you want to throw away the games and face up to how you feel. When you tell me what you want, honey, I'll know that you're willing to take the first step toward commitment."

Robyn drew the blanket up around her shoulders, suddenly feeling chilled in the hot, stuffy room. "And what do you want, Shane?" she whispered.

Very quietly, he answered, "I want you to marry me, honey."

Panic ricocheted through her mind, leaving bruises and pain. "Shane, don't—"

"Ssshh," he interrupted soothingly. "I'm not trying to pressure you, Robyn. I'll wait as long as it takes. I just want you to know that I want you to be my wife more than anything in the world. And we'll take all the time you need to work out those fears of yours."

Robyn wanted very badly to touch him, her hand lifting almost instinctively toward his bunk and then falling back. She wanted him to hold her and reassure her and tell her everything would be all right. But she knew that, once in his arms, sanity would vanish . . . and he wanted her to know exactly what she was doing.

"We only met a week ago," she murmured finally, trying to be rational, reasonable. "How can you be so sure that—that you want to marry me?"

"I'm sure." His voice was very certain. "I've been looking for you all my life, Robyn. I think you've lived in my dreams for years. And I'll walk barefoot through hell to keep you."

After a moment, he continued softly, "I've waited too long for you to lose you by impatience, honey. Now, we'd better get some sleep. We have a long day ahead of us tomorrow. Good night."

"Good night," she whispered, her mind on everything but sleep. She lay awake for a long time, staring at the underside of Shane's bunk, her thoughts, dreams, and desires confused and uncertain.

Her last clear thought before sleep ruthlessly claimed her weary mind was the vague realization that Shane had chosen to tell her of his love in the darkness because he believed that she was unable, or unwilling, to return that love.

Hours later, she woke with chilling suddenness, her hand lifting to cover her mouth and muffle the cry that would have disturbed Shane. She found herself curled into a tight ball on the bunk, her heart thudding painfully, the nightmare as vivid as though it were still replaying before her eyes.

The cabin was hot, stuffy, and suddenly stifling, and she had to have fresh air. Carefully, she straightened her cramped limbs and eased herself from the bunk. Only dimly aware that the boat was almost motionless, the storm over, she crossed the cabin to the open door, closing it behind her softly.

Wearing only the T-shirt, Robyn climbed the steps in darkness, knowing her way instinctively by now. The light, cool breeze on the deck was a blessing, and she knelt beside the padded bench, resting her elbows on the vinyl covering.

She stared out over the water, her gaze fixed on the still-blackened eastern horizon. Her nightmare hovered like a relentless nemesis, demanding to be seen, to be faced.

She bit her lip, her mind's eye re-creating the nightmare, just as it had really happened on the small television screen she had watched dumbly. Brian's crash. The twisted, flaming wreckage held in cruel focus by the camera. Firemen and paramedics . . .

And then the scene changed, and her most recent nightmare began, hurting her as nothing had before. Now it was Shane's broken, charred body they were pulling from the blackened metal deathtrap.

Tears rolled down Robyn's cheeks, hot and silent, and she tasted the coppery blood from her bitten lip. That cruel, heartbreaking vision would remain with her, she knew, as long as Shane raced. Eating away at her strength, her courage. Destroying her.

Once committed, she would cling to him as she had never clung to Brian, try in a hundred small ways to keep him by her side. Cut off his freedom. Smother him.

No. No, she couldn't do that. She had to find out if she was strong enough to watch him leave her side and climb heedlessly into a cage of death. Because if she couldn't—if she didn't face and conquer that fear—she would always be afraid of something. Weak and helpless in the grip of uncontrollable terror.

It was right, she knew, to fear for Shane when he raced. That fear was rational and understandable. But the terror she felt went far beyond anything rational. And it didn't stop at racing. She was terrified of losing Shane . . . in *any* way.

It wasn't possible to chain him to her side for fear of losing him. It was the quickest, surest way she knew of to destroy love, and two lives as well. And asking him to give up racing would be—if he agreed to—the first link in that deadly chain.

If only she weren't so afraid. If only the vision of Brian's death didn't keep haunting her. And her father's death in yet another twisted wreck only three years ago . . .

Robyn rested her head on her folded arms, letting the tears flow freely at last. She felt as if she were at the end of her rope, and she wasn't even sure she possessed the courage to face Shane.

When she finally raised her head, the eastern sky had lightened to slate gray and her knees were numb from kneeling on the hard deck. She gazed around absently, then frowned and reached underneath the bench, finding the storage locker and the sleeping bag Shane kept there. She got to her feet stiffly, automatically unrolling and unzipping the bag and spreading it out on the deck.

Stepping to the middle of the quilted softness, she sank back down to her knees. Feet beneath her, she folded her hands limply on her bare thighs and faced east. Like some brooding Buddha, she waited patiently for the sun.

It had been a long time since Robyn had watched a sunrise. It had been a favorite pastime of her childhood, but the wonder of those precious moments had somehow gotten lost during her adult years of change and turmoil.

Now a peculiar sense of peace stole over her, bestowed by the peace all around her. No sound disturbed the new day; even the sea was still. Only the gentle lapping of water against the side of the boat was audible, and the soft steady sound was as comforting as a heartbeat. Robyn thought dimly that the problems of the world disappeared in the beauty of a new dawn, and she felt her own fears and worries gradually fade away.

The horizon had lightened to a deep blue, the last stars had gently winked out overhead, and Robyn was acutely aware that she was no longer alone. As though he were an extension of herself, she felt Shane kneel behind her on the sleeping bag. Her mind curiously suspended, she wondered if he had come because she had wanted him here, because the moment needed him to be complete.

He slipped his arms around her silently, fitting her within the warm hollow of his thighs, his hands covering hers. Robyn leaned her head back against his shoulder, barely breathing as she watched the new day being born. That Shane shared her fascination, she knew; his body was utterly still, his eyes fixed on the horizon, his breath gently stirring her hair. And she could feel his heart beating steadily, keeping time with the lapping water.

Blue lightened to violet and then to pink as the sun announced its coming—hesitating now, teasing them with the delay. Then the first crescent of orange topped the horizon, and shafts of light began to coat the sea in silver. It seemed to hesitate yet again, and Robyn held her breath, almost certain that Shane did the same.

The huge orange ball rose slowly, majestically, like a king rising before an audience of rapt subjects. Robyn felt her lips curving into a smile, certain that this birth was more beautiful than yesterday's.

"So beautiful," she whispered. "So perfect."

Shane's arms tightened around her, and his voice was as hushed as hers when he murmured, "The touch of dawn washes everything clean and new."

Watching the sun rising, its orange brightening to yellow, Robyn felt Shane's statement sinking into her mind, taking hold, giving her the new perspective she had needed so badly.

She half turned in his embrace, still resting between his warm thighs as she stared up at him. "A new beginning," she whispered, her voice filling with wonder. "A fresh start."

Shane smiled down at her, his emerald eyes shining with the love he had admitted last night. One large hand lifted to cup her cheek. With the perception that astonished and exhilarated her, he murmured softly, "A new beginning for the world . . . or for us?"

Speaking as much to herself as to him, she whispered, "I've been afraid to take that first step—to move forward or back. But every day begins new. You said it yourself. The touch of dawn washes everything clean. Every *day* is a fresh start."

Shane's thumb brushed her bottom lip, and then his smile faded and his eyes dropped to the tiny wound he had found. "You've hurt yourself," he murmured, frowning.

"Not anymore." A smile trembled on her lips. "I'm not going to hurt myself anymore."

His gaze lifted swiftly to meet hers, the emerald eyes immediately darkening, becoming bottomless pools. "Robyn . . . ?" he breathed questioningly.

"I'm asking, Shane," she whispered, her hands moving to touch his bare, hair-roughened chest. "Will you make love with me?"

His eyes flared suddenly, and if Robyn had possessed any doubts about his love for her, they were erased. Because she recognized that look. From the very beginning, his vivid eyes had flared with that half savage, half tender emotion, and she knew now that it was love. The fierce yet gentle love she had wanted for so long . . .

And Robyn was taking her first step by dawn's light.

Shane pulled her abruptly closer, nearly crushing her against his broad chest, his mouth finding hers in desperate need. Robyn locked her arms around him, her desire rising in a flaming fury to meet and clash with his.

She had never been so sure of anything in her life as she was that this moment was right. The sun was rising on a new day and . . . Yes. Yes!

Robyn felt his tongue exploring, possessing, and her own tongue joined the passionate game. Her nails lightly scratched the rippling muscles of his back, and she felt him shudder and draw her impossibly closer.

Shane's mouth left hers, dropping tender, burning kisses over her eyes, her nose, the hollows beneath her ears, her throat.

"What if the Coast Guard sails by?" she questioned throatily, only mildly interested.

"We'll wave at them," he answered hoarsely, intent on exploring the warm flesh of her throat.

Robyn laughed and then gasped as one of his hands slipped up beneath her shirt and closed over a breast. When he suddenly began pulling her shirt off, she helped, anxious to do away with the barriers separating them. Shane quickly removed his shorts, tossing them aside.

He drew her down to lie beside him on the quilted softness of the sleeping bag, emerald fires raking her slender, golden body. "God, but you're beautiful!" he groaned softly.

Her eyes, in their turn, were taking in the lean strength of his body. "So are you," she told him huskily, feeling the same wonder she had felt in a lamplit hotel room a lifetime ago.

The lion's growl rumbled from the depths of Shane's chest as he bent his head, his mouth hotly capturing the hardened tip of one aching breast. His tongue swirled maddeningly around the taut bud, seemingly insatiable in its hunger. His hands explored, fondled.

Robyn bit her lip with a moan when his fingers gently probed the quivering center of her, her body instinctively arching against his. His mouth transferred its attentions from one breast to the other, his fingers continuing their erotic caress.

Tension splintered through Robyn, and her nails dug into his shoulders as Shane's lips moved in a burning trail over the sensitive skin beneath her breasts, settling for a moment on her navel where his tongue dipped hotly, then moved lower.

Through half-opened eyes, Robyn watched the mast soaring above her head begin to spin drunkenly, feeling that she was in the middle of some wild cosmic storm. Dizzily closing her eyes, she felt the heat of the sun and of her desire, and she didn't know or care which was stronger.

"Shane!" It was half a protest, half a plea to continue his spellbinding touches.

"You're beautiful," he rasped, the feel of his words against her flesh nearly driving her crazy.

Robyn felt the excitement spiraling crazily, becoming a primitive, driving rush toward release. She was carried along helplessly on the wave, moaning raggedly, the hands she held him with going white with nearly unbearable tension. And then the world dissolved.

She floated for timeless moments, drained almost to the very depths of her soul.

She opened her eyes slowly as Shane came up to rest beside her, his body taut, his emerald fires blazing down at her. When he bent his head to kiss her gently, blotting out the sunlight, Robyn felt the fires within herself kindling to new life.

Pushing almost fiercely against his chest, she rolled with him, coming to rest on top of him as the kiss ended. She felt a sudden yearning to know him as he knew her, to explore every inch of his body until it was as familiar as her own.

She pressed teasing kisses against his throat, his shoulders, her lips finding and capturing the flat male nipples. Concentrating only on pleasing him, she was barely aware of his hands unsteadily stroking her hair, her back. She slid her lips over his flat, hard belly and then lifted her head.

Slowly, almost hesitantly, she rested one hand on his chest while she explored with the other, feeling his heart hammering wildly. He jerked slightly as she touched him, held him, and his breath caught with a rasping sound in his throat.

Robyn caressed him gently, tentatively. And then she bent her head once again, her long hair forming a curtain around her face as she tasted every inch of his flesh she could reach. She felt no shame, no hesitation now. With a need beyond reason, she had to know him.

"Robyn!" he groaned hoarsely, and then she was being lifted and turned as easily as a child. She felt the softness of the sleeping bag beneath her back. Shane rose above her, the emerald fires now burning almost out of control.

She felt his weight, welcomed him eagerly, and as they became as close as separate beings could ever be, looked deeply into his eyes. There she saw undisguised love burning even brighter than desire.

In that timeless moment, Robyn became acutely aware of his stark vulnerability, and his willingness to show her that. That realization crumbled her last defense. Locking her arms around his neck, she cried huskily, "I love you, Shane! I love you."

Shane went still for a moment, something very fierce and male flashing in his eyes. He lowered his head, kissing her with that tender, savage passion she loved. "Robyn . . . beautiful Robyn . . . I love you so much!"

They began to move together with the grace of trained dancers, each of them giving and taking until they were drained and filled and drained again. Like helpless voyagers adrift in the heart of a raging sea, they clung to one another as the only stable things in a universe gone mad.

And then even that crazy universe turned inside out, and they crashed to shore like shooting stars.

Robyn was the first to stir from the limp, exhausted tangle of arms and legs, and then it was only because she felt the sun beating down on her and was suddenly worried about being sunburned in uncomfortable places.

"Do you always seduce your women on the high seas?" she asked in a muffled voice, trying to move and finding very little energy for it.

"Never," Shane responded in a lazy voice. "You did the seducing."

"I did not," she objected, managing at last to raise her head and stare down at him. "I was a total washout as a vamp. You told me so."

"Not a *total* washout." Shane didn't bother to open his eyes. "With a little practice, you'll be topnotch. I'll let you practice on me. S'matter of fact, I won't mind a bit."

"That's big of you." With an effort, Robyn disentangled herself and sat up. She found herself staring at a little island off their port side, and she suddenly had a horrible thought. "Shane, does anybody live on that island?"

"Key. And I wouldn't be a bit surprised." He opened one eye and peered at her. "Why? Worried about your modesty?"

She transferred her gaze to him, not greatly surprised to find that she felt no shyness. Not with him. From the very beginning, she'd been without modesty with him. "Well, it's a little late for that," she pointed out wryly. "But shouldn't we shove off before somebody calls the police?"

With startling energy, Shane rose to his feet and lifted her easily in his arms. "No. First, we're going for a swim. Then we'll have breakfast. We'll get around to shoving off later." He smiled down at her, apparently not the least bit concerned that if there was a watcher on the Key, he was getting an eyeful.

In the same calm voice, he demanded, "Now tell me, beautiful witch—did I really hear what I thought I heard in that dream I just had?"

Robyn stared at him for a moment, then smiled slowly. "I hope you heard it. A woman likes to be heard when she tells a man she loves him."

Shane's eyes held a trace of wonder. "And a man likes to be loved by the woman he loves," he said huskily. His arms tightened around her. "I wasn't sure we'd make it, sweetheart."

Her smile faltered for just a second. "There are still some . . . rough seas ahead," she warned lightly.

"I know." The deep voice was sober. "You'll tell me all about it when you're ready."

And with the abruptness of his earlier movements, he threw her overboard. Robyn came up sputtering. Treading water and pushing her hair out of her eyes, she glared up at him. "That was a rotten, no-good, low-down, sneaky trick!" she yelled at him.

"How's the water, honey?" Shane asked with interest, evidently completely unabashed by his nakedness or his actions as he leaned over the side.

"I'll get you for this!"

"Is that a promise?" He leered, arching his eyebrows.

"Dammit, this water's cold!"

"A brisk, reviving swim—that's what we both need."

"*We?* I don't see you out here. What's that over there? Is that a shark?" she yelped.

"No, it's a stick in the water."

"I saw it move!"

"The current made it twitch. Stop imagining things."

"You're a funny man." Robyn splashed water toward him, irritated when her aim fell short. "Well? Are you going to stand there and smirk all morning, or are you going to join me in the cradle of the deep?"

Shane grinned at her. "Having a lively sense of self-preservation, I have no intention of coming in until I'm reasonably sure you won't try to drown me."

"Who, me?" Robyn smiled innocently. "Why worry? You're bigger than I am."

"Yes, but you're a witch, and witches cast spells and things. Eye of newt and toe of bat and so on."

Robyn laughed so hard she nearly forgot to tread water. "Bats don't have toes!"

"Whatever." He raised one foot to rest on the chrome railing and leaned an elbow on his knee. "Anyway, I don't want you casting any more spells. I'm still tangled up in the first one."

"The first one?"

"Sure. I looked across a room and tumbled into a pair of golden eyes. Definitely a spell." His emerald eyes were acquiring a gleam she recognized well.

Robyn eyed him carefully. "You seem to have recovered rather quickly from your exhaustion," she observed.

"You noticed that, huh?"

"It's a little difficult not to."

"Mermaids in the water do that to me." He smiled slowly. "One sure difference between a man and a woman . . . a man can't hide his desire."

"Especially a naked man," she pointed out.

"Are you complaining?"

Robyn took another stab at the art of vamping. Smiling gently, she murmured, "I'm simply wondering why you're still on the boat . . ."

She read the intent, flaring expression in his eyes long before he left the boat in a clean dive, and she hastily began swimming away. He caught her before she'd taken three strokes.

"Come here, witch . . ."

"Shane? Shane, not in the water! We'll drown!"

Chapter Eight

They didn't make very good time that day, which was—as Robyn gleefully pointed out more than once—all Shane's fault. Periodically, he would suddenly drop the sails, allowing the boat to drift, and lunge at Robyn. And since she couldn't run very far on a boat, he inevitably caught her.

"I've spent half the day trying to keep my clothes on!"

"I didn't notice you trying very hard a few minutes ago."

"A gentleman wouldn't point that out."

"Gentlemen don't have any fun."

The boat nearly ran aground on a sandbar once while they were otherwise occupied, and then later showed a tendency to drift toward the Bahamas. After that, Shane began dropping the anchor when he dropped the sails.

George climbed the mast and sails from time to time, then apparently lost interest in the game when neither of his human companions objected. He sulked on Robyn's bunk for the rest of the day.

Robyn had never been happier in her life. She was delighted by the fact that Shane couldn't let brief moments go by without touching her and holding her—delighted because she felt the same way about him. Laughter and teasing and love surrounded her, claimed her, and she pushed the fears from her mind. Like Scarlett O'Hara, she would think about that tomorrow.

Since Shane *said* he was determined that they reach Key Largo by sundown, they didn't stop the boat for lunch. Robyn went below and made sandwiches, bringing everything up on deck and feeding Shane a bite at a time while he steered.

"You know, I really don't know much about you," she commented thoughtfully a little while later, sitting cross-legged on the bench in one of Shane's shirts. "Generalities, but no specifics."

"What do you want to know?" Shane was spending more time gazing at her with glowing eyes than paying attention to their course.

"Well, everything, obviously! Tell me about your family . . . and where you live when you're not traveling . . . and your favorite colors . . . and what you plan to do with your life . . . Good Lord—I don't know *anything* about you!"

He chuckled softly. "We can fix that. Let's see—my family. I think I told you that Mother runs the family wine business. My father died about ten years ago. I have three younger sisters, two of them married and one still in college." He slanted Robyn a grin. "I spent a lot of years playing big brother. And they all still run to me when they have a problem, which I'm glad of."

The brief sketch told Robyn more, perhaps, than Shane knew. It told her that he was accustomed to responsibilities, which he didn't shirk. Inevitably, she compared him to Brian, whose recklessness had carried over into his personal life. He had always left responsibility to others.

Shane was chuckling again. "Sharon, the youngest, is suffering the pangs of love at the moment. Or she was when she called me a couple of weeks ago. She's after some med student at UCLA, and since she's majoring in history, they don't seem to have much in common."

Robyn smiled at him. "So she called big brother for advice. And what did big brother tell her?"

"To keep looking! My baby sister has fallen in love a dozen times in the last year alone. I keep telling her not to try so hard."

Laughing, Robyn observed, "I bet she liked that!"

"Sure." Shane grimaced slightly. "I've heard cleaner language from liberty-bound sailors."

Robyn smiled at the affection in his voice, then prodded curiously. "Do you all live in California? When you're not traveling, I mean?"

"As a matter of fact, aside from Sharon, who comes home for holidays, we all live within a few miles of each other. The business is in the northern end of Napa Valley. Mother lives nearest to it. My oldest sister, Connie, married a lawyer, and they live nearby. Beth's the middle sister. She startled all of us a few years ago by marrying the eldest son of a vintner—our biggest rival! I don't know who was more dismayed, Mother or Beth's new father-in-law."

"Montague and Capulet?" Robyn teased, her lips twitching.

"Only in tragedies!" Shane laughed softly. "Actually, Mother and Alan's father accepted the situation with good grace. The rivalry is a cordial one."

"A missed opportunity!" Robyn mourned with mock regret. "Just think how romantic it would have been: a modern day story of star-crossed lovers! A family feud—"

Shane grinned at her. "No way! For one thing, Beth's no weeping Juliet. She would have told us all to go to hell and marched off with Alan to conquer a world or two. And I'm sure Alan could slay dragons with the best of them."

"Really?" Robyn lifted an inquiring brow. "And how are you at slaying dragons? A woman likes to know these things."

"Not bad." Shane pursed his lips thoughtfully. "Although I think I'm better at scaring away things that go bump in the night."

"Dragons don't go bump?"

"Have you ever *seen* a dragon? They're huge. Absolutely huge. Before you hear the bump, you're squashed flat."

"Then how do you slay them?"

"Where on earth did you go to school? I've never heard such ignorance! Dragons are slain with magic swords, of course."

"I beg your pardon," Robyn sputtered, biting the inside of her lip to keep from laughing out loud. "I thought it was slingshots."

"That was Goliath," Shane informed her pityingly.

"Oh." She reflected for a moment. "Are there dragons in Napa Valley? Do they squash the grapes?"

"Oh, we drove them deep into the mountains years ago," he told her loftily. With spur-of-the-moment invention, he continued gravely, "They only come out in years ending in a zero, and then we find a witch to curse them until they hide again."

"I *knew* you had an ulterior motive!" she accused.

"Of course. I need a resident witch. With her own familiar and a book of spells to keep the dragons away, so I won't have to dent my magic sword."

"Oh, damn," she murmured mournfully. "And I traded my book of spells to a wizard for Stardust! I'm afraid you'll just have to keep looking for your witch. I won't do at all."

"Are you kidding? It took me too long to find you. We just won't tell the dragons about the book. You can chant at them in pig Latin or something. They'll never know the difference."

"I'd never have the nerve. Dragons terrify me."

"Nonsense. I'd be standing by with my magic sword, just in case."

Robyn's laughter finally began escaping. "Oh, God!" she gasped. "I've never been party to such a ridiculous conversation in my life!"

Shane grinned at her, but then the grin faded, replaced by a frown. "Hey, witch-lady," he ordered, "get your butt over here."

"I *beg* your pardon!" Her voice was frosty, but she relented beneath his narrow-eyed, threatening stare and got her butt over there. "I'm here, skipper," she said meekly, but with a grin.

Shane hauled her against his side with one arm, resting his chin on the top of her head. "It's been nearly half an hour since I've touched you," he complained gruffly. "I was beginning to suffer withdrawal symptoms."

Robyn slipped her arms around his waist, rubbing her cheek against his bare chest with kittenlike contentment. "You never told me where you live in Napa Valley," she murmured.

"Actually, I live above the valley. I have a house halfway up a mountain. Lots of wood and stone, and huge windows with a terrific view. It stands empty for most of the year, now, but I'm hoping that'll soon change. Would you like to live in a mountain aerie, witch-lady?"

The casual question demanded a casual answer, and Robyn swallowed hard before she could supply one. "I think . . . that I'd love to live in a mountain aerie," she finally got out lightly. "As long as my dragonslayer lived there, too."

He brushed his lips against her forehead gently. "Your dragonslayer," he vowed huskily, "will always be there. He'd sell his soul to the devil for a promise of eternity with you, love."

Robyn shut her eyes against the bright reflection of sunlight off the water and refused to let herself think about eternity. Or even tomorrow. "I love you, Shane," she whispered.

"I love you, too, honey. So very much."

They stood that way for a long time, only the snapping of wind in the sails and the splash of water disturbing the peace of their surroundings. Then Shane—perhaps sensing, with his uncanny perception, her need to hold the fears at bay with laughter—became playful once again.

His hand slid downward and shaped a rounded hip. In a shocked voice, he exclaimed, "My God—the woman's wearing nothing but this flimsy shirt! Are you lost to all decency?"

Robyn batted his hand away and laughed. "You should know. I seem to remember express orders from the skipper to wear something without snaps, buttons, or zippers. That was after my shorts and top bit the dust for the third time."

"Counting your conquests—and at your age, too!"

"I'm putting notches on my belt." She gasped suddenly as his hand returned to probe more intimately beneath the shirt. "What *are* you doing?" she asked breathlessly.

"Well, if you don't know by now—"

"Shane! Look, there's another boat coming! They'll call the Coast Guard, and we'll be arrested for shocking the fish or something. Darling, put both hands on the wheel—!"

The "darling" was nearly her undoing, since Shane promptly showed signs of abandoning the wheel and shocking more than the fish. She somehow managed, however, to be sitting decorously on the padded bench when the other boat sailed by. Fortunately, she reflected, the other skipper and crew weren't close enough to observe her flush or the gleam in Shane's eyes.

In spite of everything, they reached Key Largo by the time the sun was setting. But Robyn was somewhat puzzled at first when Shane decided that they would drop anchor in a small cove rather than enter the marina they had stopped at before.

"No marina?" she questioned.

"I don't think so."

"Why not?"

"Well, those bunks below are pretty narrow."

Light dawned, but Robyn kept a straight face. "So?"

"We'll be up here on deck." Busily tying one of the sails, he slanted a gleaming look her way. "And it's remotely possible that we could shock narrow-minded neighbors in the marina."

Solemnly, Robyn said, "We wouldn't want to do that."

"Of course not."

"You're a dirty old man."

"I am not old!" Shane protested indignantly.

"You have a one-track mind."

"Quoth the vamp."

"*I* didn't nearly run us aground. And I didn't let the boat drift toward Cuba, either."

"Of course not. And you didn't look at me with bedroom eyes all day. Or call me darling and distract me all to hell."

"Well, if you don't like it—"

"I like it too much, witch, and you know it! But if you don't help me tie down these sails, I may not be a nice guy and let you out of galley duty tonight the way I'd planned."

Robyn promptly went to help him. "I don't have to cook? What did you have in mind? No, don't answer that. I *know* what you have in mind!" She dodged his playfully threatening hand and continued teasingly, "But neither man nor woman lives by shocking the fishes alone. We have to eat."

"We'll shock the fishes *after* we eat. If you ask me nicely, I just might let you watch the master chef at work."

"Doing what?"

"What master chefs do best. Grab that line, will you?"

"I will if you'll stop grabbing me!"

"I like grabbing you."

"Really? I never would have guessed if you hadn't told me. *Now* look what you've done! I only have three buttons left on this shirt, dammit."

"Your vamping abilities are coming along nicely."

"Shane!"

The night passed in a dreamy haze as far as Robyn was concerned. Making love under the stars was an experience she would treasure for the rest of her life, and Shane's tenderness seemed to deepen and grow with every passing hour. He made no attempt to hide the awe he felt at the incredible feelings between them, and his openness sparked an openness in Robyn that she hadn't known she possessed.

But "tomorrow" inevitably came, and all too soon they were beginning the last leg of their trip only miles out of Miami. The morning slipped past quickly, filled with the laughter and teasing that made Robyn feel as if she'd known Shane for years.

"I feel like the sultan's favorite girl," she grumbled once. "Will you *stop* looking at me like that?"

"Like what?" He was smiling.

"Like you're the sultan!"

"Your lord and master, in fact."

"Gloria Steinem freed the slaves."

"Well, she missed one." He ducked hastily. "Witch! You just threw a perfectly good shoe overboard, and I'm not going back for it!"

"That's all right. It was your shoe."

After Shane had wreaked awful vengeance on his unrepentant crew, they got back underway and, since the wind held, rapidly made up for lost time. By the middle of the afternoon, they were almost within shouting distance of Miami.

Robyn fell silent as they neared their destination, feeling fear take hold of her and this time refuse to be shaken loose or pushed away. Shane would race in exactly one week, and she didn't know if she would have the strength to face it.

She had to tell him about Brian's death and her fear of racing. Knowing Shane as she did now, she had no doubts that he would instantly offer to stop racing. And, though that was exactly what Robyn wanted him to do, she couldn't allow it. She had to conquer her unreasonable terror before it spread to other areas of her life and destroyed her. She would not be a coward.

"Robyn."

She looked up quickly from her seat on the bench and saw that Shane was watching her steadily. He held out a hand, and she went to him immediately, sliding her arms around his waist as he drew her close to his side.

"You're nerving yourself up to tell me, aren't you?" he asked quietly, rubbing his chin slowly against her forehead.

Robyn nodded once, listening to the comforting beat of his heart and wishing they could just sail away somewhere and abandon the world.

"We'll work it out, honey." His voice was steady, firm. "We'll take all the time you need and work it out. Whatever it is."

"I know." She held on to the solidness of his body as if it were a life line. "I know we will." But time, Robyn knew, had nearly run out. If she could face this upcoming race, she could face the rest. And if she couldn't . . . then no amount of time would help her.

Some time later, they worked together silently tying up the boat in the marina. Then they spent two hours cleaning and leaving everything just as they'd found it. Shane took care of getting rid of the perishable foodstuffs while Robyn neatened the galley and the bathroom. Finally, they gathered their things together and left the boat, Robyn carrying George securely in her arms.

The black Porsche was waiting where they'd left it, and within moments they were on their way to Robyn's house.

She had been aware for some time of the anxiety in Shane's eyes when he looked at her, but she could find no way to reassure him. Thinking of a sunrise and of new beginnings, she watched the sun as it began to lower itself in the western sky.

By the time Shane stopped the Porsche in front of the house, Robyn was strangely calm, ready to rid herself of her last burden of truth. It was time to take the next step.

Shane got her duffel bag out of the car and followed her up the walkway, not pressing for the answers he must have sensed were soon to come.

Marty opened the door just as they reached it, her eyes lighting up when she saw Robyn. The intent glance swept from top to toe, taking in Robyn's golden tan, the neat shorts and knit top, and the quiet glow in her eyes. Then she looked thoughtfully at Shane, standing just behind Robyn with one hand resting almost protectively on her shoulder.

Apparently Marty drew her own conclusions from what she saw. "Welcome back," she said, including Shane in her smile and stepping back to let them come in.

"Hi, Marty." Robyn kissed her lightly on the cheek as she passed. "Back all safe and sound."

"So I see." Marty lifted a pointed eyebrow at the cat as she shut the door behind them. "And one more than when you left."

Robyn smiled down at the cat, and then at Marty. "This is our mascot, King George."

"The third," Shane added, setting the duffel bag down by the door.

"The third," Robyn affirmed. "Marty, would you please take him into the kitchen and find him something to eat? Shane and I have to talk for a while."

Marty didn't ask the obvious question of why they hadn't talked on their trip. She simply looked at Robyn for a moment and then calmly accepted the cat and headed for the kitchen.

Robyn turned and reached to grasp Shane's hand. "There's something I want to show you," she said, managing a smile to ease the anxiety in his eyes.

"I love you, Robyn," he said huskily.

Staring up at him, she realized suddenly that his anxiety was mixed with real fear. A fear of *her* fear. He knew only that whatever it was, it was standing between them. And Robyn knew that he was worried about losing her.

She hadn't meant to build this moment of confession into what it had become: something tense and frightening to them both. Somehow, in that moment, his vulnerability sparked a strength and determination in her greater than she had ever known before.

"Shane," she said very quietly, "I've been looking for you all my life. There was a place in me that nobody saw, nobody touched—not even me. And then you came, and I was whole, alive, for the very first time. I won't give that up. I won't give you up."

He reached up to touch her cheek lightly with his free hand, and a sigh seemed to come from deep inside him. The emerald eyes flared with that fierce glow. "Show me what it is you're afraid of, love."

Silently, she led him to a closed door across from the den, opened it, and led him inside, closing the door behind them and flipping a switch to light several lamps in the room.

It was a large room, furnished as a formal living room. But the closed draperies and curiously empty scent marked it as a room seldom if ever used. It was a room for guests, for displaying one's pride away from the clutter of everyday life.

Robyn leaned back against the door and watched Shane, vaguely surprised that the room caused her no pain this time, no heartache. It was almost as if someone else's memories were stored here.

Shane stared slowly around the room, his green eyes taking in the trophies, plaques, and medals. He stepped over to a low table, heavy with photographs, and picked up one framed in silver. It was of a man, smiling, triumphant, holding a huge silver cup. A dark-haired man, lean, handsome, with a devil-light of recklessness in his blue eyes.

In a low voice, Robyn said, "Brian's father comes here some-times. I thought he might be hurt if all this stuff were packed away. So I've kept it in here. And kept the door closed."

Shane looked up to meet Robyn's steady gaze. "McAllaster," he murmured. "Brian McAllaster. He was your husband."

"Yes. And he was killed in one of those damned cars."

There was a dawning understanding in Shane's eyes as he replaced the photo and stepped toward her. "That's why you didn't want to get involved with me," he said slowly.

She nodded. "I swore to myself after Brian was killed that I'd never again get involved with a man who raced. And then I met you." She stared down at her clasped hands. "Kris told me the next day that you raced. So I . . . convinced myself that I had pretended you were Brian."

"You lied about that?"

The hope in his voice brought her head up again, and she smiled at him a little sadly. "I lied. First to myself, and then to you. I was terrified of loving another reckless man."

"Reckless? Honey—"

Robyn held up a hand to stop him. "Let me explain everything first, all right?" She waited for his nod and then moved over to the couch and sat down. When Shane had taken his place beside her, she half turned to face him and began at the beginning.

"I knew Brian for months before we were married. I knew that he was . . . obsessed with racing. He didn't have to race to make a living, but he loved the excitement and the danger. He told me it was in his blood, and I believe it was."

She smiled suddenly. "Remember the 'groupies' on Key Largo?"

Shane nodded, eyes intent.

"Brian would have eaten that up. He was never happier than when he was surrounded by adoring racing fans."

"But you didn't like it?"

"I wasn't jealous, if that's what you mean. Jealousy over Brian was about as useful as wings on a pig. He just got a kick out of it."

Her brief spurt of humor faded, and she frowned slightly. "I told you that there were problems in my marriage; that was one of them. For me to try and tie Brian down was like roping the wind— useless."

"I'm not like that, love," Shane said quietly, reaching out to take one of her hands and hold it firmly.

"You don't have to tell me that." She smiled at him mistily. Then the smile died, and her fingers closed convulsively over his.

"What is it? Tell me what you're afraid of," he begged softly.

Robyn swallowed hard and answered in a low monotone. "I'm afraid of racing, Shane. When I married Brian I was afraid. I thought that I'd learn to deal with it. But the fear grew into terror."

"Did he know?"

"He knew, but he didn't understand. He thought I was exaggerating, that I just wanted him away from the track. So I learned to keep it inside—and died a little every time he raced."

She took a deep breath and went on before Shane could interrupt. "I thought that not knowing what was going on would help, so I stayed away from the track. Hotel rooms in different cities. I didn't watch television; I didn't listen to the radio; I just had nightmares. Wide-awake nightmares. So I tried—once—being at the track during a race. But that was worse. I felt sick, shaken. I just couldn't understand what drove Brian to risk death every time he got behind the wheel of that car.

"And it got worse. It reached a point where I couldn't even function when he raced. I just stared at the walls and waited for the phone to ring. And then—that day—something drove me to turn on the television. I saw him crash."

"Robyn—"

"I couldn't look away. The car was rolling over and over, and there was fire . . . and I knew he was dead. And do you know what the worst part was?" She stared up at Shane with blind eyes. "The worst part was that I was . . . almost . . . relieved. It was finished.

What I'd been dreading had finally happened, and it was over. I didn't have to be afraid anymore—"

"Robyn!" Shane gripped her shoulders tightly. "Honey, please, stop torturing yourself!"

She blinked at him, and suddenly her eyes were clear again. "Yesterday morning . . . when we watched the sunrise?" Her voice was calm. "I'd had a nightmare. That's why I was up on deck. I dreamed that it was happening again. I was watching it happen. But this time it was you. They pulled you out of that twisted death trap. You were dead."

Robyn drew a long, shuddering breath. "Oh, God, it hurt. It's not possible to hurt that much and go on living . . ."

"Robyn." Shane's hands lifted to frame her face gently. Unsteadily, he told her, "Honey, I wouldn't hurt you or frighten you for anything in the world. I'll stop racing. I don't need it!"

When he drew her fiercely into his arms, Robyn didn't resist. She clung to him for a long while, listening to his heart hammering beneath her cheek and realizing that he had been as disturbed by the past few minutes as she had.

Oddly, she could feel the remembered pain ebbing away. It might have been because Shane had said he wouldn't race anymore. But she didn't think so. He would race again—at least once more. He would race in the Firecracker 400 at Daytona Beach on July fourth, exactly one week from today.

"Give up something you enjoy just because I'm afraid?" Astonished at how calm her voice was, Robyn gently eased from his loosened embrace and rose to her feet, pacing over to the window before turning to face him. "I can't let you do that."

He got to his feet slowly, staring at her with frowning eyes. "You're more important to me than anything. Racing is just a hobby. I won't miss it."

She folded her arms beneath her breasts and returned his steady look. "And what else will I find to be afraid of?"

"Honey, it's a reasonable fear," he said quietly.

"If it were just fear, yes, it would be. But it's terror, Shane. Crippling terror. And if I don't face it now, learn to deal with it, then it'll only get worse."

Shane ran a distracted hand through his hair and sighed roughly. "Robyn, what are you saying?"

"That I . . . have to watch you race. I have to prove to myself that I can handle the fear."

"And if you can't?"

Through gritted teeth, she responded, "I will! I won't let myself be a coward. I won't smother you because I'm terrified something will happen to you!"

He was watching her very intently, a thoughtful expression on his lean face. "This is very important to you, isn't it?"

"Shane . . ." She took a deep breath. "I don't want to tell you to race. I want to live with you in your mountain aerie and make wine and babies. I want to grow old with you. But I have to prove to myself that I'm not a coward."

"You're not a coward, love. You hung on to your sanity for a year while your husband raced. That took courage."

"I didn't love him the way I love you. And I just don't know if I can watch you race, Shane. But I have to try. Do you understand?"

He smiled crookedly. "I think so. But, Robyn, I'm going to marry you no matter what happens. Do *you* understand?"

Robyn hesitated before replying. "One thing at a time, okay?"

His emerald eyes darkened almost to jet. "Robyn, if you're saying you won't marry me if you can't face my racing—to hell with that! I'll hang up my driving gloves, and we'll stop off in Vegas on our way to California!"

She startled herself by laughing. "Commanding sort of man, aren't you?"

"Robyn—"

She lifted a hand to cut him off. "I'm just saying that I want to think of one thing at a time."

"You're going to marry me."

Grateful for the lightened atmosphere, Robyn gave him a mock frown. "Not if you keep ordering me around like that."

"We'll make wine and babies."

"There's a population explosion."

"And you can knit little things."

"I can't knit."

"Then you can *buy* little things. Or you can *sell* little things— like books."

Robyn giggled again and immediately went to him when he smilingly held out his arms. The sense of desperation she had felt for so long was gone now, replaced by the calm determination she had felt earlier. Shane had been right; they would work it out.

He tilted her face up and kissed her. "I have to go take care of some business," he murmured huskily. "Are you going to let me stay here tonight?"

"*Let* you?" Robyn's senses whirled dizzily as she gazed into the slumbering passion and love in his eyes. "I may not let you leave in the first place!"

He chuckled softly, his eyes devouring her. "You've gotten tangled up in your own spell, haven't you, witch?"

"Looks that way." She stood on tiptoe to kiss him lightly, but ended up staying on her toes for some minutes because Shane wanted more than a light kiss. When he finally put her away from him, it was with obvious reluctance.

"If I don't leave right now, I never will," he muttered hoarsely. "And if I don't take care of Mother's business, she'll shoot me."

"You haven't done that *yet*? You mentioned being in Miami because of business a week ago!"

"I've been a bit . . . distracted."

"Your mother won't believe that."

"She will when she sees you."

Robyn smiled and reached out to trace his bottom lip with one finger. "When are you going to Daytona?"

"*We* are going tomorrow. That is, if you can get Janie to run the store for you for another week." When she hesitated, he added quietly. "I need to have you with me, Robyn."

Immediately, she nodded. "I'll call Janie and see what we can work out. You—you will come back here after you've finished with your business?"

"Never doubt it, love." He gave her one last, possessive kiss and quickly strode toward the door. "I'll be back in a couple of hours."

Robyn stood where he'd left her, smiling, until she heard the roar of the Porsche pulling out of the drive. Then she turned slowly, staring appraisingly around the room. Mentally rolling up her sleeves, she briskly got to work.

When George dashed through the open door a few moments later, she was opening the drapes and letting sunlight into the room for the first time in months. Marty came into the room just as Robyn was throwing a pillow at the cat for sharpening his claws on the couch.

"He got into the kitchen cabinets a few minutes ago," the older woman said disapprovingly. "Spilled a box of cereal all over the floor."

"He's been a vagabond, Marty; we'll have to teach him some manners," Robyn responded vaguely, retrieving the pillow from the floor and busily plumping it up. "Do we have any packing boxes?"

"In the storage room. Why?"

Robyn waved a hand at the trophies, plaques, and photographs. "I think it's time this stuff was packed away. Don't you?"

Marty had been watching her rather intently since entering the room, but now she smiled. Apparently going off on a tangent, she murmured, "Does Mr. Shane like baked chicken? I'm fixing it for dinner tonight."

Robyn immediately caught the change in Marty's tone, including the half mocking, semi-formal address, and she knew that the relationship met with Marty's fullest approval. Smiling at the older woman, Robyn laughed. "You know, I haven't the faintest idea whether he likes baked chicken or not!"

Chapter Nine

By two o'clock Tuesday afternoon, Robyn was busy again—unpacking in a lovely hotel suite less than half a mile from the track in Daytona Beach.

"Why did you tell me to pack lots of jeans?" she asked Shane as he hung up the phone and turned toward her. He'd been talking to Eric, and she hadn't paid any attention to the conversation.

"Because the track's not the cleanest place, and that's where we'll be all week."

Robyn felt a quick stab of panic, but curiosity overrode her instinctive reaction. "Why do I get the feeling that I'm going to learn more about racing than I ever wanted to know?" she asked warily.

Shane leaned over to fish a pair of jeans out of his own suitcase, and he waved them about instructively. "The best cure for a fear is familiarity with the object of that fear," he intoned solemnly.

"Uh huh. How sure are you of that?"

He sobered abruptly, smiling at her reassuringly. "Pretty sure. One of my sisters, Beth, was terrified of horses when she was small. Since the rest of us rode, and we didn't want her to miss out on the experience, we all worked to cure her of it. She didn't know much about horses, so we taught her. From the basics. Care and feeding, the different breeds, equipment, and so on. By the time she finally climbed into the saddle, most of her fear was gone."

"I do ride, by the way," Robyn said, mentally going over his strategy and finding it sound.

"Good. I know some terrific trails. Why are you standing there with that shirt in your hands? Move, woman! We have things to do!"

Robyn gave him a long-suffering look and continued with her unpacking. "We're not on the boat anymore; you can stop ordering me around now."

"I like ordering you around."

"I've noticed."

"If you really don't like it, you can try out one of those karate kicks like you did in the shower this morning."

"That was not a karate kick! I slipped on the damn soap, and you know it."

"Good thing I was there to catch you," he murmured.

Robyn threw a pair of her shorts at him and then dashed into the bathroom with her makeup bag before he could retaliate. Emerging to find him hanging up several of his shirts in the closet, she said, "I wonder if Marty ever found Kris. I wanted to let her know we hadn't drowned, but she wasn't home when I called."

Shane turned from the closet with laughter gleaming in his eyes. "I think you'd better sit down," he warned gravely.

Automatically, she sank down onto the foot of the bed. "Why? Is something going on?"

He appeared to consider the thought. "I would say so. Definitely."

"Well, what?"

"It's about Kris. And why she wasn't there to answer the phone."

Robyn eyed him suspiciously. "You appear to be hugely enjoying yourself. Why wasn't Kris there to answer the phone?"

"Because she's here."

"In Daytona?" she asked blankly. "Why would she be here?"

Shane smiled gently. "Remember Eric?" he quizzed.

Robyn stared at him for a long moment with slowly widening eyes. "Eric? She's here with Eric?"

"Well, you told me to give him her number. Apparently, they really hit it off."

"If she's here with him, I guess they did." Robyn shook her head dazedly. "Is it serious, do you think?"

"Judging by Eric's voice, it is. I've never heard him sound so happy. There may well be two weddings in the offing."

"They haven't known each other a week!"

"Does that matter?" Shane asked softly.

Looking at the man she had known less than two weeks, Robyn smiled slowly. "No. That doesn't matter at all."

Slightly more than an hour later, Robyn was trying to get straight in her mind the names of the men in Shane's pit crew. There were half a dozen of them, and the only one she could remember was Shorty—who was nearly a head taller than Shane and thin as a rail.

They were all at the track, and Shane was "starting with the basics." After introducing her to the men, he calmly put her behind the wheel of his car, a gleaming Thunderbird, and began explaining all the safety features.

At first nervous, Robyn quickly became interested enough to pay close attention. She was surprised to find that the car was actually much safer than the one she drove to work each morning;

but she reminded herself that it was a machine pushed to the highest speeds and structurally strained to the limits on the racetrack.

Still, it was reassuring to find that Shane took safety very seriously. He explained the checklist he went over before each race and briefly touched on the amount of work constantly done on the car to keep it in top shape.

The work was going on as they sat there, and Robyn got out of the car—with a little help from Shane, since the door wouldn't open—and walked around to the open hood to see what was going on. She peered into the car's innards, frowning slightly.

"Routine maintenance." Shane had come up behind her. "Right now, he's—"

"I know," she said. "He's adjusting the carburetor."

Shane turned her around to face him. "You are the most amazing mixture of ignorance and gold! You've been holding out on me again, haven't you?" he accused softly.

"Not really." She smiled up at him. "I'm an Army brat, remember? And my father's only offspring. Naturally, I was given the benefit of his teachings. So I do know one end of a car from the other. As a matter of fact, I can tinker with the best of them."

"Change a tire?"

"Or the oil. I even overhauled a transmission once."

"Then why am I paying these lazy bums?" Shane sent a mocking glare toward Shorty, still bent under the hood of the T-Bird. "I'll just hire you."

Robyn shook her head as Shorty chuckled softly. "No way. I don't know anything about race cars. Besides, I'd ruin my nails."

"Women!" Shane rolled his eyes heavenward.

"Uh uh. Woman. Singular."

"I'll go along with that."

Robyn didn't feel the slightest bit of embarrassment as Shane kissed her in front of half a dozen grinning, coveralled men. In fact, she returned the embrace with great enthusiasm.

"Hello? Will you look at that? It's indecent!"

With her arms still around Shane's waist, Robyn leaned sideways to peer past him at Kris and Eric, who had just arrived. "Hello. When did you blow into town?" she asked pleasantly.

"Over the weekend," Kris informed her with equal aplomb.

Looking at her cousin's glowing face and Eric's happy smile—and their entwined hands—Robyn lifted an eyebrow. "That was fast work," she commented teasingly. "I've never seen such fatuous expressions in my life!"

"Try looking in a mirror!" Kris retorted.

Robyn kept one arm around Shane's slim waist as he turned to greet the new arrivals. When Eric immediately began talking about some problem with one of Shane's sponsors, Kris took her cousin's hand and drew her a little apart from the hubbub surrounding the car.

"Robyn, you're going to let him race?"

"What choice do I have?" Robyn was watching Shane.

"Are you kidding? Shane adores you; anybody could see that. He'd do anything for you!"

Robyn transferred her gaze to Kris's worried face. "And I'd do anything for him." Her voice was smooth. "I have to let him race, Kris. I have to know that I can take it, that I won't smother him with my own stupid fears."

Kris stared at her for a long silent moment. "And how will Shane feel," she pressed quietly, "when he has to watch you suffer? He won't do it, Robyn. I think he'll quit whether you can take it or not."

Running damp palms down the thighs of her faded jeans, Robyn met Kris's look, telling herself that her cousin was right about one thing: Shane wouldn't let her suffer if he could help it. His love for her made him as protective as her love for him made her. And she thought with remorse of the fear she had put him through because she'd been reluctant to explain her own fears.

"He won't watch me suffer," she told Kris flatly, fierce determination straightening her shoulders. "Because I *won't* suffer. I won't do that to myself anymore. I won't do that to us."

"You *could* take the easy route, you know," Kris pointed out.

Robyn sighed. "I've taken the line of least resistance all my life. I think it's time I grew up."

"Secrets, ladies?" Shane draped an arm around Robyn's shoulders and smiled down at her.

"We're plotting your downfall, of course," Kris supplied instantly.

"It's a little late for that." Shane grinned as he watched his friend take the hand of his own lady, and then he shook his head in mock sorrow. "You two ladies plotted far too well in the beginning. We've fallen about as far as we can fall."

"She plotted." Robyn sent a demure glance up at Shane. "I cast spells."

"You don't have to remind me of that, witch!" Shane chuckled softly. "I'll never be the same again."

"And aren't you glad—"

"Glad? What man happily welcomes insanity?" Shane retorted.

Eric interrupted as Robyn was playfully trying to strangle her favorite dragonslayer. "As much as I hate to put an end to this little scene," he said dryly, "I'm afraid I have to. Shane, Jordan's threatening dire things if you don't present yourself this afternoon. And since he *is* your biggest sponsor . . ."

"What's he afraid I'll do—run off with the car?"

"Ask him. I'm just passing the message along."

Shane sighed. "All right, then." He winked at Robyn. "Come along with me, witch. I'll introduce you."

"Like this?" She looked down at her jeans and casual top. "I'm not dressed to meet sponsors!"

"Nonsense. You'll melt his crusty, money-grubbing little heart."

"Oh no. You can't hide behind me. I'm not big enough!"

"You'll be all he'll see . . ." Shane purred.

As the week wore on, Robyn found that she was actually enjoying spending most of her time in the large open garage, smelling grease and oil and fuel, listening to men calling out to one another, and growing accustomed to the clank of tools and the roar of engines.

It had never occurred to Brian to ease her fear by exposing her to racing, by giving her a behind-the-scenes look at the sport. And Robyn had wanted no part of it then. But she was determined to learn now, and learn she did.

She sat in on strategy meetings with Shane, Eric, and the "foreman" of the pit crew, Sonny, who was middle-aged, stout, and had a weatherbeaten face and shrewd gray eyes. Silently, she listened as they discussed which drivers would likely be racing and what their habits were.

Shane put her behind the wheel of the T-Bird one day and had her drive once around the track by herself. Vaguely worried that he was breaking a rule by having her do that, Robyn nonetheless found herself fascinated by this new perspective. The audible power of the car made her a bit uneasy, but when it responded instantly to even her inexperienced hand, she relaxed and enjoyed the brief trip.

She met the representatives of various sponsors, learned the names of everyone in the pit crew, and was introduced to sports reporters as Shane's "lady."

Inevitably, "lady" stuck. Whenever Shane came back into the garage after being absent for some reason, his first words would be: "Where's my lady?" If Robyn wasn't immediately produced, he'd keep asking until somebody found her. After the track was nearly turned upside down one day—Robyn and Kris had gone for hamburgers and forgotten to tell anyone—Sonny made it his business always to know where Shane's lady was so he wouldn't be yelled at.

And the entire crew called her Lady as if it were her name.

"You'll always be Lady to them," Kris remarked once in amusement.

"I know. Isn't it sweet?"

Robyn was a bit puzzled, though, at the careful, respectful way the men treated her. Having been an Army brat, she knew very well that when groups of men worked together, there was always a great deal of good-natured roughness, swearing, and rather ribald teasing. That wouldn't have bothered her in the least.

Being wrapped in cotton wool did.

While Shane was in a meeting with track officials on Thursday morning, Robyn cornered Eric to demand what was going on. She found him seated behind a table that served as a makeshift desk, paying far more attention to the blonde in his lap than to the papers spread out before him.

"Excuse me?" Robyn said politely.

Eric, like Shane, was not easily embarrassed. He simply lifted his head, leisurely, and stared at Robyn. "Yes?" he queried with equally bland politeness.

"What's going on?" Robyn leaned her palms on the table and tactfully ignored the flush on her cousin's face. "Shorty nearly had a heart attack when he almost ran into me a minute ago. And Sonny hovers over me like a mother hen. Why am I being treated like I'm made of porcelain?"

Kris giggled, and Eric's lips twitched. "That's Shane's fault, I'm afraid," he confessed.

"What did Shane do?" Robyn asked blankly.

"Put the fear of God into them!" Kris laughed.

"I beg your pardon?" Robyn looked from one to the other.

"Shane had a talk with the men," Eric drawled, amusement in

his light blue eyes. "The gist of which was that if any one of them hurt, frightened, embarrassed, or otherwise disturbed you, he would be quite displeased. So displeased that he would very likely tie the offender to the rear bumper of his car and drive around the track a few thousand times."

Robyn found that her mouth was hanging open, and she hastily closed it. "Well, no wonder I'm being treated like a leper," she muttered. "Don't tell me they believed him?"

"I would have if I'd been in their shoes," Eric replied.

Torn between being warmed by Shane's concern and amused at the situation he had created, Robyn shook her head slowly. "It's got to stop. I'm going to be underfoot for a while at least, and they won't be able to get any work done if they're terrified of tripping over me."

"Sit in a corner." Kris suggested with a grin.

"Then I *would* be treated like porcelain." Robyn frowned thoughtfully. "No, I'll try something else." Without another word to the amused couple watching her, she turned and made her way back to the car.

She watched the activity for a while, then looked down at her shorts and sweatshirt with a faint grimace. Well, she wasn't exactly dressed for it, but she wasn't about to go on being treated like a delicate doll if she could help it. Pushing up the sleeves of her shirt, she set about making herself useful.

For the first hour or so, the men greeted her attempts with bemused wariness, but things rapidly loosened up when they discovered that she knew what she was doing. Amusement grew when she dropped a wrench and swore violently, and when she teased Shorty because he turned red every time she spoke to him.

By the time she had recalled several slightly off-color jokes from her Army days and busily replaced three spark plugs, she was well on her way to being everyone's kid sister.

"Hand me that wrench, Lady, will you?"

"Not that way, Lady—turn it to the left. Yeah, like that."

"I'll toss you to see who goes for lunch. What do you mean, you'll flip the coin? I don't trust you. Shane probably gave you his two-headed quarter!"

"Your father was in the Army? I remember once . . ."

"No, Lady, Shane won't be mad because you sat on his hat. It was his fault for leaving it on the seat anyway."

"And then the General's wife . . ."

"Lady, toss me that filter, will you? I said *toss* it—don't sail it like a Frisbee!"

"No, Shorty doesn't mind getting oil in his eye. Tell Lady you don't mind getting oil in your eye, Shorty. Shorty? Of course he didn't drown. People don't drown in oil. Shorty?"

"And she shoved him out the window because the General was coming, but the bedroom was on the second floor, so . . ."

"Lady, put your hair up under this cap. No, the sponsor won't mind. Besides, it never looked that good on Shane."

"The drive shaft's connected to the . . . Hey, Sonny, what's the drive shaft connected to?"

"Hell, you mean you don't know? Uh oh, we're all in trouble."

". . . and he wanted to know how Joe had managed to break his leg on level ground right beneath the General's window . . ."

"Here, Lady, you can't lift that. Let me. Wait a minute—I can't lift it, either. Shorty? Shorty! Of course he's not hiding from you, Lady."

". . . and the General never could understand why that pair of shoes under the bed didn't fit him."

"Paul, hand Lady that hose . . . Because her hands are smaller and she can get it into place better than I can."

"No, Shorty didn't mind that you stepped on his toes. He shouldn't have been standing there. You didn't mind, did you, Shorty?"

"Lady, take this rag and put it in your pocket; you shouldn't wipe your hands on your shirt. No pockets? Then . . . yeah, do that. You look like an Arab with it draped over your cap."

". . . so this Captain walked in one day, and . . ."

"Here, I'll give you a boost. Crank her up and let's hear how she sounds."

"Of course there's no radio. This is a *race* car."

". . . the base PX just didn't have what he wanted, so . . ."

"Lady, Shorty's eye isn't black. That's the oil from before. And he knows you didn't *mean* to hit him with your elbow. It was all his fault. It was all your fault, wasn't it, Shorty?"

". . . so the Captain says . . ."

Kris wandered in sometime during the morning and watched with wide eyes, shaking her head when Robyn winked at her. She headed back toward Eric, apparently to report the changed attitude among the crew.

When Shane finally got back, Robyn was flat on her back on a wooden creeper underneath the car, helping Shorty.

"Where's my lady?"

She heard Shane's bellow and the answering rumble of male voices. She peered sideways and saw his feet stop beside her own.

"What *are* you doing under there?"

"How do you know it's me?" she asked loftily. "I could be somebody else."

Shane's foot nudged her bare ankle. "Nobody else has legs like these. Why are you trysting with Shorty under the car?"

"I'm not trysting. I'm ruining my nails."

Shane bent down to grasp her ankle, pulling her and the creeper out from under the car. He took the wrench out of her hand, pulled her to her feet, and sent the creeper rolling away with a thrust of his foot. Then he stared at her.

"Should I ask why you're wearing a cloth over your hat? Or

why you're wearing *my* hat? Or why you have a smudge of grease on your nose?" His voice was solemn.

"No."

He sighed and pulled the cloth off her hat. Using the cloth to wipe the grease away, he said, "I seem to spend half my time either putting something on your nose or taking something off it. Why didn't you put on a pair of coveralls if you wanted to tinker?"

"Sonny found three pairs, and I got lost in all of them. Apparently, there aren't many small mechanics."

"Fancy that." He tossed the cloth aside and then pulled off the hat and tossed it aside, too. Abruptly serious, his emerald eyes searched hers intently. "Are you all right, honey? Really all right?"

Robyn smiled and stood on tiptoe to link her arms around his neck. "I'm really all right," she confirmed softly. She smiled sunnily. "But I think Shorty wants to talk to you about a raise . . ."

As the qualifying laps scheduled for Saturday and Sunday drew near, tension increased noticeably among the men. Activity picked up around the track as all the cars arrived, and the place was hectic with noise and semi-organized confusion. Reporters multiplied in number, and flashbulbs began going off unexpectedly.

Robyn felt the growing tension but refused to let it get to her. The days and nights spent with Shane had given her something very precious to hold on to, and her determination to conquer her fear remained fixed in her mind.

She knew that Shane was watching her carefully, knew that he would instantly withdraw from the race if she showed any signs of the torturing fear. That she showed no signs had nothing to do with her ability to pretend; it was impossible to hide her feelings from him.

But somehow, she had gained strength from Shane and from

their love. Knowing that he supported her fully, she was able to look at her fear, for the first time, rationally.

Why had she been so terrified of Brian's racing? Because she had loved him, certainly. But there had been more to it than that. From the very beginning, racing had possessed more of Brian than she had. It had been worse than his infidelity would have been. She could have fought another woman; she couldn't fight a car.

Because racing had possessed so much of Brian, she had convinced herself that it would take all of him. As she had gone with him from city to city, race to race, he had become more and more possessed with the determination to win every time. He had hungered for the Winston Cup, NASCAR's top award, the way another man might have hungered for the woman of his dreams.

And Robyn had grown more terrified.

A normal, reasonable fear of high speeds and danger, coupled with the memory of her father's death at the hands of a drunk driver, had grown into something all-consuming.

Safe in the haven of Shane's love, Robyn looked back on her fear with detached analytical interest.

What had frightened her the most? That Brian would be killed? Or that she was becoming a vague shadow by his side, unimportant, unneeded? Lost in the wake of a speeding car.

Quiet fear, loneliness, resentment, jealousy, ignorance of the sport, hatred of it—all had twisted into terror. A terror she had been unable to fight, even to understand, because there had been no solid foundation to stand on. There had been no loving arms to hold her close at night, at morning, at mid-afternoon. No booming voice demanding to know where his lady was.

How much laughter had she shared with Brian? How many times had she awakened, cold and lonely, with nothing to hold but her growing fear? How many times had a quiet instinct deep inside her murmured that Brian would have been just as happy with another woman, just as pleased by another body in his bed?

He had never worried over her fears. He had never introduced her to sponsors or reporters with possessive pride. He had never looked at her with eyes that said she meant everything to him, or silently shared the heart-stopping beauty of a sunrise.

Why had Brian's racing terrified her? Not because she had loved him. Because he had not loved her.

Robyn allowed the realization to sink slowly into her mind, her heart. Brian had never truly loved her. A little sadly, she understood at last that he had been unable to love her the way she had needed to be loved.

He had been her husband in name, in fact. But he had never really been her lover. And certainly never a friend. And she had never been a wife to him, because he hadn't needed a wife.

But Shane? He was her friend, her lover. He teased her and laughed with her—and held up a mirror to her soul. He was her match, her equal, on some level she couldn't name. The other half of herself, the part that made her complete.

She was necessary to Shane, just as he was to her. His delight in her, in what they had found together, told her over and over again how much she meant to him. With him she had found the companionship she had longed for, the love she had needed.

A mutual love.

For the first time in her life, Robyn completely understood herself. And she knew then that she would be able to watch Shane race, that fear wouldn't cripple her—not because she didn't love him enough, but because he loved her enough. Shane didn't need racing to make him happy, but he needed her. What had he told her only moments after setting eyes on her? That he had dreamed her. That he had always dreamed her.

In that moment, Robyn had felt that she knew him, that she had always known him. She had blamed some fleeting resemblance to Brian and convinced herself that she had wanted one last night with her husband.

But the strange shock she had felt had had nothing to do with a memory of Brian. Wistfully, she had dreamed the encounter the way it might have been between her and Brian. Might have been, but never was. The searing passion and shivering tenderness, the sensation that it was only the two of them alone in a world of magic. The knowledge that everything was forgotten in the wonder of love.

Only Shane's determined pursuit had shown her that her dream had contained not the ghost of her husband, but the living, breathing body of the stranger she had tumbled headlong into love with.

The man she had dreamed of. Always dreamed of.

Racing would never take Shane away from her. Not in this life, and not in the next. He belonged fully to her, just as she belonged completely to him. They would make wine and babies together, and grow old together. And though they would be apart for brief times in the flesh, they would never be apart in spirit.

This new understanding brought a serene glow to Robyn's eyes—at least, that's what the reporters wrote in their "human interest" stories about this woman who had lost one man to racing and was now involved with another.

The enterprising reporter who had dug into Robyn's past and unearthed her marriage to Brian McAllaster tried to interview her, but Shane's constant presence seemed to cramp his style. And since Robyn was only mildly amused by the interest in her past, she said little. So the reporter wove about Robyn's surprised person a tale of love and sacrifice and courage that made Joan of Arc pale by comparison.

Safe in her newly discovered strength, Robyn was able to laugh and shake her head over the story. She tried to explain to the reporter that he was dramatizing things a bit, but he was hot on the trail of what seemed likely to be the most talked about story at that year's Firecracker 400.

It wasn't until his next story appeared in Saturday's newspaper that Shane discovered that Robyn's father had been killed in a car wreck three years before.

"Dammit, why didn't you tell me?"

"It's been three years, darling. It doesn't hurt anymore."

Shane faced her as they stood in their hotel suite late Saturday afternoon. "You should have told me," he said roughly. "How did it happen?"

"Another driver had had too much New Year's cheer. His car crossed the median and crashed into Daddy's."

Shane looked at her searchingly. "I can pull out, honey. It's not too late."

Robyn smiled at him and calmly began unbuttoning her shirt. "Nonsense," she murmured. "You're going to qualify tomorrow, and on Monday you're going to win the race."

His eyes darkened as he watched her dispose of the shirt. "What are you doing?" he gasped.

"Sharpening my vamping abilities. I've nearly gotten them honed to a fine edge, wouldn't you say?"

"I'd say. But aren't we supposed to meet Eric and Kris in the lobby half an hour from now?"

"I think they'll be late. I think we will be, too." Robyn paused for a moment to regard him with a mock frown. "Or should we be conserving your energy? Jocks in training—"

"I'm not a jock," Shane interrupted hastily, moving toward her with desire flaring in his eyes.

"Oh, well. Then we needn't worry."

Sunday afternoon was hot and still when Robyn took her place in the stands to watch Shane drive the necessary qualifying laps around the track. She was aware of her friends' searching glances, but her entire attention was fixed on the Thunderbird rolling out onto the track. It was colorful with the decals of sponsors, and gleaming from the washing the crew had given it only an hour before.

Long moments later, she was turning away from the railing and heading for the pit area. Elation surged through her as she realized that her strongest emotions while watching Shane's car tearing around the track had been excitement and pride.

She was barely aware of Kris and Eric following behind her as she hurried to be in the pit when Shane arrived. She got there just as the car did, and she watched as Shane was helped from the vehicle. He tossed his protective helmet to one of the crew, and emerald eyes immediately searched the small crowd.

"Where's my lady?"

Robyn launched herself from three feet away and was instantly caught in strong arms and swung in a happy circle. "There's my lady," he murmured, utter satisfaction in his voice as he gazed down at her. He kissed her possessively, apparently oblivious to their interested spectators.

"That's showing 'em how, skipper," Robyn said when she finally found the breath for it.

"On the track?" He lifted an inquiring eyebrow. "Or here?"

"Oh, both." Ignoring the chuckles around them, she added softly, "They should see what you can do on the sea . . ."

Chapter Ten

The qualifying laps hadn't frightened Robyn. The race did. She had expected the fear, and she was ready for it. It was sane, rational fear. Shane was driving a car surrounded by other cars in a close pack at speeds in excess of a hundred and fifty miles per hour.

The slightest mistake in judgement on his part, or on the part of even one other driver, could end in tragedy. The grueling pace demanded endurance from both man and machine.

As Monday afternoon wore on, several cars dropped out of the race because of mechanical failure. Heat shimmered above the track, and the roar of laboring engines drowned out every other sound.

Rather than watching the race from the stands, Robyn remained in the pit area. She was there to smile at Shane and give him a brief thumbs-up signal each time he pulled the T-Bird in for a bewilderingly quick change of tires and refueling.

A quick smile and flash of emerald eyes, and he was back on the track again.

There was only one mishap during the afternoon, and it wasn't serious, although it easily could have been. A car blew its engine coming off a turn, and the cars behind it narrowly avoided a collision. One of those cars was Shane's Thunderbird.

Robyn's heart leaped into her throat and hung for an agonizing second until the hazard was safely passed.

"Are you all right?"

She turned her head to find both Eric and Kris watching her carefully, and she knew without being told that Shane had asked them to keep an eye on her.

"I'm fine," she said faintly.

"It isn't easy, is it?" Kris empathized.

"No." Robyn turned her eyes back to the track and rapidly found Shane's car among the others. "No, it isn't easy."

Her heart jumped into her throat more than once during that long afternoon. The courage she had gained during the past few days held—just. Her eyes remained fixed on the T-Bird with almost hypnotic intensity. But an unfamiliar excitement gripped her as Shane established a lead late in the afternoon and doggedly held it.

By the closing moments of the race, the lead had narrowed to one lap, and two more cars blew their engines in a last vain effort to close the gap. When the checkered flag waved above the finish line, it was to signal Shane's victory.

Robyn didn't need Eric's guiding arm to take her to Shane. By instinct, she was heading to meet the Thunderbird as it rolled in. The car was surrounded by jubilant fans and well-wishers, all trying to touch Shane and congratulate him. The loudspeaker was blaring, and the crowd was roaring.

The pit crew managed to cut their way through the confusion of people and help Shane from the car. Flashbulbs were popping all around them, and the din of excited voices filled the air. But his deep voice rose easily above all the chatter.

"Where's my lady?"

He had tossed his helmet aside, and the grime of the long hot hours in the car streaked his weary face. But the emerald eyes were bright with a touching eagerness as they scanned the crowd.

And his lady flung herself into his arms.

It was hours later before Eric and Kris had shoved the last well-wisher out the door and bid Robyn and Shane good night. Looking around their suite at the clutter left behind from the impromptu party, Robyn shook her head in amusement.

"We'd better call the maid."

"In the morning." Smiling down at her, Shane reached out to draw her into his arms. "I haven't had a moment alone with you all day."

"You've been busy," Robyn excused. She laced her fingers together at the back of his neck, happily breathing in the clean, spicy scent of his aftershave. "You barely had time to shower and accept the sponsors' congratulations before the fans started arriving."

"Mmmm." Shane lifted an inquiring brow. "I noticed that wacky blonde showed up. What did you say to her that took the wind out of her sails so quickly?"

"Nothing much." Robyn smiled up at him, remembering the girl from Key Largo and their little confrontation today. "Just that I was going to make an honest man out of you."

His arms tightened around her. "And are you?" he asked huskily, emerald eyes flaring with unconcealed hope.

"Was there any doubt?" Robyn felt her heart lurch with sudden, overpowering love as she met the searching look. "I'm an old-fashioned kind of girl, skipper; you'll just have to marry me."

"Nobody has to point a shotgun at me, honey," he told her gruffly, giving her a bone-crushing hug. "I've wanted to marry you since the moment I set eyes on you!"

"And here I had to do the asking!"

"I asked you more than a week ago!"

Suddenly serious, Robyn looked up at him gravely. "I had to find out a few things about myself before I could answer you," she explained quietly.

"If you could handle the racing?"

"That, and why I was so afraid in the first place. I didn't understand that fear, Shane, and I needed to."

"And you understand now?" he asked, a hint of anxiety in his vivid eyes.

She nodded, smiling as she gazed up at him. "I understand now. I thought that I was terrified of racing, Shane, but that was never the real fear; the real fear was a fear of loss."

Shane pulled her a bit closer, as if to combat that fear. "Loss? You mean because racing is dangerous?"

"Not exactly. It all started with Brian." Her eyes asked his understanding of this last mention of her husband, and Shane nodded silently as he read the question there.

Robyn sighed softly. "I told you once that Brian was obsessed with racing. And I mean just that. He had to win every race; it took up his whole life. Racing had more of him than I could ever have had, and that scared me to death. I think that what frightened me the most wasn't that Brian could have been killed. What unnerved me was that I was becoming nothing more than a shadow in his life. My relationship with Brian was so empty, all I had to hold on to was the fear. Does that make sense?"

Shane smiled gently down at her. "It makes sense."

Robyn returned the smile, gazing up at her friend, her lover. "Once I understood that racing wouldn't take you away from me, I knew I could watch you race," she whispered. Her smile turned rueful. "I won't like it, but I can take it."

"You won't have to."

She stared at him uncertainly, feeling a sudden surge of hope. "Shane, don't give up racing for me. Please."

"I'm not, honey." His smile was a little crooked. "I'm giving it up for me."

"But you love it!"

"I love you more." He shook his head. "Robyn, I never needed racing. It was just a hobby, something to occupy my time and energy. I liked winning, I'll admit. But I always intended to go back to being a full-time vintner; I never wanted to be written up in the record books as the best driver of all time.

"And when I was out there today, seeing you waiting for me every time I pulled into the pits, I realized that I'd never race again. I'd be a fool to risk everything I have by climbing into that car again. And I wouldn't lose you for all the fame and money in the world. Today was my swan song."

Robyn was afraid to hope, afraid to show him how much she hoped. She didn't want him to race. She didn't want him to spend precious hours risking his life. But she loved him enough to watch him, if that was what he wanted.

But now he was saying . . .

Shane framed her face with his warm hands. "Oh, witch-lady," he murmured, "don't you know even yet how much I love you? I lost my soul in your eyes the first night we met. The night I couldn't believe my luck, because I was dancing with the woman who had haunted my dreams for years—for always.

"And she looked up at me as though the spell had caught her, too; as if she knew, without words or stupid games, that we belonged together. She left that boring party with me, putting her hand in mine with such complete trust that it made my heart ache."

He laughed softly as he gazed with darkened eyes at her dazed expression. "My feet never touched the ground that night. I had found a treasure, and I would have fought demons from hell to keep her. She showed me an enchanted place I had never believed possible, a land of lovers and dreamers."

Bending his head, he rubbed his forehead against hers gently. "And then she was gone the next morning." His breath was soft as a whisper on her face. "Like a dream. And I think I went a little crazy. I had to find her . . . because she was the other half of myself, the part that made me real."

Robyn swallowed hard, and managed to whisper, "And then you heard I was married."

Shane nodded slowly, the green eyes darkening and darkening until they were very nearly black. "I wanted to take you away from your husband," he confessed thickly, a muscle tightening suddenly in his jaw. "And at the same time, I felt betrayed, wounded, because I thought you belonged to him.

"When you told me you were a widow, the relief was staggering. I almost told you then that I loved you, but I could see that you were wary of me. I had to find out why. I thought that you were still in love with your husband, and that made it all the more bewildering."

Robyn was suddenly, crushingly aware of how much she must have hurt him. "And when I lied to you—Oh, darling, I'm so sorry!"

"I frightened you." His voice was low, far away, as though he were reliving that terrible moment, and his eyes were as opaque as those of a blind man. "I never wanted to frighten you, honey. But I wasn't . . . quite sane. The thought that you had pretended I was your husband . . ."

"I love you, Shane," she whispered fiercely, putting her heart and soul into the words, trying to make up for the other words that should never have been uttered. Trying to erase a lie told to herself and to him.

"I knew that night that I had sent you away hating me because I was too scared to think about a future with you racing. I was so afraid of loving you. And it all happened so quickly! It almost didn't seem real." She looked up at him with pain and regret in her eyes. "How could you go on loving me after that night?"

"What choice did I have?" he asked simply, a faint smile lifting the corners of his mouth. "I could no more stop loving you than I could stop breathing."

"Oh, Shane." She stood on tiptoe to reach his mouth, wanting to reassure him, wanting to belong to him now, with everything cleared up between them.

His kiss was filled with half savage tenderness, with love and possession and need. He kissed her as though the world would end at any moment and he wanted the touch and taste of her to be the memory he carried with him into eternity.

Robyn lost herself in a surge of sensations and emotions. She felt a wild, primitive craving to merge with him and become one being. His kiss seemed to draw her very soul from her body to join his in some heaven only they knew.

She felt him lift her into his arms and carry her toward the bedroom with easy strength. Her arms locked around his neck, Robyn clung to him, dazed, needing him as she had never needed him before. She was in a dream once again—the dream, the reality, of Shane's love.

He set her gently on her feet by the huge, lamplit bed, gazing down on her with emerald fires burning in his eyes. "No more questions?" he whispered. "No more fears?"

"No questions, no fears," she answered huskily. "I love you, Shane. With everything inside me."

Shane bent his head to kiss her gently, his lips moving from her mouth to caress her throat and the hollows beneath her ears. Nimble fingers slowly began to unfasten her blouse, one button at a time, with infinite care. His hands softly touched bared golden flesh as a caressing tongue circled the tiny heartbeat pounding away at the base of her neck.

And Robyn's hands were far from still. She eagerly parted the buttons on his shirt, touching his firm chest as if hungry for the sensation. She pressed her lips briefly to him, tasting his clean skin as he pushed her blouse off her shoulders. Immediately, her hands returned to tug his shirt from the waistband of his slacks and help him shrug it off.

He unclasped her bra and smoothed it away, shaping her breasts almost wonderingly, thumbs teasing the rosy peaks to vibrant awareness. "You were made for me," he told her hoarsely, his opened mouth drifting over her closed eyelids. "Beautiful witch, you fit me so well . . ."

Robyn traced the rippling muscles of his back. She felt a tremor shake his strong frame, and an aching trembling began in the center of her being. With a catch of her breath, she reached for the waistband of his slacks, desperate to touch him totally.

She unfastened the snap and tugged the zipper down, her mouth moving in a rhythmical back-and-forth motion across his broad chest as she slowly slid the pants down over lean hips, strong thighs.

He kicked the jumble of clothing away, reaching for the snap of her jeans and groaning softly as her fingers teased and caressed with the certain knowledge of him that the last week had given her.

Her jeans fell away from her and she was lifted and placed tenderly on the bed. Strong hands brushed away the final barrier of her thin nylon panties, and then he was lying beside her on the wide bed.

"God, I need you," he rasped softly. "I'll always need you." He touched her face as though reading Braille, tracing the curve of her brows, her nose, her slightly parted lips. Sensitive fingers moved in a butterfly caress over her skin.

Robyn caught his finger as it passed gently over her lips, letting him feel the sharp edge of her teeth, staring up at him with eyes full of need. Her hands came up to clasp his wrists, feeling a pulse hammering beneath the skin. "Shane," she breathed, more emotion than she would have believed possible contained in the single word.

He lifted her hands to his mouth, pressing soft, tender kisses along each finger, touching his tongue lightly to her palms. He gazed down at her, his hunger written vividly on his face. "I love you, witch," he murmured deeply before his mouth lowered, hotly capturing a throbbing nipple.

She moaned softly, feeling the wet warmth of his lips, the tongue swirling avidly. She tangled her fingers in his dark hair, her legs moving restlessly until they were trapped by one of his. Rough hands explored her body in long strokes and then settled to tease, to incite.

Robyn explored his body fervently, breathing shallowly, feeling the splintering tension building within her. "Shane!" She heard herself pleading with him in a drugged voice. "Love me, darling, please love me!"

Shane needed no further urging. He rose above her, settling himself between her thighs like a man coming home. For a long moment, he was still, with her, holding her, kissing her with burning tenderness. Then he lifted his head to gaze into her rapt eyes as he slowly began to move.

Robyn moved with him eagerly, gasping out her love for him, the desire that never seemed to diminish transporting her higher than ever before. She held him with muscles she hadn't realized she possessed, and she saw the surprise and excitement flicker in his eyes and grip his taut features.

Their movements became faster, heated, the primitive drive for release overpowering rational thought. Instinct took over, and both gave selflessly of themselves. Muffled words of love filled the lamplit room, and then the world disappeared. They were, for the brief, timeless moment allowed to mortals, one being.

They lay together at last, limp, exhausted. But not quite sated. Never quite sated. As though they feared that they were about to be parted, they kissed tenderly, lovingly.

Robyn could feel his hands unsteadily stroking her back, her hair, as if he couldn't stop touching her. She found her own hands smoothing tanned flesh, tugging gently at the crisp dark hair covering his chest. "I love you, skipper," she murmured in a contented voice.

"I love you, too, witch-lady," he vowed softly, his hands still shaping her slender body. "Always and forever."

She cuddled even closer, murmuring a sleepy protest when he disengaged them enough to reach down and pull the covers up over their bodies.

"Get the light, witch," he murmured, drawing her close again.

Robyn waved a vague hand in the direction of the lamp. "Light. Abracadabra."

"It didn't work," he told her. "Try another charm."

"Shall I twitch my nose?"

"Whatever."

Robyn reached up to rub her nose—mainly because the hair on his chest was tickling it. "Didn't work."

"Try something else."

"Open sesame."

"That's for doors."

"Who's the witch here?"

"I'm beginning to wonder."

"I got you, didn't I?"

"There is that."

"Then don't question my spells."

"I beg your pardon." His voice held a laugh. "But the light's still on."

"How do you expect me to cast spells when I've barely got the energy to breathe?" Robyn sighed languidly. "Which reminds me—for a man who drove an exhausting race today, your energy level is amazing. What's your secret? Vitamin E? Wheaties?"

"Neither. A demanding witch in my bed."

"I am not demanding." She couldn't even summon the energy to be decently indignant.

"Of course you are." He dropped a kiss on the top of her head. "That's all right, though. I like being demanded."

"Actually, I just have this thing for dragonslayers."

"With mountain aeries?"

"With mountain aeries. Dragonslayers who go out at night to dig up litter boxes for stray cats, and buy stuffed dolphins, and lead helpless women around by their braids. It's a quirk in my nature."

"I have a quirk, too."

"You have several."

"Funny."

Robyn squeaked as a gently punishing hand smacked her bottom. "Sorry. What's your quirk?"

"Yellow-eyed witches. Shall we fly to California on your broomstick, or will you condescend to use a plane?"

"What are we going to do with my store, my house, Marty, and King George?" she asked pointedly.

"Sell the house and the store and ship the rest to Napa Valley. Unless you'd like to keep the house."

"What woman needs a Spanish style house in Florida when she's got a mountain aerie in California? We'll sell the house. Do you really not mind Marty coming with us? She's been with me for so long now . . ."

"Of course not." He erased doubts with a swift hug. "The aerie has plenty of room. And people read in Napa Valley when they're not stamping grapes, so—"

"I'd like to watch you stamp grapes," she interrupted wistfully. "With your pants legs rolled up and your feet turning purple."

He chuckled softly. "We don't do it that way anymore. But if you like, we'll order a bushel of grapes in the morning, pour them into the bathtub, and stamp away."

"Will we make wine?"

"We'll make a mess; I don't know about wine."

"Never mind. I'll wait until we get to California, and you can show me how it's really done. Will George like your aerie?"

"Our aerie. There are plenty of trees to climb."

"He'll love it." Robyn sighed and absently traced a finger along his firm jaw. A sudden thought occurred to her, and she murmured uneasily, "Your family. Won't they be upset that you've suddenly decided to marry a woman they haven't even met?"

"They've had a week to get used to the idea," he told her with utter calm. "I called them from Miami."

"You what?" Robyn finally managed to lift her head, staring down at him in surprise. "When?"

"Before I came back to your place last Monday night. I called Mother, and I'm sure she's told everyone else."

"*What* did you tell her?" Robyn demanded suspiciously.

"The truth, of course." He finally opened his eyes to return her uneasy look with one brimming with laughter. "That I'd fallen under the spell of a beautiful witch, and that I planned to marry her just as soon as I could drag her to the altar."

"Oh, Lord," Robyn muttered.

"Don't look so nervous. You'll love Mother. She told me not to lose you between Florida and California, and started planning the wedding. Huge, she decided."

"Shane, I can't let her do that! It's supposed to be the bride's family that throws the wedding, and besides, you don't want all that fuss and bother—"

"Are you kidding?" He pulled her over fully on top of him. "I intend to marry you with as much pomp and ceremony as I can manage."

"But, Shane—"

"Mother still has a bottle of wine she got the year she and Dad were married. She's been saving it all these years for my wedding. You wouldn't deprive her of that pleasure, would you?"

"Of course not! But—"

"And my sisters'll want to be bridesmaids. And I have a niece just the right age for a flower girl. And a nephew to carry the ring. Speaking of which . . ." He reached to fumble at the drawer of the night table and produced a small velvet box. "Mother sent this by special messenger yesterday; it's been in the family for years. If you don't like the setting, we'll change it."

Shane opened the box to reveal a beautiful marquise diamond set in delicate white gold. He slid it onto the third finger of her left hand with infinite care and then gently pressed his lips to her hand. "For my bride-to-be," he whispered softly.

Robyn stared dazedly at the lovely ring and then at him. "Shane . . . it's beautiful." Realizing suddenly that she was being seduced away from the subject at hand, she continued strongly, "But your mother can't—"

"Of course she can." Shane smiled at her. "Mother knows that Marty's all you have. She wants to do this, love."

"You seem to have told her an awful lot," Robyn managed weakly.

"Just that I love you very, very much. She really didn't need to hear any more than that. Will you marry me, witch-lady?"

Robyn stared deeply into his eyes and felt her protests die into silence. "On one condition," she breathed.

"Anything." A slow smile lit his eyes. "If you want the moon, I'll charter a shuttle and go get it."

"Not quite that." She pulled herself forward until she was a single breath away from his lips. "I just want you to put up a mast near the aerie so George'll feel right at home . . ."

"Hell, darling," Shane muttered thickly, "I'll buy Eric's boat and anchor it in the yard."

It was some time later before Robyn could gather the breath to murmur, "Abracadabra," and wave her hand at the lamp.

The fact that Shane's hand found the switch a moment later, of course, only proved that Robyn wove powerful spells.

On Her
Doorstep

For my sister, Linda.
In celebration of her second chance.

Chapter One

t wasn't a real body, of course.

Or, rather, Erin thought decidedly, not a *dead* body; it looked real enough, but it was breathing. She shifted her weight onto her other foot and studied the breathing body thoughtfully.

"It's alive, Chester," she said.

Chester sat down in the dirt and sighed heavily, his bloodshot eyes peering at the body with the unfocused and wholly disinterested look of an alcoholic after a weekend binge. Which was the case.

Erin could sympathize with her companion, but, unlike Chester, her own lack of focus came from a horrendous case of jet lag. Call it jet lag, anyway. Or just plain exhaustion. She felt light-headed, and her body was slow to obey the commands of her brain—which was performing at something less than the norm.

"Hey!" She nudged the breathing body with one boot rudely.

The body stirred, said something hardly polite, and subsided again.

Erin looked down at Chester and said, "Bite him."

"If he does, I'll shoot him," said the body.

Since Chester showed no disposition to bite anything at all, this threat wasn't put to the test.

"You're on my porch," Erin told the body coldly.

The body stirred again. A sunbrowned hand reached up to push back a western hat, revealing a lean face stubbled with beard from which a pair of bloodshot gray eyes peered at her unhappily.

Erin repeated her statement even more coldly. "You're on my porch."

"This place is empty," he disagreed in a deep, weary voice.

"Only because I wasn't here. I am now. So it isn't empty. Go away."

He folded his tall length into a sitting position, removed the hat to run fingers through Indian-straight raven hair, replaced the hat firmly but in an oddly unpracticed gesture, and squared his broad shoulders as if he were prepared—now—to deal with the situation.

He peered past her to see two horses, one a pack horse heavily laden with unidentifiable packages covered with canvas. He sighed and swung his boots off the porch, getting to his feet reluctantly. "Well," he said, "since you live here—apparently—maybe you can tell me where to locate someone. I've been looking for two days. They said in town it was a cabin, and this is the only one I found."

"I know nothing about my neighbors." She was slightly annoyed to find that he was bigger standing than he'd looked lying down.

He regarded her for a moment, then shifted his gaze to Chester's depressed form. "What in God's name is that?"

Chester lifted a lip at him.

"That," Erin said coldly, "is my dog."

The man appeared somewhat bemused by Chester. "Somebody's pulling your leg, lady. That's not a dog, it's a mutant grizzly."

Erin felt offended on Chester's behalf, but could hardly cavil at the apt description. Her dog did rather resemble a grizzly, especially since his head (no doubt painful) was hanging low so that he looked as if he had a humped back. In addition, he was very large and muscular, with a dense coat of grayish-brown hair. And when he yawned—as he did at that moment—he displayed a set of pearly whites that any grizzly would have claimed with pride.

Deciding to ignore the insult to her pet, Erin stared at the man and felt a vague curiosity. "How did you get up here?" She looked him up and down while he seemed to consider his answer, adding, "You look like you walked."

He glanced briefly down at himself, at the jeans and flannel shirt liberally coated with dust, then stared at her. Ignoring her question, he said politely, "Mind telling me what a delicate little creature like you is doing out here in the back of beyond?"

Since the three-inch heels of Erin's boots put her at exactly six feet, and since she was what men tended to term "voluptuous," this was clearly sarcasm of the first order. Looking up at him (something she didn't often have to do), she said sweetly, "I needed peace and quiet for my knitting."

A grin tugged at his mouth, but gave up the struggle. "They tell me there are real bears up here, you know," he offered with a glance down at Chester.

Erin wondered who had told him. "Good," she said dryly. "I could use a new rug."

He clearly decided she was kidding. "I wouldn't think it would be safe here," he pursued gravely. "And not just because of the bears. I've heard the weather up here gets wild this time of year; you could be completely cut off. There's no power here, and that old generator in the shed hasn't worked in years from the looks of it. You'd be better off—" He stopped, since she'd turned and gone to her horse. A moment later she was before him again, and he took an involuntary step back.

Erin slid two shells into the shotgun and closed the breech with a quietly deadly snap. She held the gun negligently, the barrel pointed at his belt buckle. "You were saying?"

"I'll just get my horse," he murmured, eyeing the shotgun.

"Do that." She waited calmly.

He disappeared around the corner of the log cabin, returning a few moments later atop a roan horse with a rather wicked eye. A familiar horse. Erin took due note of the horse's unpredictable nature. She also took note of the man's obvious unfamiliarity with horses in general and this one in particular. One never knew, after all, when such information would come in handy.

And it did. Rather quickly.

"Look, lady," he said, trying again, "I'm just looking for someone in this godforsaken place. J. D. Mathers. And I'd appreciate it if you—"

Smoothly, Erin raised the shotgun and fired both barrels into the air. The roan, as she'd expected, bolted. She listened to blue curses growing fainter as angry hooves carried horse and rider away, then she sighed and looked down at Chester.

Head hanging, front legs splayed, he had both eyes closed and was whimpering softly. Opening first one eye and then the other, he gave Erin a look of heartrending reproach.

"Sorry, Chester. I forgot."

He lifted a lip at her. There was no malice in the gesture; it was just Chester's way of remarking, "The hell you say." Wearing the mien of a dog to whom torture was a daily thing, he staggered onto the porch and collapsed with a groan.

Absently, Erin ejected the spent shells and leaned the shotgun up against the wall near her dog. She paused a moment to adjust her hat, pushing a stray lock of hair underneath it. Then, sighing, she went to begin unloading her things.

She was so tired that her mind was in a fog, but a faint glimmer of sheepish guilt rose when she realized just how badly she'd behaved to what had been, after all, a harmless stranger. Carrying loads of gear from horses to cabin, she mused about that. But she was too tired to accept the guilt.

He'd been on her porch, after all. *Her* porch. Without so much as a "Pardon me, lady, but may I take a nap on your porch?" He'd just *been* there. Six feet and a few odd inches of blue-jeaned, booted, dust-coated, beard-stubbled man lying on her porch.

Erin began to feel severely put-upon. She relished the feeling.

And why, she wondered tiredly, was he looking for J. D. Mathers? Nobody ever looked for Mathers. Ever. Mathers was a recluse who had made it abundantly plain to any and all that visitors were, not to put too fine a point on it, unwelcome. Mathers's wishes, generally honored, had become scrupulously honored when a curious reporter had bolted back down the mountain some months before with a load of buckshot in his Calvin Kleins.

Erin, methodically rubbing down her horses in the small but sturdy barn behind the cabin, wondered vaguely if the man on her porch had been told about that. Probably. And, in spite of the dust coating his sturdy clothes, Erin had easily detected the gloss of city beneath.

Only innate grace and an instinctive sense of balance had kept him on the bolting roan; he was no horseman. So what was a city-bred stranger doing up here in the back of beyond?

J. D. Mathers, obviously.

Erin fed her horses and stabled them, then went into the shed to start up the generator. It looked disused, as the stranger had noticed, but worked like a charm after Erin talked to it, kicked it companionably, and made a few other minor adjustments. It choked and sputtered at first, then settled down to a busy roar.

She went into the cabin just in time to save the pack Chester was clawing frantically. Carrying the pack into the kitchen area of the roomy cabin, Erin sent a frown back at her whimpering canine friend. "No. Hair of the dog would kill you in your condition."

Chester whimpered. He grumbled and groaned and growled, complaining at great length.

Erin pulled a half-full bottle of whiskey from the pack and placed it high on a shelf. "You," she told Chester, "are going on the wagon. Get that? You're five years old and a hopeless alcoholic. It's pathetic. No more booze. If I ever see Stuart again, I'll shoot him for both of us."

She hoped she wouldn't see Stuart again. She was no longer bitter after three years, but those years had been spent up here in very rough country and she had a feeling . . . Well, there was neither city gloss nor city manners in her any longer.

If she saw him again, she'd probably kill him.

Erin started laughing as that realization surfaced. It was, curiously, the sound of release. Three years ago she had run with her tail between her legs, bruised and wounded and confused, and now she could contemplate, with detachment, killing the cause of all that distant pain.

Good. She was over him.

Still, it had been lousy of Stuart to turn Chester into an alcoholic. She was very glad now that she had rescued her dog last year. Kidnapped him, really, while Stuart had been gone from the house.

Erin looked longingly at her bedroom, tiredness almost overwhelming her. But she was a tidy person and knew she wouldn't be able to rest until her supplies were put away. Methodically, she stored everything neatly in the shining pine cabinets that she had built herself. She swept up the dust of two weeks away until the hardwood floor gleamed dully, then polished tables and shelves and counters.

Somewhere during the tidying, she put on coffee and drank it black while she worked, trying to stay awake until everything was done. Compulsive, she thought. I'm compulsive. Not that it bothered her. She didn't ask anyone but Chester to live with her compulsiveness, and he minded only the whiskey bottle kept out of his reach.

The refrigerator was getting cold, and Erin went to her radio to call down to town. She alerted the grocer with whom she did infrequent business, and Mal promised to send perishables in his battered Jeep; could she meet the delivery at Black Rock? She promised to do so.

"There is," Mal remarked, "a stranger in town. Looking for Mathers."

"He was on my porch," Erin responded. "Did you—?"

Mal was shocked. " 'Course not, Erin. I'd never. But I don't think he'll give up. Should I—?"

Erin considered the matter, sighed. "Guess not. The roan'll probably kill him anyway. Tell Jake the guy can't ride, but he sticks to a horse like flypaper. Strong legs, I imagine. The roan didn't lose him, anyway."

Mal clucked in disappointment. "Jake thought for sure. I mean, well, he looked like a dude. Came in wearing a three-piece suit, Brooks Brothers written all over it. Bought his jeans and stuff here when he realized he'd have to climb the mountain. Cussed up a storm."

Behind Erin, Chester howled mournfully.

"He's on the wagon again?" Mal asked interestedly.

"Yes," Erin said, "and tell Jake if he slips him whiskey one more time, I'll shoot him. I appreciate him renting the roan to that guy, but I won't have Chester drink anymore. It's starting to affect his health."

"Thought he had a cast-iron stomach."

Erin glanced back at her unhappy dog, then told the radio, "The booze he's swallowed could eat through the hull of a battleship. Especially that stuff Jake makes. Tell him to quit it. Or at least quit giving it to Chester."

"Okay," Mal agreed cheerfully. "You want the same supplies as usual, Erin?"

She mentally went over her standard list, known to both of them, then nodded before remembering she was on the radio. "Same, I guess. A little more cheese this time. And some fresh vegetables. My garden was raided."

"You *will* feed the animals," Mal reminded her dryly. "They get to expect it after a while. Your own fault."

"Mmmm." Erin sighed again. "Signing off, Mal. I've got to sleep."

"Jeep'll be at Black Rock at ten in the morning," Mal said. "As usual. Bye, Erin."

She replied in kind, then turned off her radio and yawned. Leaving the small utility room where she kept the radio, she went into the large living room of the cabin and looked around. Clean and neat, just as she liked it.

She went into the bathroom and turned on the faucet to allow rusty water to escape, waiting for clear. Then she tried the hot and was gratified to find the heater had managed lukewarm. She filled the huge claw-footed tub and dumped in bath salts. Chester came in and began to drink out of the tub; she shoved him out, swearing mildly, closed the door behind him, and undressed, listening to him complain. He had water in the kitchen, but apparently liked the taste of bath salts.

Then she slid into the warm water and relaxed, allowing muscles to ease, dust to be washed away. To avoid falling asleep, she forced herself to sit up and soap a cloth and rub busily to remove stubborn dirt. She used a hand shower attachment to wash her hair, forgetting the pins and having to stop for a moment to remove them.

When she was clean and glowing, she climbed reluctantly from the tub and toweled off briskly. She found her hair dryer and stood before the antique mirror above the gleaming oak vanity, drying her hair, brushing the long mass with soothing strokes.

Clean. Finally! Two weeks of camping had left her feeling decidedly dusty; the stream had been far too cold to bathe in.

Erin turned the dryer off, vaguely aware of Chester making a disinterested comment outside the door. Rummaging in the narrow closet where she kept linens and sleepwear (more convenient, since she always bathed before bed), she located a pair of rather brief black silk pajamas and looked at them doubtfully.

Then, shrugging, she pulled the silk over smooth skin. If she had associated clothing with memories, she might have felt odd to still wear garments Stuart had bought for her; fortunately, Erin didn't care. So she stepped without pain into bottoms that clung lovingly to her curved hips and long legs, then shrugged into the top that was plunging of neckline and also loving. She buttoned the top, reflecting absently that she'd finally gained back the weight shed during those tumultuous first months with Stuart; the black silk gaped just a bit over her full breasts.

Then she opened the door and padded out into the living room, nearly tripping over Chester, who looked up at her and commented mildly again. She looked up at the front door for a moment, then back at her dog.

"Some watchdog," she told him.

Chester commented again, clearly saying that he *had* tried, after all, but that she hadn't listened. Then, his dogly duty discharged, he went to the cold fireplace, looked at it distrustfully for an instant, and collapsed on the hearth rug with a groan.

Erin returned her gaze to the front door. The open front door. And the dusty stranger leaning against the jamb, who was staring at her in some surprise.

"We-e-ll," he said, the word drawled out. "You certainly look different with your—uh—hair down."

"I thought I sent you away," Erin said.

He smiled, showing strong white teeth and little humor. "I came back."

Sighing, Erin padded around the low partition that divided kitchen from living room, and poured another cup of coffee. Obviously, she had company for a while. With faint irony she lifted her cup questioningly at the stranger.

"Thank you." He accepted politely, straightening away from the jamb and coming to the other side of the partition.

Erin poured another cup, looked at him in inquiry and was told he took it black, then handed him the cup.

"We got off on the wrong foot," he told her after an apprecia-tive sip of coffee. "My name is Matt Gavin, and I'm from New York. From Salem Publishing. I'm looking for J. D. Mathers."

"Whomever you may be looking *for*," she said dryly, "you're looking *at* my pajama top. At, specifically, my bust."

He grinned suddenly, gray eyes that were sheepish lifting to her face. "Sorry," he murmured. "At least—Hell, I'm not sorry. I'm human. And the flannel shirt and jeans you were wearing before didn't even hint—I mean—and your hair, is it—" He stopped suddenly.

"It's real," she told him dryly. "Given my druthers, I wouldn't have chosen red." She paused for a moment, then added gently, "Mr. Gavin, it's difficult to talk to someone who won't look you in the eye."

He seemed to withdraw his gaze with great effort and fixed it on his coffee cup. "Then," he muttered, "button that damned top."

She looked down, swore mildly, and refastened two gaping but-tons. "It wasn't intentional," she told him. "I've gained some weight."

"All in the right places." He fumbled in a pocket, finding ciga-rettes and lighter. "Do you mind—?" He didn't look at her.

Erin found an ashtray and pushed it across the narrow bar that topped the partition. Then she leaned against the counter behind her, sipping coffee and trying to hide the gap. Useless, she decided, and set her cup aside to go into her bedroom. When she returned, the silk top had been replaced by a loose pullover top.

He looked at her over the partition and sighed. "You haven't told me your name."

"I didn't know it mattered."

"Look—" he began.

Erin lifted a hand, halting him. "Mr. Gavin"—she spoke slowly, as if to someone a bit, just a bit, dense—"I have just returned from two weeks of camping. Eventful camping. I am very, very tired. If I don't get some sleep quite soon, I won't be responsible for my actions. I am in no mood to stand in my cabin and talk to a stranger."

He drew on the cigarette, staring at her. His eyes dropped fleetingly to her now decently covered superstructure and seemed to flicker in momentary sadness. Then, as if it were a throwaway line, he said, "My horse is gone."

Erin blinked. "Threw you, did he." It wasn't a question.

"No. I got off outside and he just—ran away."

"You didn't tie him?"

Matt Gavin smiled sheepishly. She was beginning to mistrust that sheepish smile. It had a motive under it.

"Then," Erin said, "you walk."

"It's ten miles down this mountain."

"Better get started then. It'll be dark in a few hours." Erin would have looked at her watch, except that she didn't own one. It would, she thought, have made her comment more pointed if she could have looked at her watch.

Seeming to ignore her advice, he half-turned to gaze around the neat cabin. A place for everything and everything in its place. Shining floors dotted here and there with bright throw rugs. Comfortable overstuffed furniture. A lovely rock fireplace with split logs piled handily in the stone wood box beside it. Floor-to-ceiling oak bookshelves on two walls. The third wall formed the front of the cabin and boasted wide windows, curtained lightly in gauzy whiteness; the fourth wall contained the small kitchenette and a short hallway with three doors turning off it.

One door was the bath, the second the bedroom; the third door was firmly closed and announced nothing.

He turned back to her after contemplating that closed door for a long, pointed moment. Then, mildly, he said, "I'll double your next advance if that door doesn't hide your office."

She blinked, stared at him. After a minute of silence, she poured more coffee and sipped. Then she looked at him again and sighed.

"J. D. Mathers, I presume?" His voice was very polite. "Who signs her contracts in the name E. Scott. Which stands for—?"

"Erin." She sighed again, aware that she was too tired to cope with this invasion. Aware she would have to cope whether she wanted to or not. "Why couldn't you have just gone away?" It was, obviously, a rhetorical question.

He recognized it as such and ignored it.

"What," he asked, "is this mania of yours all about? I mean, granted, you have the right to live alone if you want. But up here? Miles from nothing? You won't talk to us on the phone, you refuse to promote your books—not that they need it—you've refused a dozen invitations to come to New York—"

"Mr. Gavin." Erin was tired, she knew that, and wished she could shut her own mouth before her tiredness led her into areas she really didn't want to tread. "It is, as you said, my right to live as I choose. I choose to live here. Why is none of your business." It was said politely, quietly. Firmly.

He was studying her, his gray eyes nearly as weary as the green ones that looked back at him. But his eyes were sharp nonetheless. He gazed from the shining, incredibly vibrant waist-length copper hair, over the loose-fitting (pity, that, he thought) top, and down to the narrow waist that was all he could see before the partition got in his way.

Then he looked at her face, searching, intent. He found eyes so green that they could have defined the color, and they were framed by long dark lashes. A complexion that was translucent and beautifully pale (no wonder, he thought, she'd worn a hat earlier; she'd burn *very* easily no matter what time of the year). A straight, delicate nose. Lips that were full and curved with innate humor. Stubborn chin.

All in all, he decided, she had a face that men dreamed about, poets wrote about, singers sang about . . . A face that could launch ships. Lovely. Just lovely. Colorado, he thought, was looking better, too. Now that he'd found her in Colorado.

Still, he could see nothing in that lovely face to indicate why she hid herself away up here. It was, he thought, a waste. A *criminal* waste.

Erin, who was perceptive even when tired and had considerable experience in seeing men look at her, watched his lean face change expression and wished, wryly, that the roan had thrown him.

She was, she suspected, stuck with him.

"Mr. Gavin, is there some reason you came up here to find me? I'm just curious, you understand."

With a start he realized he'd forgotten business. He had, he thought, begun to forget business the instant her top had gaped at him. He cleared his throat. "About your next book." When she remained politely unresponsive, he tried again. "We're scheduling, and we need a title. And chapters, if possible. For the artwork. The cover."

She looked around the cabin for a moment, then back at him. "Couldn't you have just written a letter?" Then remembered that he had.

"I did. You didn't answer. And, besides—" He hesitated, then shrugged. "So damned reclusive. We wondered. And we've had requests for you to speak, and appear on television—"

"No."

"Your last book," he reminded her, "was on every major bestseller list for months. *Months.* In fact, it's still there. People want to see you, hear you, know about you. You won't even release a *picture*, for godsake."

Erin felt temper creeping, and with it the realization that she was going to tread where she didn't want to. The man's persistence made it inevitable. "Mr. Gavin—"

"Matt."

"Whatever. If you'll reread my contracts, you'll find that we got rid of the standard clauses about promoting books. I won't do that. They can read my books or not, criticize or not, speculate—or not. I don't care. I don't watch television. I don't like cities. And I won't promote the books."

"We could sell even more."

"I don't care."

He looked at her, a man who was handsome in spite of the stubble and coating of dust, a man with a determined jaw. And he smiled, this time with humor.

"I'll try to convince you, you know."

"I know." She sighed inaudibly. "But you won't succeed. It'll take time for you to realize that, unfortunately. Pity you won't just take my word for it."

He shook his head. Slowly and firmly.

"Uh-huh." Erin looked at him and felt even more tired. "But in the meantime, leave. I have got to get some sleep."

"My horse."

"Take one of mine. The sorrel, not the gray." Remembering whom she was talking to, she added, "The brown one."

Matt Gavin considered the matter. "Look," he said, "we're both tired. And if I have to ride back down this mountain today, I'll get myself killed. You have a couch." He looked, added, "A comfortable couch. Take your shotgun into the bedroom if you don't trust me, but have a heart and let me sleep on your couch."

"No."

He looked at her pathetically. "I'd like children someday. If I have to get back on a horse," he said, "I'll never be able to father children."

It surprised a laugh out of her. She realized, while he gazed at her appealingly, that he was determined to stay. She also realized she was just too damned tired to argue about it.

"Oh, hell," she said. "Take the couch. I'm going to bed." She turned toward the hall, then hesitated and crossed to get the shotgun leaning near the door. Pointedly, she reloaded it, then smiled at him gently and retreated to her bedroom.

She was, literally, asleep before her head hit the pillow.

Chapter Two

It had been mid-afternoon when Erin had flopped the covers over her and abandoned the world and the stranger out in her living room; it was, she judged, early morning when she woke. The cabin was silent and still.

She threw back covers and slid from the double bed, going to the window and parting gauzy curtains. She looked for and found the sun rising behind the cabin, nodding to herself. *Early* morning.

It took only a few moments for her to dress in jeans and a bulky sweater, to brush her long thick hair and wrestle it into a pony tail high on her head. In socks and carrying her boots, she padded into the living room and stood gazing down on her stranger.

Either, she thought, he hadn't wanted to dirty her off-white couch with his dusty clothes, or else he simply preferred not to sleep in his clothes. His jeans and flannel shirt were folded with an attempt at neatness and reposed on her square coffee table. As for himself, he was wrapped in the colorful afghan that had graced the back of the couch.

And it covered him decently only by liberal standards.

For a moment she studied him. He was even more beard-stubbled, his lean face relaxed and vulnerable in sleep; dark lashes lay in thick crescents against his cheekbones. His raven hair was tousled, a lock falling over his high forehead.

Broad shoulders rose nakedly from the afghan, tanned and strong (sunlamp? she wondered—he was a city man, after all). A thick mat of black hair covered his chest. One powerful arm lay outside the afghan, and one long leg was bared as well.

She found her eyes fixed on the steadily rising and falling chest, and frowned a little. There was an odd weakness in her knees and her own breathing seemed to quicken. She fought a sudden urge to touch him, her frown deepening.

Ridiculous. She wasn't attracted to this stranger.

Erin slowly turned away, going into the kitchen and setting her boots down to start making coffee. Mid-thirties, she decided. No wedding ring, but that meant little.

Nor did her weak knees mean anything, she decided firmly. Except perhaps that she'd been alone up here for too long.

Erin grimaced as she measured the grounds, ignoring the impulse to turn and stare at him again. He was a *stranger*, and he'd be gone soon.

When the coffee was perking, she quietly retrieved his clothes and took them, along with some of her own, out to the little laundry room by the back door. Chester came in through the pet door as she was starting the washing machine, looking better today but still bad-tempered, judging from the growl with which he greeted her.

Erin followed her pet from the laundry room, closing the door to cut the noise. She went out back to feed and water the horses, then returned to the cabin. She found her guest still sleeping soundly and coffee ready for drinking. She fixed breakfast for Chester but none for herself, leaning against the partition while she drank coffee and stared broodingly at Matt Gavin.

Why couldn't she stop staring at him?

She was on her second cup when she dimly heard the washing machine cut off, and went to transfer clothing into a basket and carry it out to hang on the line behind the cabin. The morning air held a faint chill, but the sun promised a warm day with a soft breeze, and Erin preferred to hang out her clothes whenever possible.

When she returned, Matt Gavin was still asleep.

Erin shrugged to herself, jotted a quick note and left it on the coffee table, then went out to saddle her horse. She took the sorrel, Amos, leaving the gray, Tucker, in his stall munching hay. Specially made saddlebags dangled behind her saddle, large bags that would hold the provisions Mal was sending up.

She mounted at the barn and rode around the cabin, finding Chester sitting on the porch. He looked at her, ears lifting.

"You stay here," she told him, and he lay down with a gusty sigh.

It took nearly an hour to reach Black Rock—which was the nearest to her cabin a wheeled vehicle could manage (and only a four-wheel drive could get that far). A battered black Jeep was parked beside the jutting black rock that had named the spot, and sitting on the hood was a young man engrossed in a book.

"Hi, Jake," Erin called as she reached him.

Spaniel-brown eyes rose to hers, eyes shining with a deceptive innocence and a not-so-deceptive intelligence. "Morning, Erin." He grinned at her. "Mal gave me your message. I promise, no more tea for Chester."

"Tea!" Erin dismounted, shaking her head. "D'you know how I used that jug you sent me? I stripped varnish off an antique rocking chair."

"Yes, it's good for that," Jake agreed, not at all offended by her use of the concoction he fondly called "tea" and which he gleefully sold to amused townspeople to supplement his income. He joined

Erin at the rear of the Jeep and began helping her transfer provisions into her saddlebags. "Erin—that guy. Didn't come back to town. The roan did, though, just a little while ago."

"He's on my couch." Erin looked at Jake, shook her head.

Jake gave her a thoughtful look. "Uh-huh. Nice-looking guy," he added casually.

Erin remembered a nearly naked male body on her couch and cleared her throat. "I suppose. But he's a city boy, Jake. He'll get tired of the wilderness soon enough."

Jake sat on the tailgate of the Jeep, still thoughtful. The book he'd been reading was stuck in the back pocket of his jeans, and he pulled it out to gaze at it absently.

Erin looked at the title, not surprised to find that the book dealt with chemical composition. Jake, although heaven knew he didn't look it, was something of a genius.

"Erin . . ." Jake looked up, frowning. "When you first came up here, you were—well, thin, pale, nervy. Like you'd been kicked in the stomach. You were like a ghost at first, slipping into town a few times, then slipping out. Didn't want to be bothered. So we didn't. Then you started talking to Mal, me, a few others. Opened up.

"Now—" He ran impatient fingers through thick brown hair and sighed. "Hell, now you're one of us. And we worry about you. There's nothing wrong with living alone if that's what you like, and you seem to like it. But you're a beautiful woman who's had most of the softness kicked out of you, and that's not good. Maybe . . . maybe you've been up here long enough."

It was, she heard, a reluctant suggestion. And she smiled a little. "What brought that on?"

He grinned faintly. "The dude, I guess. He's the first stranger to get this close since you came. We all guessed there was someone for you once; you've got the kind of scars only a man could put on a woman. And you—I don't think you're a woman who'd want to live alone all her life, Erin."

Erin didn't even think of mocking or scorning his tailgate psychology; he was serious, and he cared about her. So she smiled at him as she mounted her horse.

"Thanks for worrying, Jake. But I've found something up here I've never known before. Call it peace if you like. I'm happy here. So stop worrying. And say hello to Randi for me, okay?"

"Okay. She wanted to come up and visit, but the doctor—"

"You tell her to stay put and take care of herself. I'll come down in a week or so and visit." She kept her voice light; after three years it had gotten easier.

"The baby might be here by then," Jake said, the pride and anxiety of an about-to-be father in his voice. "Randi looks like she's swallowed a basketball."

Erin laughed, waved good-bye, and headed Amos back up the mountain.

When she carried the saddlebags into the cabin more than an hour later, she noted in passing that her guest's jeans and flannel shirt were gone from the line out back. Once in the cabin, she heard the shower going and was not surprised to find the couch bare of an almost-naked stranger.

Chester, who had met her out front and accompanied her through the unsaddling and stabling process, stood and watched hopefully while she unpacked and put away the perishables. When neither labeled whiskey nor Jake's "tea" was forthcoming, he grumbled at her and went to lie on the hearth rug.

Erin started preparing a late breakfast, hearing the shower shut off and, moments later, water running in the bathroom sink. She smiled a little. In her note she had invited him to use the shower and explained where a razor could be found; a pointed comment he had clearly taken to heart. He had also, judging by a missing cup and lowered level of coffee in the pot, taken his morning caffeine with him.

Erin had no dining table, but a breakfast bar formed a part of the

partition and in between cooking chores she set out plates and sil-
verware. By the time Matt Gavin came out of the bathroom, the
main room of the cabin smelled enticingly of bacon and eggs and
fresh homemade rolls.

Erin greeted him by saying "Hello" and taking away his coffee
cup to refill. One quick glance had showed her that he was, clean
and shaved, more than handsome. He was devastating.

It bothered her. Having lived with one extraordinary man and
been exposed to many others, Erin had learned to mistrust extremes. It did no good to remind herself that this man's extraordinary looks could hardly be compared to Stuart's incredible, driven
talent; it was, she knew, like comparing apples and oranges.

Still, she was only too aware that Matt Gavin lived in a fast-
moving and high-powered world, and a wound she had believed
healed cringed away from the threat of that world.

The calming peace she had found in the wilderness wrapped
around her, protecting her from her body's tentative awareness of
the presence of a devastating man.

So the clear, steady gray eyes that looked at her out of that
handsome face found no interested awareness in her own gaze. She
merely placed food before him, joined him at the bar, and began
eating her breakfast.

After a moment he followed suit. After another moment he
sent her a sideways glance. "You're a good cook," he noted.

"Thanks." Erin didn't look at him even though she was aware of
his oblique glances.

He tried again. "Thanks for the use of your couch. And for
washing the clothes, and the shower and breakfast."

"You're welcome."

He laughed suddenly, a short sound that was barely amused.
"Hardly. Hardly welcome."

"You weren't invited," she reminded him.

Nothing more was said until the meal was finished. Erin poured more coffee for them, but took hers to the sink as she began cleaning up. Silent, he rose and began helping. She accepted the help matter-of-factly, but didn't comment on it. When they were finished, she took her cup into the living room, and he followed suit. She sat on one end of the couch; he took the other.

Erin began feeling amused, but didn't let it show. He was, she realized, trying to get some handle on her. Watching her every movement, bothered by her silence. And Erin, who was herself a student of people in spite of her lonely surroundings, half-consciously tried to fit him into a mental niche.

She was, she decided, not seeing him at his best. His best would be in an office or at a glittering cocktail party. His best would be three-piece suits and gleaming cars of foreign origin. His best would be room service and dim restaurants and laundry that was sent out unthinkingly and not hung on a line behind a cabin.

His best was certainly not dusty trips up mountains aboard bad-tempered roan horses, or shotguns fired without warning, or couches to sleep on, or uncommunicative women with whom to have breakfast.

Particularly the latter. Women who had breakfast with this man, she thought ruefully, probably scattered rose petals in his path—metaphorically speaking, of course. According to what Erin had read—and knew from experience—extraordinarily handsome men weren't always good lovers, but there was something about this one, something she sensed or just something in his eyes, that told her he understood women too well to be inept or selfish.

And if that wasn't a ridiculous thought, she mused uneasily, to be having about a stranger—

"What are you thinking?" he asked suddenly.

"I don't know you well enough to answer that," she said, her voice easy with an effort she hoped didn't show. "Thoughts aren't meant for strangers."

"You looked annoyed."

"Did I?"

He frowned a little. "You have," he said finally, consideringly, "gone to some lengths to make this entire morning painfully impersonal."

"I haven't gone to any lengths at all." She looked at him, smiled a twisted smile. "I am what I am, Mr. Gavin."

"Matt, for godsake. Calling me by my first name won't strike you mute."

Erin said nothing.

His frown deepened. "Look, will it kill you to talk to me like a reasonably friendly human being instead of regarding me as something your dog dragged in?"

"Have I done that? Sorry."

"You're so cool." He stared at her, a fixed gaze that probed and searched. "So—unflappable. Even yesterday, when you were tired." His eyes lifted to her bright hair confined high on her head and swinging free behind her, and there was speculation in his eyes.

As if, she thought, he were wondering at the common belief about red hair being a brand of passion. Now that was *another* peculiar thought, she realized uneasily.

And Erin was surprised to find herself briefly tempted to explain the coolness he commented on, the control. She frowned a bit, not pleased by the impulse, and said, "You should get started back to town. Don't worry about my horse; he's much calmer and easier to ride than the roan was. When you get to town, just tie the reins loosely to the saddlehorn and let him go. He'll come home."

Matt Gavin slowly finished his coffee, never taking his eyes off her, then reached over to set the cup on the coffee table. Leaning back, he said musingly, "I heard about that reporter you chased off the mountain with a load of buckshot in his pants. Would you do that to me? I wonder. Just chase me off as if I were an annoyance to be dealt with?"

"Do you think I wouldn't?" she said.

"Oh, I think you would. I think it wouldn't matter to you a bit that I work for the company you write for." He paused, then went on deliberately. "What I'm wondering, really, is why. Why you're hiding up here. Why a beautiful, intelligent, talented woman would be so cold."

Erin knew he was trying to provoke her, probing for some reaction from her. She was, again briefly, tempted to tell him just why. Tempted to explain. But she was a private woman, and she said nothing.

"How old are you?" he asked abruptly.

"Twenty-eight." No hesitation, no evasion.

His eyes searched her impassive face. "When you signed the first contract four years ago," he said, "it was in another name. About three years ago, you explained in a letter that your name was now legally Scott." He hesitated for a moment. "You were married, weren't you?"

"I was married." She wondered absently why she was answering his questions, why she was just sitting here watching his face and feeling peculiarly detached.

"You're divorced now."

"Yes."

"How long were you married?"

"I lived with my husband for a year." Erin felt something gathering, tensing, threatening to spring from the dark closet where it lived. Matt Gavin, she realized dimly, was very good at probing. And all her instincts were shouting at her. She wanted to get up, walk away, to go and saddle a horse and put him on it and get him out of her life.

Because when dark things leaped from closets and stood nakedly between two strangers, they couldn't be strangers anymore.

"Just a year? You don't strike me as the kind to give up that easily."

She watched his eyes drop to her mouth, and realized that she was worrying her lower lip. Instantly, she stopped. Words came from somewhere and piled up in front of the closet to keep the dark thing trapped.

"Sometimes," she said, "it isn't a matter of giving up. Sometimes it's . . . recognition that there's nothing to fight for. Nothing that matters anymore. Sometimes you just can't keep getting up when you're knocked down."

He frowned. "Do you mean—"

"I don't mean anything." She stood abruptly and carried their coffee cups to the kitchen.

"Erin . . ."

She started when the voice came from behind her, when he said her name. She felt curiously cold, but there was heat spreading over the surface of her body, skin tingling. Her knees were weak again, and her heart thudded against her ribs. Accustomed to digging for motivation in characters, accustomed to studying reactions objectively, she found her own reaction to him deeply disturbing.

What was wrong with her?

"Erin, I don't want to pry, but—"

"Then don't." She turned, suppressing an instinctive physical withdrawal when she saw how close to her he stood. Too close—he was too close to her. Too close to her pain. "Don't pry. Stop asking questions. You turn up on my porch one day and expect the story of my life the next?"

He nodded slowly. "All right, I had that coming. It's really none of my business, is it?"

"It's none of your business," she agreed.

He looked at her intently, searching her calm face and shuttered eyes. Wondering if a failed marriage had made her this way or if something else had been the cause.

Matt Gavin was a man who was comfortable with women, a

man who understood women better than most. But this woman baffled him. There was something in her lovely, wary green eyes, a shadow of some dreadful hurt, and it touched something inside him.

He hadn't known her eyes would be green, or her hair red; only the features of her face were familiar to him—as familiar as his own. Her vivid coloring brought those features to life and indicated a passion otherwise deeply hidden . . . or unawakened. Her beauty and wariness had first drawn him, but it was that hidden passion which intrigued him.

Behind his immobile face, Matt's mind worked quickly. Everything inside him warned that his only chance was to make an impression on this guarded woman, and to make it quickly. She was adept at ridding herself of strangers.

He couldn't afford to remain one.

"I'm not normally so inquisitive," he murmured. "My only excuse is that I've never cared for shadow-boxing."

Erin thought she knew what he meant, but asked anyway. "Meaning?"

He crossed his arms over his broad chest and seemed to study her intently. "Well, when a man finds himself interested in a woman, he generally has to contend with her past, because he isn't a part of it. Unless she's a childhood sweetheart, in which case he *is* her past."

"You don't waste time with small talk, do you." It was an observation rather than a question.

"I can't afford to, can I? At any moment I may find myself tumbling down this mountain, speeded along by your shotgun."

"There is that." Erin found herself amused by his solemnity, but fought off the urge to relax and enjoy his approach. "Look, Mr. Gavin—"

"If," he interrupted conversationally, "you don't start calling me Matt, I'm going to kiss you silly."

She blinked. "Look, Matt—"

"Works every time," he told an invisible third party. "All you have to do is threaten them with a fate worse than death."

Erin bit the inside of her cheek and cleared her throat, staving off laughter. "Matt, I really hate to see a busy man waste time in a—lost cause. And I'd hate to endanger your future progeny by asking you to ride up the mountain every day, which you'd have to do since I rarely go down to town. So—"

"I thought I'd stay here."

It was, she realized, a very matter-of-fact statement. And his tone was so reasonable that Erin found herself unable to object. For a split second. "No."

"You have a very comfortable couch," he offered hopefully. "And since I've already spent one night here, your virtuous reputation in town is likely shot to hell anyway."

"You slept on my couch, and Jake knows it; he'll spread the word." She was amused to find herself patiently explaining things to him. "But you can't stay here."

"Jake." Momentarily distracted, he assumed an expression of irritation. "He's the one who rented me *that horse?*"

By the tone of voice, Erin gathered Matt had not been overly fond of the roan; he must have spent an uncomfortable couple of days aboard the animal. "He's the one," she told him.

"I have a score to settle with that young man."

Erin smiled a little. "Be careful how you settle it. Jake's older than he looks, and he was a marine." She considered a moment, then added thoughtfully, "And he seems guileless; don't drink his moonshine if he offers it."

"Too late." Mart's expression spoke plainly of remembered agony. "I sampled the stuff before I got on that horse. Why hasn't Jake been arrested for pedaling poison?"

"We like him," Erin replied simply. "Besides, we know better than to drink it."

"So he springs it on unsuspecting strangers," Matt realized with a sigh.

"Something like that."

He brooded on the thought for a few moments, then dismissed it. "Anyway, if Jake's your pipeline into town, he can report that I'm still sleeping on the couch."

"What's believed for one night," she said very dryly, "won't be believed for several." And was ignored.

"I've always wanted to spend time in—the back of beyond." He looked around the cozy cabin. "The wilderness stops at your door from the looks of it; you've got all the creature comforts."

"No," she said.

"I would, of course," he said, "pitch in for groceries and whatever. Board."

"No."

"We can talk about your next book."

"No, Matt," she said firmly.

He looked at her for a moment unreadably. "Well, at least you used my name," he said. "Unprompted, as it were. That's something."

Perversely, she found herself wishing she had not been quite so uncompromising. Still . . . "Sorry, Matt. I just don't want a guest." Strongly suspecting she'd end in defeat if she allowed the "conversation" to go on any longer, she moved around him toward the back door. "I'll saddle the horse for you."

"Do I have to leave now?"

Erin hardened her heart, which was difficult in the face of his questionable meekness. "Yes. I have things to do; I've been away for two weeks, and I have work to catch up on."

He followed her out to the barn. "Well, thanks for the hospitality, Erin."

She was busy brushing Amos, but spared a moment to direct a suspicious look at Matt's guileless expression. "Uh-huh." She had the vague feeling that the man was hugely enjoying some private joke—at her expense.

There was just something about his meekness, she thought uneasily. Like the earlier sheepishness, it had a motive under it. She couldn't think what it could be, but her knees felt weak again. Dammit. Those gray eyes . . .

A few moments later she led the saddled horse from the barn and watched while Matt climbed aboard—with grace if not with expertise. He held the reins in one hand, gazing down at her for a moment.

"Just tie the reins and turn him loose once I reach town?" he questioned, and when she nodded, nodded himself. "Fine. Thanks again, Erin. Bye."

She watched him ride away, thinking nothing, ignoring a peculiar feeling of depression. When he disappeared from her sight and the peaceful mountain sounds were all to be heard, she shook her head and went into the cabin.

Odd that it felt so empty.

Erin kept herself busy for the remainder of the day. She worked outside for the most part, replenishing bird feeders, repairing the fence around her small kitchen garden, and working in the garden itself.

Amos came home late in the afternoon, moving briskly and obviously glad to return. She unsaddled him, reflecting with a pang that it really was too much to expect that any man would spend the better part of a day on a horse just to visit a woman. Only ten miles or so to town, true, but given the terrain, a trip up and down on horseback took most of a day.

Grimacing at her own dim disappointment, Erin fed and watered her horses, then went into the cabin to feed Chester and herself. She worked for a while that night in the peaceful quiet of her study, getting her notes and research organized for the next book.

Like everything else in the cabin that was not made by herself, her computer had been transported up the mountain at considerable expense, and she used it carefully. Her generator was a powerful one, but during this time of year unpredictable and sometimes violent storms could easily cut her off from everyone and everything for weeks at a time; unwilling to be without power for lack of fuel, Erin tended to be miserly in her use of any appliance that consumed electricity—particularly the computer.

She did all of her planning, therefore, on paper, organizing as much as possible so that her actual writing utilized "quality" time. Somewhat to her surprise, Erin had found that her work went much more smoothly in this way; she wasted little time while actually writing on the computer, since her books were roughed out in some detail in longhand on paper.

She worked in preparation that night, her bright desk lamp throwing crouching shadows around the room. Neither the quiet nor the shadows disturbed Erin; she worked steadily, only halfhearing Chester's soft snores from where he lay by the door. She rose a few times to consult books on the crowded shelves lining three walls of the study, arranged her notes, and constructed a brief outline to be filled in during the next few days.

She hoped.

It was late when she tidied her desk and quit for the night. She went through her usual getting-ready-for-bed routine, and it was only when she was in bed and drowsy that thoughts of Matt Gavin crept into her mind.

At one moment half asleep, she found herself abruptly wide awake and restless the next. From experience, she knew it would be almost impossible to blank her mind; a mind accustomed to the ongoing creative process, she'd discovered, was often obsessive. She had spent many a sleepless night listening to her mind work through a story.

This was, however, the first time in a long time that something other than a story had kept her awake and thinking.

She lay there, staring up at a dark ceiling, and swore at herself solemnly. Facing her thoughts with reluctant honesty, she admitted that Matt had made a strong impression on her. Not his looks especially, she decided, because she had known many handsome and charismatic men—particularly during her whirlwind courtship and marriage.

No, she thought, it was something else, something besides his looks. He had a certain presence; in spite of the fact that her own sharpened instincts had marked him as a man out of his element, there was something about him that seemed curiously adaptable.

Unwilling to draw comparisons, she nonetheless found herself doing just that. Stuart had not been adaptable; remove him from his element, and he was clearly a fish out of water. He had been comfortable, even brilliant, in his own world, and totally at a loss out of it. Coping masterfully and enjoyably with his frenetic lifestyle, he had been bored and moody in rare moments of quiet, and explosively temperamental when his will was thwarted.

Matt Gavin, Erin thought reluctantly, would not be that kind of man. And where Stuart was an essentially humorless man, she thought that Matt had not only a sense of humor but also a strong sense of the ridiculous and an ability to laugh at himself.

More than a little surprised that her opinion of Matt should have developed so strongly and after so short a time, Erin frowned in the darkness. Fiercely pushing him from her mind, she closed her eyes and counted sheep.

And it wasn't ten minutes later that she found herself half-giggling and feeling the heat of self-consciousness in her face as she realized that her stubborn thoughts had taken a gentle turn into the speculative: She wondered what Matt Gavin would be like as a lover.

She had never considered herself a passionate woman sexually; Stuart's lovemaking had been as frantic and as overpowering as the man himself, leaving her breathless but, on some deep level, unfulfilled. At times rough, always unpredictable, he had been a slightly selfish lover, concerned first with his own pleasure. She had often longed just to be held in loving silence, but had more often than not found herself gazing at his back as they lay in their bed. Or worse, gazing at the ceiling as she lay there alone, because Stuart had barely caught his breath before leaving her to pursue a fleeting idea.

Alone now, she stared at the ceiling and wondered about Matt Gavin, unable to halt the speculation. Would he, she wondered, leave a lover in her lonely bed with nothing more than an absent kiss? Would his passion explode with no warning, overpowering but not satisfying? Did a demon drive him to be rough and frantic in love as in life? Or would he be a sensitive and generous lover, evoking tenderness as well as desire?

The thoughts that had flickered that morning rose again now with certainty. No, she thought, Matt would not be a selfish lover, or rough or impatient. She was uncomfortable with that knowledge, that certainty, but didn't doubt it. Somehow, she just knew.

He was an undeniably, heart-stoppingly masculine man who, either by instinct or experience, understood and appreciated women. It was in his eyes.

"It's in your imagination," she told herself fiercely aloud, startled by the sound of her own voice.

Erin turned, pounding her pillow and swearing unsteadily. Too late, she thought, for regrets. Too late to wish she had encouraged his interest. He would have been safe, she thought dimly, as a lover, because he had his own life in New York and would have returned there, leaving her with what might have been a good memory and her peace intact.

There would have been no threat to her heart or her life, just an interlude like a stirring breeze soon gone.

No threat . . .

Erin *found depression hanging over her head like a gloomy cloud* the next morning. She did her usual chores automatically and with no enthusiasm, disquieted at her unusual brooding. She gave the cabin a thorough cleaning, working hard and quickly to block thoughts. By ten A.M. the cabin was spotless, and she was still depressed.

The radio squawked as she was passing listlessly to take her coffee out onto the porch, and she detoured to answer the unusual summons, half-expecting Mal to announce a package or something awaiting her in town.

He didn't.

"Erin . . . this dude who went up to see you—"

She felt interest quicken. "What about him, Mal?"

"Well, did you tell him not to come back? I mean, are you expecting him up there again?"

Erin frowned at her friend's faintly unsteady tone. "I'm not expecting him, but I didn't threaten him with the shotgun if he came back. Why?"

"He's—uh—a resourceful man, your dude. The whole town's tickled about it."

"About what?"

Mal didn't have to answer, because that was when she heard the music.

Chapter Three

I t began first as more of a throbbing than a sound, a vibration felt rather than heard. Erin signed off the radio with a hasty, abrupt good-bye and carried her coffee out to the front porch, baffled. She stood there for a moment before the throbbing became sounds, and identification of those sounds did nothing to stop her bewilderment.

Ravel's *Bolero*?

It was, confusingly, just that, and the music swelled steadily, blotting out all the gentle sounds of nature. There was another sound accompanying the music, a sound Erin couldn't identify at first; when she could identify it, bewilderment clashed with incredulity.

A helicopter?

So it proved to be, and a helicopter, moreover, with character. It was painted a vile green that shocked the eyes and would cause any self-respecting soul to cringe. It was obviously vintage army surplus, a great hulking gunship bare of guns and boasting definitely obscene graffiti painted in various colors. It thundered over the cabin, blaring Ravel from a loudspeaker bolted near its blunt nose, and set down with a thump drowned by music about twenty yards from the cabin—as far away as it could get without tangling with trees or falling off the mountain.

Erin held on to one of the posts supporting the overhang on her porch, dimly aware that her mouth was open and instinctively bracing herself against the rush of oily wind caused by the thumping rotors.

While she watched in astonishment, Matt Gavin climbed from the aircraft and strolled toward her with complete sangfroid as the peculiar green machine at his back lifted again with a roar and swooped off still blaring the seductive *Bolero*.

On the corner of the porch Chester snored contentedly, never stirring at the noise or the cessation of it.

"Hi," Matt said casually as he reached the porch.

On some faraway level of herself, Erin realized then why the entire town had been, in Mal's words, tickled. She could easily imagine the faces of townspeople when that nauseating helicopter had set down near the small motel where Matt had undoubtedly stayed. Especially if it had announced its arrival there with the same sort of fanfare.

She stared at him, stunned and incredulous, feeling sudden laughter welling up. "You—you—" She didn't even know what she *wanted* to say.

Matt was no help at all. Deadpan, he gazed at her, arms crossed over his chest. He looked neither defiant nor amused, simply calm.

Erin sat down on the porch, put her coffee to one side, and laughed herself silly. When she finally got herself under control, she wiped streaming eyes and found Matt sitting beside her, grinning.

"Oh, Lord," she gasped. "Who picked the music?"

Laughter gleamed in his eyes. "Me. Didn't have much choice,

I'm afraid. It was either Ravel or some godawful marching music. As you can see—and hear—Steve likes to announce his arrival."

Erin held her aching stomach, smiling at him unconsciously. "The pilot? Where on earth did you find him?"

"He's an old friend of mine. Lives in Denver. He owns a successful charter service. I called him this morning and asked if he'd mind being my taxi for a while, since I'd met a fascinating woman who lived in an aerie, and I didn't want to end up impaired for life and permanently bowlegged."

Erin choked.

"He said," Matt went on blandly, "he would happily deliver me every morning you cared to have me, then retrieve me before dark. I'm paying for fuel, and Steve is gleeful at the opportunity to shock people with that monstrosity he fondly calls Sadie."

A little weakly, Erin said, "It'll cost you a fortune—even if it's deductible as transportation costs to find a reclusive writer."

Matt smiled at her slowly. "Oh, Salem isn't paying. I also called them this morning and announced that I was on vacation."

Erin shut her mouth and tried to think. "But you—I mean— you can't want to—"

"What I'd like to do," he interrupted smoothly, "is find out why one of my favorite writers requested several postponements on her last deadline, and seems to be . . . unable to tell us anything about her work-in-progress. That's not like you, Erin."

She had to mentally shift gears from the personal to the professional, and felt a bit chagrined about it. Though apparently footing the bill for his transport, Matt Gavin was obviously here for purely business reasons. She was irritated with herself for being upset by that.

Matt watched the play of emotions on her lovely face, his heart leaping as he realized that he had already made an impression on Erin. But he pushed eagerness aside, all too aware that there was still a way to go yet. "Writer's block?" he asked neutrally.

Instantly, she said, "That's a catch-all phrase, and you know it. Writers get *blocked* on particular stories, maybe, and occasionally burn out on the work altogether." She picked up her coffee cup and frowned at it, trying to keep her mind on professional matters and ignore those other more nebulous thoughts. "And maybe I haven't talked about what I'm working on because it hasn't taken shape yet."

"Have you worked lately?"

"Last night."

"And?"

"And what?" Erin felt defensive and tried to ignore the vague uneasiness that had plagued her for the past three months. Tried to ignore her bitter certainty that the notes and summary she'd compiled roughed-out a story that was pure garbage.

"How did it go?" Matt was gazing straight ahead, apparently at nothing, his expression neutral.

"I don't want to talk about it," she said, abrupt.

He was silent for a long moment, still gazing ahead. Then he said, "All right, we'll talk about something else. I need your help, Erin. Tell me how to box shadows. Tell me how to fight my way through some other man's stupid mistakes."

She turned her head to stare at him. He wasn't—surely he wasn't—he didn't mean— She cut off the confused thoughts. It didn't make sense. *He* didn't make sense. "I don't know," she said carefully, "what you mean."

"I have a thing about redheads."

Erin blinked. Good heavens, she thought, he did mean— "I thought this was a professional visit," she managed in a very steady voice.

"I'm on vacation, remember?" Matt was smiling just a little, but still not looking at her.

"You asked about my work."

"Yes. And we'll talk about that again. When you're ready."

He was, she thought, simply interested in the work. The work that had provided quite a bit of income for his company during the past few years. There was a bitter taste in her mouth, and she wondered tiredly if she was destined to be exploited by the men in her life. Instantly, she qualified that thought. Matt was not "the man" in her life, and Stuart had not exploited her. Not that. Not quite that.

Erin took a deep breath. "I see."

"No, I don't think you do." He looked at her then, with quiet, level gray eyes. "Your work is important to me, Erin, but only because it's a part of you. Because you're a *writer*. Not because you make money for my company."

She stared at him, suddenly puzzled by some inflection in his voice. "Your company."

He hesitated, then grinned faintly. "My company. I don't suppose any of us ever notices who signs our checks."

Erin remembered then. "My God—you own Salem."

Matt nodded.

"And you expect me to believe you don't care about the earnings from my books?"

"It does sound unlikely, doesn't it?" He seemed to think about that, to find it amusing. "But true, whether you believe it or not. Erin, I'll release you from your contract if you like. You can sign with another publisher."

"And?" She looked at him warily.

"And I'll still be on vacation. Still around. And I still want to talk to you about your work when you're ready."

"Why? Why would it interest you if I were writing for someone else?"

He was silent for a moment, reaching into his pocket for cigarettes and lighter. "You don't smoke, do you?" he asked idly, and when she shook her head, added, "It's a lousy habit."

Erin waited patiently.

Matt lighted the cigarette and smoked for a moment in silence, then sighed. "You," he said, "are a writer. It comes across in every word you write. It isn't a job with you; it isn't a profession. It's what you are. You put your heart and soul into a book, and it shows."

She felt more than a little shaken. How could he know? Was it so obvious that every word mattered to her? "Assuming—" She cleared her throat. "Assuming that's true, my question stands. Why would you be interested if—if—"

"If I didn't stand to gain?" His smile was crooked. "Erin, I have all the money I'll ever need. Believe it or not, what matters to me are the writers."

Erin looked at him curiously. Sales didn't matter? Money didn't matter? It was, she thought, an unorthodox attitude—to say the least. Unless . . . "Have you—ever written?" she asked.

"Why do you ask?"

"You *have* written." The evasion, obscurely, pleased her.

He shrugged. "Years ago. I found out I wasn't a born writer. Oh, I could write to please readers. But my basic pleasure in writing was a fascination with the whole process. From the origin of an idea to the finished product on the shelves."

Erin dredged into her memories of what she'd read and heard about Salem. "You took over Salem about ten years ago, didn't you? And the first crop of books you bought hit the best-seller lists—a first for the company."

Matt dropped his cigarette into the dirt in front of the steps and reached a booted toe to ground it out. "I publish what I like."

"First-time authors, most of them," she noted. It was coming back to her now, what she'd read about her publisher. That he was tough in a tough business, but fiercely supportive of his writers—of all writers. Salem paid writers well, and treated them with an unusual amount of respect in a business where books and authors had come to be packaged and promoted like soap powder and breakfast cereal.

It was, basically, why she had submitted her first book to Salem; she had checked the market critically and had heard again and again that Salem was a home for its writers rather than a place where one sent manuscripts and from which one received checks.

"Writers have it rough in today's market," Matt mused almost to himself. "So many houses want their—products—tailored to whatever happens to be popular at the moment. Good writing is sacrificed in favor of homogenized banality. House policy dictates that editors tone down this, cut that, reword this phrase because it isn't *acceptable* as it stands—

"We have books available for every taste," Matt said, his level voice roughening, anger creeping into the tone. "And writers are being squeezed into molds. You don't buy many books on their own merits anymore; you buy a *kind* of book. Look at the top six best sellers any given month, and at least four of them look mass-produced! Dammit, books can be entertaining without being trash.

"Writers should be left alone to explore their potential, should be encouraged to write what they feel—and they should be paid for the effort! Numbers should never be the judge of accomplishment, and houses should never restrict a writer's vision just because it doesn't match their own—"

Matt broke off abruptly and laughed. He looked at Erin, no apology or defiance in his expression, but rather a faintly amused self-mockery. "Sorry. Didn't mean to get on my soapbox."

Erin drew a deep breath. "Lord, don't apologize," she said, sounding as dazed as she felt. "What you believe would be music to any writer's ears. I had no idea . . . Talk like that at any writer's conference, and they'd be beating down your door."

He smiled. "Luckily, I have the capital to gamble. If Salem loses money, I can poke more into the company. But we haven't lost money yet—which proves, I believe, that writers and books don't have to fit into molds to find an audience."

Erin shook her head, bemused. Offhand, she couldn't recall ever meeting anyone—particularly a businessman—who seemed more concerned with talent than with the product of that talent. "You're . . . an unusual man," she said slowly.

Matt shrugged. "Not really. Even businessmen can be idealistic; it's just that most of them have to think about earning a living and listening to a boss."

She looked at him, realizing that she still was not certain just what interested Matt Gavin here in Colorado: her or her writing. And she was startled when he seemingly picked up on her confusion, almost as if he could read her mind.

"I want to spend time with you, Erin. Is that so hard to understand?"

"Why—professionally?"

He nodded slightly, his expression clearly saying that she was right to divide his motives into professional and personal. "Professionally . . . because you're a born writer apparently having trouble writing—for whatever reason. And I've had some success in helping writers over walls; I want to help you if I can. Personally . . ."

"Because you have a thing about redheads?" she ventured when his voice trailed off.

He hesitated, gazing out over the loneliness of the place she had chosen to call home. "I could say it was because you had to fasten those buttons," he murmured.

"Would that be true?" she asked steadily. She remembered her gaping pajama top and his fascinated gaze, her heart leaping at the realization that he had found her attractive—even if it was only physically.

"Partly. But even before that . . . even seeing you wearing jeans and a flannel shirt, I was drawn to you. You made me think of a rose bush in full bloom. Very lovely—and potentially painful. Some roses have more thorns than others; you'd better wear gloves when you touch them. That's you."

Erin was a little surprised by the analogy, and unsure whether to be flattered or insulted. "So you put on gloves?" she asked, carefully polite.

"Well, I think I'd better. At least until I find out if you're prickly because you're a writer, or because of something else. Given my druthers, I wouldn't get involved with a writer." He sent her a swift smile, "temperamental creatures, writers. But I don't seem to have a choice where you're concerned. If you want me out of your life, Erin, you'll have to use that shotgun. I won't go willingly."

Erin returned the steady gaze, her thoughts and emotions chasing themselves in circles. Her gaze wavered and focused on something in the distance as she remembered her thoughts and regrets of the night before. She was, it seemed, being given a chance for that interlude she'd wondered about.

He was safe, she thought. Safe. He'd get bored in time, and go home to his city life. It was bound to happen. And three years of private peace had strengthened her; she could cope, now, with a relationship—a fleeting one. Couldn't she?

She wondered, then, if the failure of her marriage had marked her indelibly; would she always, forever, question her own ability to cope? Could she never be sure of herself? Had Stuart drained away even confidence in herself?

"How he must have hurt you," Matt said quietly.

She started in surprise.

"Shadows," he said. "In your eyes. I wonder if I'm any good at shadowboxing."

"Matt, I don't . . ."

"I've already put on the gloves, Erin. The boxing gloves—and the gloves to handle thorns. Are you going for the gun? Or should I square off and start fighting?"

"Damn you," she said.

Correctly interpreting that muttered curse, he smiled again, eyes steady. "I don't suppose you'd like to shine a light on those shadows and make it easier for me?"

"If you shine a light on shadows, they disappear," she managed carefully.

"I know."

He was safe, she told herself fiercely. Safe.

Erin held her voice even. "Matt, I won't—I won't chase you off with a shotgun. But I—don't know you."

He was silent for a moment, obviously thinking that over. When he spoke, it was in a quiet tone. "But you'll give us a chance to get to know each other?"

She nodded, not hesitant, but silent. Wondering if the kindest lesson Stuart had taught her had been to never again throw her entire heart into a relationship. She wouldn't, she decided, do that again. Not this time. This time she would still be whole when it was over.

He rose and drew her to her feet so that they both stood at the bottom step. "That's all I'm asking, Erin. A chance. If I ask questions you don't want to answer, then don't. If I say or do something you don't like, tell me. As long as you'll give us a chance."

Erin could hardly help but think how different this beginning was from the last one. She felt absurdly grateful to Matt for the patience he promised. And he must have seen that.

"I'm breaking new ground?" he asked gently.

Even that mild question almost caused her to withdraw, but then, with a feeling of release, she knew she would answer. "Something like that." She nodded jerkily and stepped away from him, retrieving her hands from his quiet grasp and sliding them into the pockets of her jeans.

"He swept you off your feet?"

That question, like the first, was mild and undemanding, and his expression was neutral but intent. The lack of demand and the lack of persuasion allowed her to answer with no feeling of being forced against her will.

"Like a steamroller." Erin found herself smiling ruefully. "They say every girl hopes Prince Charming will come along on his charger and carry her away; I can tell you it isn't all it's cracked up to be. Princes can be imperious . . . and falling off a charger hurts like hell."

"Did he rescue you from a dragon?" Matt was smiling.

She laughed a little. "No. No dragon. I wasn't running away from anything; I had loving parents and a good home. I didn't think there was anything missing until he came riding by all white and shining, and made the rest of the world look dark and slow and dull."

"And then? Did the prince get tarnished?"

Almost absently, Erin began walking, and he fell into step beside her. She followed a favorite path that wound gradually farther up the mountain, thinking that the light and casual talk of princes made it easier to talk of difficult things. Did Matt realize that? Probably. Certainly.

"No," she said at last, dryly. "He didn't get tarnished. He didn't change at all. He had feet of clay, like all princes; I just couldn't see that at first. The shine of him blinded me. He threw me across his saddle and galloped off, and I was so breathless and grateful."

"Why grateful?" Matt was still neutral, still calm.

"Every girl wants a prince." She shrugged, mocking herself faintly. "And I got one. A handsome, talented prince who could— and did—set the world on fire with his brilliance."

After a moment Matt said, "May I ask—?"

"Stuart Travis." There was another long moment of silence. Erin didn't look at Matt, but she could feel his surprised recognition of that name.

"Quite a brilliant prince." His voice was still calm, reflective. "Singer, songwriter, world-famous entertainer. If I remember correctly, he's won more awards than any other singer in history."

"He has. He's thirty-six." She related the information calmly, with no envy or bitterness in her tone. "He's been a genius all his life, and his star keeps on climbing. Years ago a reporter realized in shock that Stuart had written, recorded, and performed eight out of ten of the top songs for the past decade. A remarkable achievement."

"A . . . driven genius."

Erin glanced at him, curiously not surprised by his perception. "Driven by powerful demons. Temperamental, moody, constantly creative. Burning continually like a comet, rushing through space and time as if there weren't enough of either." Softly, she added, "I could never catch my breath."

After a moment of silence, Matt returned them impassively to the safety of analogy. "So the prince just kept charging through life. And what about the princess?"

Erin laughed under her breath, wryly amused at herself as she hadn't been then. "She didn't get to live in her castle. She got a succession of hotel rooms and learned to live out of a suitcase. She ate her meals courtesy of room service or takeout places because the prince was too famous and too restless to eat in restaurants and too impatient to let her cook."

She stopped walking, looking out over the spectacular view where the path ended; they were miles in the air, looking down at a distant world. Vaguely, she wondered if that accounted for her fondness for this place; it was above the world. Unreachable.

"Hard to share a genius with the world," Matt commented, a faint question in his voice.

Erin shook her head, gazing blindly out on all that distance. "There was never anything to share. Never a part of him that was mine. I was . . . just there." She looked at Matt suddenly, and her smile twisted. "He loved me."

Matt frowned slightly. "But—?"

Flatly, she explained what had taken her many long and painful months to realize and understand. "But he used me, used what he felt for me. Like everything else in his life. Fodder for his songs. He tore emotions to shreds—his and others'—to find songs. He demanded. And what he got, he chewed up and spit out to the world in a song. And he never gave in any other way. The world could have what he was, what he felt, but those closest to him could only give and give until he couldn't drain them anymore."

Matt reached out suddenly and pulled her into his arms, holding her with a fierce gentleness. "I'm sorry, Erin," he said huskily.

She put her arms around his lean waist, holding him because she needed that contact, hiding her face against his neck. "Not a cruel prince," she said unsteadily. "Not deliberately cruel. Just driven. He was what he had to be, what his talent made him be. Still is, I guess. And I couldn't give anymore. I didn't have anything left. I—" She broke off abruptly, unwilling to explain what had finally broken her, what had collapsed the empty shell she had become.

Matt stroked her long hair gently and held her with no demand and no more questions. "No wonder you came up here," he said finally, quiet. "And no wonder you're so wary. You've already given more than anyone should ever have asked of you."

She stood in the quiet embrace for long moments, feeling peculiarly suspended and not a little shocked. A stranger. He was a *stranger*, and she'd told him things even her parents had not been told. She pulled away slightly and gazed up at that handsome, still face, unable to guess what he was thinking, unable to see what lay behind the quiet of his gray eyes.

"I don't—" she began in a troubled voice, but Matt interrupted.

"You don't talk about it, do you? But you told me." He smiled down at her. "You needed to tell someone, Erin, that's all. It was time for you to tell someone. I happened to be here, and asked."

She was surprised again. Was she so transparent that he saw she needed reassurance? Or was he that perceptive? Still bothered by her willingness to tell him what she had told no one else, Erin was only partly aware that he had turned them back toward the cabin. She was very aware that as they walked he kept one arm loosely around her shoulders.

Safe . . . he was safe . . .

Abruptly, she said, "You don't know what I gave Stuart. What he—took. For all you know, I may well have been the proverbial misunderstood wife. A brilliant, talented husband, no room in his spotlight for me. For all you know, I could have run like a coward from my own imagination."

"You didn't."

"You can't *know* that," she insisted fiercely. They had reached the cabin, and she shrugged off his arm, turning to face him. "I don't want you to get the wrong idea, Matt. Don't think I'm some poor, wounded creature in need of sympathy and solace. Don't think I need another prince on another charger." She stopped, stared at him, realized what she'd said, and what it implied. "I don't believe in fairy tales anymore," she ended in a whisper.

Matt reached up to slide a hand beneath the heavy weight of her hair, a warm hand with no pressure. "I'm not offering fairy tales, Erin," he said quietly. "When I look at you, I don't see some frail maiden in need of a prince and cotton batting to be wrapped in. I see a woman to walk beside a man, not behind him. I see a wary woman who's been hurt, but not a weak woman."

He smiled at her slowly. "A woman who would never have run from a man or a marriage, except as a last resort. Stop doubting yourself, Erin."

"Have you ever been in love?" she asked him.

He hesitated, shook his head. "No. I have no scars from a past."

"The scars don't hurt. They're just reminders of mistakes. I wanted you to know. I won't make those mistakes again. I won't let myself be hurt like that again."

"You think I'd hurt you?"

"How can I know that?" She was honest. "I only know that I won't let you hurt me. Or anyone hurt me." She turned away from him again, looking toward the porch and Chester, and wondering dimly how her faithful canine friend could possibly be sleeping through so traumatic a moment.

Easily. It wasn't his trauma.

"Erin?"

She leaned down to pick up her discarded coffee cup, then half-turned back to look at him.

"Now you're running," he said.

She didn't deny the quiet accusation; she just gazed at him steadily. After a long moment she said, "When Stuart and I met, he wrote a song about us. I was flattered. I always thought that a man singing to a woman was corny—but when you're in love, nothing's corny. That song hit the top ten; millions of people heard it. Shortly after that we had our first fight—and millions of people heard it. Later. During a live concert. In a song."

Matt's brows drew together. "You mean he—"

"Fodder for his songs. The fighting . . . the making-up. Everything that we were was set to music and sung to the world. He—he wrote songs about our lovemaking. About sleepy eyes in the morning. About a peach nightgown I wore. About—being torn between his wife . . . and another woman."

She felt the hot sting of tears, but smiled faintly. "I didn't need to stand in his spotlight; he focused it on me. Stripped me naked in front of the world. I ran. Oh, I ran."

"I wouldn't do that to you, Erin," Matt said, something intense in his level tone. "You don't have to run from me."

"Don't I? It would have been so much simpler, Matt, if . . . If you'd just seen those unfastened buttons. There's no threat in that. That's two people—finding something without having to look too deep. I thought you were safe. Here for a while and then . . . gone. No threat. But you want—something else. Don't you?"

"Yes," he said steadily.

She nodded a little. "Yes. Probing like that. Shadow-boxing. To have something simple, you wouldn't have to fight." She paused, thinking, acknowledging her own vulnerability. "Funny that I know that." He had hardly touched her, yet she knew. She went into the cabin, carrying her coffee cup to the kitchen, knowing he was following.

She spoke before he could. "I think you're a wizard. I didn't want to— It was so damned *emotional* with Stuart. Euphoric highs and devastating lows—and no in between. I didn't want to feel like that again. I don't know if I can stand feeling like that again."

"So you just want something nonthreatening this time. Something simple. Something physical. And when it's over—an empty bed, but not an empty heart. Is that it?"

Erin couldn't tell from his voice how he was reacting to that. Without looking at him, she went into the living room, moving restlessly, aware that he was standing only feet away and watching her. "It sounds so—crude, put like that," she said in a low voice.

Matt felt the ache in his jaw, realizing only then that his teeth were gritted. Consciously, he relaxed his expression even as he leashed a very primitive desire to snatch whatever he could get. Not yet, he knew. Not just yet.

Fighting himself, determined that she wouldn't be rid of him so easily, his own emotions crept into his voice. "It is crude."

She swung around, staring at him now, surprised by the harshness of his voice. She felt abruptly defensive, uncertain. "Maybe—maybe I just want to take this time." She forced a short laugh. "Matt, I'm trying to be honest. If you want an affair, I won't—I can't—say no. I have both feet firmly on the ground this time, you see. Men and women ... there's no magical mystery; people are attracted to one another. Either they do something about it, or they don't."

Erin squared her shoulders and held his impassive gaze. "I'd be sorry if you left, Matt, but I won't let you destroy my peace."

"Is it peace? Or a limbo?"

"Whatever it is," she said steadily, not rising to the bait, "I'm happy with it."

Matt crossed his arms over his broad chest and stared at her, no expression at all on his handsome face. "And you don't believe a polite, civilized, impersonal affair will disturb your peace? Is that it?"

Defiant now, feeling oddly in the wrong, Erin lifted her chin. "No. I don't."

"Okay."

She blinked. "What?"

"I said okay." He glanced around in a businesslike manner. "You have a radio, don't you? The grocer down in town mentioned something about it."

"I—yes, I do." Tensely, she gestured toward the small room containing the radio. "But why do you—"

"I'll get in touch with Steve and have him bring my stuff up from town." He paused to lift an eyebrow at her. "I can't stay away from New York indefinitely, so we may as well get on with it, right? No sense in keeping that motel room."

"I—"

"Of course, the whole town will know about us, but I don't suppose you care about that. I'll be gone in a couple of weeks anyway; they'll find something else to talk about then." Briskly, he headed for the radio.

Erin paced the living room, her emotions in turmoil. She heard his deep voice in the other room, and when he returned, she whirled to face him with an accusation.

"You said you wouldn't push!"

Matt looked at her in mild surprise. "But that was before I knew you wanted only an affair, Erin. Affairs tend to be quick things, you know; they start and they end—there isn't much in between.

Surface, mostly. And since we both agree on the ground rules, what's the sense in waiting?"

Erin wanted very badly to have the courage of her convictions. He was offering what she had claimed to want, after all. She wanted to agree with him, to nod practically and say of course he was right, and why should they waste time?

She couldn't say it.

In a tone very different from the brisk one of before, Matt said, "It isn't what you want, is it?"

Chapter Four

"**D**amn you."

Matt smiled a little, for the first time since they had entered the cabin. "Maybe it wouldn't cut up your peace too much, Erin, but you don't want . . . just an affair."

She looked at him, suddenly curious, realizing how easily he could have taken her up on the offer. "And you don't want one either?"

"No."

"Then what do you want?" she asked in what was very nearly a wail. "You've put me through more emotions in an hour than I've had to cope with in three years! I don't understand! You say my books don't interest you commercially, even though my writing *does* interest you—so I assume you aren't up here offering a little R and R to the troops!"

Matt burst out laughing. Erin glared at him for a moment, then smiled reluctantly herself. She felt as if she'd been through a wringer since that helicopter had landed, and she hadn't the faintest idea how this man's mind worked.

It was, she realized, a reversal of the first day; he had been puzzled by her then, but the shoe was on the other foot now. He seemed to understand her, and she was bewildered by him.

"What I want," he said, smiling at her, "is to get to know a rather beautiful woman who's as prickly as a very thorny rose. I'll probably end up getting myself skewered, but I'm willing to take that chance. If, that is, I can convince her that I don't wade into relationships swinging a baseball bat or make it a practice to strip away the privacy of just anyone at all."

He crossed the room to stand before her, looking at her gravely. "Erin, I'd be as blind and deaf as a post if I didn't want to spend the rest of the day in your bed making love with you. And I'm neither blind nor deaf. But the *last* thing I want is to have you believe that another man is using you—for whatever reasons. When we make love, it'll be because we want to, for all the reasons that bring two people together. Not because a physical relationship is easier than an emotional one and less troublesome. Not because we want to avoid the clutter of emotions."

Erin felt her heart turn over as she gazed up at him. "You," she said carefully, "are an anachronism. Or else," she added, "you've perfected the best and most original approach I've ever been privileged to hear."

"Don't lump me into the predatory-male group, please," he requested mildly. "I don't like labels. Besides, if you'd read the latest studies, you'd know that men tend to want emotional ties in a relationship. Nobody wants to sleep with a stranger if there's an alternative."

She looked at him for a moment, then caught her breath as he reached out and pulled her firmly into his arms. She couldn't seem to get her breath back, too conscious was she of the hard-muscled strength of his body pressed against hers. And her knees were weak again.

"Have you," he murmured, "ever heard the expression 'priming the pump'?"

Erin swallowed. "Uh-huh. It means to get something started."

"It's always nice to have one's actions understood," Matt said meditatively, and bent his head to hers.

Erin didn't know what she had expected to feel; other than her speculative thoughts of the day before, she'd not actually considered what it might be like to be kissed by Matt Gavin. But she had not, certainly, expected to feel something entirely new to her. She had not expected to discover with a shock that she was indeed a passionate woman—with this man, at least.

Shaken, she was only dimly aware that her arms had risen to encircle his neck, only faintly and bemusedly aware of feeling small in his embrace. Confused, she wondered how she could feel so small when she knew she *wasn't* . . . and what was this man doing to her?

Matt didn't waste time with gentleness, although there was nothing rough or crude in his kiss. He kissed her with a force and passion that demanded, yet did not take. He parted her lips with fierce need, yet it was not the plundering kiss of a victor; it was not possession but persuasion, fervent and urgent.

Erin, suddenly dizzy, felt the force of that kiss. She felt the persuasion that was insidiously heating her blood and draining the strength—what little was left—from her legs.

And though she was astonished at the realization, Erin knew that she was being, for the second time in her life, swept off her feet. But this time it was not by a shining prince; this time it was by a powerfully charismatic man whose touch she could feel down to her marrow.

And this time she was not grateful.

An abrupt surging anger rose in her, fed by her body's desire and her mind's revolt. She would not—*would not*—be carried away by someone else. This time she'd control her own damn destiny.

It was only partly a conscious decision; Erin's body was acting even before her mind realized what she was doing. And what she was doing was meeting his force with her own. For the first time in her adult life she tapped into the deep well of passions that her red hair hinted at so truly. Always before overwhelmed by someone else's passion, this time she loosed her own.

It was a palpable force as vital and tempestuous as a summer storm, as untamed as a forest fire.

And though another man might have been scorched by that blaze, Matt was delighted. He felt that hidden, guarded part of her rise up to meet him fiercely as she came alive in his arms, felt the heat of this vital woman igniting his own deepest desires.

Instinct demanded a struggle for supremacy, a clash of wills that would allow no winner or loser but simply swallow them both in the conflagration that would change them forever. And the hardest thing Matt had ever done in his life was to back away from that, to chain an instinctive beast howling an intolerable need for its mate.

Matt drew a deep and shuddering breath as he wrenched his lips away, holding her hard against him because he couldn't bear to release her just yet. He looked down into stormy green eyes and felt an exultation that nearly made him laugh aloud. No timid maiden hiding from life—not she! Waiting, perhaps, just waiting for the moment some wise fate had decreed to breathe fire into a woman meant to burn gloriously.

He had seen it—felt it—in her books, that fire. And then, seeing her face, her serene composure, he had found himself captivated by the seeming paradox. It had intrigued him, and meeting Erin here in her aerie had only increased the fascination. Fire within, composure without, there was a self-contained air about her, as though she had shown her inner self once too often and been kicked for it.

Knowing, now, what lay behind that, Matt wondered if Erin herself understood. Did she understand that Stuart Travis's shallow grasping at emotions had never touched her deeply? That because he had overwhelmed her instantly, her own emotions had lain dormant in a kind of bewildered limbo?

Did she understand that the breathless rush she had described had protected her, in a very real sense, from the devastating hurt of love betrayed? Could she see, he wondered, that her "fall" from that prince's charger had been the collapse of a girl's starry dream rather than a woman's shattered love?

Matt could see that so clearly. It had to be that. Stuart Travis had married a girl in love with a shining prince, but that was not the girl Matt wanted for himself. He wanted the woman who had blazed to life in his arms, who had responded with desire and temper, with the wholehearted life force that would never be flung at the feet of a man but would reach out and snatch his heart boldly.

Not a docile princess, but a regal queen.

It would take more than a shotgun to drive him away from her now.

He could see the furious temper in her eyes and, knowing without having to ask why she was mad, grinned down at her quite unconsciously. She knew! Whether she realized it or not, Erin Scott knew the difference between naive girl and vital woman.

Erin all but stamped her foot.

"Damn you!" she gasped for the third—or was it fourth?—time. "I *won't* be rushed again! D'you hear me? Stable your damned charger and slow down!"

Still holding her, very conscious of her fingers threaded through his hair, Matt did laugh aloud. "It takes two," he reminded her, cheerful in spite of his body's fury at obstinate self-control.

Rather hastily, she disentangled her fingers and pushed vainly against his broad chest. Matt laughed again, infuriating man that he was.

"And you thought we could have a simple little affair," he

pointed out dryly. He shook his head in gentle disbelief, still easily resisting her attempts to escape him.

Erin stopped struggling and glared up at him. She was absolutely furious, as much at herself as at him. "You listen to me! I'll take control of my own life, dammit! I'll never again be carried along by someone else like some starry-eyed idiot! Never again! I'll *take* this time, I'll *demand* what's mine and won't wait to have it handed to me on a plate like a reward for being a good girl!"

"Good."

The soft, delighted word stopped her abruptly, and she saw bemusedly that Matt really meant it. He *wanted* her to fight for herself, for her rights as a woman.

Matt kissed her briefly, hard, then grinned down at her. "You fight me every inch of the way, wildcat. Yell at me—hit me if you want. Because the passion in you is worth whatever it takes to free itself."

In something like horror, Erin realized then that she had just announced to both of them that there would be no patient, cautious exploration of whatever lay between them. No matter what his intentions were or how strongly she wanted no complications in her life, it seemed a decision had been made. This was something to be fought furiously, emotionally, mastered like a green colt until it could be handled tamely.

"Oh, no," she said numbly. "Not—"

"Don't say *again*," he interrupted instantly. "It wasn't like this before, Erin. What just exploded between us is something I'll bet Stuart Travis would have sold his soul for—if only to write about it. But he never felt what I just felt from you. I don't know why—" Matt hesitated for the first time, then went on. "I don't know why that's so. Maybe you were so overpowered by him, by what you thought he was. Maybe it just wasn't in you then.

"But the point is that it's in you *now*. And I *want* it, Erin! I want that passion. I don't care if I get my fingers burned, or my heart—I want it. If I have to needle you until you strike out at me, kiss you until you fight me, force you to feel it in spite of yourself—I'll get it."

It should have frightened her, Erin thought dimly, his utter determination. But something in her recognized the difference between taking and giving in to his demand; he would take, certainly, but only what he could make her give to him. Only what he could draw from her because she willed it.

She stepped back, and this time he allowed it. But they were still touching, she realized. There was some elusive link between them now, something tying them inexorably together. Something born in a rush of fierce temper and unleashed passion. She could feel the storm of her own temper in her eyes, and his eyes were alight with a satisfaction and anticipation he made no effort to hide.

Erin no longer felt daunted by the thought of violent emotions; instead, she felt curiously energized. She felt as if something long trapped and hidden inside her had burst suddenly into life. "And what," she asked evenly, "am I supposed to get from this?"

"Anything you can take." He smiled slowly. "Whatever you can hold on to. You want me at your feet, Erin? Put me there. You want my heart? Take it. Fight for it. You want to send me tearing back to the city carrying a load of emotional buckshot—fire away."

Staring at him, she said slowly, "I let Stuart use me. I didn't lift a finger to stop him."

Matt nodded. "Now you see it. And now you've got the chance to see if that would happen again. I know it wouldn't; I know that I'd never do that to you, and that you'd never allow it to happen. But you aren't sure of that. So we'll fight it out until you are sure."

"Will we fight—in there?" she asked, nodding toward the bedroom, feeling, with a sense of surprise, no embarrassment at the blunt question.

"We'll fight to get there." He nodded, seeing the comprehension on her face. "It'd be too easy to start there, wouldn't it? Too easy for us. But we will get there—eventually."

"You're very sure of yourself," she muttered, silently acknowledging that he had reason to be. Matt, thankfully, didn't point out the obvious.

"I know what I want," was his only response to that. "But there is something we'd better agree on up front."

"Which is?" she asked warily.

"We have to reach a compromise. Somewhere between your aversion to cities and my ineptitude with wilderness lies a middle ground. We have to find it."

For a moment Erin silently resisted that suggestion. It implied, she knew, a more solid and long-lasting relationship than the one she had had in mind. But she saw the challenge in his eyes and squared her shoulders unconsciously. "All right. But I don't see how to compromise on that. You live in New York, and I live here."

"Ummm." He looked at her for a moment, then said, "We'll have to work on that, I see. And we will. In the meantime, however, I suggest we suspend hostilities in favor of lunch."

Erin started, surprised to realize that it was only just past noon. And then she remembered something else. "Didn't you get in touch with—what's his name? Steve?"

Matt grinned at her. "Sure I did. We had a nice little chat. He's down in town letting kids climb all over Sadie. I told him to come pick me up around five this afternoon."

She glared at him briefly. "Swine. You knew I wouldn't—"

"Well, I was reasonably sure you wouldn't. Lunch?" he added hopefully.

"I ought to let you starve." Erin went into the kitchen and started banging pots, taking a perverse pleasure in the noise. But Matt merely remarked that his sisters always made a hell of a racket in the kitchen when they were irritated at something—or someone—and that it sounded like home to him.

"How many sisters?" Erin asked ruefully, abandoning her noisy temper because he so obviously understood the reasons behind it. Swine that he was.

"Four. Three older, one younger. My father died when I was young, so my mother and sisters pretty much raised me." He grinned as she sent a discerning glance his way. "I won't say I always enjoyed my upbringing, but it did teach me quite a lot about the feminine mind."

"As opposed to the masculine mind?" she inquired politely.

Blandly, he reminded her, "I didn't tell Steve to bring up my stuff, did I?"

Erin turned her back on his grin, uneasily aware of its charm. Damn the man! How on earth could a woman hope to hold her own against that kind of charisma, coupled with what looked like a shrewd understanding of both temperamental writers and women? And with an absolutely *lethal* physical attraction thrown in for good measure?

Thinking back on the day as she lay alone in bed late that night, Erin decided that she had managed to hold her own. She was still somewhat bewildered by the flare of emotions between her and Matt, but admitted—to herself—a certain excitement in what was clearly going to be a furious exploration of those emotions.

Matt had wasted little time once his intentions had been made clear. With an easy, confident knowledge of women guiding him unerringly, he had hardly waited for lunch to be over before he'd begun needling her about her "retreat" from life.

Erin had never bothered to explain, even to herself, why she had fled so radically from the life she had led during her marriage. From a hectic, public lifestyle to this lonely wilderness was indeed a drastic change, and she found herself looking at it clearly for the first time.

Still, she defended her actions staunchly to him, snapping like a cornered wild thing whenever he got too close—as he inevitably did—to the wounds that had caused that move. Her temper had elated him and surprised her, but neither attempted to damp the flare of emotions.

"Sure you ran—you had reason to run—but why in hell did you run so far?"

"Because I wanted to, dammit!"

"Why? Why here?"

"I wanted to be alone—and *don't* make a crack about bad lines from movies!"

"Thinks she's Garbo," he had mocked mercilessly, then attacked again before her fury could find voice. "So you came up here and put a nice, safe distance between you and everyone else—above the rest of the world, like some bloody ice maiden, daring anyone to touch you—"

"That isn't true!" Erin had tried frantically to control her own temper then—just once.

"Don't you dare freeze up on me!" he had snapped violently.

Erin had snatched up a book and thrown it at him. She'd missed him, and had been so surprised by her own action that she hadn't minded his laughter.

Alone now in the darkness of her bedroom, Erin laughed a little in surprise and bemused amusement. Throwing things, for heaven's sake!

She knew what Matt was doing, of course, because he made absolutely no attempt to disguise his actions. He needled her coolly, openly enjoying her angry responses. He was neither cruel nor unfeeling, but simply determined to wake her up with a vengeance.

When the helicopter had come to retrieve him, he had patted her familiarly on the bottom and grinned unrepentantly at her audible snarl. And when the helicopter had swooped away, Erin sat down on the steps and laughed without being sure why.

Not, she thought, because her would-be (and probably *soon* would be) lover came courting—or whatever—in a helicopter no self-respecting pilot would have flown and no one else could look at without gasping. Not because of the music that had been, this time, that "godawful marching music."

She laughed, she decided later, at the bewildering turn of events that had deposited a very peculiar prince on her doorstep. His charger was not a galloping white beast, but rather a violent green machine that came and went with a fanfare of music. If he carried a shield, it was cheerful confidence, and his lance was a rather unnerving understanding.

"What're you hiding from, Erin? Him?" Matt had asked.

"No. No, I—"

"Yourself? He shattered your self-confidence, didn't he?"

"I couldn't cope!" she'd admitted at last, fierily.

"He couldn't cope! Stop blaming yourself!"

But she did, in some way, blame herself. It took two to make—or break—a marriage.

And Erin wasn't blinded this time by the brilliance of fantasy. She had a notion that this prince wore his tarnish proudly and openly, counting it as a warrior would count a battle scar: something earned in cheerful pursuit of life. His aim was not to sweep her off her feet, but to rouse in her a strength and willingness to jump aboard his charger freely and with both eyes wide open.

And if nothing else, he certainly woke her up. Erin had been conscious of no limbo, no suspension in her life; she could look back now and see both.

She could also see that Matt had chosen a perfect method to challenge her self-confidence—and capture her heart. She didn't want to think about the latter, but this day had opened up a part of her, and she faced the realization without flinching.

Like Stuart, Matt had come abruptly into her life, showing almost instantly a style and manner she found enormously attractive—but hardly the same style and manner as Stuart's. Where Stuart had been brash and overpowering, Matt had been at first cautious and then, unerringly, challenging. He had not swept her off her feet but had shown her that he *could*—and dared her to stop him.

He didn't draw emotion from her, but goaded her to throw it at him, mocked her mercilessly until she could have strangled him and instead found herself responding with a passion she had never suspected in herself.

She was, she realized staunchly, fascinated by the man. He had come with a weary, beard-stubbled face and eyed her in puzzlement the first day; on the second day he had probed tentatively; and on the third day he had first listened with patience to her and then had quite contentedly gone about rattling the secure—if cowardly—foundations of her life.

Erin was rather amusedly certain that this prince would tuck his crown in a pocket or lay it aside absently because he'd feel ridiculous wearing it; not like Stuart, who had worn his crown with arrogant self-satisfaction. Facing a ten-mile ride up a mountain to see his lady, Stuart would sulk; Matt, finding his charger temperamental, had simply gone looking for the mechanical equivalent. And faced with a stubborn and wary woman, Stuart would have cajoled and charmed; Matt stood back for a measuring look and then waded happily into the fray.

Matt could claim ineptitude with wilderness, but Erin had the shrewd suspicion that he would land on his feet no matter where fate chose to drop him. She wondered then in sudden curiosity if he felt an aversion to her lifestyle, or simply intended to force her to examine it for good points and bad.

And being Erin—this new Erin, who gloried in the straightforward battle they were engaged in—she wasted no time in asking him. And she was in a temper when she asked, because Matt's charger woke her at the crack of dawn the next morning, after a somewhat sleepless night, with its vibrating roar and fanfare of *Bolero.*

Climbing from her bed, she swore steadily and stumbled through the house to wrench open the front door, glaring out on the world in general, and Matt in particular.

Chester, taking an interest today in the music, lifted his muzzle and howled mournfully from behind her. Erin winced, her glare deepening.

"Good morning!" Matt shouted lightheartedly as he reached the steps and Ravel thundered away over the trees.

"Go away!" she shouted back, the final word rather loud since Ravel was fading into the distance.

"Not," Matt said politely, "on your life."

Erin got a grip on herself and the doorjamb. With steely politeness she said, "I do not appreciate being awakened at dawn by that ungodly racket."

"Sorry." Matt responded with no sign of contrition, eyeing her in obvious enjoyment.

Looking down at herself, Erin realized that she was wearing a T-shirt that barely covered the tops of her thighs. With nothing underneath it. Refusing to be embarrassed, she looked him fiercely in the eye. "Gentlemen," she told him, "don't come calling at dawn!"

"I'm not a gentleman, I'm a general. And an army marches on its stomach. How about breakfast?" Stepping onto the porch, he continued to gaze at her appreciatively, with a definite gleam in his eye. "Tell you what—I'll cook. You can just stand around looking seductive in that outfit." Thoughtfully, he added, "I'll burn everything, but what the hell."

Erin ignored the laugh that was trying to choke her. "You're an impossible man!" The accusation lost something of its force, since she had to step back into the cabin as he advanced.

Chester lifted his lip at the visitor, and it got stuck on his upper teeth. He sat there, seemingly glaring at both of them but managing to look surprised. Helpfully, Matt reached down to smooth the wrinkle and hide a few gleaming canine incisors. Chester thumped his tail once in gratitude or perhaps acknowledgment. Matt patted him on the head in a friendly manner.

Erin got a grip on herself and fought an inner battle to keep laughter at bay. Crossing her arms beneath her breasts in an unconsciously provocative gesture, she demanded intensely, "D'you hate my lifestyle?"

Addressing the cleavage visible at the V neckline of her sleepshirt, Matt said absently, "What? Oh, no, of course not." After a long silence, he lifted his gaze and grinned a bit sheepishly. "Well, dammit, Erin—"

"Lecher!" she accused him somewhat breathlessly. Grin or not, there was something very male in his eyes, and it affected her strongly.

Assuming an expression of extreme patience, Matt said, "My darling Erin, I can hardly walk and talk at the same time around you. If I manage not to stutter, it's only because I'm not prone to it. In case you're interested, my heart's doing flips like a landed fish, and my pulse rate and blood pressure would probably put me in a hospital if a doctor were around to measure them."

Erin uncrossed her arms and cleared her throat, wondering what in the world she could say to that. Luckily, Matt wasn't waiting to find out.

"I came up here this early because I couldn't sleep, and Steve brought me happily because he always gets up with the chickens. And since it's your fault that I couldn't sleep, I decided to wake you up. Although," he added musingly, eyeing her, "I never expected such a nice reward."

Erin wanted to lift a lip at him in an adaptation of Chester's snarl, but found herself giggling instead. "You sound like a besotted adolescent!" she exclaimed, choking.

"I'll probably start to drool in a minute," he agreed amiably.

Then added in a different tone, "For godsake, Erin, go get dressed before I carry you and the battle into the bedroom."

The fact that she obeyed this command, Erin decided moments later as she pulled a sweater over her head, had nothing to do with docility. It was, she acknowledged ruefully, more along the lines of discretion being the better part of valor. She brushed her hair, debated briefly, left it down.

Pausing before leaving her bedroom, Erin studied herself in the mirror. She was, in a sense, perversely armed for battle. Her jeans were tight, molding hips and legs lovingly. Her sweater boasted a V neckline far deeper than the sleepshirt, and was a soft coral that made the visible flesh warmly pale and added an extra gleam to her hair and eyes. Or maybe, she thought in sudden amusement, the glint in her eyes owed nothing to the sweater.

Girded for battle, Erin strolled out of her bedroom and stood near the breakfast bar, gazing at Matt. He was working busily, whistling between his teeth. Pancakes, from the look of it, she thought, watching him expertly mixing ingredients.

"I'm going to feed the horses," she announced.

Matt glanced over his shoulder with "okay" forming on his lips—but only the first letter and sound made it. He stood there with a whisk in one hand, the other gripping a large mixing bowl . . . and managed to look amazingly masculine. He took an unwary step toward her, trod on Chester's tail, and jumped at the yelp.

"Sorry, Chester," he said automatically.

Erin smiled in a gentle manner and turned toward the back door.

Matt found himself leaning back to look around the bar and watch her, caught himself, and swore softly. He concentrated on mixing the batter, wondering if his ears were red. Probably, he decided; they felt hot. *He* felt hot.

He was grinning a little. Did she, he wondered, realize just how true his earlier words had been? Never one to hide from himself, Matt acknowledged silently that if he hadn't stuttered in her presence, it was only because he'd managed to straighten out his tongue at the last possible second. And just because he hadn't tripped over his own feet didn't mean it couldn't happen at any time now.

God, she was lovely! Caged fire. He felt like an adolescent around her, forced to constantly remind himself he was a grown man, dammit, and could keep his hands to himself. But every time he looked at her he felt a jolting shock that took away his breath and made him dizzy.

She was more beautiful with each glance, more desirable, more everything. Even half asleep and mad as hell as she greeted him— violently—at the door, she'd caused tension to coil in his stomach and heat to burn through him.

He was still astonished that he hadn't attacked her with a primeval howl and gnashing teeth.

Ruefully, he decided not to congratulate himself on his restraint just yet. She was, obviously, carrying the battle into treacherous territory; the vixen had worn that sweater with malice aforethought.

It gave him hope, though, that sweater. In addition to a near heart attack. It gave him hope because it stated plainly her lack of fear in consequences. She was, he decided, waving her red cape at the bull with full knowledge of the creature's horns.

At least . . . he hoped so.

He felt rather like pawing the ground.

Matt managed to keep his boots still when she returned. He even managed to hold a semi-intelligent conversation over breakfast.

"Could you pass the butter, please?"

"Certainly."

"Thank you."

"You're welcome."

"Chester, stop chewing on my ankle. Does he want a pancake?"

"He probably wants a beer."

"I beg your pardon?"

"He's a recovering alcoholic. Don't give him any firewater."

Matt leaned back to gaze down at the unnatural animal sharpening his teeth on his leather boot. "Um. Right." He welcomed the distraction of Chester's peculiarities, since every glance at Erin glued his tongue to the roof of his mouth. But then she twisted on the barstool to look down at her dog, and Matt choked on his coffee.

"Go down the wrong way?" she asked sympathetically.

Wiping streaming eyes, Matt looked for a gleam in hers and found only mild concern. He fought the urge to lunge and said, "Um."

"I'll clean up," she said a few moments later. "You cooked. And very well, too."

"Thanks." He didn't offer to help, not sure he could get off the barstool without making a fool of himself. He propped an elbow on the bar, drinking coffee and smoking a cigarette, barely feeling Chester's continued munching.

Matt watched her move about the kitchen and tried reciting the multiplication tables silently. When that failed him, he dredged his mind for every impossibly corny love poem he could recall.

He would, he decided, have to make her mad again. At least when she was yelling at him he could chain that part of him bent on lunging.

Maybe.

He was, after all, a grown man.

Chapter Five

Matt was finishing his third cup of coffee when Erin turned to look at him, a little puzzled, a little amused. "Are you wedded to that barstool?"

He thought about it, answered, "No." Then he managed to get off the barstool without falling over his own feet. The accomplishment was mildly pleasing to him. "Eve must have looked like that," he observed.

"Like what?"

"Amused." Matt sighed. "I don't think we've learned a damn thing since Adam chased Eve through the garden."

"What are we talking about?" Erin asked.

Matt resisted an urge to get on all fours and howl, reminding himself that men walked like men, dammit. "I," he said, "am talking about a siren let loose in my garden. Can we go outside? I need some air."

Erin followed as he bolted (Matt couldn't think of another word for it) out the front door.

"Claustrophobia?" she asked, still honestly bewildered.

Matt looked down to find that Chester had also followed and was now chewing on the other boot. He sighed. Then he looked at Erin, which was a mistake. The morning sun made her hair gleam like copper and her skin like fine porcelain.

There was, Matt decided calmly, a limit to patience. He nudged Chester aside, stepped toward Erin, and allowed his instincts a modified lunge.

"Not claustrophobia," he said in a voice Chester might have claimed for a growl. "A siren."

This time Erin felt no conscious urging to fight his fire with her own—she simply and instinctively did so. Her body felt hot, liquid, molding itself to his with a sense of affinity too strong to resist. Her knees went weak and her lips responded to his as if they had been created just for that reason, that response. There was no way she could have pulled back.

But Matt, with too much at stake, could pull back. He didn't want to, and God knew it was almost impossible to do so . . . but he did it. Barely.

By the time he came up for air, Erin needed it. She stared up at him, a bit dazed, a little surprised because he had seemed so calm and cheerful in spite of his earlier claim of a fast pulse and high blood pressure. She wasn't at all surprised, though, to find her arms around his lean waist.

"Release me, madam," Matt ordered somewhat hoarsely, "or I'll ravish you."

Erin felt a heart pounding and wasn't sure if it was hers or his. With an effort she managed to release him and step back.

"I hate rejection," Matt told Chester. Chester growled sympathetically.

"You told me—" she began indignantly.

"Do you always do what you're told?" he demanded, being quite fierce about it.

Unaware that her reasoning was the same as his, Erin decided to resume the argument of the day before. "Look, if you don't hate my lifestyle, why're you so scornful of it?"

Matt blinked, adjusted his mind rather hastily, and waved a hand at the lonely grandeur surrounding them. "This is a fine place to come to," he said firmly, "but a bad place to *run* to. And three years is too damn long to hide up here."

"I'm not hiding!"

"No?" Matt slid his hands into his pockets to hide the stray tremor and rocked back on his heels. "Prove it."

"How?"

"Spend the day with me tomorrow in Denver. Steve'll fly us, and we'll lose ourselves in the city." He paused, adding blandly, "And see a concert tomorrow night."

Erin, on the point of accepting the dare, hesitated and felt suspicious. "Concert?"

"Uh-huh." Matt lifted a gentle brow and related a piece of information he'd discovered the day before. "Stuart Travis."

"You—swine!" Erin said when she could.

Satisfied with the reaction that was anger rather than fear or pain, Matt nodded firmly. "I'll box shadows, Erin. I'll even punch out flesh and blood. But I want to be sure of what I'm fighting. And I want you to take a good long look at what you ran away from."

Erin stared at him. "Fine!" she snapped. "I'll go to Denver, I'll go to the damned concert. But right now I'm going riding!"

Matt stepped off the porch when she did. "Good. So will I."

"You can't ride," she reminded him, annoyed.

"Then you'll just have to teach me, won't you?"

Erin made a sound that might have been a snort if it hadn't come from a lady, and she headed for the barn.

Looking at the clean, defiant line of her slender back, Matt nearly tripped, and swore inwardly. Walking behind her for reasons he didn't have to think about, he blocked a wistful sound at the back of his throat and concentrated on walking like a man.

It didn't seem to get any easier.

Erin saddled both horses, her temper easing so that she could explain to Matt how horses were saddled and tell him the basics of handling the animals. Such as to beware of sharp teeth.

"Hell!" he yelped, jumping aside as the gray, Tucker, attempted to bite him.

"He bites," she explained, not without a certain pleasure.

Looking at the horse he'd ridden down the mountain the day after he'd found Erin, and which he was holding by the bridle, Matt said, "This one doesn't, huh?"

"Amos? No, he's sweet-tempered. Easy to ride. Tucker, on the other hand, is a mass of bad habits." Tightening the girth, she briskly brought one knee up against the gelding's side, and he released air in an indignant snort. "He holds his breath," she said, quickly tightening the girth an extra couple of inches.

"That's bad?" Matt wouldn't have thought a horse's personal habits were of any concern to humans.

Erin gave him a patient look. "It is if you're planning to keep a saddle on his back. They aren't put on with glue, you notice."

Matt chuckled a little at the tolerance in her voice. "All right, so I'm ignorant. Willing, though." He led his own mount from the barn behind hers, carefully keeping his distance from Tucker's heels; he didn't need to be told that *that* end was dangerous.

Erin gathered the reins and said, "Don't mount up yet. Tucker usually fights me. Stay put until he settles down."

Before Matt could say a word, she swung up on the horse. On the fury, he amended almost instantly, his heart leaping into his throat as the gray animal instantly gave his imitation of a rodeo bronc—and it was a fine imitation. It was, in fact, an award-winning performance. He bucked wildly, snorting, lunging, whirling in a mad circle. He tried fiercely to get his head down between his knees to buck harder, frustrated by Erin's expert hand on the reins. He tried even more furiously to get her off his back, twice nearly going over backward in the attempt.

Matt knew—he *knew*—that Erin was a horsewoman. He knew she was safe, that the horse wouldn't hurt her. But his heart pounded sickly in his chest, and he felt cold with fear. He gripped Amos's reins with white-knuckled fingers, rooted to the ground. And even through his dread he felt a surge of emotions that had nothing to do with fear.

She rode like a Valkyrie, seemingly a part of the furious beast who fought her. Her copper hair flew wildly, and her face, her lovely face, was curiously intent in a kind of elemental pleasure. With grace and skill and determination she mastered half a ton of enraged animal, and the barbaric beauty of the contest was breathtaking.

And then, suddenly, it was over. Tucker stood very still and stiff for a moment, then let out his breath in a snort and stamped one hoof in what was clearly irritation. Then he relaxed and yawned.

Erin, a little flushed but calm, glanced over at Matt. "He's finished," she said. "Ready to go?"

"You'll get indigestion riding like that so soon after breakfast," Matt said. It sounded like a croak to him, but Erin seemed to notice nothing.

"I'm fine. Mount up."

Matt got into the saddle, noticing absently that the imprint of the reins lay whitely across his palm. He felt decidedly precarious on his horse, wondering with something between bewilderment and admiration how Erin managed to look so damned *at home* on hers.

They started along a trail that wound away behind the barn, able to walk side by side. Still conscious of his pounding heart, Matt cleared his throat.

"Why in God's name do you keep that hellion?" he asked.

She looked faintly surprised. "Nothing's perfect, Matt. Tucker has excellent gaits, and he'll go anywhere I ask once he resigns himself to a rider."

Matt shook his head on an instinctive thought. "It isn't just that, though. You *like* the fight."

Erin frowned a little, clearly dealing with something new. "I suppose," she said slowly. "I never really thought about it. I've had Tucker since I came up here, and he fights me every time I saddle him. Oddly enough, he'll carry a pack with no trouble and no fuss."

"Maybe he enjoys the fight, too."

She reached down to stroke the gray neck that was only slightly damp with the sweat of exertion, and smiled suddenly. "Maybe you're right."

Matt knew he was right. She and the horse fought, neither of them willing to submit. But the horse submitted first. Perhaps it was a point of equine honor with Tucker to fight; Matt thought it was something deeper and more basic with Erin.

Caged fire.

They rode companionably for nearly two hours, taking various trails that wound up and down the mountainous terrain, talking idly when they rode side by side and falling silent when the trail forced them to go single file. Chester accompanied them, going off on his own occasionally and then returning to make certain they weren't lost—or at least that was the impression he gave.

Erin watched Matt without, she trusted, being obvious about it. She was impressed by his grace and ease in the saddle, knowing very well that he was unaccustomed to horses or riding. Still, he rode well and handled his horse with a firm hand.

She had always thought that riding a horse brought out the best or worst in the human body, revealing it as either impossibly awkward or else beautifully fluid; Matt looked strong and lithe, with a sense of restrained power.

And he seemed attuned to the beauty of nature, watching everything but commenting only with a quick smile or an intentness in his gray eyes.

He guided Amos to follow or walk beside Tucker across streams and along narrow cliff-hugging paths, never complaining of an uncomfortable ride or suggesting an easier way. There was no bravado in him; she could neither see nor sense an attitude of the macho I'll-do-it-if-it-kills-me. Thinking again of his adaptability, wondering at it, Erin at last turned them back toward the cabin.

Matt had enjoyed the ride. He still felt precarious on horseback, and some of Erin's decisions as to the proper trail to take had sorely tried what he chose to call his courage. He would, he knew, be painfully aware of the ride for hours—if not days—and wondered if he would ever be able to walk without *looking* as if he'd just gotten off a horse.

The beauty of the place was beginning to affect him. He could better understand now why Erin chose to call it home. But he was, at heart, a creature of the city, and knew that even the lovely wilderness would begin to pall if not for her beside him.

Back at the barn, he dismounted, hoping he didn't look as stiff as he felt, and began unsaddling Amos rather gingerly. Glancing over his shoulder to where Erin briskly unsaddled Tucker, he said idly, "It is a lovely place. I'm surprised no one has thrown up a resort hotel or something."

"I wouldn't let that happen," she responded absently, carrying Tucker's saddle into the small tack room.

Matt followed with the second saddle. "You wouldn't?" He felt a little startled.

She looked surprised herself, then sighed. "When I came back here, Matt, I came home in a way. My grandmother used to live in the cabin. She owned the mountain. Now it's mine."

He thought about that while they groomed the horses and stabled them, not commenting until they'd returned to the cabin and carried coffee out to the porch.

"No one told me you owned the mountain," he ventured finally.

Erin, leaning back against one of the support posts and sipping her coffee, watched him light a cigarette, and shrugged. "People around here mind their own business."

Matt leaned against the post on the opposite side of the steps, gazing at her quietly. "Did you live up here while you were growing up?"

"No. Visited sometimes, but not often. My parents preferred the city. Still do. I grew up in Los Angeles."

Neutrally, he asked, "School?"

"Stanford," she answered briefly.

"I went to William and Mary. Grew up in D.C."

Erin shook her head a little, smiling. "See how incompatible we are? Me from California—an unconventional state, if nothing else. You from the traditional East."

Matt smiled in return, a smile that was a little wry and a little amused, as if he could have disagreed with her. But all he said was, "We're meeting on fairly neutral ground. And we've both seen more of life than childhood. I don't think our backgrounds will come between us."

She stared into her coffee cup for a moment, then set it aside. She looked at him. "I'm not hiding."

"That rankled," he noted dryly.

"Of course it rankled. Nobody likes to be called a coward. All right—I was hiding when I came. But not now. Not for a long time now."

"As long as you know that."

After a minute Erin said, "Damn you."

Matt grinned faintly. "You didn't know, did you? You weren't sure. But after you had to defend your choice, you did know." He watched her, watched her think about that. Watched her smile and felt his toes curl. And he wondered if he would ever grow accustomed to this reaction to her that was physical but emotional and intellectual as well. Somehow, he didn't think he would. Not in this lifetime.

She saluted him with an inclination of her head. "All right, General—that's one point for your side. What do we fight about next?"

"Are you writing?"

She stirred, uneasy. "No. I don't feel like working."

"Maybe," he suggested neutrally, "you're ready for a change in your life. Less—peace and quiet?"

Erin frowned a little. "I just don't feel like writing. I need a break, that's all."

"All right," he responded easily.

She was silent for a while, wondering what he was thinking. Unnervingly, he seemed to pick up the mental question and answered it with a flickering smile.

"Tight sweaters," he murmured.

"Yours or mine?" she asked, deadpan, managing to hide her inward start of surprise.

Matt looked down rather pointedly at his flannel shirt, then lifted a brow at her. "I'm not wearing one. If it'll cause you to feel a faint pang of lust, I'll get rid of what I do have, though."

"Wouldn't want you to catch cold."

"And it wouldn't spark an interest in my manly body anyway, huh?"

"Don't fish."

Matt brooded at her. "Maybe I'll bring ravishing maidens back into style."

"Will you pillage too?"

"Desperately."

They both watched impassively as Chester climbed onto the

porch and collapsed between them. He sat up abruptly as though remembering something, scratched fiercely behind his left ear, then lay down again with a contented sigh.

Matt looked at Erin. "A recovering alcoholic?"

"Yes."

He wished he could think of further conversation regarding Chester. It was, he'd decided, far safer to stare at a mutant grizzly bear than at a redheaded Erin. But certainly more fun to stare at Erin. Even if it hurt.

"You look," she observed dispassionately, "as if you were starved for sweets and someone had closed the doughnut shop in your face."

He started laughing, shaking his head when she looked quizzical. "Never mind. Maybe it's the mountain air, but I'm already hungry again. Why don't we pack a picnic lunch and go find a spectacular view?"

Erin decided not to question. She merely agreed and went inside the cabin with him. She wondered more than once during the following hour why she couldn't seem to breathe whenever he was close, ignoring all the instincts that were telling her why.

She caught herself watching him beneath her lashes, watching strong hands move with grace. Watching shoulders that were wide and powerful. Watching, obliquely, a face that was very handsome and very masculine.

She listened to his voice, responding automatically to words she hardly heard, meeting his smiling eyes occasionally, her own skittering away. Fighting was one thing, she decided, but becoming a kamikaze was something else entirely.

She hadn't been able to cope with Stuart's demands on her, and a part of her was still uneasy about coping with this new relationship. He could hurt her, she knew. Hurt her more unbearably than Stuart had. If she lost anything to Matt, it would not be a dream. It would be a part of herself.

She wondered if moths knew flames would destroy them, and went on in spite of knowledge.

She thought they did.

They carried a picnic basket and blanket farther up the mountain, at last reaching Erin's favorite place. The trail ended abruptly at the edge of the cliff, a spectacular view framed by the deep green of pine trees, like a picture of raw beauty. They looked down on the valley far below, at tiny dollhouses and minute roads. And when they looked straight out from the cliff, mountains shouldered one another in sharp angles and arrogant peaks, closer to the sky than anything man could carve from the ground.

They spread the bright yellow blanket on a layer of pine needles that promised softness and just enjoyed the view for a long time in companionable silence.

Later, while they rapidly disposed of the satisfying lunch, Erin looked at her glass of wine and felt guilty.

They had left Chester in the cabin entirely against his will—he'd seen the bottle—and he had let them know in no uncertain terms how unhappy he was about the situation.

Unerringly reading her expression, Matt grinned and said, "I wonder if he's still howling."

"Probably," Erin said wryly, "He won't be destructive because we shut him up in the cabin, but he'll sulk for the rest of the day."

"How in the world did he—?"

"Stuart's idea of something funny. It wouldn't have mattered if Chester hadn't liked the taste. But he did, and— Oh, well. I went back to the house once when I knew Stuart was on the road, and I stole Chester," she added abruptly. "He really belonged to Stuart."

They were silent for a while. The remains of lunch were packed neatly away, leaving only the wine they sipped.

Finally, as abruptly as she had spoken before, Matt said, "Did it hurt so badly?"

Erin, lying on her stomach only a few safe feet from the cliff edge, nodded slowly without looking at him. "It did then. Oh, not the other woman. Oddly enough, that barely hurt at all. But the rest of it. The feeling my life was no longer mine. The understanding that . . . that Stuart had taken what I was, what we were, and turned us into songs people sung with their radios."

She pushed away her empty wineglass and rolled onto her back, staring up at the ceiling of green needles. "Cheap," she said curtly. "It cheapened me, what I felt. Or thought I felt. Maybe another woman could have coped. I couldn't." Her sigh was a soft rush of sound. "I was in the studio when he recorded that song. The one about his new love. He looked at me while he sang. Oh, he didn't mean to be cruel; Stuart never meant to be cruel. He was just explaining the only way he knew how. He looked surprised when I walked out."

After a moment she turned her head and looked at Matt, wondering vaguely what went on behind his immobile expression. "A few months after the divorce, I was in town and heard his latest song on the radio." She smiled a small, wry smile. "It was about the death of love—and a marriage. The music industry gave him three awards for it."

Matt sat with his back against a tree and gazed at her, telling himself that she had hurt because a dream had died—not love. He didn't want to think that she had known love and that some other man had killed it.

He moved suddenly until he was lying beside her, raised on an elbow to look down at her. "He couldn't touch the passion in you," Matt said softly. "He couldn't destroy that. He killed a girl's dream, Erin . . . not a woman's love."

She stared up at him. *You want my heart? Fight for it.* With a shock she could feel all through her body, Erin realized then that she did want his heart. And that this was no wistful yearning for the heart of an elusive comet; this was a compulsive need, a desperate hunger for a strong heart she would have fought for had it lain inside hell's gates.

"Fight for it."

Erin fought the only way she knew.

She was reaching up even as he leaned toward her, seeing in his flaring eyes the reflection of her own, seeing a face she hardly knew because it seemed transformed by a sudden and terrible need. A slumbering fire ignited instantly when his lips captured hers . . . or hers took him captive.

Erin felt the rough flannel beneath her fingers and, beneath that, the hard power of muscles and sinew and bone, of flesh and blood too real to ever be a dream shattered by a song. She felt the seeking demand of warm, hard lips, the primitive possession of wine-sweet breath moving hotly from his mouth to hers. The heavy weight of him lay half over her, his heart thudding like a living thing caged against her. His thick, silky hair was tangled between her fingers, and his belt buckle dug into her hip with the sharpness of reality.

A strong hand slipped beneath her back, beneath the sweater to touch and inflame like a brand. Her breasts were crushed against his chest, throbbing in a sweet near-pain, trapped by clothing, aching for his touch.

Again and again he kissed her, deep, drugging kisses that sapped her strength and her soul. But the force of her, the elemental power so recently freed she willingly gave him, her response as fiery, as strong and hungry as his own desire. Everything that she was leaned toward him as a flower to the sun.

His lips traced the line of her jaw, her throat, her forehead, leaving behind them a trail of stinging awareness. His hand slid around to lie warmly against her stomach while his free hand tangled in her long hair.

"Erin . . . dear God . . ." He caught his breath on a ragged sound when her own hand found the smooth, tanned skin of his back, traced his spine with caressing fingers. With her nails she scratched lightly, feeling him tremble, and his lips were hot and shaking against her throat.

Matt could barely breathe, feeling his heart pounding like a runaway engine in his chest. Her every touch made him that much more hungry, that much more desperate for her. Rational thought sank like a stone beneath the overpowering weight of fierce desire. He wanted her so badly that nothing else mattered; nothing else could be felt except the aching demand within him to know her completely.

Nothing else mattered.

She heard a faint whimper, knowing only vaguely that the sound came from her, from somewhere deep inside her, where hunger coiled and writhed and tension gathered like anguish.

She whispered his name, unable to find her voice or her breath or any will at all except the will to have this go on forever, past the point of pain and far beyond thought. Her lithe body, made strong by the work of wilderness, arched of its own accord to press against his. Her arms held him tightly, and her thigh quivered at the hard power of the desire it pressed against.

"Erin," he murmured. "Erin . . ." His hand stroked her stomach, the silky flesh beneath his touch vibrating with tremors of need. The pulse in her throat beat frantically like the wings of a small bird under his lips, and the soft sounds she made ran like fire through his veins.

On some dim and distant level of his mind, Matt knew they were fighting still, fighting as men and women had always fought. Man and woman, eternally different, eternally destined to join in spite of differences and because of them. Destined to strike sparks off one another's souls in a clash taking them very nearly to death.

But he knew something else as well, something he tried desperately to ignore because molten heat flowed through his aching body, and his need for her tortured him. He fought the knowledge for eternal moments, for heartbeats, his senses flaring with the touch of her, the taste of her, the sounds of her desire in his ears.

He wondered if one could die of passion, and thought that here, at least, and now, one could. He could. He didn't think he'd mind dying very much if that were the cost of loving her.

Loving her . . .

The knowledge, the certainty formed, made sense in his mind. And along with that knowledge came the other certainty, the other knowledge he silently damned.

Loving her as he did, he could not make love to her. Not yet. Not with so much still unresolved. They couldn't take the easy way.

With a wrenched groan he rolled away from her, covering his eyes with a forearm and fighting for control of that howling beast. Instinct made him reach out swiftly with his free hand, catching hers and holding it hard to ease the uncomprehending pain of rejection.

Erin lay in silence for a long tense moment, staring upward at the canopy of green pines and feeling bereft, torn. Then she felt the slight pain of his tight grip, and that other pain lessened. She turned finally on her side to face him, holding his hand as tightly as he held hers. She brought her other hand up slowly, enclosing his in both.

His face was half hidden from her, but the white tautness of what she saw both reassured her—and awed her. What was this between them, she pondered, this raw, wild thing that could make of them something they had never been before?

Something *she* had never been before. She didn't think she could bear it if this was something he knew well, had known often. She didn't think it was possible.

He had said—what? That he had never been in love. Was this,

then, love? If it was—if it was, she thought, then she had never loved. What she had called love before today seemed a pale and sad thing, a weak and shallow thing.

And that other prince, that bright and shining prince of no substance, faded away almost to nothing, without pain or regret, lost in the shadow of flesh and blood and bone and sinew. And the girl who had fallen off a charger picked herself up and waited with the patience of something deep and sure for the ride that would last forever.

Matt spoke at last without uncovering his eyes, his voice hoarse. "You have to face him. Tomorrow. Put him behind you. Then we go on."

Erin thought about that for a moment, understanding the need for certainty, for resolution. That other prince was gone, but there had been a man as well, and he was still a shadowy, elusive part of her. She had to see that man without the shining armor she had encased him in.

"All right," she said, hardly recognizing the soft, husky sound of her own voice.

"I'll be with you," Matt said. "I won't let you go. Even if he fights for you."

"He won't," she said, knowing that.

"I would." Matt drew a deep harsh breath. "Lord, I would. Erin—"

She brought his hand to her cheek as he turned at last to face her with bright, intense eyes. Before he could follow the choked sound of her name, she said, "After tomorrow. We'll go on after to-morrow."

He nodded slowly, very conscious of what he had nearly said. He didn't know, even now, what it would lead to. He only knew with certainty the depth of his own feelings, the incredulous astonishment he felt in looking at her.

The thorns were still there, of course. And even now he knew that Erin's meeting with her ex-husband would determine the future of their relationship. Even now. Even if Erin were no longer blinded by shining armor, she could find the man beneath to be too much a part of her to abandon easily—or at all.

And even if she would feel nothing for the man, Matt understood her too well to think that everything would be easy now.

There were still the thorns.

Chapter Six

Erin found she couldn't stop watching him. Just looking at him gave her a pleasure that was nearly painful, and kept hunger rumbling with soft insistence deep inside her. An inner voice impossible to ignore.

The fiery passion he had aroused in her was banked now, and with clear thought came wariness. She had been at the mercy of her feelings once before, and even though every beat of her heart told her this was different, this was real, she was nonetheless frightened.

And Matt knew.

He caught her hand firmly as they walked back down the trail to the cabin, the picnic basket swinging from his free hand. "Tell me, Erin."

After a moment, staring ahead because looking at him weakened her knees and her judgment, she responded slowly. "Back there . . . I was swept away. Nothing mattered." She felt heat in her face, painfully aware that she was handing him a powerful weapon—one an unscrupulous man wouldn't hesitate to use. She felt his gaze and cleared her throat strongly.

"I don't know . . . I can't be sure that I feel what I think I feel . . . I mean—it's happened so damn *fast!*"

"The way it did before?"

She glanced at him, unable to judge from the neutral tone how he might feel about that. His face told her nothing, and she sighed and looked ahead again. "Matt, does it bother you that I can't help comparing?"

"I'd be a liar," he said dryly, "if I said no. At the same time, I understand why you have to. I realize how difficult it is for you, Erin. You were swept off your feet by him, and when you woke up to what was happening, it was to find the whole world staring at you. Then, when you'd finally found peace, I dropped into your life."

He stopped walking and turned to face her, his expression serious. "It's happened fast," he agreed quietly. "We're still strangers, you and I. But we have something, Erin. And whatever it is, it's worth fighting for. So if you have to compare me with him because it helps you to understand, then I can take it. I have to take it. I don't have any choice."

Erin swallowed. "A year isn't very long—but he was all my life during that year. And there was nobody before him. Whatever else he was, he was my husband. And vows *mean* something to me. I thought we were forever." She drew a deep breath. "But it ended. There's nothing between us now but memories. I'm through with him, Matt."

Rather abruptly, Matt started them toward the cabin again. "I wonder if he's through with you . . ."

It was little more than a murmur, and Erin wasn't entirely sure she had heard the words clearly. She felt an inner bitterness that Stuart still had the power to shadow her life, and wondered if facing him now would do any good at all.

Self-doubt and uncertainty crowded into her mind. Could she

trust herself not to make the same mistakes again? In the blaze of the incredible passion between her and Matt, could she find enough strength to keep control of her life? Or had Stuart somehow influenced her perception of emotions, teaching her subconsciously that there was only a wild roller-coaster ride with nothing at the end of it but memories?

"You think too much," Matt said suddenly.

"Oh, no! Before, I—" She broke off.

Matt seemed unperturbed by the intended comparison. "You didn't think enough? Probably not. He didn't give you time to think. And now you're going overboard in the other direction, worrying about everything. Well, we both knew we wouldn't take the easy way, didn't we?"

"The easy way." She looked down at their clasped hands. "Physical being less complicated than emotional?"

He smiled a little, but didn't look at her. "Isn't it? We could just follow our urges; I'm having a hell of a time fighting mine."

"Is—that a suggestion?" she asked, wondering if he had changed his mind.

"No, just an observation. I don't know if I'm right in thinking that *would* be the easy way for us, Erin." As they came out of the trees and faced the cabin, he stopped, staring at the neat home as if it represented something more than it was. Then he looked down at her.

"All I do know is that what I want and need from you isn't simple physical passion. And for you to give me what I need requires a trust we don't have yet."

"What do you need?' she asked softly.

"Your love," he answered simply. "Given freely. I don't want the blind worship of a girl for a prince, Erin; I want the love of a woman for a man. I want you to trust me because you see me clearly—in all my human imperfection. No prince in shining armor. Not even a knight. Just a man."

"I'm human, too," she said shakily, then swallowed hard. "And imperfect, Lord knows. It's just—you don't know it all, Matt. It's hard to trust myself not to let it happen again." Blindly, she pulled free of his gentle grasp and went quickly to the cabin. She went inside, leaving the door open and noticing only vaguely that Chester lay by the hearth with his back firmly turned to her. He didn't stir.

Sulking, of course.

Feeling exhausted, drained emotionally and still tautly aware of unsatisfied desire, Erin sank down on the couch and stared down at the hands clasped in her lap. She felt his weight beside her but not touching, and all her nerves shrieked awareness.

"Erin—"

Quickly, softly, aching with a pain that had never entirely left her, she said, "I'd never before lost anything or anyone that mattered, Matt. Never. I guess I led a charmed life; tragedy was something that happened to other people. I knew—intellectually—that death followed life; I never had to deal with the death of anyone I knew personally. The odds are against it, I suppose. In more than twenty years of living, one usually has to face death and loss. But I never did."

Matt shifted a bit on the couch, and his arm lifted to lay across the low back. His hand moved to grasp her shoulder very gently. "I see."

She knew that he didn't see, couldn't possibly know. But he had to know. She had to tell him, because her marriage had shaped so much of what she was. They both had to face that.

"Matt . . . it wasn't the end of a marriage or the death of—of a dream that caused me to run up here and hide. Those were . . . final blows, but they broke me only because any blow would have broken me then."

"Something else happened," he said slowly.

Erin nodded blindly, feeling suddenly the welling of grief that had never been allowed to escape in a normal and healthy release, grief that had lain deeply buried in her for more than three years, alone in the darkness. It was a primitive, soul-deep emotion, and it had torn her up inside.

"Tell me," Matt urged quietly.

"I'd never lost anyone before." She was talking more to herself than to him, reliving the shock and pain, the fear and horror of abruptly facing the fragility of life. "But I lost him. He moved inside me for months and then . . . I just lost him. If I could have held on to him for one more month, they could have saved him . . ."

The hand on her shoulder tightened suddenly, convulsively, and Mart's deep voice was unsteady with anguish. "You lost your baby? Oh, Erin—I'm sorry!"

Her eyes filled with hot tears that spilled free to run down her cheeks. His had been an instant and honest expression of sympathy for a real and devastating loss. Such simple words. But Stuart hadn't been able to say them.

To him it had meant only a minor inconvenience, a bad dress rehearsal before the real performance.

"Don't look so stricken, honey. We'll have another kid. The doc says they're letting you out of here in a few days, so you can meet me in Detroit. I have to catch the jet this afternoon. You need anything before I go? No? See you in Detroit then, baby."

Erin felt strong arms drawing her close, and she hid her face against Matt's warm throat. She didn't sob, but her voice was jerky, and the tears flowed as though released from a dam.

"He didn't *care!* He never even said he was sorry. And he'd acted excited about the baby." She laughed, and it was a terrible sound. "A baby was something new, you see. He'd never been a father before. He wanted to—experience it. He was even going to take childbirth instructions, because he wanted to be there. But then I miscarried. And he—he didn't even say he was sorry. The baby wasn't *real* to him. He felt it kick in me—but *he wasn't sorry it died!"*

And then she cried.

Matt held her tightly, stroking her hair but making no attempt to halt her difficult, rasping sobs. Held her and wondered savagely what kind of bastard could feel no pain at the death of his child.

He didn't even have to imagine how he would feel himself. He loved children, and had often abandoned office and work to baby-sit for his sisters when they'd come to New York on visits; between his four sisters he had three nephews and four nieces ranging in age from two to nineteen, and every one had discovered as toddlers that their uncle was the world's softest touch.

He had paced the floor with more than one brother-in-law, and had once disrupted airline schedules by pulling every string he could find in order to get to the West Coast in the middle of the night because his younger sister had come frighteningly close to losing her first child.

He held Erin even more tightly, aching for her pain and grief, feeling a savage anger that any man had hurt her like that. A dream shattered had hurt, certainly, but it was nothing compared to the devastation of losing a child.

And at a moment when her husband should have held her, grieved with her, he had instead dismissed months of life and an agonizing loss with a callous insensitivity.

Matt had never considered himself a violent man, but he knew that if Stuart Travis had stood before him right then, he would have beaten the bastard to a pulp.

And enjoyed every blow.

After a long time Erin lay limp in his arms, drained but curiously at peace. She had finally let go. She accepted the handkerchief he gave her, wiping her cheeks.

"I got your shirt all wet," she murmured, her head resting on his shoulder because he still held her tightly.

"It'll dry." Matt rubbed his cheek against her forehead, his voice very gentle.

She realized distantly that Matt could hold her without desire exploding between them, that he could be tender and evoke tenderness, and she pondered that silently. She felt so . . . at home in his arms. Beneath the hand clutching a handkerchief, she could feel his heart beating steadily, his chest rising and falling with each breath.

And she became aware then, very slowly and gently, that she was less confused and uncertain about her own feelings. The dark pain she had hidden away in its locked room had finally burst free, the pain that had been standing between two strangers—and they weren't strangers anymore. There would always be in her a small, empty place nothing would ever fill, but there was no pain now.

One man had hurt her unbearably and another had healed the hurt with a simple touch and gentle sympathy.

Matt was now even more real to her. He was flesh and blood, bone and sinew, and he had shared her pain as instantly and completely as he had shared her anger and her passion. He had not withdrawn from her, had not been awkward or uncertain; his responses to her had been immediate and tender.

Unexpectedly sleepy, Erin tried to hold on to another, more elusive realization. But it slipped away. She fell asleep with the feeling of a heart beating under her hand.

Matt continued to hold her, to softly stroke the silky fire of her hair. He smiled a little, realizing that she'd probably be disgruntled to wake finding herself clinging like a limpet. He was under no illusions; though her painful disclosure had brought them closer than ever before, it had been a temporary closeness. Waking with a clear mind, she would very likely scurry behind her prickly, wary wall, the chip on her shoulder a bit precarious but still visible to the naked eye.

Thorns.

Sometime during the last few moments, Matt had realized wryly that, though their fight had shifted, the battle continued. In passion or pain they could forget differences and share what they felt, but otherwise they circled each other warily.

One year, he thought with a sense of bitterness. One year of her life stood between them. One year and a man who had always been to her something larger than life.

And yet—Matt unknowingly echoed Erin's conclusions—that year had helped to make her the strong woman she was. For good and bad, that year had shaped her. Without a brief, wild ride behind a shining prince, what would she have been today?

Not wary, probably. Not prickly. Not a woman who was finding, now, the depth and power of a woman's feelings. Perhaps without pain she would have remained a princess in search of a prince, or perhaps, as so many had, she would have settled happily for less and built a good life.

Matt rested his chin atop her head and thought about that. He had been, he knew honestly, drawn to her wary independence, her control. An obsession with her face had brought him up here, but it was the personality behind her beauty that had kept him stubbornly in her life. His interest had made him probe, and her challenging response had drawn him even more.

And, of course, there had been his physical reaction to her.

He immediately regretted even the thought. Following the ebbing of pain, desire had crept up on him unawares. The ache that had not entirely deserted him for some time now began throbbing again as he held a sleeping Erin in his arms.

Matt cursed quietly and solemnly. She was half-lying across his lap, and the pressure of her warm body did absolutely nothing to aid him in controlling building desire. In fact, he could almost feel his blood pressure going through the roof, and his body spoke to him emphatically and at some length about stubborn self-denial.

He began reciting verses in a soft and toneless voice, gazing fiercely at a perfectly inoffensive seascape decorating the far wall.

Not that it helped.

Erin thought she was dreaming. A rumbling had disturbed her, finally becoming definite sounds with a kind of rhythm. She listened, frowning a little.

"The Drawling-master was an old conger-eel, that used to come once a week: *he* taught us Drawling, Stretching, and Fainting in Coils."

Definitely, Erin decided, she was dreaming. She frowned harder, eyes tightly closed, and concentrated on the sounds. Surely they'd make sense . . .

But four young oysters hurried up.
All eager for the treat:
Their coats were brushed, their faces washed,
Their shoes were clean and neat—
And this was odd, because, you know,
They hadn't any feet.

Erin sat bolt upright and stared at Matt incredulously. His face, she noted, seemed a bit darker in color than usual, his eyes very bright, and a sheepish smile tugged at his lips.

"Hello." He frowned, cleared his throat, and tried again. This time there was less hoarseness. "You're awake."

"Yes. Are you?"

He tried a careless kind of laugh that broke in the middle—then deepened suddenly in real amusement. "Oh, yes. Yes, I'm awake. Quite painfully awake, in fact."

She frowned at him. "Then why on earth were you reciting Lewis Carroll?"

"It—uh—came most readily to mind. My nephews and nieces all love the verses, so I've memorized most of them."

Erin thought about her question, then clarified it. "Why were you reciting verses of any kind?"

He looked at her for a moment, then sighed. "Because, my darling Erin, it was either recite nonsense verses or else attack you with a howl. A rude awakening for you. I thought the verses would be less likely to earn me a slap."

She blinked. Unaware that she was reacting exactly as Matt had decided she would, she moved abruptly to put nearly a foot of space between them, feeling a bit uneasy over her nap in his arms. And she felt defensive somehow. The combination caused her very understandable reaction.

"Matt, stop pretending you can't keep your hands off me!"

He looked so astonished that she giggled.

"Pretending?"

"You're a grown man, for godsake!"

"I keep telling myself that." Matt looked thoughtful and a bit pained. "You probably haven't considered it from my point of view, but I can tell you it's pretty unnerving to find at this late stage in my life that I have so little control over my own body."

Erin lifted a disbelieving eyebrow; she was very conscious of him *and* of her desire, but she felt no urge to howl. An urge to growl, maybe. But not howl. It would be undignified.

In a confiding tone, Matt said, "I probably shouldn't tell you any of this, because you could get drunk with power."

She kept the eyebrow up, but it took an effort.

He crossed his arms over his chest. "I am," he told her courteously, "putty in your hands. You smile at me, and my toes curl. I touch you, and I have to fight the urge to grab you by your hair and drag you off to my cave. When you walk in front of me, I have to concentrate on putting one foot in front of the other. Sleep in my arms, and I have to recite silly verses. I won't even *mention* what happens to me when you're awake and passionate in my embrace."

Erin no longer felt defensive. She felt surprised. Clearing her throat, she murmured, "But you never show it."

"Good. I have some pride." He considered. "Not much, mind you, but some."

She hesitated, then said almost inaudibly, "We can still take the easy way."

He reached over to brush his knuckles down her cheek briefly. The eyes that had half-laughed at her before darkened now, and his voice was a little husky. "No. When you can wake up in my arms and not pull away—then it'll be time for the easy way. And the easy way will be the right way."

Her throat felt tight in the most ridiculous way, and she fought to ignore it. Inexplicably cross, she muttered, "I'm not likely to wake up in your arms again unless we *do* take the easy way!"

His eyes were laughing again. "There is that. I'll have to arrange something."

Erin felt slightly baffled and extremely wary. Though more certain now of her own feelings, she was still unsure of his. He wanted her—she didn't doubt that. He *said* he wanted her love; he made use of occasional endearments; he had certainly shown her tenderness and understanding. Yet she was still uneasy. He had not offered his own love, although she thought he had nearly done so after telling her she'd have to face Stuart before they could go on.

She remembered his challenge then. He hadn't offered his love—but he had invited her to take it. His heart.

"You're thinking again," he noted dryly.

Slowly, Erin rose to her feet and stretched like a cat. She didn't think about what she was doing until Matt muttered something, and she looked at him in surprise that became quick comprehension. "Sorry," she murmured, pulling her sweater hastily back down over her midriff.

He was looking at her with a curiously twisted smile. "I," he said, "am certifiably out of my mind." He laughed.

She stood with her hands on her hips and stared at him, still frowning just a bit, her mind working. "Yes," she said finally. "Yes, I think you are."

"Meaning?"

"Why look so surprised?" she inquired mildly. "I was just agreeing with you."

"Yes," he said, studying her oddly immobile expression. "But what did you mean by it?"

"I mean . . . you're crazy because you've put both of us on an emotional roller coaster. Neither of us—apparently—can think straight when we—when we touch each other." She took a deep breath, then rushed on. "Nothing matters then, nothing seems impossible. But then we aren't touching, and—and it doesn't seem real."

He rose to his feet, frowning. "Erin—"

"You seem real," she hurried on. "And when I look at you, I know—I know there's . . . something between us. Something real. It's *me*, Matt. It's what I feel that I don't trust, don't believe in."

"Give it time," he urged quietly.

"I . . . don't think we have much time." *Before we lose control*, she added silently. *Before we take a step that can never be taken back, a step that will change us forever.* She brushed a hand through her hair, frowning. "Matt . . . I have to think this time. I *have* to. I won't be swept away again. And I think—I think I can write now. I think I need to."

"Are you telling me to get lost?" His voice was still quiet, but a little strained now.

Erin turned away, going to the door and gazing out blindly. "I'm . . . asking. How long will Stuart be in Denver? Do you know?"

"He's giving three concerts, the last one a week from tonight.

Apparently, the demand for his concerts took three scheduled performances to satisfy."

She nodded. "It has before." After a moment she said, "Then give me a week, Matt. A week to be alone, to write. To think."

"Are you afraid of facing him?"

"No." She turned then, leaning back against the doorjamb. "No, I'm not afraid. Instead of tomorrow night, we—I'll—face him in a week."

"We," Matt said flatly. "We'll face him. If you want me to leave, Erin, then I will. But I'll be with you in Denver next week, at that concert." He was silent for a moment, then added ruefully, "Well, I came up here to find out why you weren't writing and to try to help. Try to shake something loose. It looks like I've done that, at least."

"At least." She smiled a little. "I guess after three years of peace and quiet I needed a jolt. You were right about that, I think."

He studied her, his eyes restless, then sighed. "I'll call Steve and have him come pick me up. But I'll be back, Erin. Next Friday."

She stared after him for a long moment, hearing his deep voice in the radio room. Then she went out and sat on the steps, asking herself if she was doing the right thing. She thought she was. It was true—she needed time. She had been carried along in a breathless rush after meeting Stuart; she didn't want to wake one day and find that the explosion of feeling between her and Matt had carried her blindly a second time.

She felt his presence even before he sat down beside her, and spoke without thinking. "I should have met you first."

"But you didn't." There was a faint smile in his voice. "You met him. And you were looking for a prince."

"Was I? If so, it was stupid of me. Fairy tales. I reached for glitter . . . and that's what I got. Just something shiny and empty." Staring blindly she said, "There's nothing *there* anymore, Matt.

Just a year gone from my life. Why can't I forget it? Why can't I put it behind me?"

"Because vows mean something to you." He didn't touch her, and his voice was low, taut. "Because you married a man and lost a dream . . . and a child." After a moment, and with obvious reluctance, he went on quietly. "There is something there, Erin. Something you haven't resolved. Him. To you, he was always larger than life. He wrecked your dreams, but he never quite forced you to let go of them. Not all of them. There's still something in you that blames yourself instead of him. That's what you can't let go of."

Against her will, listening to his low, relentless voice, Erin realized he was right. There *was* a part of her that was afraid she had been somehow inadequate, a part of her that had numbly accepted a large part of the blame.

"It takes two," she whispered. "Two to make a marriage. Two to destroy it." She had thought it before. Seen it before. But she hadn't realized, hadn't understood.

They both heard the sound of a helicopter approaching, and Matt rose to his feet. Catching her hands, he pulled her up as well. Quickly, he said, "Sometimes it only takes one. Erin . . . he'll try to get you back."

She looked up at him, bewildered. "No. Not Stuart."

"Yes." Matt was speaking a little louder now as the thumping sound of rotors grew closer. "He's shallow and he's a fool, but he'll see the change in you. It'll gall him, Erin. He'll hate the fact that another man found something in you that he missed, something he never touched." Matt glanced up, impatient, as the roar of Steve's helicopter grew louder.

"Matt, you're wrong! He doesn't care—"

Running out of time, Matt bent his head to kiss her hard. "Just listen to me," he said. "I know what I'm saying, Erin! And I want you to think about that. God knows I don't want to do anything to send you back to him—but you have to know. You could handle him now. You could have him on his *knees!* You're a hell of a lot stronger than he is. Remember that."

Then, after another hard, possessive kiss, Matt was gone.

Making use of the earphones he and his passenger wore, Steve said cheerfully, "Now *that* was a leave-taking! When're you going to introduce me to that gorgeous redhead?"

Matt managed to find a calm voice in the tumult of his emotions. "Pull your tongue back in. Ally wouldn't like it."

Virtuously, Steve retorted, "Ally knows I'd never stray. That doesn't mean I'm dead, however. Do I hear wedding bells, Matt?"

A bit grimly, Matt answered, "I certainly hope so. You wouldn't happen to have a lance lying around handy, would you?"

With a sidelong glance from merry brown eyes, Steve said gravely, "I put mine away in mothballs after I won Ally. Why? Don't tell me you've been challenged?"

"I think I'm about to be. An ex-husband, damn his soul." Matt wondered a bit desperately if he'd done the right thing in warning Erin. He just didn't know. But he was certain that Stuart Travis would try his damnedest to recapture his ex-wife, and he didn't want Erin swept blindly off her feet again.

At least she'd *know* this time.

If only, he thought, she could come to terms with her marriage before she met Travis again. Heaven knew she had the strength, now, to resist the man's apparent charm—except that she didn't realize that. Matt knew he could spark her anger, and in anger she would fight fiercely for control. But Travis had been unable to spark those strong feelings while they were married.

Could he sweep her off her feet a second time? Was there

enough guilt within Erin to force her to make a last effort to live up to those vows she believed in?

Or would these new, stronger feelings give her the strength to finally let go of her image of her ex-husband?

"You look dangerous," Steve commented lightly but with an undertone of concern.

Matt watched as the little town at the base of the mountains grew nearer. "I feel it," he confessed. "My entire future depends on what happens next Friday. And I have an awful feeling that a lance won't help me. Dammit, I should have taken the easy way."

Steve glanced at his longtime friend and said dryly, "I won't ask you to define that." He cleared his throat. "Will you be going back up there tomorrow?"

"No. No, she doesn't want that. I'll be going back to New York for a few days." As the helicopter set down near his motel, Matt turned in his seat to gaze at Steve. "But there *is* something you can do for me."

"Name it."

Erin moved by rote, taking care of her horses and making peace with a sulky Chester. She didn't want to think about what Matt had said to her, and managed to blank her mind until she was in bed that night. But then . . .

Would Stuart want her now? Would he, as Matt had so flatly stated, try to get her back?

And how did she feel about that?

Erin could admit to herself now that she felt guilty, inadequate about the past. Her marriage had failed. She had failed. No matter how many times she had told herself that Stuart had stripped her bare and stood her before the world, a small part of her wondered if she should have been able to cope with that, change it.

"You could handle him now. You could have him on his knees! You're a hell of a lot stronger than he is—remember that."

Being human, Erin thought for a fleeting moment of bringing Stuart to his knees, and how it would feel. Then she realized that it would feel empty. She didn't want Stuart—not even at her feet.

Her guilt and uncertainty were still with her, though. Was she so afraid that a second relationship would find her inadequate, so afraid of failing again? Was that why she was, even now, wary of her feelings for Matt?

There was much she still didn't know about him. He was not, as Stuart had been, an image of something more than a man. But he was, in his own way, elusive, not quite real. He had startling good looks, charm, humor, intelligence, and compassion.

He was a flesh-and-blood reality—and yet she knew little about him, and that made him elusive. He was so adaptable that she had no idea what his preferences were. He had come out of nowhere to enter her life and jar her from the peaceful limbo she had built for herself, yet he had revealed very little of himself in the process.

Or . . . had he? What did she really know, with certainty, about Matt Gavin? As to background, she knew only where he'd grown up and gone to school, that he had four sisters. As to the man that background had produced, she knew that he understood women uncannily well. That he felt a deep respect for writers and was a staunch supporter of creative freedom.

She knew that he was sensitive, understanding, compassionate. That he could make her laugh and rage and cry in spite of herself. That he could evoke passions more powerful than she would have believed possible.

In astonishment, Erin realized that she knew an awful lot about Matt, especially considering the short time since they had met.

Why, then, did he seem so elusive?

Because you aren't looking at him. Stuart's glitter blinded you, and you're so afraid it'll happen again that you won't look at

Matt. He isn't elusive. You just don't trust yourself to reach out and touch him.

Erin drew a deep, slow breath and stared at a dark ceiling. Was that it, then? She had to look at Stuart without his glitter, and she had to look at Matt without the fear of being blinded.

Princes. All the thoughts, comparisons, analogies. She had always thought of Stuart as a prince, and when Matt had appeared, she had quickly, instinctively, thought of him that way as well.

Why?

Simple. So simple now that she faced it. Princes were dreams— vague, untouchable things conjured from wisps of imagination. Not real. They blinded one with the glitter of their perfection.

There was, in a prince, no need for reality. And relationships with princes conjured emotions just as unreal. In love—with the idea of being in love.

Safe. Nothing real to touch.

But Matt, whether consciously or not, had refused to be safe. Needling, probing, purposely pricking his fingers on the thorns she surrounded herself with. He was a flesh-and-blood man who demanded equal reality from a woman. A man who demanded the *real* passions instead of girlish wistfulness.

And that was what Erin was wary of, mistrustful of.

She had failed to cope with a dream. And she was afraid she would fail even more devastatingly to cope with reality.

In Mart's arms, with the explosion of desire between them, she touched reality—and gloried in it.

But then, inevitably, she backed away, unnerved. Tried to convince herself that it was the *desire* and her own feelings that were unreal. Because dreams were safe.

She fumbled toward understanding, even as sleep finally claimed her.

Chapter Seven

In the three years since she had lived on the mountain, Erin had never felt loneliness. After the frenetic pace of her marriage, she had been more than ready for aloneness. But now, as the days passed, she felt lonely.

There was an emptiness she'd never known before, a place where something *should* have been . . . and wasn't.

She leaned heavily on her writing during those days, working long hours and skipping both meals and sleep. She felt a rueful gratitude that Matt, in throwing her emotions into chaos, had somehow forced her to break through her "story block" and begin writing again. Her book began taking shape, paragraph following paragraph on her computer's screen, her thoughts fixed firmly on the story.

But when the computer was shut off and the silence of night closed in around her, Erin found herself restless and anxious. She had talked to Mal on the radio on Saturday and his news of Matt's leaving had depressed her. She didn't—oddly enough—doubt that he would return; it was just that he was so far away.

She dreamed about him, unsettling dreams she could never remember clearly. She thought about him almost constantly, wondering what she would see when she finally *did* look at him, finally did reach out to him.

It didn't occur to her until Tuesday night that she had not thought of Stuart, had not compared him and Matt in days. And she realized that she hadn't because Matt was so strongly in the foreground of her thoughts, so solidly real; there was no longer room even for the glitter that was Stuart. The realization made her feel stronger, more positive about her relationship with Matt.

She was dividing men from princes.

Erin honestly didn't know if Stuart would remain wrapped in the armor she had seen so clearly. She didn't know if he would, now, become just a man in her eyes. She thought somehow that he would not, that Stuart Travis *was* something larger than life. That he was, in fact, untouchable.

The thought brought her no grief, no interest. Whatever Stuart was, she no longer wanted.

She *would* face Stuart and put him and her guilt behind her. And then, with luck, she could build something with Matt.

On Wednesday morning Erin woke to a thumping roar, and she recognized the sound of *Bolero* and the arrival of a helicopter. She threw back the covers and hurried to the front door, her heart thudding, hoping that Matt had returned in spite of her week limit. But when she yanked open the door, it was to see the helicopter lifting off and swooping away.

Bewildered, she gazed after it until she could neither see it nor hear the fanfare of music. Disappointment tightened her throat and she swore unsteadily. It was then, backing away a step and beginning to close the door, that Erin looked down to see the roses.

Six perfect red roses wrapped in tissue, and atop them lay an envelope.

Erin carried the roses into the cabin and lay them on the bar, feeling unexpectedly teary. She opened the envelope carefully, and unfolded a short message.

> I never minded thorns, but six days without you are hard to bear. I hope you're missing me. A favor? I've asked Steve to come and pick you up early Thursday morning; please stay with him and his wife in Denver until I arrive. They want to meet you, and have invited you to stay as long as you like. Bring Chester; Jake tells me you can pasture the horses. Please, Erin, do this for me.
>
> There was never a week so long.
>
> Matt

Erin had to laugh a few minutes later when she found herself standing before her closet debating what to take with her to Denver. There was, she realized, just something about Matt Gavin. He was like an elemental force driving all before it. He asked her to go and stay with total strangers and await his arrival—and she was going to do just that.

After packing with a cheerfulness she couldn't remember ever feeling before, Erin completed the other chores necessary for leaving. Perishable foodstuffs were carried some distance from the cabin and left for foraging animals. Riding Amos and leading Tucker, she took the horses farther up the mountain to a large canyon, where there was plentiful pasture, a sparkling stream, and shelter from harsh weather.

With Chester for company, she made her way leisurely back to the cabin, asking herself if she could leave all this. The answer, honestly, was no. Not forever. But she had gradually come to realize that she no longer felt any fear or discomfort at the thought of living in a city; that fear had simply been caused by memories of too many hours alone during her marriage. It was not the *place*, she realized now, that mattered.

This mountain had helped to heal her, and it would always be a place to come back to. But she thought that—perhaps—she could stand time away. Even months. As long as there was this to return to.

Not to run to. Erin didn't plan on running again.

She was ready early the next morning, bag packed and by the door. The generator was off, the cabin silent. Chester was grumbling uneasily and tried to hide from her as she found his leash, recognizing, as animals often do, the indications of departure.

Erin cornered him and fastened the leash, laughing. "No, Chester—not the vet, I promise. We're going visiting."

Chester howled when Ravel approached, but stopped suddenly as the music and engine did. Holding the leash firmly since her pet was not above making a dash for freedom, Erin opened the door to look curiously at the approaching pilot.

He was a lean six-footer, dark-haired, with cheerful brown eyes, dressed as casually as she in jeans and a sweat shirt. His voice was deep and lilting when he spoke.

"Steve Burke," he said, holding out a lean hand.

Erin shook hands, smiling because people would always smile at so cheerful a man. "Erin Scott. It's nice to finally meet you after hearing you come and go so many times."

He grinned. "Have to do justice to Sadie, you know. Besides—I like to see people react." He glanced at her bag, his lean face relaxing somewhat. "Good—then you are coming."

"Did you doubt it?" she asked curiously.

"Well, Matt didn't," he said, then immediately grimaced. "I didn't mean that the way it sounded."

She was laughing. "Yes, I know. He wasn't arrogant about it. He just knew I'd come. Damn him."

Clearly reassured by this reaction, Steve smiled again. "Ally's really looking forward to it. My wife—Alison." He looked past her to Chester's crouched, rebellious form and said cheerfully, "Hello, Chester. Ready for a ride?"

Chester lifted a lip at him.

Laughing, Steve carried Erin's bag to the helicopter, then returned to help her muscle the reluctant dog into his place behind the seats. Within moments Sadie lifted away, the sounds of Chester's unhappiness drowned by rotors.

Making use of the earphones, Steve explained that he and his wife had a house in the suburbs of Denver. He replied to Erin's hesitant question that they had two children—Danny and Julie, eight and six respectively.

He cheerfully dismissed Erin's fears that having her stay with them would be an imposition, then talked to her easily during the ride to Denver.

"How long have you known Matt?" she asked at one point.

"Twenty years. We met in high school. Went to the same college. Same branch of the service, too."

"Service?"

"Air Force. We were both pilots." He sent her a sudden grin. "They were glad to get rid of me, but tried everything short of blackmail to keep Matt; he's a natural pilot. We both learned as teenagers, because Matt's mother is a pilot."

Erin listened, fascinated. "Is she? He didn't mention it."

Steve laughed. "I'm not surprised. There isn't a lot he could say about her with a straight face. His mother—like yours truly—is a seat-of-the-pants pilot. I'm being careful today," he added cheerfully, "since Matt told me he'd draw and quarter me otherwise."

She blinked, then laughed. "I see. Go on about his mother."

"Her name's Penelope, absurd as it sounds. But Penny to everyone who knows her—including air traffic controllers who have conspired with Matt from time to time to keep her grounded. Matt even hid her plane a few years ago. Not that it did any good."

"What happened?"

"She bought another one."

"Good heavens." Erin hesitated, then asked carefully, "Is she so dangerous a pilot?"

"Oh, no, not dangerous. Just . . . gleeful. Apt to do chancy things. Matt only just stopped her once from joining a stunt team."

Erin felt her eyes widening, and a giggle caught in her throat. The "traditional" East indeed! she thought. No wonder Matt had looked peculiar when she'd made that remark. And no wonder he'd developed the gift of laughter; he'd had a choice of laughter or despair with such a mother!

"Does she still—?"

"Oh, yes. Penny's forever young. She's in her late fifties, of course, but she married young. The twins were born when she was just nineteen."

"Twins?"

"He didn't tell you? Well, Matt doesn't talk about family much. His oldest sisters are twins, Adrian and Barbara. After them came Kathy, then Matt, then Ally." Abruptly, Steve winced and sent her an uneasy look.

Erin hadn't missed it. "Ally. Alison? Your wife?"

He sighed. "Well, she would have told you once we got home. It's just that Matt said you wouldn't come if you knew."

"He was right." Erin had to laugh, though. "So he's your brother-in-law."

"And best friend," Steve said with the deceptively casual sound of bedrock certainty. Then in a suddenly teasing voice he added, "Of course, he never listens to my advice. I warned him, for instance, that a Scots-Irish girl was more than most men could handle. *Especially* a redhead. But he's mostly Welsh himself, and those Celts always do like a challenge."

Erin managed to speak lightly. "You speak from experience?"

"About Celts, I sure do. *All* the Gavins enjoy challenge. About redheaded Scots-Irish girls . . . well, let's just say I know what dynamite looks like."

Erin would have responded to that—although she wasn't sure just how—but the helicopter began descending then, and she took the time to gather her composure. It had been no part of her plans to meet any of Matt's family, particularly now, when she was still uncertain.

However . . .

In the sprawling two-story house that was comfortably cluttered, evidence of an active family, Alison Burke greeted Erin with cheerful friendliness. She was nearly as tall as Erin, dark-haired and blue-eyed, and looked ten years younger than she was.

"Nice meeting you, Erin. Is this—well, of course it is. Matt described him, but— Hello, Chester. He can have the run of the house, Erin, and our backyard's fenced."

They had left the helicopter a mile down the road at a private airstrip, and Erin's dog had only just stopped grumbling about his unexpected ride. Steve took her bag upstairs, disappearing just as two dark-haired urchins erupted from another room to fall on Chester with uninhibited cries.

Erin, secure in the knowledge that Chester was a marshmallow with children, watched with a smile as Ally tried to talk above the noise.

"Danny and Julie," she told Erin wryly. "And they love animals so much they're inclined to forget manners. Get up, you monsters, and say hello to Erin!"

Two pairs of identical blue eyes gleamed up at her, and childish voices found politeness for a moment. "Hello, Erin," they said in unison, then instantly fell to arguing over who was to have the honor of shaking the paw Chester amiably waved at them.

Ally drew Erin into the family room and smiled. "I'm glad they're fussing over him; our ten-year-old collie died last year, and they've refused another dog. I think it's time now." Her blue eyes were bright as she studied Erin with friendly curiosity.

Seeing hesitation, Erin put the older woman at ease. "Steve let the cat out of the bag," she said dryly. "And I just may kill your brother when he gets here."

Ally laughed and waved her guest to a chair. "He does have an uncomfortable way of understanding what you'd rather he didn't," she agreed. "But in this case, I'm glad. Any woman who can get my brother on a horse is one I want to meet!"

Hearing something in Ally's voice, Erin looked at her curiously. "He just wanted to find a reclusive writer," she explained, "and horseback was the only way."

"Yes," Ally agreed, smiling. "But it's funny, don't you think? Odd, I mean. He stayed here for a few days before he set out to look for you. He mentioned that one of his writers lived up on some mountain near here. But he didn't say anything about going to find you. Steve and I've read your books, by the way, and enjoyed them immensely."

"Thank you," Erin said rather blankly, wondering at the gleeful look in Ally's eyes.

With elaborate casualness Ally said, "He soaks up information like a sponge, you know. Matt. Always interested in whatever's happening. We're all pack rats in a way, saving newspapers and magazines. And Matt's always looking for ideas, of course, to suggest to some of his writers. So he goes through my stuff whenever he's here."

From the doorway, Steve said ruefully, "Matt's going to kill you, Ally."

She laughed and agreed, "Probably!"

"What's going on?" Erin asked, baffled. She looked from husband to wife, seeing a laughing despair on Steve's face and gleeful enjoyment on Ally's. "Somebody clue me in?"

Ally looked back at their guest as Steve came to sit beside her on the couch. "Gladly. You see, Matt found something unexpected among my newspapers and magazines."

"What?"

"His Waterloo." Ally giggled suddenly. "I came in here and found him surrounded by dusty newspapers—the Denver papers—and he looked like the house had fallen in on him. Sort of stunned and incredulous."

"What was it?" Erin was completely at sea.

"It was," Ally told her enjoyably, "a picture and part of an article. Only part, unfortunately; probably the kids had torn away the rest."

Apparently deciding that his wife wouldn't listen to the voice of reason, Steve chimed in ruefully with the rest. "The picture was one an enterprising reporter had snapped in a town not far from here. A picture of a reclusive writer. He used a telephoto lens, by the way. Apparently, he'd had some experience of the writer's wrath earlier, and was still smarting under a load of buckshot. Can't blame him, I suppose, for standing well back when he took the picture."

"That'll teach me to make an enemy of reporters," Erin agreed dryly. She took a good look at their faces, and her own went still. "Matt would have recognized the pen name, of course," she said slowly.

Seriously, Ally said, "He cares very much about writers, you know. And he was worried about you because he believed you were having trouble with your work." Then, in a very deliberate tone, she added, "But he hardly got on a horse—after avoiding them religiously for thirty-five years—and climbed a mountain just to find a reclusive writer. He went to find the woman in that picture."

Perhaps it shouldn't have been a shock. Erin had wondered, after all, at Matt's apparently sudden interest. She thought back to that first meeting and shook her head disbelievingly. "He didn't know me. He asked about—"

"Devious, my brother. And when he wants, he's got the best poker face this side of a riverboat gambler. Erin, Matt went up there to find *you*, not a writer. He carries that picture in his wallet."

Erin had to think about that. And both Ally and Steve, realizing, immediately dropped the subject.

The rest of the day was enjoyable for Erin. The Burke family accepted her casually. Erin found herself asking about the entire Gavin family and being answered easily, and she learned all about the fascinating Penny, about Matt's sisters and their families. And about Matt.

Moment by moment he grew more real to her. And with Ally's astounding information in the back of her mind, she found herself inwardly going back over her time with Matt.

She found it difficult to believe that he had, as Ally had heavily implied, fallen in love with a picture. Yet she couldn't help but remember his determination to remain with her, to get to know her.

To box shadows.

He called late that afternoon, talking briefly to his sister before asking for Erin. And Erin, who could also play poker, held her hand very close to her chest.

"Hello, Matt," she said calmly, glancing around at the den, which had been tactfully vacated by Steve and Ally.

"I miss you," he told her, his voice husky.

Erin ignored her weakening knees and kept her voice calm. "Do you? I got some writing done this week."

"Good." But he sounded restless. "You aren't mad at me, are you? For not telling you who Ally and Steve were?"

"Do I sound mad?"

"You sound like a prickly rose bush," he answered wryly.

"You said you didn't mind thorns." She spoke without thinking.

"No. No, I don't mind *your* thorns." He paused. "I'll be back to-morrow afternoon, Erin. And I've gotten our seats for the concert." It was a question.

Steadily, Erin answered it. "All right."

"And then we go on." He sounded restless again. "Erin . . . re-member what I told you, will you? You're stronger now. Stronger than he is."

"All right," she repeated, unemotional.

Matt swore softly. "I'll see you tomorrow, then."

"Yes. Good-bye, Matt."

She stood for a moment, staring down at the telephone. Then, taking a deep breath, she picked up the receiver again and made a collect call. In California, the call was accepted, with surprise, and Erin kept her own voice even and mildly friendly.

"Hello, Con, how are you?"

"Fine, just fine, Erin. And you?" Conrad Styles, Stuart's man-ager, hid his surprise swiftly with the expertise of years.

She more or less passed over his question. "Con, I'm in Denver, and I'd like to see Stuart. Can you tell me where he's staying, please?" Experience told her that Stuart's whereabouts would be a closely guarded secret, as always, to prevent hordes of fans from descending on the hotel.

After a slight hesitation Con said slowly, "Stuart told me that if you ever got in touch, I was to let him know pronto. Seems your lawyer's a bit protective and won't give out your address."

Erin was a little surprised, and slightly wary. "Did Stuart want to get in touch with me for any special reason?"

"He didn't say. I told him he could write through your lawyer, but he wasn't having any. It must have been a few months ago, I guess." He hesitated, then said unemotionally. "Lisa didn't last out the divorce proceedings. Did you know?"

"No." But Erin wasn't surprised. Lisa, the "other woman" Stuart had written about. Dryly, she added, "No reconciliation,

Con. I just want to talk to Stuart. Will you tell me where he's staying?"

Quietly, Con gave her the hotel and room number. Then, slowly and to Erin's surprise, he added, "Stuart's a fantastic talent, Erin, but he'll always be a taker. Don't let him take anything else from you, huh? I didn't like what he did to you before."

Erin was touched, remembering only then that it had been Con who had sometimes made things bearable by seeing to it that she was rarely trapped in hotel rooms while Stuart practiced and performed; he had often cheerfully played tourist with her just so she could see the various cities.

"Thanks for caring, Con. But I've made a new life for myself— and there's someone else now. Stuart won't hurt me again."

"I hope not," Con said soberly. "Take care, Erin."

"I will. Good-bye, Con."

Erin debated briefly, but she knew that her mind had been made up even before her call to Stuart's manager. She had to see him alone, without Matt to cling to. Matt, she thought ruefully, would not be happy about it. But he would, she knew, understand.

Casually, Erin told her hosts that she was going into Denver for a while that night, and was instantly urged to take one of the family cars. Gratefully accepting, she left soon after dinner, armed with a map and feeling curiously calm and detached.

She had dressed with no special care, wearing dark slacks and a coral silk blouse. Light makeup, as usual. She wore her hair in a single braid hanging down her back.

She had no trouble finding the small hotel, and went inside with the casual air of belonging. She went directly to the elevators, up to Stuart's floor, and found herself knocking on his door—only then wondering with amusement if she would be interrupting the current romance.

She did not.

Stuart opened the door swiftly, saying impatiently, "It's about time—" Then broke off to stare at her in surprise. "Erin!"

"Hello, Stuart. Mind if I come in?" Her voice was calm, casual.

"Of course not." He stepped back, gesturing, and Erin entered his room. Suite, really; it was brightly lit, because Stuart couldn't bear dim rooms, and empty of people but for them.

Erin crossed to the center of the sitting room before turning to face him, feeling a faint, thoughtful surprise. How odd, she mused; he was only as tall as she was herself. She could have sworn he was taller.

Maybe it was true, then, that the people and places in one's past were always smaller than they were remembered to be.

"I was expecting room service," Stuart said more or less automatically, doing a bit of stocktaking himself. Vivid blue eyes looked her over thoroughly, a speculative gleam hovering somewhere in their depths.

He has an idea, she realized with more resignation than annoyance.

"What're you doing in Denver?" Stuart asked.

"Visiting friends."

"Does that include me?"

"No." She smiled a little. "We were never friends."

"We were lovers," he said with surprising truculence. "We were married."

Erin studied him in silence, trying to remember back to the days when that fierceness in his voice had shaken her, made her anxious. At that moment she could remember the emotions analytically— but felt nothing except faint interest.

How volatile he was, she thought. Like a child—or a superstar. He was constantly needing, his hot emotions quickly past and forgotten. Consciously or unconsciously, he was certain that the entire universe revolved around him.

He was lean with the wired tautness of explosive energy. Dark and brooding of face. Undeniably, strikingly handsome. Women had been known to do incredible things to get his attention.

But . . . A little surprised, Erin saw a man instead of a prince, and wondered how she could have been so blind.

She went to a chair and sat down, feeling unthreatened and unafraid. "Con said you wanted to see me. Any particular reason?"

His brows drew together as he stood staring at her. Indecision and uncertainty flickered in his eyes, then anger. The anger of a man accustomed to holding the complete attention of whomever he spoke to. "I want you back," he said roughly.

It was, Erin thought vaguely, a suitably dramatic line delivered with suitable fire. Ruined, though, by the knock at the door announcing room service.

She was so delighted to find that his words left her unmoved that she was smiling when the door closed behind the waiter and Stuart faced her again.

"Erin—" He stepped toward her, eyes lighting.

"No." She shook her head, stopping him in mid-stride. "I'm sorry, Stuart. There's nothing between us now. Surely you can see that?"

"I want you back," he said stubbornly, fiercely.

She shook her head again. "I have a new life now, one I'm quite happy with." She thought of Matt, and her lips curved unconsciously.

Stuart went very still, something hot and angry leaping out of his eyes. "And another man?"

Erin looked at him. "Did you think," she said dryly, "I'd waste away for wanting you? If you'll cast your mind back, you'll remember that I left you. And that's where it ended, Stuart."

"I'll change your mind," he promised, arrogant and certain.

It took only a moment for Erin to realize what he was doing. She found herself wondering ruefully how she had truly believed him in the past. Stuart was surely playing a role. He was fathoms deep in the role of a lover betrayed, a lover desperate to reclaim his lost love no matter what the cost to his pride.

He probably believed it himself, she thought, after so many years of the same sort of ordeal. And it was an ordeal for him, she knew. He would tear himself to shreds—for a while. Then he would set the emotions to music, and blast them into an audience of millions of adoring fans.

And the emotions would be forgotten, with no lingering pain.

It was sad. For the first time, she understood what his genius cost him. His own demon drove him to experience—however briefly—all the extremes of emotion; and his life was a series of roles designed spontaneously for just that effect.

He had, she realized then, played the part of a shining prince with the same deliberate spontaneity. He had found a princess and had supplied a prince, automatically and with pleasure, as any actor would throw himself delightedly into a new and challenging role. And then the part of husband and—briefly—expectant father. Then erring husband, ashamed and suffering. Ending, finally, with the noble pain of a husband releasing his wife.

And now he was arrogant and demanding, but pleading underneath, striving to win back the ex-wife that his own careless cruelty had driven away from him.

Erin felt no desire to laugh. And, perhaps oddly, no desire to lash out at him for the pain he had caused. One could hardly, she thought, punish a demon.

Instead, she found herself rising with a grave face. Found herself—for the first time—knowingly and willingly supplying fodder for his song. She looked at him with eyes holding just a touch of sad regret—and it was not acting on her part. She was sad for him, and regretful that he would never know the true magic of feelings that he allowed himself to feel only for a while.

"I'm sorry, Stuart." She found, instinctively, lines to add to his play.

"Once we might have tried again. But it's too late now. And you . . . you belong to the world. There was never a part of you that was mine. I need a man who can give himself to me. A man who needs me."

"I need you!" His face was drawn, pale.

"You need your music." She moved toward the door slowly.

Stuart reached out suddenly, blind obsession in his eyes. He caught her before she could escape, pinning her wrists at the small of her back and kissing her with bruising passion.

Erin stood unmoved, not struggling, no flicker of response rising in her. She could have told him that it was never his passion that had attracted or held her, never physical desire she had responded to. That he had made her breathless, but had never touched her with fire.

But that would have ruined his play.

When he finally lifted his head and gazed with clouded eyes into her own distant face, Stuart's mouth twisted bitterly. "I killed it, didn't I?" he asked huskily. "I killed it three years ago."

Erin looked at him mutely.

With a curse Stuart released her. He turned toward the room's small bar and fumbled to make himself a drink. Abruptly, he turned back, staring at her. And there might have been a flicker of honest regret in his eyes.

"You woke up. Grew up. Because of another man."

Her instant surprise quickly faded. Of course he saw a change in her—just as Matt had predicted. And he was, underneath the layers of genius, man enough to understand.

"We'll be at your concert tomorrow night," she said slowly, unsure why she was telling him.

"He wants a look at his competition?" Stuart laughed harshly before she could respond. "I always thought you had fire buried somewhere. And, damn you, I could never find it."

She blinked, again surprised, but Stuart was instantly back in his role.

"I won't give up, Erin. I'll win you back."

Erin gathered her thoughts and played her part. "No, Stuart. It's too late. I won't be seeing you again after tomorrow. There wouldn't be any use."

He watched, grim and unsmiling, as she headed for the door. When she turned for a last look, his eyes were bright . . . and she could almost hear the music. She went from the room, closing the door behind her quietly.

She stood silently in the hall for long moments, until she heard what she had expected to hear. The sounds of tentative chords being struck on a guitar.

He had given her a glorious, painful ride on a white charger. He had given her a crown of sorts. He had blinded her with shining armor and left her breathless. He had rocked her off the stable foundations of her life and forced her to stand alone. He had stripped her naked before the world.

And now he was just a memory, the ragged, painful edges of it smoothed by understanding and pity. Now he was just a man who sang songs born in fleeting emotions. A man who would never know he had missed the best song of all.

Erin touched the door briefly with her fingers and turned away from the sounds of birth.

Now he was just a man.

And she wondered . . .

What price genius . . . ?

When Erin left the hotel, she drove aimlessly for a while. Thinking. Remembering pain that was distant now and unimportant. Thinking of the deep and honest emotions Matt had sparked in her.

No wonder, she thought, Stuart had never managed to touch the deepest part of her. His talent had made him a manipulator, a taker; he delved within himself for the frantic surge of momentary emotion and played off those nearby for the responses he needed. And anyone near, dazed by his charisma, inevitably played the roles assigned to them.

But those others lost something of themselves, and Stuart never did. He was, as always, a man driven, obsessed.

She wondered again if he would ever know the real thing. Ever allow himself to feel honest emotion that would never find its way into a song. Perhaps. But Erin didn't think so, and she was glad that Stuart himself would in all probability never realize he had missed something so special.

Erin drove back to the suburbs and parked in the Burkes' driveway. It was late, but they had left the front porch light on for her and given her a key. She let herself in quietly, closed and locked the door, and turned off the porch light.

A small lamp stood on the hall table by the stairs, providing a warm, dim glow. And when he spoke, she turned toward the den to find his face in shadow, his body taut.

"You went to see him."

Chapter Eight

"I went to see him." *She moved slowly toward the den, past Matt* when he stepped back. The room was lighted only by a lamp next to the couch. An ashtray on the coffee table was overflowing. Clearly, Matt had waited restlessly a long time for her to come back.

She sat down on the couch, laying her purse absently aside, only then meeting his eyes as he sat down a foot or so away.

He looked strained, and his face was almost imperceptibly thinner, the fine bones more prominent. The gray eyes were intent, worried.

Without hesitation, she smiled at him.

Matt relaxed somewhat, eyes instantly brighter, smiling in response. He half-turned toward her, but didn't touch her or move closer. "You had to see him alone," he said.

Erin nodded, hearing both his understanding of that and his dislike of it. "It was important, Matt. It had to be just him and me, with no audience. No one to . . . act for."

"And?" He looked at her, eyes restless.

Erin didn't hesitate. She told him exactly what had happened, sparing neither Matt nor herself. She told him all the things she had realized and understood. And she finished by telling him of the song being written even now.

After her voice had trailed away, Matt said reluctantly, "I can almost feel sorry for him."

"I do." She smiled a little. "But that's all I feel. I don't love him or hate him or feel bitter toward him."

Huskily, Matt said, "Then that year isn't standing between us anymore?"

"No."

"But . . . you still have to hear him sing. It was his singing, wasn't it, that first drew you?"

Erin no longer felt surprise at Matt's perception. She nodded. "He's larger than life onstage. It was easy to look at him and see a prince. But it won't make a difference now, Matt."

"Still." He sighed. "Until you're absolutely sure . . ."

"I can't sleep in your arms?" There was a faint note of teasing in her voice but a stronger note of longing.

"I don't think," he said, clearing his throat, "that I could stand it."

"You said you missed me," she murmured.

Matt looked at her for a moment, then said rather grimly, "You know what hurts almost more than anything? My jaw. My teeth have been gritted ever since I left you."

She reached out to touch his lean face, her fingers gentle. "I'm sorry."

He half-closed his eyes at her touch, and a muscle leaped under her fingers. "You've been driving me crazy," he said in a strained but conversational tone. "Ever since the day we met."

Erin hid an inward smile and said gravely, "Steve said he warned you. About redheaded Scots-Irish girls. You should have listened to him."

"Next time," Matt said a bit thickly, "I will."

"And I," she said, "will be nicer to journalists next time. Then they won't hide behind things and take pictures."

Matt's eyes, dark and heavy-lidded, widened suddenly and gazed at her with something more than desire glowing in them. Something like sheepishness. "Um . . . pictures?" he managed, his voice still deep and rough.

Limpidly, she said, "I hear you found one of them. Before we met. Before you rode Jake's roan up the mountain."

"I'm going to kill Ally."

Erin's fingers were still touching his face, trailing along his jaw and tracing his features with seeming idleness. Reproachfully, she said, "And you *said* you came all that way to rescue a writer in distress!"

Matt cleared his throat again. Not that it helped. "And what was I supposed to say? That I fell in love with a picture? You would have shot me!"

If Erin's fingers quivered at that declaration, she at least managed to keep her expression calm. "Big, tough businessman like you?" she mocked softly. "Falling for a picture? I'm afraid I find that hard to believe."

His eyes were growing more heavy-lidded and his hand, which lay on the back of the couch, was tense. But Matt still didn't touch her. "I . . . don't blame you," he said hoarsely. "I didn't believe it myself. I thought I was losing my mind."

Thoughtful, she said, "I imagine a man like you—who understands women so well—is constantly in demand. You must have . . . gotten your feet wet a few times."

Matt swallowed hard. "Um . . . yes. Well, of course. I'm thirty-five, after all."

"After all," she agreed gravely.

"And I *like* women. As companions, I mean." Matt cleared his throat yet again and wondered if she even realized how dizzy he was. "I happen to be glad somebody decided there should be—two sexes."

"It makes life interesting. To say the least."

"Erin—"

"You're being very good at keeping your hands to yourself," she noted approvingly.

The heavy lids lifted for an instant as Matt glared at her. "Dammit, Erin—"

"Wonderfully noble." Her voice was gently admiring.

Matt released a sound that Chester would have claimed happily as a lethal growl.

"It would serve you right," she said virtuously, "if I jumped on-stage as soon as Stuart sang the first note tomorrow night, and fell into his arms."

There were, Matt thought, things beyond bearing. There were limits past which a man could hardly be expected to control his baser instincts. Especially when a vixen pushed remorselessly past those limits.

He lunged.

Laughing, Erin found herself lying back against the comfortable arm of the couch with her arms happily up around Mart's neck.

"Witch!" he said feelingly.

"We have to see if I can wake in your arms and not pull away," she countered reasonably, laughter fading as her own eyes grew sleepy with desire. She absorbed the heavy weight of him as he lay half on her, her fingers tangling in the silky thickness of his hair, and her limbs felt suddenly heavy. How wonderful, she thought, to be able to feel like this.

"Did you set out to torture me?" he asked gruffly, his lips feathering along her jaw. Then answered himself. "Of course you did!"

"You told me I had to fight for what I wanted," she reminded him throatily, tilting her head back as he began exploring the V neckline of her blouse. His rueful laugh tickled her flesh and made her shiver.

"Honey, you didn't have to bring out the big guns. You can have anything on this earth I can give you."

Erin waited until he lifted his head. She gazed gravely into his taut face and flaring eyes. "I asked for time and you gave me that. I asked for understanding and you gave me that. What I need from you right now . . ."

"Is what?" He kissed her very gently, clearly holding passion rigidly in check.

She pushed a lock of raven hair off his forehead and smiled slowly. "What I need . . . is balance. You've been giving, Matt, and getting nothing. Let me give."

After a moment he asked very quietly, "What do you want to give?"

Her smile grew, green eyes very bright. "What do you most want from me?"

Matt hesitated, then sighed a bit raggedly. "Your love."

"Then that's what I want to give you."

"Erin—"

"I love you, Matt. I've known it for a long time. I was just afraid to believe it. Afraid I'd created another prince because I was afraid of reality. Afraid you'd go away when I touched you."

"And you aren't . . . afraid of that anymore?" His voice was unsteady.

"I'm not afraid. You're real. And when I touch you, you're still real. And I still love you."

Matt framed her face with shaking hands. "I fell in love with a picture," he said softly. "And then with a prickly rose." He drew a deep breath. "God, Erin, I love you! I've been going out of my mind all week, afraid you'd decide you didn't want me. And when I called this afternoon—you sounded so distant. After I hung up, it was like a kick in the stomach to realize that I'd asked you to come here—within miles of Travis. So damned close to him and to that year you spent with him. I had to come. I had to get here as fast as I could."

"It's just a year now," she said quietly. "A part of my past like any other year. It doesn't matter anymore. He doesn't matter anymore."

Matt kissed her, his lips warm and hard, and Erin instantly took fire, fighting the reins he held on his desire. She fought willfully, even though a small and rueful part of her mind reminded her of just where they were. She didn't listen.

Her arms wound more tightly around his neck, her mouth opening to him, her body straining to be closer to him than was possible. She could feel the thud of his heart against her, feel the runaway pounding of her own heart.

He tore his lips from hers at last, but only so that he could explore the silky flesh of her throat. "Oh, hell, Erin," he groaned. "My sister's house . . . and kids upstairs . . ."

"I know," she murmured achingly. "I have lousy timing. But I love you so much . . ."

Matt groaned again, his hands slipping down to unsteadily open the buttons of her blouse. His mouth trailed hotly down from her throat, lingering in the valley between her breasts. The front fastening of her bra yielded to his touch, and the flimsy lace confection fell away.

Erin gasped, biting her bottom lip when she felt the pull of his mouth, the erotic caress of a swirling tongue. She could feel her flesh swelling at his touch, and a hot, restless emptiness grew in her. She held his head, her fingers locked in his hair, fighting herself now. Fighting a fire burning out of control.

"Matt . . ."

His lips found hers again, kissing her so swiftly that she gave him his name with her breath, the aching sound passing from her to him. The duel of their tongues was hot, hungry, desperate with a primitive need denied too long.

Matt tore his lips from hers abruptly, burying his face between her breasts, breathing as if he had just run a marathon. "Erin . . . dear God, I want you so much!"

The words were muffled; Erin felt as much as heard them, and she held him as hard as he held her. "We could . . . go somewhere," she managed, having to concentrate to produce coherent words.

His laugh was a ghost of sound, and when he lifted his head, she could see the strain. "Don't tempt me."

"But I want to," she said honestly.

"Oh, hell, don't—" He drew a deep breath. "You have to hear him sing. You have to be sure."

Or maybe you *have to be sure,* she thought suddenly. Sure that year no longer stood between them. She could forgive Matt a twinge of doubt; she had certainly placed heavy enough emphasis on it herself.

Accordingly, she nodded with reluctant acceptance. "All right. But the concert won't make a difference, Matt."

Fingers unsteady, Matt started to draw her bra closed again. But his mind and his body were on two different wave lengths. The creamy mounds of her breasts, their tips pointed with the need he had aroused, beckoned to him. And this time he couldn't block the wistful sound in the back of his throat. His head lowered again, hands releasing the lace to find willing flesh.

Erin promptly forgot his determination in sheer, boundless pleasure. Her hands moved over the rippling muscles of his back, kneading the hard flesh beneath his white shirt, entranced by the strength and power of him. She was so involved in her own feelings, so conscious of the fire he could summon with a touch, she all but forgot that Matt still felt the elusive presence of a rival.

But Matt, his body aching and his mind trapped within the steel threads of passion, was too near the edge to fully control ancient instincts. And those primitive, unreasonable feelings tormented him. She loved him . . . she was *his* . . . but another man had touched her first—however shallowly. Another man had been her first lover . . . had made her pregnant . . . And vows *meant* something to her . . .

"Hell!" The explosion was savagely quiet, utterly primitive, and Matt lifted his head to show her glittering eyes for an instant. "*He's* the one who touched you first, a girl with dreams in her eyes and no shadow in her smile! *He* was first—" Whatever words may have followed tangled in his throat, and Matt kissed her fiercely, almost ruthlessly, in a driven, instinctive attempt to wipe away a ghostly touch that had come first.

After the first shocked instant, Erin understood. It wouldn't have mattered to some men, perhaps most men. It mattered to Matt. It mattered to him that there would be memories he could have no part of, memories of a first lover and a first child. With the best will in the world, she could not turn back the clock.

With the best will in the world, she couldn't be a girl again.

Her body responded to his touch, as always, her fire rising to meet his own, but Erin felt a fleeting despair. She could put Stuart behind her . . . but could Matt? Groping desperately for something, anything, she found it at last.

And though they were still lying on his sister's couch in his sister's house with her children asleep upstairs, Erin forgot everything but convincing him.

His mouth was buried in her throat, bruising in its fierce pressure, but Erin held him with all the strength she could find in herself. "Matt," she whispered achingly, "this is something I've felt only with you. His kisses never made me burn. His touch never made me tremble. I was starving . . . starving and never knew it . . . It was someone else he touched, not me. You have my heart, all my heart, all that I am . . ."

Gradually, almost imperceptibly, the savagery drained from Matt's taut body. His kisses gentled; his caresses were no longer fierce. He took part of his weight off her by rising on his elbows, and carefully fastened her bra and blouse, dropping soft kisses on the creamy flesh before it was covered.

When he finally met her eyes, his own were hot and restless, anxious. "I'm sorry," he murmured finally, his voice deep and husky. "I never thought I'd be jealous—of a memory."

Erin stroked the padded muscle of his shoulders almost compulsively and smiled. "Matt, in every sense except the very technical one, you're my first lover. What you touch in me no one else has ever touched. I love you."

"I love you." He kissed her lingeringly, then shifted them both in a gentle movement until they lay close together, side by side. He held her, resting his cheek against her hair. His body still ached and pulsed relentlessly, but something even wilder had been tamed, and Matt thought he could handle the need for her.

Quietly, he said, "I'm not going up to that empty bed. I think we'll find out, after all, if you can wake in my arms and not pull away."

"I won't pull away." Erin snuggled even closer, finding that her body fit his as if some fate had decreed it. Her body felt heavy, unsatisfied yet still hovering on the edge; she felt no disappointment. Just contentment and a glorious certainty that she had found her match, her mate.

"I wouldn't be able to run from you," she added softly, utter certainty in her voice. "I wouldn't get over you. I'd carry you with me all the days of my life. If you left me tonight . . . or tomorrow . . . or years from now . . . it wouldn't matter."

His arms tightened around her. "I need you, Erin," he said equally softly. "I'm not whole without you. You've haunted me since I first saw that picture. So lovely, and so wary. I want to make certain no one ever hurts you again. For good or bad—I'm yours.

All of me. There's no part of me you can't touch. I love you so very much. If I lost you—" His voice broke, steadied. "If I lost you, I'd lose myself."

Erin moved her cheek against his shoulder. "You won't. You won't lose me."

Exhausted both from physical tension and emotional strain, they both slept deeply. And held on to each other all night.

Matt woke slowly, instantly aware of her warmth at his side. He found himself listening instinctively for the even sound of her breathing, and felt peaceful, some imperceptible tension easing when he heard it.

It was only then that he looked up to find his sister leaning on the back of the couch and regarding him with amused eyes. "Old poker-face," she said in a stage whisper. "Better put away your cards, old chum. Every thought shows on your face."

Unwilling to disturb Erin, Matt whispered as well. "Why don't you go away and bother someone else?" he invited politely.

Ally grinned. "We *have* five bedrooms," she reminded him.

"No kidding. With beds and everything?"

"Last time I looked. How come you two didn't end up in one of them?"

"Alison—"

"All right, all right. Breakfast in an hour. You'd better shave." She headed for the kitchen, laughing softly.

Matt remained where he was, for a while at least. He knew that soon the kids would be up, and noisy. The day, with all its distractions and potential problems, was here.

Would she pull away?

He didn't think so. But the subconscious sometimes lays mine fields where one would expect to walk without fear, and Erin had been through a wide range of emotions these last weeks. Perhaps her subconscious was still guarding itself.

He was afraid to put it to the test.

"Good morning," she murmured then, suddenly.

Matt felt himself tense. "Good morning. Ally says breakfast is in an hour."

"I should go and help." Erin raised up on her elbow to smile down at him. Her braid had come loose during the night, leaving the glorious mass free and shining. She was still heavy-eyed with sleep, but no shadows lurked in the green depths of her eyes.

So beautiful it stopped his heart.

And she didn't draw away.

"I love you," he said, whispering because it was the only sound he could manage.

She bent her head to kiss him, a light kiss that rapidly became something else. A little breathless, she said when she could, "I love you, too."

"I suppose," he said, after staring at her for several hungry moments, "we'd better get up."

With a reluctance that both warmed his heart and tested his control, Erin sat up and swung her legs to the floor. "I suppose we'd better."

They met the children in the upstairs hall, noisily deciding who was to have the honor of giving Chester his morning constitutional. The huge dog, sitting patiently between them, gave Erin and Matt a look, but was undisturbed by having his ears pulled as the kids argued.

"Both," Matt said firmly. "Both of you take him."

"But he slept in Danny's room—"

"He likes company," Erin said diplomatically. "I'm sure he'd prefer you both to take him."

With each ear held firmly in a childish hand, Chester lumbered down the hall between them.

Erin and Matt, still laughing, parted company outside their bedroom doors and got their morning decently started with showers and whatnot . . .

They spent the morning at the house, and Erin was both amused and touched to find that Matt was putty in the children's hands. It was clear that his niece and nephew adored him, and equally clear that he returned the affection. He had the rare ability to talk to children without talking down to them, and he was clearly unable to resist whatever blandishments they chose to aim his way.

"He'd give them the earth," Ally told Erin dryly, "if he could. The man's a born father."

Erin offered only a smile to the bright blue gaze turned her way, and Ally sighed gustily. "Well, I have eyes, don't I?" she demanded aggrievedly.

It would have been too much to expect, Erin acknowledged ruefully, that she and Matt could keep their feelings to themselves. They never strayed more than ten feet away from each other all morning, and both the smiles and touches they exchanged, however casual they *thought* they were, would probably have been obvious to a blind man.

They left just before lunch, Matt telling his sister and brother-in-law that they'd be late in returning. He steered Erin determinedly to the family car, saying only that his rental car was a Mercedes with bucket seats.

Smiling, Erin had already moved across the seat to his side by the time he got in.

They did indeed lose themselves in the city—walking, window shopping, talking casually. They had lunch in a small restaurant, and the casual talk dropped away from them. Every meeting of eyes grew more intense than the last, and words that weren't at all casual emerged as husky sounds.

"Erin . . . could you move to New York?"

"As long as you're there," she answered simply.

He drew a sharp breath. "And your aerie?"

She smiled. "It'll always be there. For vacations. Visits from time to time."

"There are demands on me," he warned reluctantly. "Business demands. Sometimes—late nights. Trips I have to take."

Erin was thoughtful. "I'll cope, Matt. If you want me with you, I'll be there. You won't ask more of me than I'll be able to give."

"Just—tell me if I do. I won't mind so much to know you're waiting, but if you feel stifled and leave—"

She looked at him, realizing suddenly that he wouldn't ask. Matt was so apprehensive of asking too much of her that he was unwilling to ask for a binding commitment. Too conscious that another man had taken constantly from her, Matt was determined to take only what she would give him.

Erin reached across the table to lay her hand over his. "Marry me," she said softly.

Something leaped in his eyes, but Matt cleared his throat before speaking. "If you ever felt trapped," he said roughly, "or had to break your vows, I don't think I could stand it. I *know* that what I feel for you is forever, but—"

"But what?" She smiled gently. "But I may not be sure? I love you, Matt. And what I feel *is* forever. Marry me."

He carried her hand to his lips, his eyes very bright. "Just say when," he murmured.

Erin laughed aloud. "When!"

The audience was restless, thousands of voices blending into constant sound, a quivering roar. Eyes turned constantly to the curtained stage and the indications of movement behind the concealing draperies.

Erin and Matt, sitting in the center of the third row, waited like the rest for the concert to begin.

"You told him we'd be here?"

She nodded. "If you want to meet him—afterward—we can go to his hotel."

Matt hadn't made up his mind on that point. "We can decide that later," he said, holding her hand firmly.

"All right."

He looked at her, still somehow anxious. If he lost her now— lost her to a prince whose glitter he could never hope to equal— Matt knew he'd go out of his mind.

He thought of minds, of subconscious desires and wishes.

Dammit! Dammit, stop thinking! he ordered.

Instead, he gazed at her. So lovely. So terribly, vitally important to him. She was far calmer than he, her breathing steady, face composed. Her hand was warm and still, no tremors betraying a disturbance of any kind.

She turned her head and smiled at him, and Matt, reassured, lifted her hand briefly to his lips.

What would his life be like without that smile?

It didn't bear thinking of.

The lights dimmed and thousands of voices were suddenly muted, then fell to silence. With the harsh suddenness of a blow, an announcer's voice blared out over the speakers, thundering an introduction no one listened to. The curtain swept back, revealing instruments, cables tangled from amplifiers to instruments, musicians . . . and a lone man in the center of the stage.

The crowd went wild.

Matt realized instantly what Erin had meant by calling Stuart Travis something larger than life. His charm was a palpable, almost visible thing as he talked and joked with the audience, his voice warm and deep. Disdaining the glittering or deliberately sloppy dress of some of his contemporaries, he wore dark slacks and a light open-throated shirt; his dark hair was cut casually and he was clean-shaven. He neither wandered restlessly all over the stage nor moved jerkily, but stood at ease and comfortable in the spotlight.

And then he sang.

He sang to Erin.

He came to the edge of the stage, unerringly finding the warm glow of her hair in the third row; the stage-lights spilled out over several rows. They were close enough to see him clearly, and it was obvious that he saw them.

After a flickering glance, Stuart Travis ignored Matt as though he were an unimportant part of the faceless audience. He gazed only at Erin, sang only to her.

And it didn't take Matt more than the length of one song to realize that Travis was still trying to win his ex-wife back. The first song was about a man falling in love with a woman with hair the color of a sunset. The second song was about a wedding. The third, about a fight—and making up afterward. The fourth, about a peach nightgown and a lovely sleeping face.

It was a strange, stomach-jarring shock for Matt to realize what was happening. He heard the man singing with passion and power and longing. Heard a voice that was incredible in its surging emotions.

Heard a man making love to Erin with music.

And Matt wondered—even he wondered—how Erin could possibly resist the passion and pain and longing in his voice. How any woman could.

He fought the urge to turn and gaze at her profile, taking what comfort he could from the fact that her hand was still warm and steady in his grasp. But he was, in a sense, helpless to fight Travis now. He couldn't fight with the same weapons. He couldn't claim a year of Erin's life—much less remind her of it in such a strong, revealing way.

Even though Matt believed Stuart Travis had never felt the

depth of emotion between himself and Erin, he nonetheless heard it in Travis's voice, in his songs.

Then, catching a second flickering glance from the man onstage, Matt realized something else. Travis was attempting a double blow. He was deliberately, mockingly flaunting his entire relationship with Erin beneath Matt's nose—and reminding her passionately of every day they'd spent together. And every night.

Matt kept himself still by sheer willpower, staring at the singer, dimly aware that if eyes had been knives, Travis would have lost his life.

The singer sang, on and on, songs of his life with Erin. And she hadn't exaggerated, Matt thought. Every facet of their life together had been set to music.

Even the loss of a baby.

Matt tightened his hold on her hand as he heard that song, appalled that the man could have been so callous—and so hypocritical. To Erin he had shown no regret, no grief; to the world he could show both.

From Erin, Matt could feel no reaction at all. He glanced at her profile quickly, seeing only a calm and detached interest, and some of his own tension drained away. That was when he felt her squeeze his hand gently, and he realized that she was very aware of his reaction to all this.

Travis kept singing. Song by song, the passion and appeal in his voice grew stronger, his lean face more intent, his gestures more controlled.

Finally, as the crowd was wildly applauding a song about the painful end of a marriage, Travis smiled a curious twisted smile. He looked directly at Matt for the first time, a long and steady look. Then he saluted the other man in a gesture that seemed to mock both of them.

And sang a last song. A song about an ex-wife's unexpected visit . . . and a very final ending. There was, it seemed, another man. A man who knew how to summon fire, and hold it. A man who had found a woman's love.

Then the stage went abruptly dark, the last echoes of the song ringing out in the blackness of despair.

The crowd went crazy, and was still wildly applauding when the houselights came up. There was no curtain call; Stuart Travis never returned to the stage to accept accolades. The curtains remained closed.

As the rest of the crowd began to rise, Matt did also, almost afraid to look at Erin. She stood at his side, her hand still within his grasp, and said nothing.

Matt nerved himself and looked at her.

She was smiling. "He's very talented. I'd forgotten. And that last bit, killing the lights like that, was very effective, don't you think?"

Matt drew a deep breath. "Very effective. The hair on the back of my neck stood up."

She laughed a little. "Another award winner, that song."

The crowd was moving, surging toward exits, and they had no choice but to move along with the tide. There was no time and no privacy to say what needed to be said, so they were silent. It took nearly half an hour to get out of the building and find their car in the lot.

They sat in the car and watched the tangle of vehicles that would take at least an hour to clear out, and Matt made no effort to join the rush to leave. He talked very quietly, in a voice that was conversational with an effort.

"I knew he was talented . . . but not like that. I listened to him and—I told myself he wouldn't get you back. I told myself you knew him too well now to be fooled by his songs. But I was so afraid he'd win."

Utterly calm, Erin said, "There was never a chance of that."

In the brightness of the parking lot, with the headlights of passing cars flashing from time to time, he could see her very clearly. She looked completely calm. Then she met his gaze and smiled, and he felt his heart lurch at the love he saw.

"Never a chance," she repeated. "Matt, I knew what he was trying to do. And I didn't feel a thing. Oh, I admired his talent, but that was all."

"You're . . . sure?" he asked softly.

"Completely sure." She turned, sliding her arms around his neck, smiling. "I love you, Matt."

Matt drew her even closer and kissed her, his heart pounding, only then realizing how tense he had been, how troubled. Even knowing the shallowness and selfishness beneath Stuart Travis's extraordinary talent, Matt had felt the incredible pull of emotions the other man had flung at them.

And he felt humbled, suddenly, that this woman had chosen him over that other man. It was not a rational thought; he knew that Erin had found in himself qualities Travis could never lay claim to, qualities she needed. But there was an instinctive part of him that was triumphant, as one male always is when he defeats another male.

"I love you," he whispered when he could, drinking in the glow of her green eyes, the tender smile.

"I've nothing at all against your sister and brother-in-law," Erin murmured, "but do we have to go back to their house?" With direct and husky honesty, she added, "I don't want to wait anymore, Matt."

Chapter Nine

He felt as nervous as a sixteen-year-old.

Matt hung up the phone after offering a somewhat incoherent explanation to Ally, then sat and counted to ten silently as he tried to slow his runaway pulse. It didn't work. He stared at the bathroom door and listened to the shower. That didn't help his pulse either.

Rising from the bed where he'd been sitting, he paced slowly over to the window and stared out. They had found this hotel and checked in, with Erin grinning a little at their lack of baggage; Matt had arrogantly stared down the politely surprised desk clerk, resisting an urge to sign the register in the name of Mr. and Mrs. Smith.

It was ridiculous, of course, but he'd found himself forced to deal with several peculiar thoughts and urges since meeting Erin. He had never thought much about conventions of behavior—until now. Modern morals being what they were, he was even vaguely surprised that the desk clerk had looked surprised.

He couldn't help but be amused by himself, realizing that being in love had changed him in many ways. He found himself caring more about conventions, about the opinions of others. Not for himself—but for Erin. He wanted nothing, absolutely nothing, to tarnish their feelings for each other.

He wanted her to have nothing to regret.

He knew that neither of them would regret this night.

Restless, Matt took off his jacket and tossed it over a chair, hardly noticing the bright furnishings of the room. He stood for a moment, staring at that other door, then started toward it, shedding clothing erratically.

The bathroom was steamy, the mirror fogged. Behind the opaque shower curtain, he could barely make out the shape of her body. Hesitating only momentarily, Matt pulled the curtain aside and stepped into the hot, wet enclosure.

She turned, her arms lifted as she thrust fingers through the heavy mass of her wet hair, and smiled slowly. "What took you so long?"

For a moment Matt could only stare at her. His gaze moved slowly over her lovely face, lingering to watch droplets of water trickle gently down the slope of her firm, full breasts. His eyes traced the narrow width of her rib cage, the tiny waist, rounded hips, and long legs, all creamy white and utterly beautiful.

His gaze returned slowly to her face, meeting green eyes that were deep and dark. With infinite restraint his hands lifted to her waist, the touch of her wet flesh a physical shock he could feel down to his bones. He drew her slowly closer, feeling her hands resting lightly on his shoulders, his eyes intent on the droplets of water clinging to her lips.

He bent his head, his mouth touching hers very lightly, tongue searching out the glittering drops of water. He felt her breasts touch his chest, two points of fire branding him, and a harsh sound found its way from the depths of his chest and lost itself in her mouth.

His hands were stroking her body compulsively, learning the shape of her with an unsteady touch. He could feel the fire in her, the response that was instant and total rising up to meet his desire like a wall of flame.

Holding her slippery body, he trailed his lips down her throat, tasting the clean wetness of her flesh. He felt her fingers lock suddenly in his hair as his mouth found a hard nipple, and felt more than heard her gasp. Her head fell back, causing the shower spray to sprinkle over them both.

Matt hardly noticed. Senses starved for the touch of her could hardly be sated now; he couldn't get enough of her. One hand slid down to the small of her back, pulling her lower body hard against his until they were almost as close as they could be.

Almost.

Sanity reared a reluctant head then, and he realized their need was too frantic to allow for athletic contortions in the shower. He turned off the shower blindly and swept back the curtain, keeping an arm around her, reaching for towels.

It took an agony of patience to delay long enough to dry each other in hurried silence and every instant his eyes met hers seemed to stop his heart. He flung the towels aside and gathered her up, lifting her into his arms and carrying her through to the bedroom.

Seconds later, the covers of the wide bed thrown back, Matt gazed down on her lovely face and groaned softly. "Erin . . . my God, you're so beautiful . . ."

Her lips parted beneath his, jade eyes only half open as they looked into his own. Her hands molded his shoulders, traced his spine slowly. One silken leg moved to brush his hip in a smooth, tingling caress.

He lifted his head at last, breathing harshly, their gazes locked. He felt one of her hands slide over his chest, the other along his ribs. Her lips were swollen, beautifully red, her breasts rising and

falling quickly. She was looking at him, he thought dimly, as if he
were everything she had ever wanted out of life.

"Matt . . ."

He reached desperately for some kind of control, a part of him
strongly aware of the need to take all the time they could master.
His hands moved to shape rounded flesh, his mouth surrounding
the hard, throbbing tip of her breast. His own body demanded,
pushing recklessly for satisfaction, but Matt found a thread of control and hung on fiercely.

He traced the valley between her breasts with his lips, moving
slowly downward over the quivering flesh of her stomach. His
tongue dipped hotly into her navel, and he felt a stronger quiver,
heard a faint sound from her. He slid his hands along her long legs,
rubbing slowly over the satiny skin, moving back up along her hips
and under them. He kissed the sensitive hollows above each leg.

He could feel the restless heat of her, and murmured something
low in his throat soothingly, his fingers seeking the slick, hot center of her desire. Erin moaned softly when he found it, her body
twisting in a sudden helpless reaction.

She could feel his lips touching her thighs, caressing, moving
ever closer to the tormenting fingers. Her legs trembled and there
was a molten heat in the pit of her belly, burning her. She wanted
to scream, to cry out some wild cry of need and pleasure and
agony. And she did cry out softly when she felt his lips touch the
ache. She cried out wordlessly, her nerves splintering, all her
breath leaving her for an instant in a gasp.

She felt as if she were stretched tightly, about to break, her heart
pounding against her ribs with thuds she could feel strongly. All her
consciousness seemed to focus on him, on what he was doing to her,
and if she could have found words, she would have asked him why
he was doing this, why he was tormenting her this way.

But she could find no voice, no words, and the plea in her mind
was a desperate, growing agony. She didn't think she could stand

it; her entire body rebelled against the torture, twisting restlessly, and her heart was choking her.

He moved, finally, rising above her with a taut face and blazing eyes, every muscle rigid and quivering. He hesitated, gazing down into her awakened, striving face, seeing the tense desperation there, seeing the jade fire in her eyes.

His own control broke into splinters and his body joined hers in a sudden thrust. Erin cried out, her eyes widening, conscious of nothing but the sheer pleasure of him deep within her. There was an emptiness now filled, and the ache in her was partially satisfied. She cradled his body, her limbs moving to enclose him, feeling the strength and power of him, feeling their hearts pounding together.

There was no time for gentleness, no desire for it. From the first instant they were matched, their bodies moving instantly into a savage rhythm. Tension built strongly, winding tighter and tighter, hot and powerful.

Erin could feel her body reaching, stretching mindlessly for something almost beyond her grasp. But it was there and she knew it, knew somehow that Matt could take her somewhere she'd never been before, somewhere glorious. And she clung to him, murmuring a plea she didn't hear, the emptiness in her filling . . . filling . . . bursting suddenly in a splintering explosion of sensations beyond pleasure. Her entire body shook, heat searing her, and her cry was a breathless sound of exaltation.

Matt groaned harshly when her body contracted around him, his own body surging toward release. He buried himself in her, the white-hot strain of his need giving way suddenly in a burst of sheer ecstasy . . .

She wouldn't let him leave her, her arms tightening mutely when he would have. He kissed the hot flushed skin of her breasts and shoulders, looking at last into her wondering eyes. She was smiling when he kissed her lips, her hands moving over his shoulders slowly, smoothing his damp flesh.

"I love you," he murmured huskily.

Erin traced his lips with a finger that wasn't quite steady. "I love you, too, Matt . . . so much."

He kissed her again, then lifted his head, his eyes flickering with surprise. Erin felt the stirring within her, the renewal of passion, and her body responded instantly.

Matt caught his breath, his eyes half-closing in pleasure. He moved only to gently torment the hard buds of her breasts, his lips and tongue languidly caressing.

Erin locked her fingers in his hair, a soft, kittenlike sound of pleasure escaping her lips. She could feel the slow throbbing within her, feel her body catch the rhythm of it, match it. Tense, she held herself still, eyes closed, breathing shallowly. It was, this time, a soft, slow building of need, a gradual rising of heat.

Tremors shook them both, rhythmic tremors growing in intensity until they gasped suddenly with one breath, bodies straining together for an endless moment before relaxing, going limp, and sated . . .

Erin thought that Matt must have turned out the bedside lamp and drawn the covers up around them; she didn't think she had but couldn't remember. She knew only that she had never before slept so deeply and peacefully.

She woke in the gray dawn hours, aware that her body had prodded her, hungry for these new and wonderful sensations. Matt was awake, stroking her body gently, familiar now with all her most sensitive spots. Drowsy and willing, Erin responded instantly to his touch. She accepted him with natural grace, cradling him, holding him. Moving with him in a gentle, steady rhythm that quickened only gradually until the tension grabbed them sharply

and flung them upward in a surge of delight that left them clinging wordlessly to each other.

W*hen Erin woke again, it was late in the morning. She lay in con-*
tentment for a while, her head on Matt's shoulder and his arms
around her. Stirring finally, she carefully eased herself from his
embrace and slid from the bed. He murmured something and
turned his face into her pillow, and she smiled a little.

She found his discarded shirt on the floor near the bathroom
and picked it up, shrugging into it. A few moments later she spoke
softly into the telephone, ordering breakfast for them.

Matt slept on.

But he woke with a start when a loud knocking sounded at their
door sometime later. He sat up abruptly, blinking.

"Am I decent?" Erin asked him, looking down at herself wearing only his shirt.

Matt took a long look, the sight very effectively waking him up,
and said simply, "No."

She giggled.

"You are not," he said, "going to the door in nothing but my
shirt. Hang on a minute," he added in a much louder voice directed
at the door. He slid from the bed, reaching for discarded clothing.
"Who is that?" he asked, nodding toward their visitor.

"Room service. I was hungry." She sat on the bed and drew her
legs up to sit like a Buddha.

Matt straightened, dressed now in his trousers, and gazed down
at her for a considering moment. Then he sighed, bent to flip a corner of the bedspread over her legs, and went to answer the door.

Erin sat, pensive and silent, until Matt had gotten rid of the
waiter. He wheeled the table into the room after shutting the door
behind the young man—who hadn't been able to keep his eyes
strictly front and center.

"You're dangerous," he told Erin dryly.

She smiled at him, and Matt felt his heart lurch. *I'll never get over this feeling*, he thought, and it was a wonderful thought. He looked at her, sitting so sweetly in the tumbled bed, her glorious hair falling over her shoulders in a shining curtain of copper, and he felt deeply sorry for any man who didn't have an Erin of his own.

Caveman thoughts, those, but he didn't think she'd mind.

After breakfast—eaten in comfort on the bed—Matt announced his intention of remaining in the hotel for a week. At least.

"We don't have any clothes," she reminded him thoughtfully.

"We don't need any."

"People might wonder."

"Let them." Then he frowned a little. "Would that bother you?"

Erin was surprised. "Of course not, darling. We'll pitch a tent in Times Square if you like—" Her offer ended on a gasp as she found herself tackled gently; she was lying flat on her back with Matt smiling down at her.

"That's the first time," he said between kisses, "you've called me darling. We're going to stay here two weeks."

"But, darling—"

"Three weeks."

Erin giggled and abandoned the world.

They did stay in Denver for two weeks—and a rushed two weeks at that. Blood tests and a license took little time, but a gleeful Ally had sent out a call to the Gavin clan and all showed up for the wedding.

Penny swooped all over the city in a small plane trailing a banner behind her that said IT'S ABOUT TIME, MATT! Her dutiful son was ready to go up and chase her down, but Erin, who had yet to meet the Gavin matriarch, only laughed helplessly.

Erin found herself warmly welcomed by Matt's sisters, all of whom resembled one another—and their mother. They were all tall and dark, and all had clearly married for love—love that had endured. An affectionate family, there was no formality and few manners among them, all of them forthright and cheerful.

Penny Gavin turned out to be a slender, dark-haired woman with an infectious grin and the energetic spirit of all her grandchildren combined. She rushed into Ally's house and hugged Erin delightedly, talking a mile a minute and totally ignoring Matt, who was trying to find out where she'd hidden her plane.

"—and it's going to be just *wonderful* to have you in the family! Good for Matt, you know—"

"Where is it, Mother?"

"—and a redhead! Such lovely hair—"

"Steve, did you see the plane when you picked her up?"

"But I didn't pick her up, Matt—"

"—and I hope you mean to teach him some manners, Erin, because *I* certainly never could—"

"Mother—"

"—interrupting people in the middle of their sentences—"

"Mother, where's the plane?"

Danny came into the room, his large eyes taking in the sight of his favorite uncle. "Uncle Matt, there are two police cars down the street."

"Well, what's happened?"

"I don't know. Unless," he added thoughtfully, "it's grandmother's plane."

"*What?*"

Danny nodded. "She landed in front of Timmy's house—"

"Oh, for gods—"

"Don't fuss, Matt," Penny begged sweetly, and took the arm of a laughing Erin to lead her away. "He fusses so, my dear. You'll have to teach him better—"

"*Mother!*"

With such a beginning, it was hardly surprising that Erin was nearly breathless with laughter by the time they finally got to church. Her own parents had arrived and fit in very well with the Gavins, accepting Penny's talk of altitude and wind velocity without a blink and clearly pleased with Erin's choice of husband.

The ceremony itself was beautiful and grave, both Erin and Matt conscious of the vows they exchanged and of the strong support of their families.

Erin had left the choice of location for a honeymoon to Matt, and was a little curious as to where they'd go. She was even more curious when the whole family escorted them to the small airport near Steve and Ally's home, and laughed helplessly when they were put solemnly aboard Sadie and Steve climbed gravely into the cockpit.

"Where are we going?" Erin asked her husband, having to nearly shout.

He put an arm around her and grinned, but refused to answer. Bemused, Erin watched the miles fall away from the helicopter, knowing only that they weren't going back to her cabin. They swooped away to the southwest, ending up some considerable time later, and after a stop to refuel, on an island off the coast of California.

It was a small island with a golden beach—and a single neat cottage shaded by tall palm trees.

Erin was wordless when Sadie landed and they climbed out. She stood gazing around her, delight growing, while Matt and Steve transferred bags into the cottage. When Steve and his trusty steed had disappeared into the distance—blaring Ravel for the first time during the trip—she turned to Matt with an incredulous smile.

"Matt . . . it's beautiful!"

He smiled, leading her into the cottage and watching her look around at the comfortable furnishings. "I thought you'd like it. It belongs to a friend of mine—loaned to us for as long as we like."

"I'll never get my book finished," she murmured, going into his arms.

"Your publisher," Matt said graciously, "has decided to postpone your deadline. Indefinitely."

"He's *such* a nice man. I must buy him a tie or something for Christmas."

"I can think of things he'd rather have."

"Oh? What, for instance?"

"A little . . . TLC. For the man who has everything."

Erin smiled slowly. "Well, that's fine—except that all my tender loving care is spoken for."

"Oh?"

"Mmm. My husband, you know."

"Lucky so-and-so."

Erin kissed his chin. "No, I'm the lucky one. I came home one day and found him sitting on my doorstep, and I was angry. I told him to go away. But thanks to whatever fates were watching over us, he didn't go."

"He was stubborn?"

"Wonderfully stubborn."

He kissed her, then said in a conversational tone, "Do you know that my toes still curl when you smile at me?"

She bit the inside of her cheek. "Um . . . really? Is that why you looked so peculiar at the altar?"

"Well, it's an odd reaction to have while committing one's life to someone. I mean—honestly. You'd think a grown man could control his toes."

She choked. "Yes. You'd think."

"And his urges." Matt began unfastening the buttons of her blouse, frowning in concentration. "But . . . somehow . . . I can't seem to do it."

"I can't imagine why," she responded solemnly, her own hands busy with his pants. "It's not at all civilized, you know."

"Yes, but what can I do about it?"

"I suppose"—Erin caught her breath as warm lips found her throat—"you should follow . . . your urges . . ."

"Oh, I agree," he murmured. "I really do."

*   *   *

In the two weeks of being with Matt almost constantly, Erin had discovered a wonderful new world of sheer pleasure. Pleasure in his company, in their conversations, in their laughter.

And in their loving.

Most of all, their loving.

Every time he took her in his arms, she wondered if it could possibly get any better. And every time, it did. With growing knowledge of each other came growing pleasure, even when it seemed impossible that there were still pleasures to learn.

When Matt carried her to the bed in their honeymoon cottage, Erin wondered again if it could . . . possibly . . . get even better.

It could.

And did.

Five years passed. Two little girls—Amanda and Nicole—played in the Gavin house in New York State, with summers spent in the mountains of Colorado. Three more best sellers had been written, the second one completed just as the first stages of another kind of labor began, and the third written in the midst of children's demands in a cheerfully cluttered household.

Six years saw the addition of a son. Lee.

Also two ponies. And a litter of puppies after Chester brought his mate home and she decided to stay. Also a kitten Amanda "found" at a friend's house.

On their tenth anniversary, Matt and Erin returned to the cottage on the little island.

And it just kept getting better.

Return
Engagement

For Jewel—
A friend indeed . . .

Chapter One

"You're off your mark, Miss Collins!"

The harsh voice scraped across Tara's nerves like finger-nails on a blackboard, and she resisted an impulse to scream in sheer frustration. It was the third time Bradley had interrupted the rehearsal—and he wasn't even the director, for heaven's sake! Whirling to confront her tormentor, she shouted, "I was *not* off my mark! This is exactly where Derek told me to stand!"

The big, casually dressed man who was leaning easily against the low wall of the veranda a few feet away returned her glare with a cutting smile. "But he didn't tell you to plaster yourself all over Gallows like a second skin. This isn't an X-rated film, Miss Collins. Force yourself to remember that."

Tara made a choked sound that was half a gasp of outrage and half a smothered oath. "You've got a hell of a nerve!" she managed to say at last, her blue eyes shooting sparks of rage and embar-rassment. How dare he speak to her like that in front of all these people! "Get your mind out of the gutter, Mr. Bradley. This is supposed to be a love scene—which you'd know if you'd read the script—and I did *not* plaster myself all over Randy!"

Bradley laughed briefly. "From where I'm standing, Miss Collins, you looked like an advertisement for a red-light district."

"I'm sure you'd know what *that* looks like," she retorted nastily, and was immediately angry at herself for turning the criticism into a personal remark. And *why* couldn't she tear her eyes away from his lean body? Reading the gleam in his silvery eyes, she saw that he was about to reply to her remark, and spoke quickly to head him off. "Just because you're backing this film doesn't give you the right to stand around criticizing everything we do!"

His wide shoulders lifted in a shrug. "I have to protect my investment, Miss Collins," he returned coolly. "And that investment does, in fact, give me the right to criticize. I'd also like to point out that my money pays your salary."

"So?" she demanded.

"So watch yourself, Miss Collins," he told her in a silky tone that didn't quite hide the steel. "As much as I enjoy crossing swords with you, there comes a time in every match when one opponent must concede defeat."

"Oh? Are you waving the white flag already?" she asked with sweet innocence.

He shifted slightly, impatiently, and Tara found her eyes once again drawn to his powerful body. "I hold the upper hand in this match, Tara, and you know it," he snapped.

Tara sensed heads turning and ears pricking as the cast and crew noticed Bradley's lapse from formal address to the use of her first name. Furious with him for stepping over the line she had drawn between them three years before, she bit out coldly, "Your ego defies description, *Mr.* Bradley! Don't be so damned sure of yourself!"

His silver-gray eyes narrowed sharply, and Tara knew he understood the reason for the sudden intensity of her anger. Before he could take yet another step across the invisible line separating them, she put the conversation firmly back on a professional footing.

"Mr. Bradley," she began, in a sweet tone expressly calculated to drive a saint to murder, "why were all of us hired?"

Arms folded over his massive chest, Bradley smiled across at her, his even white teeth reminding Tara of a wolf on the prowl. "I should think you'd know the answer to that, *Miss* Collins. You've been in the business long enough."

Her teeth came together with an audible snap. "Look, you complained not three days ago that we were behind schedule and over budget. Don't you think we'd finish this picture a lot faster if you didn't drive out here every day just to interfere?"

Tara was just beginning to work up a good head of steam, and she relished the feeling. "If you think you can do everything so much better than us, then do it!" she invited acidly. "Handle the cameras, direct the picture, even star in it! But you're going to have a hell of a time fitting into my costume!" Her slender hands indicated the silk dress she was wearing, which clung flatteringly to every inch of her lush body.

"Finished?" Bradley inquired courteously.

"Only if you're leaving." She glared at him.

"I'm not leaving."

"Then I'm not finished!" She took a deep breath and gave her temper full rein. "I'll admit that this is a good part, but I have better things to do than stand around in the desert and listen to you snipe at me!"

One dark brow lifted sardonically. "Are you threatening to walk out, Miss Collins?"

"Oh, you'd like that, wouldn't you? Well, I'm not about to break my contract, Mr. Bradley. If you don't like the way I'm handling this part, fire me!"

"Keep it up, Miss Collins, and I just might." His deep voice was a little grim.

Elated at having finally goaded him, Tara opened her mouth to prod him a bit more, hoping that he'd get angry enough to leave them in peace, but she was forestalled by her obviously worried costar.

"Tara, why don't we take a little break while Derek gets set up for this scene?" Randy suggested hastily. "It's been a long morning. I'm sure Mr. Bradley understands that we're all tired—"

"You stay out of this!" Bradley interrupted fiercely, his silver eyes shooting metallic sparks in a dangerous warning. "You're not up to her weight!"

"Neither are you!" Tara snapped back. From the corner of her eye she saw Randy throw up his hands in defeat and retire to the opposite side of the veranda. Then she forgot about him. She was too wrapped up in writing another chapter in her years-long feud with the annoying Devlin Bradley. "And stop ordering people around!" she added for good measure.

"I sign the paychecks, spitfire. That gives me the right to order people around."

Irritably Tara wondered why that particular insult sounded more like an endearment from an amused and indulgent lover. She began heatedly, "You can take your paycheck and—"

"Fifteen minutes, people," Derek, the director, intervened hastily, rising from his chair, "then we'll shoot the scene."

Tara turned to him, but when Derek met her glare with a wry plea in his eyes, she gave up. Stalking over to the farthest corner of the veranda, she found a spot in the shade and sat down in a wicker chair. She was hoping that her abrupt change of mood had angered Devlin Bradley, but when she glanced his way she found him strolling over to talk to one of the cameramen.

Irritated, she watched Derek approach her with the watchful, wary gaze of a man whose pet kitten has suddenly turned into a lioness, and her sense of humor abruptly righted itself. Grimacing apologetically, she murmured, "Sorry, Derek—but he makes me so mad." With effort, she kept her voice low.

"No—really?" Derek leaned against the low wall beside Randy and gave her a look of comical surprise. "Well, now, I never would have guessed that if you hadn't pointed it out."

"It must be her red hair," Randy murmured thoughtfully.

"No, I think it's Bradley," Derek disagreed in a contemplative tone, for all the world as though Tara were invisible. "There must be something peculiar in his chemistry. Or hers. Every time they're within ten feet of each other, the sparks start flying."

"Hey!" Tara waved a hand to attract their attention. "I'm here, you know. Don't talk about me as if I weren't."

Derek and Randy exchanged looks, and then Derek looked down at Tara with the same wry plea in his eyes. "Honey, we only have two scenes to go, and then we can all leave this damned desert. Do you think you can put a rein on that temper of yours for the rest of the day? You're twenty-six years old. You should be able to control it by now."

"Bradley's thirty-six—why can't he control *his* temper?" Tara asked mutinously.

Randy lifted a sandy brow, his rugged face curious. "How do you know how old he is, Tara?"

Tara felt a flush rise in her cheeks, but forced herself to look calm. "How do you think? If he so much as sneezes it makes the papers. His life's no secret."

Randy nodded absently, watching as Derek was called over to settle a slight dispute between two of the technicians. "How did you meet him, Tara? I've been wondering."

"At a premiere party a few years ago," she replied in an offhand manner. "I had a small part in the picture he backed." She stared across to where Bradley was talking to Derek, and grimaced irritably. "Just look at him," she muttered, forgetting her audience. "Not so much as a drop of sweat to prove he's human. And he never loses control. Never. Just once I'd like to see him really blow his stack."

"I wouldn't," Randy said flatly. "Not unless I had a concrete bunker to hide in, anyway. Devlin Bradley strikes me as the sort of man it doesn't pay to rile." He grinned suddenly. "But you just go right on stoking the fire, don't you, Tara? Do you have a death wish?"

With just the right touch of scorn in her voice, Tara responded, "The man is arrogant, egotistical, domineering, and rude. I'm not going to fawn all over him just because everyone else does." She wondered vaguely why she couldn't put such a disagreeable man out of her mind, and why her pulse rate increased so frantically whenever she saw him or heard his voice. It had been three years, for goodness sake!

"Not a member of his fan club, are you?" Randy was asking in an amused tone.

"You could say that," Tara agreed dryly. "His fan club is full of adoring women."

"God knows you'd never be mistaken for one of *those*." Randy laughed. "Tell me something, Tara—did you hate him at first sight, or did it take a year or so for the feelings to build?"

"Oh, at first sight," she replied airily. "The only thing we've ever agreed on is the fact that we can't stand each other." She looked up at him with an easy smile, succeeding at last in tearing her eyes away from Bradley.

"And you've been fighting ever since then?" Randy asked curiously.

"Ever since." Tara changed the subject determinedly. "What's this I hear about a possible engagement for you?"

Randy grimaced slightly. "You've been reading the gossip columns. I only went out with the lady twice, and the press has me engaged to her." In almost the same breath he went on casually, "I wonder if the stories of Bradley's love life are exaggerated. What do you think?"

"I think it's none of my business." Swearing silently at Randy's persistence in talking about her own personal nemesis, Tara managed nonetheless to keep her voice calm.

Ignoring her apparent disinterest, Randy said thoughtfully, "That model he's been seen with for the past few months seems to have the inside track as far as he's concerned. I've even heard whispers of a wedding. That article last month—"

"I read it," Tara interrupted firmly, her mind's eye filling with the image of the gorgeous blonde who had been hanging on Bradley's arm in public with increasing frequency. Pushing the oddly disturbing picture away, she looked up and nodded to acknowledge Derek's signal, then went on smoothly, "Let's go, champ—Derek's ready for us."

To Tara's relief, Randy abandoned his speculation about Bradley and followed her across the veranda to their marks. This time the scene came off without a hitch. Tara wasn't completely satisfied with her performance—she felt a little stiff in Randy's arms after Bradley's earlier remark—but Derek seemed delighted, so she left well enough alone. The cast and crew immediately dispersed for lunch, some heading for cars and the drive to Vegas, some heading for the cool interior of the bungalow or the trailers, parked a few yards away.

Tara headed for her air-conditioned trailer. She wasn't really hungry, and a brief, stabbing pain between her eyes warned her that she needed to get out of the sun.

"Tara."

With one hand on the trailer door she turned in surprise to watch Bradley approach her. A swift glance showed her that no one was close enough to overhear them, but she still wasn't happy about being alone with him. Experience had taught her that with Devlin Bradley around, she was safer in a crowd. "Yes?" she asked haughtily.

Apparently undisturbed by her quelling question, he halted a short distance away and looked at her with unreadable eyes. "I'm driving in to Vegas for lunch," he said calmly. "Come with me?"

Her fingers tightened on the door handle. "No." She hesitated, then added a grudging, "Thank you."

"Such pretty manners," he mocked softly, and then added, with a faint twist of his lips, "Still afraid someone will think you're in cahoots with the boss?"

Tara stiffened, her blue eyes flashing with anger. "You've never forgiven me for that, have you?" she asked stonily. "It dented your ego to think that I preferred my independence to your . . . protection."

He slid his hands into the pockets of his close-fitting black pants and continued to regard her with an unreadable expression. "My ego," he murmured thoughtfully. "Yes, I suppose it did dent my ego. But I offered more than protection, Tara." The silvery eyes raked over her, from her short red curls to her sandal-clad feet, without missing an inch along the way. "I offered marriage."

She smiled bitterly. "And I was supposed to be delighted that you'd decided to make an honest woman of me? No way, Devlin. I'd rather be dishonest."

"Really?" He lifted a mocking brow. "Well, they say there's a streak of the harlot in every woman."

Tara took a hasty step toward him, her face white and her eyes blazing. Anger and bitterness combined to form an icy ball in the pit of her stomach, and the stabbing pain between her eyes increased with the force of her emotions.

Before she could utter the scathing words on her tongue, Devlin said, "I'm sorry." His lean face wore an expression of self-contempt, brief but real. "That was uncalled-for, I know."

"But not totally unexpected." She smiled tightly. "You don't pull any punches, do you, Devlin?"

His remarkable eyes had darkened to a cloudy gray, suddenly somber. "Not with you. But then, we've always been brutally honest with each other, haven't we, Tara?"

"Brutally," she agreed in a flat tone.

After a moment, he said dryly, "Then be honest with me now. Why won't you have lunch with me?"

She hesitated. "I'm not hungry."

Devlin laughed shortly. "If you were starving you wouldn't have lunch with me, would you?"

Her mouth curved in a sudden, mocking smile. "If I were starving I just might. But then, if I were starving I'd have lunch with the devil himself."

"Thanks!" He shifted impatiently. "After three years of your brand of warfare it's a wonder I have any ego at all."

Tara crossed her arms over her breasts and leaned back against the trailer door, staring at him wryly. "You have what they call 'total ego,' Devlin. You know exactly who you are and who you're not, and no one's opinion is going to change that."

"Well, *that* makes me sound lovable as hell!"

"There are a lot of adjectives I could use to describe you," she told him sweetly, "but 'lovable' isn't one of them."

He stared at her for a moment and then grinned suddenly. "That must be one of the reasons I keep hanging around, Tara. You keep me on my toes," he said ruefully. "Pax, huh? Have lunch with me."

Tara swore silently at the faintly pleading look in his eyes, reflecting bitterly that when Devlin turned on the charm, he was incredibly hard to resist. And he knew it, damn him! That smile could charm the devil out of hell, and Devlin used it ruthlessly to get his own way. But not this time. She'd fallen for that smile once, and remembered all too well the heartache it had caused.

"I'm not hungry."

His smile disappeared. "The years haven't changed you, Tara. You're still as stubborn as ever."

"Nothing's changed, Devlin." She looked him squarely in the eye. "Nothing at all."

He nodded slowly, still staring at her. "Yes. Yes, I'm beginning to see that." His silvery eyes reflected a new concern. Almost to himself, he murmured, "You're thin as a rail."

Tara started at the abrupt change of subject and then lied stoutly. "I'm on a diet." She felt torn between irritation and pleasure that he had noticed her weight loss. Irritation won. "Not that it's any of your business," she snapped.

The worry in his eyes spread, until he was scowling slightly. "That's stupid, Tara," he said harshly. "You don't need to lose weight. If anything, you need to gain it. And you're as tense as a drawn bow. What are you trying to do, make yourself sick?"

Relieved that they were back on angry footing, where she felt more secure, she responded flatly, "My appearance is my own business, and I'll thank you to remember that!" Before he could utter a word, she had entered the trailer and slammed the door.

Inside, leaning against the door, Tara glanced around the cozy interior of her motor home and thought vaguely that there was nothing like slamming a door to make a woman feel vindicated.

"Waurr!"

She looked down to see her Siamese cat sitting at her feet, one chocolate-colored paw damped firmly over the tail of a struggling, indignantly squeaking mouse.

"No, Ah Poo," Tara told him flatly. "You can't go out and play. The heat out there would broil you alive. And let Churchill go!"

With a snort peculiar to Siamese cats, Ah Poo released his reluctant toy and watched with indifferent, slightly crossed china-blue eyes as the mouse scurried frantically for the safety of a pair of Tara's shoes, on the floor beside the couch.

Tara leaned over to fish him out, holding him in one hand and absently stroking his tiny head as she stared cautiously through the window beside the door. Devlin was striding toward the bungalow, his stiff shoulders visible evidence of his anger. Apparently he had decided not to drive to Vegas after all.

With a faint sigh Tara turned away from the window and carried the mouse over to a small cage on a low table. Placing Churchill inside, she sank down on the couch and frowned at her cat. "Ah Poo, if you let him out of his cage one more time, I'm going to buy a padlock. You hear me?"

She smiled slightly as Ah Poo merely stared at her. Then she leaned back and rubbed fretfully at the point of stabbing pain between her eyes. She tried to forget Devlin's charming smile. . . .

*The rest of the afternoon crept by with agonizing slowness. Noth-*ing went right. The major problem, Tara decided by four o'clock, was Devlin Bradley, who was making his presence felt with a vengeance. He was obviously in a lousy mood, and taking it out on everybody—particularly Tara. When he verbally lambasted her acting for the sixth time, she began entertaining thoughts of homicide.

She was honestly afraid that if she said a word to him, it would lead to murder—his. Finally she collapsed into a chair on the veranda and tried to get a grip on her raging temper. The pain between her eyes had become a blinding agony, and she only half saw Derek coming toward her. He was frowning.

He leaned against the low wall beside her and smiled sympathetically. "Shall we take up a collection and hire a hit man?" he asked ruefully.

Tara managed a weary smile. "You don't have to do that. I'll pay the whole tab. All I ask is the pleasure of watching him get it."

Derek grinned. "You look as though you've already gone ten rounds with him." He gestured at Tara's costume, which was mostly rags—jeans and a cotton top. The scene they were trying to film dramatized her return from a terrifying night alone in the desert.

Tara leaned her chin on one hand and stared grimly across to where Devlin was berating one of the cameramen. "How does one hire a hit man, anyway?" she asked absently. "That would solve all our problems." When the silence remained unbroken, she looked up to find Derek frowning at her.

"Do you feel okay?" he asked slowly. "Your color's not right."

"A headache, that's all." She shrugged. "And you didn't answer my question. How does one go about hiring a hit man? I don't think they move in my circles."

"It's not exactly something they taught me in director's school," Derek responded dryly. He hesitated for a moment, then went on casually, "You wait here. I think I'll go and have a word with the man. Be right back."

As he rose to his feet, Tara warned, "Better speak softly and carry a big stick. That's the only kind of conversation 'the man' understands."

Derek grinned and left her. Tara leaned her head against the back of her chair. With her eyelids drooping to cut out most of the glare from the fiery sun, she acknowledged to herself that she should have passed this picture by and taken a vacation. She had been lucky to have work for the past three years, to be too busy to take more than a brief rest between projects. Now she had a sneaking suspicion that her body was warning her to slow down . . . or else.

She always found it difficult to work on one of Devlin's films, because their constant and often heated arguments drained the energy she needed for her work. But over the years she had learned to cope. Or at least she thought she had. Now she wasn't so sure. Why did she feel so tired?

"Can't you handle a prima donna, Derek?"

The sneering voice brought Tara upright with a jerk. Across the veranda her eyes met the searing brightness of Devlin's mocking gaze. Almost at once she realized that Derek had tried to postpone production—probably for her sake—and that Devlin thought she was faking an illness.

That one phrase—prima donna—was all it took to send the adrenaline flowing through her veins once again. She jumped to her feet, cheeks flushed with anger and eyes glittering. "I'm ready to shoot the scene, Derek," she called.

"We're all tired—" Derek began.

"Then, the sooner we wrap this scene, the sooner we can all go home," Tara cut in ruthlessly. "I'm ready when you are."

Derek shot an angry look at Devlin, then nodded reluctantly and stalked toward the cameras. "Let's go, people!" he shouted.

Without glancing at Devlin, Tara headed out into the desert to where the cameras would pick her up. With the ease of long practice she cleared her mind of everything except the character she was portraying and silently reviewed her lines.

Five minutes later the cameras were rolling and Tara was stumbling across a harsh, unfriendly desert. She was a woman alone, abandoned by her lover to live or die, her strength sapped by terror and heartache. She had risked everything for love, pinned her trust and faith on a man as cold and fickle as the stars, and he had left her raw and bleeding.

Lurching, falling, picking herself up to stagger on, her blue eyes were fixed on the looming bungalow with a hopelessness and desperation that teetered on the brink of madness. Tears cleaned furrows down her dirty cheeks. Her breath came in harsh rasps.

Stumbling the last few yards, she leaned against the low wall of the veranda and in a hoarse voice called out the name of her lover, knowing all the while that he wouldn't answer. He didn't. Sobbing in pain and exhaustion, she gripped the wall with white-knuckled fingers and cursed his name bitterly. And then a scream of sheer agony ripped from her throat, and she slid down the wall to stare across the unfeeling desert landscape with bleak, empty eyes. "Damn you," she murmured weakly, raggedly. "Damn you to hell . . ."

There was a long silence. Then Derek yelled, "Cut! Print it!"

Tara swallowed the sick feeling in her throat and painfully rose slowly to her feet, wondering vaguely why the scenery around her seemed to be swaying crazily. As if from far away she heard the crew burst into spontaneous applause. But her eyes passed by them to search out Devlin Bradley. He stood apart from the others, his arms folded across his chest. Their eyes locked, and the expression of respect in his steady gaze was the last thing Tara saw before she began to fall. And then blackness overwhelmed her.

Chapter Two

Tara was dimly aware of many voices speaking at once, of hands touching her gently, of someone harshly, urgently calling her name. But it seemed too difficult to respond. Her hearing kept fading in and out. She was vaguely aware that someone was issuing a great many orders in a commanding voice. The sound irritated her, although she didn't know why.

And then she was floating. The sound of distant, steady thunder echoed in her ears, and the confusion of many voices faded away. Something warm and smelling of a curiously familiar spicy scent was wrapped around her. She felt safe and cared for.

Dreams came and went. Some were absurd dreams of talking annuals and spaceships and people with wacky personalities. Some were nightmares—a rat's maze, a dark cave, a house with hundreds of rooms and no windows. Thunder rumbled and lightning flashed, making her cringe in terror. She wanted to call out to someone, but the name would not form in her clouded mind.

Finally the dreams faded away into darkness. More than once

she was conscious of her hands being pressed gently, of something brushing her cheeks, her forehead. Faint echoes of voices—some calm, some harsh and demanding—touched her dimly, as if from a great distance. And then everything became peaceful.

She woke from time to time, dimly aware that she was in a hospital room but not really troubled by it. Often someone was by her bed, a comforting presence she didn't try to identify. She woke once to find the presence gone, and felt restless and uneasy until it returned, crying out fretfully against the unfamiliar voices trying to calm her. After that the presence was always there.

Several times she found herself in a dreamy, half-awake state, conscious of lights and shadows and the scent of roses. Voices were more distinct now, and she was able to catch snatches of conversation going on around her. The conversation wasn't very interesting. Two men seemed to be talking about someone who was ill. She roused herself enough to mutter to them to go away and leave her in peace, and was answered with a huskily amused laugh from a voice that sounded vaguely familiar.

At first it took a great effort to struggle to regain semiconsciousness. The demands of her body for rest were too strong to fight. Slowly, though, she realized that she was sleeping only because she wanted to, not because she had to. Her workaholic nature immediately rebelled at that thought. What was she doing in a hospital, anyway? She wasn't sick. And she had a picture to do in just a few weeks. She couldn't afford to lie around in a hospital bed all day.

Irritated with herself, and at whoever had officiously stuck her in here, Tara opened her eyes. She felt wide awake and reasonably fit, a little tired, perhaps—but that was only to be expected. She had been working hard, after all.

Sunlight filled the room and fell across vases of flowers lining a low chest by the door. Tara decided absently that she must have slept all night. Her eyes followed the shafts of light across the room to the window, falling at last on the man standing there.

His dark hair was a bit rumpled, his coat discarded and lying over a chair in the corner. The stark masculinity of his profile was etched for her in the light shining through the window—a high, intelligent forehead, an aquiline nose, a firm-lipped mouth. The strong jaw was shadowed with at least a day's growth of beard. Sleepy lids hid a pair of eyes that, she knew, were of such a light gray as to appear silver. Hard, keen eyes that could—but only rarely did—glow with molten fire.

At five feet eight inches tall, Tara was not a small woman, but the man standing before the window had always possessed the power to make her feel small. It might have been his own size—he was six feet four inches and built like a football player—or it might have been the sheer force of his personality. One glance from those silvery eyes warned her that he was a man to be reckoned with.

And Tara knew that well. Oh, yes—she knew that very well.

She watched him for a long time, secure in the knowledge that he was unaware she had awakened. It was a rare opportunity to study him unobserved, and Tara was appalled by just how much she wanted to look at him. Not for the first time, she wondered if she had been wrong three years ago when she had refused to give up her career for him.

It wouldn't have worked out, she assured herself miserably. She was an actress, dammit, not a little housewife. She immediately amended the unfair thought. She wouldn't have been a "little housewife," and she knew it. Just another business wife, bored to tears at business dinner-parties and listening to other business wives talk about who was sleeping with whom and the shocking cost of decorators.

It wasn't as if he'd given her a good reason to abandon her career for marriage. He hadn't even mentioned love, for instance. Or children. In fact, he'd given her no reason at all to suppose that she would have been anything more than a bird in a gilded cage. And be it ever so lovely or comfortably furnished, a cage was still a cage. What was she supposed to do—sit around all day filing her nails?

Why had he wanted to marry her, anyway? Probably, she decided irritably, because he had grown tired of having women chase him. And since she'd been the first one in line, she had received the offer.

Angry at her thoughts, Tara turned her eyes to the ceiling. It was done. Over. There was no reason to think about it any longer.

"How do you feel?"

Blinking, she discovered that Devlin was standing by the bed, staring down at her with unreadable eyes. She turned her gaze back to the ceiling and answered flatly, "Like I've been run over by a truck—twice. Were you driving it?" From the corner of her eye, she saw his face tighten.

"In a manner of speaking." He pulled a chair forward and sank into it. "Dammit, Tara, why did you do it?"

The outburst startled her. Without thinking, she turned her head to stare at him blankly.

"Why did you let me goad you into driving yourself too hard?" he demanded harshly.

Irritated, she responded evenly, "What did you expect me to do after you called me a prima donna?"

"I didn't know you were really ill."

"Have I *ever*," she shot back coldly, "held up production with a fake illness?"

His lips formed a tight line. "No. But you were angry enough that day to fake an illness. You should have—"

"What do you mean 'that day'?" she interrupted. "You talk as if it were days ago."

He stared at her for a moment. "It was. You collapsed the day before yesterday."

She was shocked, but tried to hide it by murmuring, "I was just a little tired, that's all. I must have needed the sleep."

"A little tired?" Devlin shook his head, looking grim. "You were exhausted—pure and simple. The doctor said you should have taken a long vacation months ago. Stupid little fool."

The last comment, apparently tacked on as an afterthought, did nothing for Tara's uncertain temper. "I'm neither stupid nor little," she informed him irritably. "Stop treating me like a child."

"Then stop acting like one! For God's sake, Tara, anyone with a grain of sense would have realized what was happening. I'm beginning to believe you need a keeper."

"You've thought that all along," she snapped, tears welling up in her eyes. She was immediately angry with him for being present to witness her unusual weakness.

Reaching over to cover one of her restless hands with his, Devlin said quietly, "You're experiencing the aftereffects of the exhaustion, Tara. The doctor said you won't feel like yourself for a while. Don't be afraid."

Tara wasn't particularly surprised by his seeming ability to read her mind, because he'd often displayed that uncanny knack in the past. But his gentleness disturbed her, and his touch brought back memories she wanted badly to forget. Snatching her hand away, she muttered tightly, "Why are you here, Devlin? Guilty conscience?"

He sat back in his chair with a frown. After a moment his lids dropped to veil his eyes, and he responded coolly, "I was the only one without commitments elsewhere. The others stayed as long as they could, though. Derek and Randy have called every day to check on you, and the whole production crew sent flowers." He nodded toward the colorful offerings on either side of the door.

"That was kind of them." A sudden thought made Tara's eyes widen in horror. "Ah Poo! What—"

"It's all right," Devlin interrupted calmly. "I've got him at my apartment." He grinned suddenly. "Randy had the noble intention of taking the cat to L.A. and keeping him for you, but after Ah Poo nearly scratched his eyes out, he decided to let me take care of the problem. Ah Poo's fine."

Tara looked at him wryly. "I don't suppose you explained to Randy why the cat happens to like you?"

Devlin shrugged. "If you mean did I tell him that I gave you a Siamese kitten three years ago, no. I just told him that the cat obviously had good taste."

Typical Devlin, she thought, and then frowned. "Are we still in Vegas? I didn't know you had an apartment here."

"I don't. A friend of mine does, though."

"I see." Tara thought that she did see, and she was angered by the jealousy that that lanced through her.

With a peculiarly satisfied smile, Devlin said dryly, "A *male* friend, Tara. Jim's in Europe for the summer."

The blush that Tara had never been able to control reddened her cheeks. "I don't care if you have a harem in that apartment," she snapped defensively.

"Well, I don't," he responded calmly. "Just an unhappy housekeeper, a temperamental feline, and a mouse in a padlocked cage."

Tara felt tears rise to her eyes again. "You—you've got Churchill too?"

"Sure. Randy told me about him, and Ah Poo found him for me. When Jim's housekeeper climbed down off a chair for the third time and threatened to quit—also for the third time—I bought a cage and a padlock. Mrs. Henson is happy these days, but Ah Poo's frustrated as hell."

Picturing the whole scene, Tara smiled at him. Devlin's gaze dropped immediately to her mouth. Huskily, he murmured, "That's the first time you've really smiled at me since . . ." His voice trailed away.

Tara immediately returned her gaze to the ceiling, silently damning herself for that unguarded smile. She was in no shape to cope with Devlin Bradley right now, and she knew it. More than anything in the world she wanted him to walk out the door and out of her life. She was afraid of what would happen to her if he stayed.

"Why did we split up, Tara?"

The quiet question made her heart skip a beat, and she willed herself sternly not to look at him. "You know very well why."

"Because you had the fixed idea that if you landed a role in a film—especially one of *my* films—it would be because of our relationship and not your own talent? Because you believed I interfered in your career? Because I asked you to give up your career?"

"All of the above," she answered flippantly.

"You were wrong," he said quietly, ignoring her don't-give-a-damn attitude. "Your talent is too well known for anyone but a fool to believe you'd earned your roles on your back."

Tara winced at the blunt statement. "You have such a delicate way with words."

"Why wrap it up in euphemisms? That was what you were afraid of, wasn't it?"

"Present tense, Devlin." She turned to stare at him bitterly. "That's what I *am* afraid of. I won't be labeled an easy conquest, and I won't be accused of trading on my looks or my relationships with anyone in the industry. I'm an actress. An *actress*. And that's the only way I'll be judged."

"You've already proven that, Tara."

"And I'll have to go on proving it every day. There's a double standard, Devlin, and you know it as well as I do. As long as an actress is hired for her talent, then everything is fine. But it takes only a whisper of casting couch for her career to topple. I won't take that chance."

"You're being paranoid."

"No, *you're* being unrealistic."

A certain grimness had crept into his face, and there was an expression in his eyes that she couldn't quite fathom. It looked almost like anxiety, but Tara knew that couldn't be right. It didn't make sense. Devlin was never anxious. Never.

"Okay," he said slowly, "let's skip that for the moment and go on to the other reasons we split up."

"There's no need to discuss it." Tara moved restlessly in the bed, wishing she had the strength to get up and run away. She didn't want to open old wounds. "It's been dead for three years, Devlin. Why rake over the ashes?"

"Is it dead, Tara? Is it really?"

Suddenly he was sitting on the edge of the bed, staring down at her with silver flames in his eyes. Tara tried to look away, but the magnetic pull of his gaze held her as if in a trap. She was powerless to move even when his hands came out to gently brush aside the loose hospital gown until he found the delicate bones of her shoulders. Striving for some kind of sanity, she said weakly, "It's dead. It *is!*"

Devlin didn't waste time with words. Even as his dark head bent toward her, Tara felt her own lips parting in a helpless acknowledgment of a need too long denied. The touch of his mouth was a searing brand, setting fire to her delusion of having gotten over him. That hard-won belief crumbled into ashes.

Tara felt his tongue probing gently along the sensitive inner surface of her lips, pleading for rather than insisting on a response. The fire of that silent request acted on her body like a torch. She told herself that her illness was excuse enough for her arms to curl around the strong brown column of his neck, that she was obviously addled in the head and in no condition to resist him. Then, having made peace with her conscience, she gave herself up totally to the familiar magic of his touch.

As her mouth blossomed beneath his, Devlin deepened the kiss, his hands moving up to touch her face, her throat. His touch conveyed a hot demand, a hunger that was ravenous in its intensity. It was as if he had been starving for three long years.

The same hunger blossomed within Tara. That deeply buried, carefully hidden part of herself rose to the surface now, as it had always done before, frightening her with its turbulent, aching need. It was not simply a need for his possession—although that was certainly part of it—but a restless yearning for something she had never been able to put a name to. And could not now. She knew only that no other man had the power to touch her as deeply as Devlin did.

His lips left hers to trail across her cheek, one hand sliding down to warmly cup her breast through the thin hospital gown. Tara arched involuntarily against him as she felt the dizzying sensations of his thumb brushing across her nipple and his teeth toying gently with her earlobe. A shaking gasp left her throat. Dimly she was aware of his husky whisper.

"Tara, honey, I want you so badly. It's been hell without you. Stop fighting me, sweetheart."

Caught up in the wild, sweet passion her body remembered so well, Tara made no attempt to fight him. She locked her fingers in his thick, dark hair and pulled his mouth back to hers, welcoming his heavy weight as he leaned fully on top of her.

"Excuse me . . . please."

The dry, laughter-filled voice jerked them apart like puppets on a string. Her cheeks nearly as red as her hair, Tara looked past Devlin's retreating body to see a young doctor whose brown eyes were twinkling merrily. Embarrassment and rage swept over her, and she glared at both men as Devlin straightened casually and raked a hand through the thick hair that her passionate fingers had disarranged.

"Hi, Doc," he said laconically.

If there had been a vase within reach, or a rock, or a club—anything!—Tara would have mustered her strength and done her damndest to brain him. How dared he stand there as calmly as though nothing had happened. How *dared* he! Of all the sneaky, low-down, underhanded tricks—to take advantage of a sick woman. Because, of course, she never would have responded to him if she'd been well . . .

The injustice of that last thought brought a rueful frown to Tara's face, and she shot a glare at Devlin that promised great things along the lines of revenge.

The young doctor came across the room to the bed, smiling apologetically. "I really didn't mean to interrupt. I'm Dr. Easton. How are you feeling, Miss Collins?"

With a very sweet smile Tara replied, "I feel weak, Doctor . . . and very unlike myself." The remark was meant solely for Devlin, and Tara felt a glimmer of satisfaction when she caught his wry smile from the corner of her eye.

"That's to be expected, Miss Collins." Dr. Easton was clearly unaware of any double meaning. "You've had a rough time of it. It'll take awhile for your body to recover its strength. Your fiancé has been telling us about your tendency to push yourself too hard."

Fiancé? What in the world—? Tara opened her mouth to voice her angry questions aloud, but a motion from the corner of her eye caught her attention. Glancing sideways, she saw Devlin give his head a tiny shake, clear warning in his eyes. Oh, God, what had he gotten her into this time? she asked herself wildly.

The doctor continued cheerfully, unconscious of his patient's perturbation. "The human body is a wonderful thing, Miss Collins, but it does have its limits. I'd say you reached yours a good two months ago. You're going to have to learn to slow down."

Tara shifted restlessly beneath the covers. "I'm trying to build a career, Doctor. I don't have time to slow down. How soon can I go back to work? I have a major role in a picture due to begin filming next month."

Easton was shaking his head. "Unless you want to end up right back in the hospital, Miss Collins, you'd better postpone that for a while. At least for a couple of months."

"But . . . the film," she protested, "can't be postponed! Doctor, they won't wait for me. They'll find someone else to do the part. I can't afford to let that happen."

Devlin spoke for the first time, his voice rueful. "I warned you, Doc. She's as stubborn as she is beautiful."

Not the least impressed by the backhanded compliment, Tara glared at him. "You stay out of this!" she warned irritably. "I'm not going to let the best part of my life slip by just because I'm a little tired."

If Easton was surprised by Tara's treatment of her fiancé, he didn't show it. With a trace of a professional chill in his voice, he said calmly, "You'll do as you please, of course, Miss Collins. But if you ignore my advice, your next collapse will prove to be far more serious."

Tara felt Devlin's hand come out to cover hers. She neither questioned the silent reassurance nor withdrew from it. "I see," she said softly.

Easton glanced across the bed at Devlin, then said quietly, "I know it won't be easy for you to do nothing, Miss Collins. From what I understand, you've been one of the busiest actresses in Hollywood during the past few years. But you'd better stop to consider something. Movies are a dime a dozen, but you've only got one body. Don't wear it out."

Tara was tempted to ask him what bad movie he'd gotten those lines from, but bit back the acid question. There was no reason to get angry at him, after all. He was only doing his job and trying to help her. But she still didn't like what he was saying.

"You need rest, Miss Collins," he continued. "Take a couple of months at least—more if you can manage it—and just rest. Catch up on your reading, lie in the sun. You need to avoid the kind of physical and emotional strain you've been under these last months." He shrugged slightly. "Vegas is full of show people, and I've seen quite a few of them professionally. I know what a performance takes out of a person. You just don't have that kind of energy."

Over the public address-system a tinny request filtered into the room. "Dr. Easton, call three-zero-one, please. Dr. Easton, call three-zero-one."

The young doctor smiled faintly. "They're playing my song." Very soberly he added, "There will be other roles, Miss Collins. Take care of yourself for them." He turned and left the room.

Tara stared at the closed door for a long time, her mind in turmoil. Yes, there would be other roles, but who knew how long she'd have to wait for one as terrific as the lead part in *Celebration!*—a big-budget film adapted from a recent bestseller and a sure bet to capture every major award next year.

Angry and resentful, Tara badly needed to lash out at something—or someone. Devlin would do. Snatching her hand from beneath his, she demanded irately, "Do you mind telling me how in hell I managed to acquire a fiancé while I was unconscious?"

Devlin folded his arms over his chest and regarded her with amusement. "Well, I see you're back to your spry and sassy self," he commented dryly.

"Answer me, dammit!"

"There's a perfectly reasonable explanation, Tara."

She didn't wait for it. In a few short, well-chosen words she told him exactly what she thought of his temperament, manners, intelligence, dubious ancestry, and general claim to humanity. She neither swore nor yelled, but her soft voice would have stripped the bark off a sapling at twenty paces.

Devlin listened with an air of great interest and ill-suppressed amusement, which maddened Tara all the more. She wanted him to yell at her, dammit, not smile with that infuriatingly calm expression. Trying to think of some way to goad him, she paused for a breath, which he took advantage of.

"Did you want the news of your collapse splashed all over the newspapers?" he asked mildly.

She had the odd feeling that the wind had been taken out of her sails. "No, of course not," she muttered. "But—"

"I had to be in a position of authority to keep the whole thing under wraps, Tara. Being your intended husband was the only idea I could come up with on the spur of the moment. But, of course, if you have a better idea . . ." He shrugged.

He sounded reasonable. He sounded so reasonable, in fact, that she was immediately suspicious.

"And just how did you account for the lack of an engagement ring *and* the fact that there's been no public announcement?" she asked nastily.

"The absence of a ring," he explained placidly, "was easy to explain. You were filming a scene at the moment of collapse, so naturally you weren't wearing your jewelry."

Tara was both baffled and disturbed. Baffled because he refused to fight with her; any one of the insults she had heaped upon his head moments before should have drawn a fire-and-brimstone response. Disturbed because she sensed he was quite pleased with himself, and *that* was enough to put any sane woman on her guard. "And the lack of an announcement?" she persisted.

"Also simple. I merely informed interested parties—meaning the chief administrator here and Dr. Easton—that we intended to keep the engagement secret for as long as possible, in order to avoid irritating questions from the press. I might add," he went on coolly, "that neither the administrator nor Easton was surprised by my request—show people being notorious for such secrecy."

"Oh." Tara was painfully aware of just how small and meek her voice sounded, and made a determined effort to strengthen it. "Well, thanks for . . . for keeping it quiet. But there's really no need to go on with it now."

"I suppose not," he answered indifferently, and for the second time since waking up Tara had to restrain herself from looking for something to throw at him. That her reaction was extremely unreasonable did not escape her, but she didn't bother to defend it or explain it—even to herself.

"Are you going to take the doctor's advice?" Devlin asked as if he didn't particularly care.

She must not have heard right when she thought he said he wanted her, she assured herself with silent fierceness. The man standing beside her bed obviously wanted nothing more than to file away this exceedingly distasteful episode into the slot marked "duty" and go on with his life. It was maddening.

Realizing that he was waiting patiently for an answer to his question, Tara murmured hastily, "Yes, of course I will." And then, bitterly, "I don't really have a choice, do I?"

Devlin strolled casually over to the window and stood looking out with a curious air of detachment. "So you'll give up your part in *Celebration!?*"

"How did you . . ." Tara stared at him as realization dawned. "My God, you're backing it!"

"I'm one of the backers," he answered easily.

"Well, I'll bet this illness of mine has made you terribly happy," she accused acidly.

"Not particularly." His voice was unruffled. "You're a fine actress, Tara, and perfect for the part. We'll have a hard time replacing you."

"Then don't!" The plea was out before Tara could stop it. "You can postpone production for a few months."

Softly, flatly, without looking at her, Devlin said, "I thought you refused to ask for favors, Tara."

"Forget it!" she snapped immediately, turning her gaze to the ceiling, hating herself for having forgotten her pride. And to ask *him* . . . him, of all people!

Ignoring her outburst, Devlin spoke in a disinterested tone, as if to himself. "I suppose it could be arranged. The projected release date isn't until next summer, and it'll take less than six months for production—"

"I said forget it! Don't do me any favors, Devlin. I don't need you. I don't need anyone!" Turning to glare at him, she caught the tail end of a keen, oddly searching look from his remarkable silver eyes. And then he was staring calmly out the window again.

"Would it make you feel any better if each of us benefited from the postponement?" he asked absently, his attention apparently focused on something outside.

Tara attempted to see his expression and found it impossible. "Benefited? What do you mean?"

"I'll postpone production for six months, giving you until the first of the year to recuperate."

"And in return?" she asked warily.

"You do me a . . . small favor."

"I knew there was a hook in it," she exploded. "If you think I'll become your mistress just for a lousy part—" Her voice broke off abruptly as she received a steely-eyed look from him, which made her feel suddenly small and uncertain.

"Wait until you're asked, Tara."

Flushing uncomfortably, she muttered, "What's the favor?" Damn, why did she always end up on the defensive with him!

"You sure you want to even hear it? Put aside your scruples and all that?" His voice was coolly mocking, his attention once more fixed on whatever was so engrossing outside the window.

For a brief moment Tara thought fondly of making a wax doll in his image and sticking pins in painful places. She pushed the pleasant image from her mind and said flatly, "The favor, Devlin. Stop playing with me."

He raised one hand, the fingers tapping softly, absently against the glass in front of him. Just when Tara was on the point of screaming at him in frustration, he finally spoke.

"It's really very simple, Tara. In return for my postponing the film, you will become my fiancée."

Chapter Three

"Are you out of your mind?" Tara yelped, and then, before he could respond, she went on quickly, "No, don't answer that! Insane people never admit to insanity, do they? They hold to it tooth and nail that they're just as sane as everyone else."

"Hear me out, Tara."

"Why?" she demanded angrily. "I don't like what I've heard so far."

Folding his arms across his chest, Devlin turned slightly and leaned a shoulder against the window, smiling across at her. "I'm not the devil, Tara, and I'm not asking for your soul in payment for a favor."

"Aren't you?" Longing for the strength to get up and slap his infuriatingly amused face, she spoke from between gritted teeth. "I don't want to marry you."

"I didn't ask you to marry me."

The mild comment caused her to stare at him in bewilderment. "Then just exactly what did you ask?"

"I really didn't ask anything," he pointed out in the tone of a man explaining something simple to a dimwit. "I simply said that I would postpone production of the film if you would agree to become my fiancée."

"But not to marry you?"

"That's right."

Tara wondered vaguely if her illness had left her with a sluggish mind, or if he wasn't making any sense. "You're going to have to clarify that."

"Okay, I'll put it into terms you can't possibly misunderstand." His voice was dry. "For six months you will act the part of my fiancée—if you accept the deal, of course. Needless to say, the bargain hinges on your ability to be convincing in the role."

Tara decided to let the dig at her acting ability pass. "But *why*? I mean, why do you want a fiancée? And why *me*?"

With hooded eyes and an expressionless face, Devlin murmured, "There is a certain young lady whom I wish to . . . discourage. I've found it difficult to accomplish that without seriously offending either her or her father, who happens to be rather important to me, owing to an upcoming business venture."

She looked at him warily. "I find it hard to believe, Devlin, that with all your . . . charm, you're unable to get yourself out of an entanglement."

"Did I say it was an entanglement?" He shook his head, looking faintly amused. "The young lady simply misconstrued a purely paternal interest and—"

"Paternal!" Tara's eyes widened. "How old is this young lady of yours?"

"She isn't mine," Devlin said, showing impatience for the first time. "Julie is seventeen."

"You should be ashamed of yourself," Tara scolded automatically, something inside her laughing at the idea of Devlin—strong, assured Devlin—caught in the passionate toils of a seventeen-year-old's blind infatuation.

Defending himself irritably, Devlin muttered, "I didn't do anything to encourage her, for godsake—"

"Doesn't she think a nineteen-year age difference is important?" Tara interrupted, still tickled by his predicament.

"Not so that you'd notice." He shrugged ruefully. "Part of the blame can be laid at her father's door. Jake Holman would like nothing better than to see his daughter married to me—with the idea of welding together two financial empires, I suppose. I've tried to tell him that I'm not particularly interested in settling down at the moment, and certainly not with a girl young enough to be my daughter, but the hints just roll off his back without making the least impression."

"Poor Devlin!" Tara mocked with a grin.

He grimaced. "I thought the situation would appeal to your sadistic sense of humor."

"It does." She enjoyed his wry discomfort for a moment longer, then went on dryly, "I grant the problem, Devlin, but I really don't see that there's any urgency in solving it. All you have to do is stay away from her for a while, and it'll all blow over."

"That's just it—I can't stay away from her. Holman is worse than an eel, when it comes to being pinned down, and he won't talk business in an office, God only knows why. Anyway, my mother has invited him to spend a couple of weeks with her and my stepfather at their ranch in Texas next month. It'll be my best chance to have him in one place long enough to convince him to join me in this export deal I've worked out with a European country."

"I don't see—"

"Julie," Devlin interrupted flatly, "will be tagging along with her father. And since she has a tendency to cling like a limpet and look embarrassingly adoring, it will make a sticky situation—to say the least."

"Then don't go," Tara advised practically. "Surely you could find another time to talk to Holman about the deal."

"I probably could, although it wouldn't be easy. The man's the proverbial rolling stone. But I agreed to attend this little house party before I knew Julie was coming, and my mother would never forgive me if I backed out."

"Your mother?" She stared at him, fascinated by this completely unexpected leaning toward filial obedience. "Why is your mother so set on having you in Texas?"

"She wants me to get married."

"To Julie?"

"To Dracula's mother, if the union would produce reasonably normal grandchildren," Devlin answered wryly. "I don't think she has her eye on Julie, though. If I know Mother she'll trot out the entire female population of northern Texas."

Amused, Tara exclaimed, "But if you explained—"

Devlin shook his head. "You don't know my mother. Whoever coined the phrase 'iron hand in the velvet glove' must have been thinking of her. I shudder to think what she'd do to me if I didn't show up at her house party."

Tara tried, and failed, to picture a woman formidable enough to command the obedience of a son as strong as Devlin. The image just wouldn't form. Giving up, she said slowly, "And you expect that your arrival with a bogus fiancée will put a stop both to Julie's infatuation and your mother's matchmaking. Isn't that a little drastic—especially as far as your mother's concerned?"

He shrugged. "Not really."

She studied him carefully. "What about your mother's feelings when the fictitious engagement ends? Won't she be upset?"

"If I know Mother," he replied coolly, "she'll rake me over the coals for making a horrible mistake and try to convince me to patch things up. When that doesn't work, she'll start lining up suitable candidates again."

Tara wondered if the situation could possibly be as simple as Devlin maintained. She shook her head in bemusement. "I'll accept that for the moment, but only because I don't know your mother. But why *me*, Devlin? Surely some other woman—"

He cut her off abruptly. "I couldn't risk it with another woman. I don't mean to sound conceited, Tara, but another woman could easily try to take advantage of a fake engagement."

Not really surprised by his cynical statement, Tara studied him thoughtfully. "And I wouldn't do that?"

"Not a chance," Devlin replied with reassuring promptness. "When it comes to dealing with other people, Tara, you're one of the most honest women I've ever met."

Tara had an uneasy feeling that he'd qualified the compliment, but she wasn't sure just how. "So you trust me not to take advantage of you."

"Completely."

It occurred to Tara then—belatedly—that it was Devlin who was taking advantage. She was ill and she wanted that part in his film badly. He was using both circumstances ruthlessly for his own gain. The realization rekindled her anger toward him. She turned slightly in the bed so that she was lying on her side facing him. "Your little plan's full of holes."

He walked over to the chair beside the bed and sat down. "Really? I thought it covered all the bases rather nicely."

Her fingers clutched the covers nervously. If only she could wipe that mocking smile off his face once and for all! "Well, you were wrong! In the first place it puts me exactly where I *don't* want to be, which is in the position of a woman using your influence to advance my career. I won't do it, Devlin."

"We'll keep the engagement secret, of course," he responded patiently. "Only my family and my mother's houseguests will know about it."

"And if there's a leak to the press?"

He shrugged. "Then we'll have a terrific fight—publicly, if you like—and simply recapture our reputation for being mortal enemies. The broken engagement will become one of Hollywood's tragic tales, and that will be that."

Against her will Tara had to admit to herself that, with the reputation the two of them had built up, the public would most likely consider the brief engagement a case of temporary insanity and dismiss it. But she still had an objection, and it was, in her opinion, a major one.

"I don't trust you, Devlin. You take what you can get with both hands and then reach for more." Her voice was even. "What about that little scene the doctor interrupted? Can I expect that sort of thing if I accept your deal?"

"Only if that's what you want, Tara," he answered casually. "I won't deny that I still want you. You're a beautiful woman and I still have memories of you lying naked in my arms."

Tara flushed with embarrassment at his blunt words and anger at her own surge of memory.

Ignoring her reaction—if he noticed it at all—Devlin went on, "but I'm sure you're fully capable of keeping me at arm's length even while pretending to be my loving fiancée."

"I certainly am," she snapped, and was immediately alarmed at how defensive she sounded even to her own ears.

His eyes narrowed slightly, a mocking glint showing in the silvery depths. " 'The lady doth protest too much, methinks,' " he quoted softly.

Tara's flush deepened, and her blue eyes sparkled angrily. Oh, damn the man! You're an actress, she told herself fiercely, so act! It wasn't exactly easy to be dignified with her face flaming, but she gave it her best shot. "I'm not protesting at all, Devlin," she managed coolly. "I'm simply stating a fact. Any relationship we had ended three years ago. This bargain of yours is just that—a deal, a business agreement."

"I see we understand each other completely." His eyes were hidden by lowered lids, his face calm. "Do I take it that you agree to the deal?"

A sneering voice inside Tara's head warned bitterly that she was making a terrible mistake by even considering Devlin's insane proposition, but she wasn't really surprised to hear the words that emerged from her mouth. "I agree. I'll pretend to be your fiancée for six months in return for your postponing *Celebration!*" For the first time, she wondered why he had asked for six months even though he only needed her for a couple of weeks. But before she could ask the question, Devlin was speaking briskly.

"That's settled, then. The doctors want you to remain here until the end of the week. I have to fly out to New York about then, so I'll settle you in Jim's apartment, where you can spend a couple of weeks lying in the sun and recovering your strength."

"That's not necessary," she objected immediately. "I can go home to recover."

Devlin lifted a skeptical eyebrow. "And run the gauntlet of L.A. reporters?" he asked. "Do you really think you'll be up to that, Tara?"

She frowned at him, undecided.

Sighing, he said patiently, "I won't be around, Tara, if that's what you're worrying about. I'll be in New York for at least two weeks, possibly longer. What would be the point of your flying to L.A. only to get on another plane two weeks later? You can rest just as easily here. Better, in fact, because the press thinks you left with the production crew."

"And when you come back?"

"Then we'll catch a plane to Texas."

She stared at him a moment longer, then shrugged, feeling suddenly very weary. "All right."

He nodded and rose to his feet, smiling. "I'd better leave you alone to get some rest. I think you've been through enough for one day."

"You can say that again," she muttered.

Not rising to the bait, Devlin went toward the door, then hesitated and gave her a thoughtful look. "I do have one question, Tara."

"You can ask. I don't promise to answer."

In a very neutral voice, he asked, "Has there been anyone since me?"

"Loads. I'm a popular lady."

"Don't be flippant, Tara."

She had an absurd desire to burst into tears. "You have no right to ask me that question," she said tightly.

"I was the first man in your bed, Tara. That gives me the right." It might have been her imagination, but she thought his voice was slightly strained. Holding onto that thought, she made her own voice indifferent.

"That and ten cents will get you a dime."

For a moment his lean face had a masklike look that was oddly disturbing. Then he was smiling wryly. "That's my Tara," he murmured. "Stubborn to the end." Without another word he opened the door and left the room.

Tara stared at the closed door for a long moment, trying to rid herself of the sudden notion that every move made in this room during the past hour had been carefully planned in advance, like a game of chess. And she had been the pawn . . .

A sudden crash of thunder rumbled outside, and Tara started, pulling the covers up around her neck with a faint moan. Oh, no— a storm! For as long as she could remember, she had been terrified of them. That would really put the finishing touches on an awful day. She only hoped Devlin wouldn't come back and find her cowering beneath the covers like a frightened child. Some actress she was!

Tara pulled her sunglasses down her nose and blinked in the bright light, her attention caught by the rainbow glitter of the diamond ring on the third finger of her left hand. She stared absently down at the ring.

It had been on her finger for nearly two weeks, ever since Devlin had left for New York, and she still felt odd whenever she looked at it. She had told herself time and again that the feeling was caused simply by the fact that she didn't want to wear *his* ring, but part of her found a different cause, one she didn't want to accept.

The ring, part of her insisted, was a fantasy, an illusion. It was no more real than the props she used in films, something to be worn for a brief time and then put away. Make-believe. A phantom symbol of ancient origin, meant to convey love and possession and the bonding of two lives.

It was a mirage, because it wasn't really hers.

Dropping her sunglasses onto a small table by the chaise longue, Tara concentrated on the sparkling ring. The stone was oval, the setting very old and delicate, like cobwebs spun of fine gold. It even looked unreal, she told herself silently, and then abruptly remembered what Devlin had said when he had tossed the tiny box into her lap as they were driving away from the hospital.

"Here's the main prop for your role. Wear it in good health."

He hadn't even asked her if she liked it.

The doorbell chimed suddenly, jerking Tara out of her depressed thoughts. She turned to look over her shoulder and came nose to nose with Ah Poo, who had jumped silently up on the table at her side. Momentarily forgetting the unexpected visitor, she smiled faintly, and murmured, "Hello, cat. Come to cheer me up?"

Ah Poo blinked at her, and when she felt her eyes beginning to cross like his, she drew back and blinked too. "Drat you, cat. Don't stare like that. I'll end up staring at my own nose permanently."

She rose to her feet and flexed her shoulders experimentally, waiting for the telltale prickle that would warn her she'd spent too much time on the balcony. It didn't come. She passed a satisfied hand over her flat stomach, pleased with the contrast between her smooth golden flesh and the bright-yellow bikini. Luckily for Tara, she was that exceedingly rare bird—a redhead who tanned instead of freckled. Thanks to her hours in the sun, she had completely lost her hospital pallor. That, along with the uninterrupted rest and Mrs. Henson's talent for cooking, had made her feel almost as good as new.

"Prroopp!" Ah Poo's loud approval was echoed almost immediately by a hushed and appreciative masculine voice coming from the open glass doors. "I couldn't agree with you more, Mr. Cat. She is a definite addition to my balcony."

Remembering the ringing doorbell, Tara swung around in surprise to confront a total stranger.

He was about her own height, with sun-lightened brown hair and a tanned face that looked as though it wore a cheerful smile most of the time. Warm brown eyes swept over her slender body in a thoroughly male appraisal and crinkled in apology for his familiarity.

"An early Christmas present?" he inquired hopefully. "A late birthday present?"

Coming rapidly to the conclusion that she was facing her formerly absent host, Tara relaxed and smiled in amusement. "I'm afraid not," she said with a slight wave of her left hand. The engagement ring caught the light and turned it to brilliant color.

The man's face fell in dramatic disappointment. "Oh, no! Someone's already caught you, the lucky so-and-so." He staggered forward and dropped into the lounge chair, returning Ah Poo's stare.

Interrupting the dueling match of feline and human eyes, Tara said with a laugh, "I do hope you're Jim Thomas."

"Fair lady, I've never answered to anything but Jim in my life . . . but you may call me anything you like." He cocked an intelligent brow at her. "And you are Tara Collins, unless there's a wedding band next to that disgusting rock."

She grinned. "Not yet."

"Devlin, eh?" He smiled crookedly.

She nodded and ventured hesitantly, "He told you about us?"

"Not a word," Jim replied with a shrug. "But since I expected Devlin here and found you instead, and since you're wearing a ring that I happen to recognize as belonging to Dev's family, *and* since Mrs. Henson informed me that Mr. Bradley's fiancée was on the balcony, I just naturally assumed . . ."

Tara smiled in spite of herself and tried to think of some way to explain her engagement, to a man who was obviously a close friend of Devlin's. But before she could gather her thoughts, he went on conversationally, "Funny thing about this engagement of yours and Dev's." He linked his hands across his trim abdomen and ignored Ah Poo's mutters of dislike with supreme indifference. "I talked to Dev less than a month ago, and I could swear he wasn't thinking along the lines of matrimony. And I distinctly remember reading somewhere that there's been a running feud between you two for years."

"Things change," Tara offered lamely.

"Obviously." He grinned at her discomfort. "Don't worry, I won't pester you with questions. I'll just assume that love conquered all and leave it at that."

Wanting desperately to change the subject, Tara said easily, "Devlin said you'd be in Europe for the summer, but since you're home now, I'll be glad to get a hotel room."

"Nonsense!" Jim cut her off promptly. "You'll stay here as long as you like. This place does have an extra bedroom, you know." His grin was both friendly and charming. "I'm sure Dev won't mind. After all, if a man can't trust his fiancée and his best friend, who can he trust?"

"Well, if you're sure you don't mind . . ." Tara wasn't particularly concerned with Devlin's opinion of the matter. He had no control over her life.

"Of course I don't mind. As a matter of fact it'll be nice just to be able to carry on a conversation with someone who speaks English. I made the mistake of going to Paris and trying to struggle through with basic French. The results were disastrous."

Eyeing him with curiosity, Tara pulled forward a deck chair and sank into it. "You don't exactly sound like the typical tourist," she observed. "Was it a business trip?"

"Unofficially. Devlin had already laid the groundwork for an export deal, and I went over to cement the ties of friendly relations." He smiled modestly. "You may have noticed that Dev's a bit . . . overpowering sometimes. Especially in business matters. I usually wind up being his goodwill ambassador."

Tara was puzzled by the relationship. "You mean you . . . work with Devlin?"

"Dev would probably object strongly to the term 'work,' " Jim told her wryly. "He's taken a great deal of delight in telling me for nearly twenty years that I'm a good-for-nothing lazy soul. We met in college, and I've been more or less tagging along behind him ever since. I had enough sense to invest in some of his earlier ventures, and since they were successful, I'm quite happy to help him out whenever I can." He calmly removed Ah Poo's flexing paw from his arm and went on without the slightest change in tone. "Your cat doesn't like me."

Tara had the feeling Jim had deliberately understated his importance in Devlin's business affairs, but she had no intention of prying. Frowning a warning at her cat, she said sternly, "Behave yourself!" and then looked apologetically at her host. "I'm sorry. I'm afraid Ah Poo isn't terribly impressed with the majority of mankind."

"Ah Poo?" Jim stared at the glaring animal. "Well, I must admit the name suits you, cat, although I don't know exactly why."

"Devlin named him when he was a kitten." Immediately Tara could have bitten her tongue. *Damn* Devlin for getting her in the middle of this fake engagement and then leaving her to sink or swim! What if Jim asked why a cat that was obviously at least a couple of years old should have been named by her fiancé, who was supposed to have been Tara's worst enemy at the time?

But he didn't. Tactfully ignoring her flushed face, he said calmly, "That sounds like something Dev would do. I'll bet Ah Poo thinks Dev's the next best thing to tuna, too."

"He adores him," Tara managed weakly.

"I knew it." Holding up a finger for emphasis, Jim said in a warning tone to the cat, "You are a guest in my home, Ah Poo, and you had better remember that. I also happen to be Devlin's best friend—human friend, that is—so remember *that*. If you're nice to me, I might even be persuaded to buy you some tuna. Or liver."

Crossed china-blue eyes regarded Jim for a long, unblinking minute, and then the cat stepped delicately onto his lap. Settling down comfortably, he began to purr.

"Hey!" Jim looked astonished. "He understood me!"

"I hate to burst your bubble," Tara said, amused, "but I'm afraid it's strictly cupboard love. You offered liver, which is a particular favorite of his."

"Oh." Jim stared down at the cat. "Toady!" he accused.

The phone rang just then, and Jim hastily picked up the cat and set him down gently beside the chaise. "I'll bet that's Dev," he exclaimed. "Let me answer it, Tara. I want to have a little fun."

Tara nodded in bemusement, wondering just what kind of fun he had in mind. She didn't really think Devlin was on the phone, since she hadn't heard a word from him once he'd left for New York. But maybe he was calling to say he'd be late or early . . . or whatever.

Curious in spite of herself, she rose, put on her thigh-length terry wrap, and followed Jim into the apartment. He was speaking cheerfully into the receiver.

"Hi, there, old man, how's life treating you these days?" He smiled wickedly at Tara as she perched on the arm of the couch and listened in amusement. It must be Devlin after all. "What's that?" Jim continued. "Well, of course it's me. Who else should answer the phone in my apartment? Who? Sure, she's here. As a matter of fact I was just going to treat her to a night on the town." He grimaced and held the receiver abruptly away from his ear. "Sure," he added hastily, "sure, you can talk to her." With one hand over the mouthpiece he extended the phone to Tara. "My, but he's touchy. He wants to talk to you."

She accepted the phone, wondering absently why Devlin should be touchy. He certainly wasn't jealous! Mindful of her role in this farce, and of Jim's unabashed eavesdropping, she spoke softly into the receiver. "Hello, darling."

After a moment of silence Devlin said dryly, "I take it Jim doesn't know the truth about our engagement."

"I miss you too, darling," Tara purred, trying desperately to convince herself that she was simply acting a part.

"He's in the room?"

"Yes . . . that's right."

Devlin chuckled. "I'm looking forward to watching you play the loving fiancée, Tara. From the sound of it you do it very well. Will I get a welcome home kiss too?"

Knowing Devlin would catch her meaning, she made her voice as seductive as possible. "You'll get exactly what's coming to you," she murmured, and then smiled for Jim's benefit.

Devlin laughed again. "Just don't have a knife handy, okay?" Before she could respond, he went on, "I just called to tell you I'll be back sometime tomorrow afternoon."

"I'll look forward to it"

Softly, he added, "Tell me you love me, Tara."

She was immediately furious with his underhanded tactics. Nevertheless she was obliged to bite back her anger, because of Jim.

Injecting a light, teasing note into her voice, she said, "That's not fair, darling."

"Backing out of the deal already, Tara? It hinged, if you'll remember, on your ability to be convincing." When she remained stubbornly silent, he added smoothly, "Jim will expect it."

She gripped the receiver until her knuckles turned white, but her expression remained tender—a credit to her acting abilities, although Devlin, on the other end of the line, was unable to appreciate it. Vowing with silent wrath to get even with Devlin Bradley before she was much older, she said adoringly, "I love you."

There was a long silence, and Tara could have sworn she heard him catch his breath. Then he was saying calmly, "I could easily become addicted to the sound of that. I'll see you tomorrow, honey. Put Jim on, will you?"

Tara handed the receiver to Jim and fled immediately to her bedroom. She was very much afraid she was going to burst into tears of sheer frustration and rage, and she didn't want her host to witness it. She wanted to break things, to scream at Devlin for being the sadistic beast that he was.

He had done it deliberately, damn him. Deliberately. Oh, why hadn't she realized just what this ridiculous masquerade would mean? She would have to gaze at him adoringly whenever they were together, pretend to be in love with him. And he'd probably demand over and over again that she vow her love in front of everyone.

Fuming, she changed quickly from her bikini into a pair of slacks and a peach-colored blouse. Slipping her feet into a pair of house shoes, she brushed her hair quickly and headed back toward the living room. She wouldn't cry. She wouldn't *let* herself cry.

Jim had just hung up the phone when she returned. He turned to face her with a concerned frown. "Why didn't you tell me you were convalescing?" he demanded.

Tara sank down on one end of the couch and smiled wryly. "I've known you exactly half an hour. When did I have time to tell you? Besides, it's not anything serious."

"Exhaustion isn't serious?" He grunted in sardonic amusement. "No wonder Dev nearly took my head off when I repeated my little remark about taking you out on the town."

Her blue eyes sparkled with anger. "He told you not to take me anywhere?"

He wandered toward the bar in the corner of the room and reached for a decanter. "Something like that," he murmured.

Frowning, Tara watched her fingers tap out an irritated tattoo on the arm of the couch. "I think I *would* like to go somewhere tonight," she remarked in an innocent voice. "Take in a show, maybe."

Jim turned to her, laughing. "I have to admit Dev knows you well." He chuckled. "He warned me you'd say something like that."

"Like what?" Her mouth turned sulky, and she was immediately annoyed with herself for making the childish gesture.

"Like that you suddenly felt like going out tonight. He said he would have told you not to go out, but that he knew you'd do it anyway, just to spite him. So he told me instead."

Tara looked at him speculatively. "There's a new comic playing just down the street," she mentioned in an offhand manner. "It isn't very far, and Devlin wouldn't have to know . . ."

Jim was shaking his head. "I've got my orders."

"Coward," she muttered.

"You're so right. Devlin's a hell of a lot bigger than I am, you know. I try not to irritate him any more than necessary." His voice was threaded with amusement.

Tara studied her nails thoughtfully. "I don't need an escort, you know. I can go by myself."

"Sorry, Tara. You're under house arrest, I'm afraid." Jim shook his head ruefully. "Devlin sure has you pegged. He told me my innocent little joke would have you hell-bent to go out. He also told me to keep you here even if I had to lock you in your room."

"That's barbaric!" she snapped, momentarily forgetting her role. "Devlin Bradley can't control my life from a distance of two thousand miles. If he thinks I'm going to—" She broke off abruptly to stare with impotent fury at Jim's amused face.

"Drink, Tara?" he asked mildly, holding up a decanter.

"White wine, please," she murmured, deciding that she needed a drink. But what she really needed was to have Devlin's neck within reach of her itching fingers.

Jim crossed the room to hand her a glass, then sank down on the other end of the couch with his own drink. "Devlin told me to remind you—in case you were thinking of climbing out your bedroom window—that it's twelve stories down."

Tara glared at him from beneath her lashes. "Funny," she muttered. "That's very funny."

Jim chuckled softly. "I'll bet you plan to have the word 'obey' taken out of the marriage vows."

Suddenly Tara saw the humor in the situation and laughed. "Do you really think Devlin would let me?" she asked.

Jim grinned. "No. But I'll tell you what I think *would* happen. I think you'd slip the minister twenty bucks to leave out the 'obey,' and then Dev would slip him fifty to leave it in."

Tara sighed ruefully. "He does seem to have the irritating ability to read my mind."

"At least you won't be able to say that your husband doesn't understand you," he remarked cheerfully. "I think you two are going to have a terrific marriage."

Tara sipped her wine hastily as she suddenly remembered that she and Devlin weren't really going to be married. For some inexplicable reason that thought made her feel very depressed. Unwilling to either analyze or face her emotions, she asked quickly, "Did Dev tell you he'd be back tomorrow?"

Jim nodded. "We're not to meet him at the airport, though." He paused, and his brown eyes were curious. "How did you two meet, anyway—or is that a nosy question?"

"Not at all." She smiled at him, glad for the slight change of topic. "We met at a premiere party for a film he backed."

"And it was love at first sight?"

Tara grinned in spite of herself. "Not quite. To be perfectly truthful, I didn't want to have anything to do with him. Have you heard the expression 'casting couch'?"

A gleam of understanding shone in Jim's eyes. "Of course. And I've heard it used in connection with some of Dev's films. I never believed it, though."

"Neither do I—now. But at the time, I'd heard of several actresses who had gotten parts solely because of their association with Devlin. It wasn't really his doing. It's just that producers and directors tended to hire women Devlin was interested in, to . . . court his favor, so to speak."

"And you didn't like that?"

Tara shook her head. "I wanted to be cast for my ability, not my relationships with anyone in the industry. So I decided that the safest way to avoid any prejudice would be to avoid Devlin."

"Did he lay siege to you?" Jim asked with a grin.

"Something like that," she murmured, remembering the two weeks after she had met Devlin. Each day a huge basket of roses had arrived at her apartment, accompanied by a card with a phone number and a single-word question—"Please?" Finally, hip-deep in roses of every color, and sympathetic to the plight of the delivery boy, Tara had finally given in and called Devlin.

She looked up to encounter Jim's gaze and went on lightly, "We started seeing each other. Quietly. I was still determined not to be accused of trying to find an easy way into films."

"The secrecy must have been hard on the two of you," Jim offered quietly.

Tara nodded slowly, staring down at her glass. It had not only been hard, she thought, but also had led to a degree of intimacy she had not been prepared for. "Devlin didn't like 'sneaking around,' as he put it," she murmured, almost to herself. "I wasn't happy about it myself. There were . . . disagreements."

Painfully she remembered the argument that had caused their final break-up. The casting director had promised her a part in one of Devlin's films, but at the last minute she had discovered that Devlin had recommended another actress for the role. Hurt and angry, Tara had lashed out at him. Instead of taking her seriously, he had asked her to quit acting and become his wife. She had refused. Emphatically.

"Tara?"

She shook the memories away and smiled brightly. "Everything worked out all right, though," she told Jim.

"Obviously." He smiled.

Tara returned the smile, but her thoughts were on the public fights and the private misery of the past three years. She had still been attracted to Devlin after they had parted, and the only way to fight that attraction had been to fight him. After the blow to his pride her rejection had brought, Devlin had been more than willing to fight with her.

Now she watched Jim get up to refill their glasses and wondered vaguely, but not for the first time, what had happened between Devlin and the blond model he was supposed to have been so seriously involved with. The press had certainly indicated that marriage was imminent. What had happened between them? Did Jim know?

But it didn't matter. Tara wasn't interested in that other woman. Not at all.

Chapter Four

"How do you like the ring?" Jim asked as he handed Tara her glass and sank down on the couch.

Roused from her thoughts, Tara looked down at the glittering diamond and then at her host. "It's beautiful." She tilted her head to one side, curious in spite of herself. "You mentioned a while ago that you recognized the ring. Is there something special about it that I don't know?"

"Well, it has a curse," Jim confided with a grin.

"A what?" She stared at him blankly.

Chanting as though casting a spell, Jim recited, "As long as the ring is passed from eldest son to eldest son, and given with true love to the wives of their choice, the Bradley clan will always have good luck. But if ever an eldest son gives the ring without first giving his heart, bad luck will befall the entire clan."

Tara thought that over for a minute. "You're pulling my leg—right?" she asked wryly.

"Not at all." Jim chuckled softly. "I'm surprised Dev hasn't told you. The curse originated sometime in the seventeenth century. One stormy night an eldest son performed a daring act of heroism and rescued a beautiful—and wealthy—maiden. She rewarded him with the ring and her heart."

"And the curse?" Tara asked.

"An old gypsy was responsible for that, a little later on. A Bradley ancestor took the ring to be blessed and ended up with a blessing—or a curse—depending on your point of view, I suppose. Anyway, it's been a fairly consistent curse. As long as an eldest son gave the ring with love, the whole family prospered."

Tara was fascinated. "What if he gave the ring for a reason other than love?"

Jim grimaced. "Bad luck. It happened several times down through the years. Dev's grandfather, for instance, sold the ring after his first wife died. He had remarried by then—for money, not love—and then decided that he needed capital for investments. So he and his second wife decided to sell the ring. His timing was rotten. The stock market collapsed two days later. Ruined him completely."

Tara stared down at the ring. "But . . . the ring . . ."

"Oh, you have the original ring," Jim confirmed. "It turned out that Dev's grandmother had the ring copied and hid the original. It turned up again in an old trunk, just a few years ago."

Tara watched absently as Ah Poo leaped up between them on the couch. "I've heard of stories like that," she said, "but I certainly never expected to land right in the middle of a family curse."

Jim laughed. "Well, you certainly don't have to worry. It's obvious that Dev loves you."

Tara stared down at her empty glass for a moment, then leaned forward to place it on the coffee table. Her face was calm, but her thoughts were troubled. No, Devlin didn't love her. He trusted her. He trusted her not to take advantage of a fake engagement. He trusted her with an old and very valuable family heirloom. But he had never trusted her with his secret thoughts, his hopes and ambitions. Though he had spoken to her of his mother's hopes regarding a marriage for him, she had no idea whether he wanted to share his life with someone.

Their former relationship had been based largely on physical attraction, and their rare time together had not allowed for tender confidences and whispered dreams. The passion between them had been fiery and primitive, sweeping all before it in a hungry, turbulent current of sheer need. And even in that moment of ultimate arousal, that eternity of drowning pleasure in which two separate people melded into a single entity, each had held something back. Tara because of some nameless private fear that she herself didn't understand, and Devlin . . .

Devlin. He had been tender and passionate, gentle and demanding—everything a young woman could want and need from that all-important first lover. He had never hurt her, never disappointed her. He had taken her to the heights of ecstasy time after time, each soaring flight more wondrous than the last. And always some sixth sense—or perhaps it was only the intuition that women have possessed down through the ages—had warned her that he was holding back something of himself.

She didn't know what that "something" was.

Tara came back to the present, to hear Jim say cheerfully, "Now that we have that little matter settled, I'm going to ask Mrs. Henson what we're having for dinner. And then how about a fast game of strip poker?"

Tara managed a faint smile. "How about an equally fast game of gin rummy?" she countered dryly.

"Spoilsport!" he grumbled in a voice of mock disgust, and then grinned and headed for the kitchen.

Alone but for Ah Poo's silent presence, Tara stared down at the ring on her hand until the glowing diamond seemed to have imprinted itself on her brain. So much history, she thought vaguely, so much of human passions and greed had accompanied this polished gem throughout its four-hundred-year life span. And how much influence had the brilliant stone actually exerted on those events?

Not much, probably. When a man married for the wrong reasons he was asking for trouble. And people were always suffering unexplained deaths and accidents. Fortunes were won and lost, sometimes only on the roll of the dice or the turn of a card. There was nothing unusual in this history, this ring. The curse of an old gypsy was just a fable.

Ah Poo butted his head gently against Tara's arm, and she reached out to scratch him beneath the chin. Staring into his blissful blue eyes, she murmured, "I'm not superstitious, cat." And then, almost in the same breath, she added, "But your beloved Devlin's taking an awful chance."

Midway through the following afternoon Jim managed to unearth a Monopoly game, and he and Tara spent an uproarious hour winning and losing fantastic sums and arguing fiercely over who owned what, where. After landing in jail for the sixth time and realizing, to his dismay, that he was nearly broke, Jim was in the process of trying to wheedle a loan from Tara when he was suddenly distracted by Ah Poo's abrupt activity.

The cat, who had been lying on the coffee table beside the game board and interestedly watching the proceedings, leaped up suddenly and stalked over to the front door. He planted himself firmly about three feet from the portal and stared at it intently, his tail moving restlessly.

Jim lifted an eyebrow and looked quizzically at Tara. "Does he want to go out?"

Tara shook her head, trying to ignore the way her heart had suddenly begun to pound. "No. Devlin's back." She was pleased that her voice emerged casual and steady.

"He *knows* Devlin's back?" Jim asked with a blank look.

She nodded vaguely, staring toward the cat. She remembered too well that, even as a kitten, Ah Poo had always displayed an uncanny ability to know when his adored Devlin was nearby. Struggling to keep her voice under control, she murmured, "He's probably at the elevator right now."

Jim glanced down at his watch and muttered, "Then he'll be at the door about . . ." At that exact moment, a key grated in the lock.

Jim's expression of astonishment made Tara want to giggle, but since she was dimly aware that her voice would be brittle with strain and tension, she managed to bite it back.

Devlin appeared in the open door a moment later. He barely had time to set his briefcase and larger suitcase down on the floor before Ah Poo launched himself with a howl that sounded like the battle cry of a kamikaze pilot. Jim jumped to his feet, but the alarm on his face melted into laughter as he recognized the feline delight of Ah Poo's exuberant greeting.

Tara remained where she was, seated on the floor between the couch and the coffee table, every nerve in her body throbbing with a sudden, agonizing awareness. She watched, mesmerized, as Devlin's hard features softened as he looked down at the adoring cat in his arms.

Shock ripped its way through Tara's mind with the force of a lightning bolt. She knew now why she had accepted Devlin's insane proposition, why she had gone out of her way to be hostile to him during the past three years. She knew now why she looked at other men with a disinterest she could not explain, why she had worked herself almost to death during those years just so she could sleep, and sleep without dreaming. She knew now why his presence, his touch, his voice could reassure her and excite her and anger her.

She loved him. She had loved him from the very beginning. And she had to get through the next few weeks—no, *months*—acting the part of a loving fiancée, when she wanted to be the real thing. A loving fiancée. A *loved* fiancée.

A deeply rooted instinct of self-preservation rather than acting ability kept Tara's face expressionless and her eyes wide and blank. She watched Devlin cross the room to shake hands with Jim. She met Devlin's stormy gray eyes as he looked down at her. It took only a moment to identify mockery in the luminous depths.

"Hi, sweetheart. Don't I get a kiss?"

Tara felt no anger at his underhanded tactics. She was overwhelmed by sheer panic. He'll know! her mind kept repeating over and over again. A temporary solution popped into her mind suddenly, and she dropped her gaze to the stacks of play money on the coffee table in front of her. In a casual voice she told him, "I'm mad at you. You told Jim not to take me anywhere."

Devlin lifted a brow and glanced at Jim, who was trying to hide a grin. Then he gently set Ah Poo down on the game board and stepped around the coffee table to grasp Tara by the upper arms. "If you won't give me a kiss, I'll take one," he said calmly, pulling her effortlessly to her feet.

His hands held her firmly, as if he half expected her to try to get away. But Tara made no move to escape him. You're an actress, she told herself with desperate calm. But it wasn't the actress in her who lifted her arms to encircle his neck. It was the woman in her . . . the woman who wanted to touch the man she loved.

A flicker of satisfaction showed briefly in the stormy eyes. His hands slid around to her back as he bent his dark head to take her lips. It was not a light "welcome home" kiss, and Devlin didn't try to disguise it as such. The hot demand of his lips tore through her hastily erected barriers and stirred the embers buried deep inside her to a white-hot blaze. She was powerless to fight him.

Her lips parted. Her body, guided only partly by the hand at the small of her back, molded itself against him. She felt his hands on her back burning through the thin silk of her blouse, felt his belt buckle digging into her middle with a certain painful pleasure. A hot, familiar ache began to grow in her loins.

And then she dimly heard Jim's voice, filled with laughter. "Is this an X-rated movie or can anybody watch?"

Devlin lifted his head long enough to glance over his shoulder and call his friend a very rude name that amused Jim considerably.

Tara took the opportunity to slip from Devlin's embrace and resume her former position on the floor. She moved with a grace that concealed the fact that her knees would no longer hold her up. With iron control, she said calmly, "Shall we start another game or are you two going to talk business?" She looked up to see Devlin removing his jacket and loosening his tie.

"Deal me in," he told her cheerfully, tossing the jacket onto the couch.

"We aren't playing poker," she snapped, annoyed by his utter calm. Apparently the kiss hadn't affected him in the least, though her heart was still thundering in her ears.

With a grace unusual in so large a man, Devlin dropped down on the carpet at the narrow end of the coffee table and removed Ah Poo from the game board. Ignoring Tara's comment he glanced up at Jim and said, "We can discuss business after dinner tonight. Right now I want to take all your money."

Jim took his former position across from Tara. "You'll probably take mine," he said, "but look out for Tara. She wiped me out a few minutes ago."

"Oh, I know all about how Tara plays games. Don't I, honey?"

Tara was busily clearing the board. "You should, darling," she said with false sweetness. She had no idea how she was managing to keep her voice light and even, or why her hands were steady. She was painfully aware of Devlin's nearness, of the tangy scent of his aftershave.

Silently readying the board for another game, she listened to Devlin talking casually to Jim, the actual words passing over her but the deep voice shivering along her nerve endings like an arrow across a taut bowstring. Good heavens, why hadn't she realized she loved him long before? How could she have accepted her thin disguise of hostility as truth all this time? The very fact of her reluctance to face her own feelings should have told her something long ago.

Well, she had faced the truth now. She loved him. And she couldn't tell him, because anything he might have once felt for her had been killed by her own words and actions three years ago. He hadn't loved her then, she thought sadly, but he had cared enough to ask her to be his wife. And she had rejected him angrily, bitterly, because he had meddled in the career she had worked so hard to build.

Liberation, she thought wryly. She was a member of the liberated generation, which meant that she had to prove her ability to take care of herself. How often had her mother pounded that idea into her head? How often had she lain awake at night on her narrow, uncomfortable cot and listened to her mother crying in bitter anguish over the impossibility of leaving the man she had dropped out of school to marry?

Hastily, fiercely, Tara slammed the lid down on these painful memories, which had not raised their ugly heads, except in nightmares, for sixteen years. She couldn't reopen those old wounds, not yet. Perhaps . . . perhaps not ever.

Emerging from her thoughts, Tara found to her surprise that the game had begun. She had been playing automatically. At the same moment she became aware of Devlin's voice.

"So if you don't mind, Jim, we'll stay here tonight and then start for Texas in the morning," he was saying.

"You know I don't mind," Jim responded easily.

Reaching to pick up the dice for her turn, Tara glanced warily at her bogus fiancé. "We aren't leaving until morning?" she asked.

"No reason to." Devlin reached down to scratch Ah Poo behind one ear as the cat purred contentedly in his lap. "Mother isn't expecting us for a couple of days yet." His eyes gleamed with a mischief she couldn't fathom for a moment, and then, just as she rolled the dice, the answer came.

She stared blindly down at the dice, dimly hearing Jim's voice exclaim with a laugh, "Hey, that puts you in jail!"

"It certainly does," she muttered, woodenly moving her game piece to the corner of the board. Her silent dismay had nothing to do with her bad luck in the game, but rather with Devlin's decision—deliberate, she knew—to stay the night. Jim's apartment had two bedrooms, and she knew very well that Devlin would not offer to sleep on the couch.

What had he said in the hospital? That he still wanted her but that surely she could hold him at arm's length. A week ago, even a few days ago, she had been certain of her ability to do just that. But if he took her in his arms now, she would be lost. Her love made her vulnerable, and her helpless desire for his possession left her no defense.

"By the way, Tara, what happened to Churchill?"

Devlin's casual question made her blink, and she tried to force herself to think clearly. "Oh . . . well, I know you said your mother wouldn't mind pets, but I thought that taking Churchill might be stretching things a bit. A little boy down the hall wanted a pet, and his mother didn't mind." She shrugged.

Devlin's silvery eyes warmed with amusement. "That was nice of you. I'm not saying Mother would have been upset, but she isn't terribly fond of mice."

"Mice? Churchill? What are you two talking about?" Jim looked from one to the other.

Devlin explained the story of Ah Poo, Churchill, and the padlocked cage, eliciting a roar of laughter from Jim. When his friend had finally calmed down, Devlin turned to Tara with a smile. "I'll bet Ah Poo sulked while I was gone," he remarked.

In spite of her confused emotions, she felt a smile tug at the corners of her mouth. "For three days."

Devlin's silvery eyes dropped fleetingly to her mouth, warm and caressing, and her fingers twined together nervously under the table. He was a natural actor! She could almost believe he was in love with her. No other man had ever looked at her in quite that way, she realized. It gave her a strange feeling to have him gaze at her as though she were everything he had ever wanted out of life. Strange . . . and oddly, alarmingly pleasing.

Wistfully, she allowed her eyes to follow the movements of his strong brown hands as he took his turn and rolled the dice. Looking up, she found Jim's smiling gaze on, first, Devlin and then herself. He had been completely fooled. It was there, in his eyes. He was genuinely pleased that his friend had fallen in love at last.

Tara felt sick as dismay swept over her. How many people would they hurt with this false engagement?

"Tara? It's your turn."

She reached out hastily to pick up the dice, avoiding Devlin's eyes. Why . . . oh, why hadn't she considered the pitfalls of this ridiculous situation more carefully?

"Is anything wrong, honey? You don't seem to have your mind on the game." Devlin's voice was concerned, but Tara caught the note of mockery meant for her ears alone.

"Nothing's wrong," she murmured, moving her game piece automatically on the board and wondering rather grimly how she could bear listening to the sweet endearments that fell almost constantly from Devlin's lips. She had always hated the sort of honey-eyed talk used carelessly in show-business circles, knowing that it was as meaningless as it was popular. She had never responded in kind to those empty endearments, but she had learned not to become angered by them.

But the same words she had accepted indifferently from other men aroused a bitter fury in her when they came from Devlin. She wasn't certain why. Perhaps because it seemed out of character for him to use such words and phrases. Or perhaps because he had never done so before. Not even three years before . . .

With a supreme effort of will Tara managed to keep her mind on the game, pushing her disturbed thoughts and emotions into a darkened corner and firmly slamming a door on them. It was a trick she had learned long ago, useful whenever she had been faced with a difficult part, and she was grateful for the ability now.

Throughout the afternoon she was able to maintain the charade of a loving fiancée. She talked easily and casually to the two men, even managing not to stiffen when Devlin put an arm around her to lead her into dinner that evening.

She fell silent during the meal, listening as Devlin and Jim talked business. Although she knew Devlin was an excellent businessman, she was nevertheless impressed by this new evidence of his obvious ability. He spoke clearly and concisely to Jim of his plans regarding the European deal, explaining exactly what he hoped to accomplish by talking to Jake Holman in Texas. Only then did Tara realize why Holman was so important. His shipping business was vital if Devlin's plans were to be successful. She mused over that fact until her attention was caught by something Jim was saying.

". . . and Allen Stewart was very interested in your plans to form a production company of your own, Dev. He told me his London studio would be available if you needed it for a film, and that he knows several terrific technicians who'd be delighted to work with you. He even offered to subsidize the project, knowing, of course, that you've proven your ability to back winners."

Before Devlin could respond, Tara asked quietly, "Are you really planning to form your own production company?"

He looked at her with an unreadable expression, his silver eyes curiously guarded, and then shrugged. "It was just a thought. I haven't really decided," he told her casually.

"It could become a family business," Jim said cheerfully. "Dev could produce and you could star, Tara." Without knowing it, he had put his foot right in the middle of a major dispute.

"Oh, no," Tara said lightly. "I've worked with Devlin before. He's a harsh taskmaster. I shudder to think what he'd be like after we were married." Jim only laughed, but Devlin's glance made Tara feel uneasy.

Deciding abruptly that discretion was indeed the better part of valor, she rose to her feet, waving the men back when they would have risen also. "I think I'll make it an early night," she said. "I'll read for a while. If you gentlemen will excuse me, I'll leave you to your business talk." Barely waiting for their murmured acceptance and resolutely avoiding Devlin's faintly mocking gaze, she left the room.

Alone in her bedroom, Tara considered several unsettling facts, the most important one being that within the next few hours she and Devlin would be sharing this room . . . and this bed. As if drawn by a magnet, her eyes moved to the wide bed, which had seemed huge to her for two weeks and now suddenly seemed small.

Tearing her eyes from the hypnotic sight of a bed that appeared to be shrinking moment by moment, she looked at her nightgown, lying over a chair in the corner, and abruptly faced the second unsettling fact—her only nightgown was really just a few scraps of lace and satin that practically screamed a message of seduction. Ice-blue and nearly see-through, it barely reached the tops of her thighs. The matching panties only aggravated matters.

Tara wondered if Devlin had planned all this long ago. With his usual high-handedness, he had sent her motor home ahead to his mother's ranch—why, she couldn't fathom—and only informed her of the deed after the fact. Since he chose to tell her right after tossing an engagement ring in her lap, she hadn't been thinking clearly enough to question his motives. She had made an irritated remark to the effect that he might have asked her, and then had let the matter drop.

Devlin had also packed her suitcase for her. Not until after he'd left for New York did she discover that practically every sexy item of clothing she owned was in the case.

Tara liked nice things. She enjoyed the feel of silk or satin against her skin and, luckily, had the money to indulge her tastes. But she had not bought the sexy underthings and sleepwear in her wardrobe with the idea of enticing a man. Not any man.

If she could have chosen her sleepwear on this particular night, Tara would certainly have picked something other than the blue gown. Maybe one of those high-necked flannel atrocities that Victorian women were supposed to have worn. Not that she wanted to look horrible, but she didn't want to test her shaky resistance to Devlin. And the blue gown was not exactly calculated to cool a man's blood.

Tara immediately shook the thought away with a faint grimace. She couldn't do much about it. Either she slept in that gown or slept in the buff, and she wasn't about to do *that* with Devlin in the same bed!

Sighing faintly, she kicked off her shoes and padded barefoot across the gold carpet to the connecting bathroom. Perhaps a hot shower would help her to think more clearly. She closed the bathroom door, carefully locked it, and rapidly stripped off her clothes. She made the water as hot as she could stand it, gasping under the first steamy onslaught, and then relaxing as her body adjusted to the heat. Moments later she stepped out of the stall.

Glowing pink, she shivered in the relatively cool air and reached hastily for a towel. Only then did she realize she had left the gown in the bedroom. Muttering irritably to herself, she dried off and wrapped the towel around her, reaching for the door with one hand and maintaining a death grip on the skimpy towel with the other. She paused just outside the door, keeping her head bent as she struggled with the towel's obvious desire to obey the laws of gravity. She tried several different arrangements in an effort to keep all proper areas decently covered.

Suddenly her eyes became riveted to a pair of shiny brown shoes planted squarely about a foot from her own bare toes. Male shoes. With comical slowness her eyes slid up over neatly creased brown slacks, a cream shirt open at the throat, no tie. Of course, she thought vaguely, he had discarded the tie earlier in the evening. A strong jaw, faintly shadowed. A smiling mouth.

Smiling? Oh, damn him! It was just like him to show up at the most unreasonable time!

Her red curls—even more unruly than usual, from the steamy shower—fairly quivered with rage as her head snapped back. Glittering blue eyes met darkening slate-gray ones. Then his gaze traveled away from her face to inspect her nearly nude body in a leisurely appraisal that brought the blood rushing to her cheeks.

Wishing desperately for a larger towel, Tara managed to hold the material in place over the most critical points, and resorted to anger, her oldest and best defense against that probing, caressing stare. "Did you want something?" she demanded furiously.

"Well, now . . . *there's* a question," he drawled softly, raising his eyes to her face at last.

"You know what I meant!"

Though still darkened with an emotion she recognized all too easily, his eyes contained a glint of pure laughter. "Calm down, honey. I just came in to get my briefcase, and stopped to see the show."

"Show! Why, you—"

"You should demand a towel scene in every movie, honey," he told her, laughing loudly. "You'd bring down the house."

Tara considered abandoning the towel and lunging for his throat, but contented herself with glaring at him from a safe distance. "I can't stand sexist remarks like that, and you know it! I'm an actress, not a stripper!"

For some reason that comment amused him even more. He was still laughing as he stepped to one side and picked up his briefcase from the floor beside the dresser. Straightening, he regarded her from bright silver eyes and said, "You are really something special, honey. I can want you like my last hope of heaven and still find myself laughing at you."

The appreciation in his voice did nothing to soothe Tara's temper. Especially since she wasn't fooled into being flattered by his remark. She made an attempt to gather shreds of towel and dignity around her, and requested in an icy voice, "Please close the door on your way out." Unfortunately the command lost some of its effectiveness when she was forced to make a wild grab for a sliding corner of the towel.

Chuckling, Devlin started for the door. "Jim and I have a few things to go over tonight. I'll probably be late, so don't wait up for me."

"I hadn't planned to!" she snapped.

He paused in the open doorway and glanced back at her, the darkness of desire creeping back into his eyes. "Now, that," he murmured softly, "is a real pity." The door closed silently behind him.

A split second later a much-maligned yellow towel hit the door with an unsatisfying thud.

Several hours later Tara heard Devlin reenter the bedroom. The room was dim and shadowy, lit only by the bathroom light, which she had left on. She had been in bed for some time, lying on the far side with her back to the room, taking up as little space as possible.

Pretending to be asleep, she lay perfectly still and listened to Devlin moving quietly around the room. It became darker suddenly as the bathroom door closed. She heard the shower running and watched the moon through the wide window.

The scene that had taken place in the room earlier still occupied her mind, but she was no longer angry. The defiant and totally useless gesture of throwing her towel after Devlin's departing figure had brought her sense of humor to the rescue. Lord, she had felt like a fool, standing there stark naked, glaring at a crumpled yellow towel. She had no reason to be angry, after all. Other than that cute comment of his, Devlin had been a perfect gentleman. He hadn't even touched her.

Which annoyed Tara.

Suddenly aware that the shower had ceased, she tensed as the bathroom door opened and the light went out. Struggling to breathe deeply and evenly, she felt the other side of the bed give. At the same moment she remembered Devlin slept in the buff.

Oh, no! How was she supposed to sleep, with Devlin naked beside her? Especially when she remembered only too well . . .

"I know you aren't asleep, Tara," he said dryly. "You're as stiff as a board."

She remained stubbornly silent.

He sighed softly. "If your sense of modesty is offended, I'd like to point out that I'm wearing pajamas. Does that make you feel better?"

The mockery in his voice grated on Tara's nerves. With an exaggerated flounce she moved farther away from him, realizing belatedly that another inch would find her sleeping on the carpet. "I'd like to get some sleep, if you don't mind," she snapped.

There was a long silence, and then his voice came, flat and oddly bitter. "Shall we get it over with?"

The tone warned her. "Get . . . get what over with?"

A hard hand gripped her shoulder and flipped her over flat on her back. Before Tara could completely grasp the situation, she found Devlin looming over her in the darkness. One pajama-clad leg pinned both of hers firmly to the bed, and steely fingers held her shoulders.

"The attempted rape," he bit out icily. "That is what you've been waiting for, isn't it?"

"I . . . I don't know what you're talking about," she responded defiantly, pushing uselessly against his broad shoulders. He wouldn't budge, but since he wasn't wearing a pajama top, the contact of flesh on flesh did crazy things to her senses.

"Come off it, Tara! From the moment you realized we'd be sharing this bed, you've been expecting me to try to make love to you, haven't you?"

Using the only defense she had against him, Tara whipped up an anger she didn't feel. "Now who's using euphemisms? Love has nothing to do with it!" she told him angrily.

Devlin stiffened suddenly, and Tara realized too late that she had pushed him too far. In the same flat, bitter tone, he gritted out, "Well, I was taught never to contradict a lady . . . or to disappoint one."

And then his lips were on hers in a demanding, punishing kiss. There was desire in his kiss, but it was an angry, bitter desire, which frightened Tara. She kept her mouth firmly closed against him, pushing at the muscular shoulders and trying desperately to turn her face away from him.

But it was no use. Without hurting her, he managed to hold her still beneath him, and the pressure of his mouth forced her lips apart. His tongue intruded with shattering sensuality, hungrily exploring the sweetness of her mouth. Rough hands brushed aside the frail barrier of lace and satin to find the full curve of her breasts.

Desire threatened to drown Tara's rational thoughts, sweeping over her in scarlet waves of aching need. The small part of her that had not yet submerged was suddenly, desperately afraid, knowing that she was vulnerable as she had not been three years before, knowing that if he possessed her now, she would be inextricably tied to him in the most basic way possible for a woman . . . tied with unbreakable silken threads of love and need.

She gave a last desperate cry, but it wasn't strong enough to counteract her inflamed senses. The hands that had been pushing fruitlessly against his shoulders curled involuntarily, seeking to draw him even closer, her nails digging unconsciously into his skin. Her mouth came alive beneath the fierce pressure of his, returning the kiss with matching fire.

Her response did little to drain the anger from him. If anything, he seemed even more angry. Tara was dimly aware of his anger, aware of the bitterness that was as strong as it was incomprehensible. But it was hard to concentrate on anything when his hands were moving over her body with sure knowledge and a hunger that even his bitterness could not hide.

His lips moved down her throat in a trail of fire, finally coming to rest on the pulse beating wildly at the base of her neck. Tara moved restlessly with a faint moan as she felt his hand sliding warmly over the thin satin covering her stomach. As if from a great distance she heard him speak, and even through the hazy curtain of desire she was conscious of being shocked.

"I asked you a question in the hospital, Tara, and I think you lied to me," he said harshly against her soft skin. "This time I want the truth." He lifted his head and stared down at her face. "Has there been anyone since me?"

Chapter Five

"W-what?" She stared dazedly up at him, seeing his face as a taut mask in the dim light.

"Has there been anyone since me?" he repeated harshly.

Stripped of any ability to lie, Tara could only shake her head, hating herself for the confession she was making. "No," she whispered painfully, "there's been no one."

He stared down at her for a long minute, and she could sense more than see his eyes probing her face for the truth. Then, in a suddenly gentle voice, he said, "Why not, Tara?"

She wanted to get angry at him for asking such a question, but this time the anger wouldn't come. Desire ebbed slowly from her body, leaving it cold and aching, and she wondered wearily if his revenge for her rejection three years ago was going to take this tormenting form. Unwilling to give him the weapon of her love, she said tightly, "I've been busy—you know that. I haven't had the time or the energy for any kind of a relationship."

"Was that the only reason?"

She frowned up at him, trying to identify the faint emotion in his voice. What was it—anxiety? Impossible, she told herself. There was no reason for Devlin to care how many men she'd been with in the past three years. Unless it was his pride. Did he want her to admit her love as a sop to his wounded ego? Had her response to him convinced him that she cared more than she would admit?

Bitterness rose in her. "If you're looking for your pound of flesh, Devlin, you can forget it. You had nothing to do with my lack of affairs."

"Pound of flesh?" Even in the darkness she saw his lips twist with wry bitterness. "You mean because you rejected me three years ago? Lord, you really don't trust me, do you?"

"Why should I?" She pushed uselessly at his shoulders yet again, becoming angry when he caught her hands and held them firmly folded over her stomach. "I trusted you three years ago, and you betrayed that trust."

She hadn't meant to say it, but since it was the truth, she made no effort to call back the words. He had betrayed her when he had interfered in her career, and she could neither forget nor forgive him for it.

"So that's it," he breathed softly. "You've convinced yourself that I betrayed you."

"I didn't have to *convince* myself." Tara sensed that he was suddenly pleased, as though he'd found the answer to an old riddle. She understood none of it. He was the most infuriating man! Angry and bitter one minute, pleased the next. Like a chameleon, he changed, bewilderingly, moment by moment.

And then, suddenly, the bitter, angry Devlin was back.

"My God, Tara—you mean you stuck a knife in me three years ago because of a lousy *film?*"

Unnerved by his blazing silver eyes, she defended herself desperately. "It wasn't the film, it was *trust!* I trusted you. I thought you understood how important my career was to me—and then you took that part away from me!"

"Damn it, Tara, didn't you stop to wonder *why* I recommended someone else for the part?" he demanded fiercely.

She stared up at him blankly, realizing abruptly that she hadn't ever asked him, hadn't even considered that there could have been a reason unconnected with their relationship. Had there been? "I— I just assumed . . ."

"What did you assume?" He was glaring down at her. "That I was so desperate for your body that I'd deliberately take a part away from you just to keep you in my bed every night?"

A vivid flush colored her cheeks, and she was suddenly grateful for the darkness. "You wanted me to quit acting. You told me so! What else was I supposed to think?"

Abruptly, he flung himself away from her to lie on his back, his body stiff with anger. "I don't care, Tara." His voice was flat and cold. "I really don't care. If that's the only reason your tiny mind can come up with, you're welcome to it."

"But if there was a reason—"

"Forget it!" he retorted bitterly. "You should have asked me then, Tara. The reason just isn't important anymore. Not to me. Now, go to sleep. We have a long day ahead of us tomorrow."

With trembling fingers Tara pulled up the lace straps of her nightgown and turned on her side, away from him, staring out the window. Had she been wrong three years ago? The possibility tormented her.

But it really didn't matter. Whatever his feelings before, she was certain Devlin hated her now. . . .

The flight from Las Vegas to Amarillo, Texas was uneventful. Tara was weary after a sleepless night, and, judging from his drawn face, Devlin hadn't gotten much rest either. He had dropped the loving-fiancé act the moment they had parted from Jim at the airport, withdrawing into himself and projecting a cold, unapproachable front.

Tara hadn't tried to approach him. Wrapped in her own gray misery, dreading the days ahead, when she would have to act the loving fiancée to a man she knew hated her, a man she loved nonetheless, Tara was unwilling to give him any further excuse to stick verbal pins in her. She didn't blame him for his anger of the night before. Looking back, she knew that she had hurt his pride by rejecting him so vehemently, and for such an uncertain reason.

But even if that misunderstanding was cleared up, Tara knew that their relationship had well and truly ended three years before. It was only now, pitch-forked abruptly back into Devlin's life, that Tara realized why they had broken up. In spite of what she'd said the night before, she knew she was to blame for what had happened.

His interference in her career had made her angry, but at any other time she would have demanded his reasons and would probably have understood. Her anger had been fierce, unreasonable, and prompted by panic—because he had proposed. She had not known it then, or at any time during the past three years, but she knew now that she was afraid of marriage to the point of absolute terror.

The realization had come to her in the gray hours just before dawn as she lay sleepless beside Devlin. She had asked herself over and over again why she couldn't bring herself to fight for the man she loved, why she was afraid to take a chance and try to atone for her past mistakes. She was a grown woman, accustomed to fighting for what she wanted. Why couldn't she fight for Devlin? She could swallow her pride, couldn't she? Make herself vulnerable and prove to him that she loved him . . .

But fear had swept over her like a physical shock, and she had shied violently away from the thought of commitment. In a mo-

ment of painful insight she had seen a part of herself she hadn't
known existed, something small and frightened that lived in the
dark corners of her mind, where it could not be touched or con-
fronted.

What was it?

"Tara?"

She started violently and looked across to the driver's seat of
the small rented car to see Devlin frowning at her, his eyes shuttered.

"You're shivering. Do you want me to turn down the air conditioning?"

She looked at the gooseflesh on her arms and knew that it had
been prompted by her thoughts. "I—yes, it is a little chilly. If you
don't mind . . ."

"I don't mind. You should have said something," Devlin responded curtly, reaching to flip a switch.

Tara smiled a little wryly and looked out the car window to see
the last of Amarillo's city streets fading out of sight behind them.
It was the first conversation she had shared with Devlin since they
had gotten off the plane, and she had to wonder if this would set
the tone for their moments alone during the next couple of weeks.

With a faint sigh she glanced over the seat at Ah Poo's carrier
in the back, reflecting absently that the cat had finally given up his
frustrated howling. He hated being in the carrier. If she had been
alone, Tara would probably have let Ah Poo out so that he could
ride on the seat, but she knew instinctively that Devlin would have
very strong views against letting a cat loose in a moving car, so she
left well enough alone.

Satisfied with the cat's silence, Tara stared through the wind-
shield, suddenly worried about her upcoming meeting with Devlin's mother and stepfather. Particularly his mother.

What kind of woman was she? Was she a formal woman, or casual? Broad-minded or straightlaced? Was she an affectionate

mother, or domineering? No, Tara reflected silently, she couldn't be a domineering mother—not with a son as strong-willed as Devlin.

Would she approve of the young woman slated to become her daughter-in-law? Smoothing down the silk skirt of her dress, Tara wondered vaguely at her own desire for approval. Even the hidden, frightened part of herself desperately wanted Devlin's mother to approve of her. But why? What was that ghost in her mind that hungered for approval and affection yet shied fearfully away from any kind of commitment?

"My mother's anxious to meet you."

Tara glanced quickly at Devlin, saw the guarded look in his eyes, and realized he was trying to ease the strain between them. Eager to see the last of the stone-faced stranger who had accompanied her from Las Vegas, she responded, "Is she? When did you tell her about . . . about us? I mean—"

"I called her while I was in New York," he said casually, ignoring her stumbling. "She and Rick were very pleased." He sent her a sideways glance and then concentrated on the highway once again. "Rick is my stepfather."

"Do they know I'm an actress?" Tara looked down at the ring on her finger with a grimace, irritated with herself for her defensiveness regarding her career.

Devlin gave her a quick look. "Of course they know. They've seen most of your work, as a matter of fact. Mother says you should have received an Oscar for that drama last year."

Tara smiled in spite of herself. "My agent told me not to do that picture," she murmured. "That's why I broke with him and joined Karen Farrel's agency. I thought I'd made a mistake when she started pushing me to try out for *Celebration!*"

"You were worried about the singing?" Devlin asked shrewdly.

Tara turned sideways in the seat so she could study him. "Sure, I was worried," she admitted. "I've seen quite a few actresses fail as singers. I certainly didn't want to be one of them. But the part of

Maggie was too good to pass up, so I gritted my teeth and tried to sing."

With a satisfied smile, Devlin murmured, almost to himself, "I thought that part would appeal to you."

Tara was just about to say that apparently her singing had been good enough, when his remark suddenly penetrated. Thinking back, she wondered why Karen's insistence that she try out for the role hadn't struck her as odd before now. "You got me that part, didn't you?" she accused Devlin.

He glanced over at her, his eyes veiled again, and responded casually, "No, of course not. The casting director had the final say."

"Oh." She folded her hands in her lap. "Then there's no need to thank you."

This time the look she received was one of surprise. She had to bite back a giggle. He had been thrown by her gentle remark and suspected irony or sarcasm, but she was in no mood to explain herself. She only knew she felt suddenly light-hearted, and she had gone through far too much self-analysis during the past twenty-four hours to try to understand why.

After a moment Devlin sighed and asked, "Do you invent the rules as you go along?"

"Rules?" Tara asked innocently. "Are we playing a game?"

"One of us is."

"It isn't me." She smiled brightly, suddenly feeling much better about everything—including the troublesome gremlin inside her head.

Devlin fell silent, and Tara could almost hear the wheels turning as he attempted to understand her change of mood. In a thoughtful voice he finally muttered, "It must be lack of sleep."

Tara hesitated, then conceded. "Well, I didn't sleep much."

He grinned. "I was talking about myself. I can't think of any other reason why I'm suddenly hearing you react calmly to my interference in your career."

"Hah! Then you admit it!" she pounced.

After a startled moment he began to laugh. "I walked right into that one, didn't I?"

"You certainly did!"

Still chuckling he murmured, "All right, I admit it. I did recommend, rather strongly, that you be given the part of Maggie." He gave her an intent look. "And you aren't angry about that, are you?"

"Not a bit," she confirmed lightly.

"Mind telling me why?"

" 'Woman's at best a contradiction still,' " she quoted gaily.

"Well, that certainly answers my question."

Tara laughed softly. "What do you expect when you ask unanswerable questions?"

Devlin was smiling. "I have to guess, huh?"

She shrugged. "There's no need to make a federal case out of it. I just don't feel like getting mad today, that's all."

"You're stepping out of character, you know," Devlin told her calmly.

"I know," she responded, just as calmly. "But I'm sure it's a temporary thing, so don't get used to it." When he laughed, she glanced questioningly at him and then changed the subject abruptly, determined to keep the conversation light. "By the way, what kind of attitude should I adopt toward Julie?"

He shrugged. "I'm hoping she'll take one look at you and just pack up and go home."

"Now I see why you couldn't get out of this entanglement by yourself," Tara said with a sigh. "If you think a seventeen-year-old is going to be discouraged by the appearance of a fiancée, you can forget it. She'll just try harder, Devlin."

A corner of his mouth quivered slightly. "How will she try harder?" he asked gravely.

"Go ahead and laugh," she told him tolerantly. "You'll think it's hysterical when she pays a late-night visit to your bedroom and either cries all over you or tries to seduce you. Or both."

The horror in the glance he shot her made Tara laugh. "With her father in the house?" he asked.

"Of course, with her father in the house. With me in the picture, Devlin, she'll feel she hasn't a moment to waste." The look of consternation on his face tickled her sense of humor almost beyond bearing. Biting the inside of her lip to keep from laughing again, she added hastily, "So tell me a little about her. Does she act her age, or does she try too hard to be the kind of woman she thinks you want?"

He sighed. "Both. One moment she's a teenager in jeans and a T-shirt, the next she's wearing too much makeup and a dress that would look better on Mae West. And she has a very unnerving habit of launching herself at me with no provocation whatsoever."

"And what's your response to these unprovoked attacks?"

"I detach myself as soon as possible."

Tara laughed out loud in spite of herself, and Devlin sent her a withering glance. "I can see you're going to be a lot of help," he told her. "Well, what am I supposed to do? Turn her over my knee?"

"Don't do that," Tara advised, still laughing. "She'll be in love with you for life!"

His lips twitched again. "Maybe I should have tried that with you," he murmured whimsically.

Tara's breath caught in her throat. "We aren't talking about me," she managed to say casually, turning her head to stare out the window.

"Would it have worked, Tara?"

"If you think I'm going to tell you that, you're crazy," she answered flippantly. She felt him gazing at her profile.

"Hope springs eternal," he murmured after a moment. Before she could react, he went on calmly, "Back to Julie, then. Since you seem to understand the incomprehensible workings of a teenage girl's mind, tell me how I should discourage her."

Tara was silent for a time. She wasn't satisfied with the only plan that occurred to her, but she couldn't think of anything else. She wondered vaguely if she was going to suggest this plan because it would be the best thing for Julie—enabling her to emerge from this first serious bout with love relatively unscarred—or because Tara herself wanted the bittersweet experience of pretending that Devlin was in love with her.

"Tara?"

Hastily she looked across at him. "I suppose you'll just have to moon over me whenever she's around. And don't look at me like that. I'm not any happier about it than you are."

He turned his gaze back to the highway. "I don't suppose you can think of anything better, can you?" he asked.

Did she just imagine it, or did his voice contain a suspicious quiver? Tara's fingers tightened on the strap of the purse in her lap. She wanted to hit him with it. But that would be too dangerous while he was driving the car. So she'd just wait. One of these days she'd catch him with his back turned and just lay him out . . . and then run like hell.

"I'm afraid that's the best I can do," she replied very calmly. "But I'm open to suggestions."

"No," he murmured. "No, you're doing fine." He seemed to be having trouble controlling his expression. "But what happens if Julie pays that late-night visit you were talking about?"

"You're on your own," Tara told him flatly.

"We could nip that problem in the bud, you know." He sent her a sideways glance, a teasing glint in the silvery depths. "All we have to do—"

"I'm not sharing your bedroom, Devlin," she interrupted calmly.

"What makes you so sure I was going to suggest that?"

"Weren't you?"

"Well . . ." He smiled like a guilty boy.

Sternly Tara reminded herself that this man had all the innocence of a shark in bloody waters. She changed the subject abruptly. "Is Julie an only child?"

Devlin considered her question, the remains of that absurdly guilty smile still playing around his mouth and a peculiar gleam shining in his eyes, which made Tara immediately wary. Then, apparently accepting her change of subject, he answered easily, "As far as I know, she is. Why?"

"Uh huh," Tara murmured, ignoring his question. "I'll bet Holman is a widower, too. Or divorced."

"When did you become psychic?" he asked with another sideways glance.

"Around you it pays to be," she answered absently, as they turned off the highway onto a two-lane road. "Are we nearly there?" Nervousness assailed her once again, and her mouth went dry.

Displaying a certain psychic ability of his own, Devlin said softly, "Don't worry. They'll love you." Without waiting for her response, he added, "Another ten minutes or so."

Tara bit her lip with faint irritation as she turned to gaze through the window. Were her feelings as transparent as they seemed to be, she wondered, or was Devlin really reading her mind? She had laughed about the possibility with Jim, but now she felt distinctly uneasy. Did Devlin know she loved him? Did he care?

Avoiding that unproductive line of thought, she concentrated on the large herd of sleek horses in the distance. They appeared to be quarter horses, mares and foals, their excellent breeding showing in every line. "What beautiful horses," she murmured, noting whitewashed wooden fences and lush pastures.

"They're Rick's," Devlin replied laconically.

Tara shot him a surprised look and then turned her eyes back to the rolling meadows, which continued as far as she could see, dotted here and there with horses. Dizzily, she wondered how many horses Devlin's stepfather owned and whether she was looking at a ranch the size of northern Texas.

Why hadn't he warned her? Immediately, she realized that to Devlin an estate this size was as ordinary as a pair of brown shoes. He had amassed a fortune of his own during the past ten years, while his family had been wealthy in its own right for most of its long and colorful history.

And what was she? Just an actress, one of thousands. More successful than most, perhaps, but all she had was the name she had built for herself. She had no idea whether her family could trace its roots back to royalty or to horse thieves.

Her unsettled childhood had left Tara with a sense of insecurity and inferiority that she had been fighting most of her adult life. She had wondered more than once if that was why she had sought a career in film, where she could be anyone she chose to be. Whatever the reason, her career had given her the opportunity to meet famous and powerful people, which she had found to be an unsettling experience.

Her veneer of sophistication was as thin as frost, and she knew it. Underneath that facade existed a wary young woman who was terrified of committing a social blunder, making a tactless comment, or bumping into the furniture. She felt uncomfortable around wealth.

It was a funny sort of reverse snobbery, but knowing that did not help Tara overcome it. She had never felt uncomfortable around Devlin, but that, she knew, was because of his natural ability to blend in with his surroundings. Still, she had always been conscious on some level of his wealth and power, had always been dimly aware of the difference in their backgrounds.

What was she doing here? How could these people accept her as a prospective in-law? She felt completely out of her depth, as tense as a drawn bow. She would never be able to cope with Devlin's act of loving devotion . . .

"Stop it, Tara."

The soft voice snapped her out of her nervous reflections, and she looked down to see one of Devlin's large hands covering her own, gripped tightly together in her lap. Blinking as she raised her eyes, she discovered that he had stopped the car just inside of what appeared to be a driveway. A large sign arched over the road, proclaiming that this was the Double L Ranch.

Devlin was sitting sideways, one arm over the steering wheel, staring at her with dark eyes. She knew that her own eyes reflected the panic churning inside her, knew that he was seeing a vulnerability in her that she had never shown before.

In that same impossibly soft voice he said, "You're getting yourself all worked up over nothing, honey. Mother and Rick will love you. I told you that."

"I don't belong here," she whispered, all her defenses down.

His hand tightened over hers. "You're beautiful, intelligent, talented, and spirited," he told her in a gentle, measured tone. "What's not to belong? You can hold your own anywhere, Tara, anywhere. You have nothing to be ashamed of. You would fit in at a diplomatic ball, a presidential dinner, a barn dance, or a royal wedding. You can hold your own with politicians, professors, soldiers, cowboys, kings, and queens. You could topple governments with a smile."

The nonsense he was saying finally got through to Tara, and she smiled at him. His hand tightened again.

"That's better. The members of my family aren't monsters, sweetheart. They won't eat you."

Tara felt a peculiar jolt as she absorbed the endearment, wondering why he had used it when there was no audience but herself. Was he trying to make her feel better? To her own surprise, one of her hands turned beneath his and clasped it briefly. "Thank you," she murmured huskily. "I'm a bit of a coward about some things."

"You hide it well." He released her hand and turned back to the wheel. "I didn't think you were the least bit insecure."

Unwilling to expose more of herself than she already had, Tara said lightly, "I'm all right now. Let's go and beard the lioness—I mean . . ." She flushed and bit her lip, but Devlin was laughing.

"I'll remind you later that you said that," he said, chuckling.

Now, what had he meant by that? Tara mused as the car continued along the side drive. Then she forgot about it. She was only just beginning to realize that Devlin had been reading her mind again, understanding her fears with uncanny insight, and she was vaguely alarmed to realize that she wasn't angry about it. And, oddly enough, she was no longer afraid of not fitting in.

Devlin stopped the car on a circular drive in front of the house, and Tara absorbed the view in silence as he got out and came around to open her door. The house was tremendous, white and stately. It had aged gracefully over the years, until now it seemed a natural part of the landscape. It was three stories high, supported by tall white columns and embellished with wide sparkling windows. Tara wondered briefly why no one had thought to drape Spanish moss from the tall trees, and her confidence lagged once again.

Devlin opened her door and extended a hand to help her out. Before she could do more than swing her legs out of the car, he said in a conspiratorial whisper, "By the way, I forgot one of your virtues when I was listing them back there."

Her hand lost in his large clasp, Tara looked up at him blankly. "What did you forget?" she whispered back.

A mischievous demon danced in his eyes. Still whispering, he told her, "You have a temper that could flay a man wearing a suit of armor."

Her confidence unaccountably restored, Tara laughed up at him and allowed him to help her the rest of the way from the car. "Temper! You call that a virtue?"

"On you even that looks good." He slammed the car door to punctuate the remark. Suddenly a shriek from the wide porch caught their attention.

"Devlin!"

A tiny, well-endowed young woman wearing skintight jeans and a halter top that was a single breath away from being indecent flung herself from the third step into Devlin's arms, uttering breathy cries of excited welcome.

Julie. Her brunette hair was caught up in a tortuous mass of twists and ringlets, vaguely Greek in design and completely un-suited to both her age and her clothing. She wore heavy makeup, including thick eyeliner, which made her resemble a cross between Cleopatra and a demented panda.

Tara felt a twinge of compassion for the girl and then nearly reeled as a wave of heavy perfume wafted her way. Good lord, she thought, highly amused. Devlin must be smothering! She tried to size the girl up quickly as Devlin began trying to disentangle him-self, deciding finally that Julie would probably rush away in tears before sounding the call to battle.

Tara continued to watch her fiancé's gentle attempts to remove the arms clinging around his neck and bit her lip to keep from laughing. Well, he hadn't lied to her. Mr. Devlin Bradley quite def-initely had a problem. No wonder he needed help.

Freeing himself at last, Devlin took a deep breath that sounded suspiciously like a gasp for air and reached over to yank Tara closer to his side with a complete lack of gallantry. "Tara," he began, "this is Jake Holman's daughter, Julie. Julie, this is Tara Collins—my fiancée."

Tara wasn't really surprised at the blunt, graceless introduction. She had never seen Devlin so completely rattled. A glint of des-peration shone in his eyes, and a lock of his disheveled dark hair fell across his forehead, giving him the appearance of a despairing poet.

Still trying to keep from laughing, Tara said unsteadily, "Hello, Julie. It's nice to meet you."

Julie looked as if she had just stepped into a nest of vipers, one of which was rearing back to bite her. She cast a betrayed, shattered glare at Devlin, burst into tears, and rushed into the house.

"I take back everything I ever said about your charming ways," Tara commented in a voice choked with laughter.

Devlin raked a hand through his hair and grimaced. "Sorry about that. They weren't supposed to arrive here until tomorrow, and I assumed Mother would break the news to her."

"Never assume anything," Tara counseled, finally gaining control over her laughter. She cocked her head to one side and studied Devlin carefully. "That's a very interesting shade of lipstick you're wearing. Not your color, though."

"Hell." He fished in the pocket of his sports jacket and produced a handkerchief. "Get it off, will you?" he asked, handing the folded square to Tara.

Tara tilted his chin to get at the bright red splotches on his neck. "She's an enthusiastic girl, isn't she?" she commented dryly.

"She's a pain in the—"

"Hold still. How am I supposed to get this off if you don't . . ."

Devlin sighed and reached up to loosen his tie. "She wears enough perfume to float a ship," he grumbled. When Tara released his chin and began to rub the several splotches on his cheek, he lifted a rueful brow. "Well, it wasn't as bad as I expected."

"The worst is yet to come." Tara turned his head slightly to dab at a spot near his ear. "For me, anyway. The next time she sees me, she'll bring all guns to bear."

"Sounds like you're expecting a war."

"At the very least. And you're the prize. Aren't you flattered?"

Tara refolded his handkerchief and tucked it back in his pocket, giving him a serene smile.

Devlin stared at her for a moment, then muttered, "I should have run like a thief."

Tara ignored the comment. "There's more lipstick on your collar. It's a good thing your fiancée doesn't have a suspicious mind. That's not her color, either."

Devlin opened his mouth to respond but was interrupted by a cheerful voice from the side of the house. "Well, what a charming couple you make!"

Tara turned in surprise, seeing first her trailer parked to one side of the drive, and then a woman strolling toward them. Her first thought was a wild: That can't be Devlin's mother. But she realized immediately that the woman was indeed his mother.

She was tall and slender, and moved with the unthinking grace she must have passed along to her son. Dark auburn hair, untouched by gray and gleaming with youthful highlights, crowned her head in a braided coronet. She had the complexion of a girl, clear and unlined, with the delicate tone of a ripe peach. And gray eyes just like Devlin's glinted between long, thick lashes, as changeable and as mysterious as the sea.

Tara knew very well that Amanda Bradley Lawton was in her late fifties, but she could swear that she was looking at a woman twenty years younger.

"Mother, why didn't you warn Julie about the engagement?" Devlin demanded, removing the last doubt from Tara's mind.

"What? And miss that perfectly entertaining introduction?" Her voice was as refined and regal as the rest of her. "Don't be ridiculous, dear boy." She reached up to tug at Devlin's ear, pulling his head down so that she could kiss his cheek. After a brief hug, which her son returned enthusiastically, she released him, murmuring, "No lipstick. Tara won't have to use the handkerchief this time."

Devlin chuckled and then reached for Tara's hand, pulling her closer. "Mother, this is Tara," he said simply.

Tara found her fascinated gaze being returned by a shrewd yet friendly appraisal, and fought back an absurd impulse to curtsy.

"What a beauty you are," Amanda exclaimed with a smile, and Tara saw that Devlin had also inherited his mother's charm. Before she could respond to the compliment, she was enfolded in a warm hug as sincere and unpretentious as the woman herself. "I don't know whether to congratulate you or mourn with you for catching him, but welcome to the family anyway, Tara."

Emerging from the hug a bit breathless, and completely unstrung by the unexpected welcome, Tara stammered, "I—thank you, Mrs. Lawton."

"Amanda, my dear. Devlin, you'll have to carry in the luggage. Josh has a cold, and I've put him to bed."

"Personally, Mother?" Devlin inquired with a wicked lift of his brows as he headed toward the trunk.

"And why not? The poor man could hardly see to stagger to his room, let alone find his pajamas. Tara, did you bring Ah Poo? I'm looking forward to meeting him."

Tara felt as if she had wandered into a movie in the middle of the second reel. Nothing made sense. Abandoning herself to fate she opened the back door and pulled out Ah Poo's carrier. "Here he is," she murmured. "Devlin said you wouldn't mind pets."

"Not when they're cats." Within a minute the temperamental feline was in Amanda's arms, purring contentedly and returning her smiling gaze with the look of slavish devotion he normally reserved for Devlin.

"Uh . . . who's Josh?" Tara ventured hesitantly.

"My butler." Amanda smiled at her. "I found him in an English pub, weeping into his ale, about ten years ago, and he's been with me ever since. A marvelous man, really, and wonderful with cats. Can you manage the cases, Devlin?"

"Yes, Mother." He slammed the trunk shut and met Tara's be-wildered gaze with a smile of amusement.

"Good. I was going to sacrifice Tara. Come along, my dear." Carrying the cat, Amanda started up the steps to the house.

Barely remembering to pick up her purse and the deserted car-rier, Tara followed, desperate to ask why Josh had been weeping into his ale.

Amanda led the way through the huge entrance hall. Tara was too busy listening to her fascinating hostess's gentle stream of talk to pay more than cursory attention to the polished wood floor dot-ted here and there with Queen Anne chairs and heavy tables on which riding whips and western hats vied for space with priceless vases and figurines of jade and ivory. Tara stepped on a Persian rug that she thought should have been hanging in a museum and thought vaguely, Persian rugs? On a ranch?

"I've put you in the west wing," Amanda was saying. "If you lose your way, just stand still and scream until someone finds you. For the first year after Rick married me, he was forever having to hunt for me. I threatened more than once to leave a trail of bread crumbs. It wouldn't have done any good, though, because Rose is a devoted housekeeper and would have cleaned them all up. Devlin was a beast to break the news to Julie like that, but it wasn't his fault that she picked him to fall in love with, so I suppose it just couldn't be helped. Poor child, she tries too hard to be grown up. Too much makeup. She looked like an owl, didn't you think?"

Untangling the remarks as best she could, Tara murmured help-lessly, "I thought a panda," and heard a muffled choking sound be-hind them as Devlin bumped along up the stairs with the luggage.

"A panda. Yes, you're right. Devlin, dear, Rick and Jake are out in the yearling barn. That filly you wanted came up for sale last week, and Rick bought her for you, but you may need a crowbar to get her away from him now. Do you plan to have children, my dear?"

Realizing that the question was addressed to her, Tara nearly stumbled at the top of the stairs. She heard another choke behind her. "Oh, I intend to have a houseful of them," she answered defiantly.

"You don't plan to give up your career, I hope?"

"Oh, no."

"Good." Amanda sounded deeply satisfied. "I've always wanted to see Devlin cope with bottles and diapers. His father was quite good at it, as I remember—although he had an irritating habit of pushing me out of bed for the three-o'clock feeding. And I hate cold floors. I'll have a talk with Julie and see if I can calm her down. But I don't know how much good it will do. She doesn't seem to understand me very well."

"I wonder why," Devlin murmured from the rear.

"Don't mumble, dear boy. Tara looks tired. She should rest for a while." Amanda halted on the second floor and opened a door on the right. "Here we are. Why are you lagging behind, Devlin?"

"It seemed appropriate," he murmured, brushing past Tara to take her bags into the room.

"May I take him with me, my dear, and show him the rest of the house? He'll love the pool, I think."

For a moment Tara was confused as to what Amanda was referring to—Devlin or Ah Poo. Restraining herself, she said weakly, "Of course, Mrs.—uh—Amanda."

"You see, that wasn't so hard. It'll get easier with practice. Rest as long as you like, dear. We'll be serving something downstairs around four. Come along, Devlin, and don't dawdle. Rick's wild to talk to you about that filly." She strolled off down the hall.

Tara stepped inside the bedroom and gave Devlin a blank look. "Your mother . . ." she murmured dazedly.

Leaving her suitcases at the foot of the huge bed, he headed back toward the door and said in a stage whisper, "I'm not flattered by that look of astonishment on your face."

Tara bit back a giggle. "But she's marvelous!"

"I told you she wasn't a monster—or a lioness." He winked at her and then gently closed the door as he went out.

Tara stared at the heavy door for a long moment and then sank down on the bed. She gazed around the luxurious blue-and-gold room without really seeing it, flopped back on the bed, and laughed quietly until she was out of breath.

Chapter Six

Two hours later, Tara finally gave up her useless attempts to rest and scooted off the bed. She had already unpacked and put her clothes away, and had even taken the time for a quick shower in the lovely blue-tiled bath adjoining her bedroom. She'd hoped the shower would help to relax her, but that didn't turn out to be the case. If anything, it made her feel wide awake and very puzzled.

The cause of her puzzlement was Devlin. She brooded about him as she put on a pair of black slacks and a green pullover. From the moment they had gotten out of the car, she mused, Devlin had been acting . . . odd. She couldn't put her finger on exactly what the difference was. It was as if the man she had known for nearly three and a half years had suddenly assumed an unfamiliar and disturbing mask.

Or was it a mask? She sat down on the edge of the bed to put on her shoes and continued to think.

What had been the first indication that something had changed? His teasing, of course. Devlin had always been witty, but she could only remember satire and a sardonic mockery. His light-hearted, cheerful teasing had come as a surprise.

And then she must consider his helpless reaction to Julie. *That* had been a definite surprise, although Tara herself had been a bit off-balance at the time and hadn't paid much attention to it. But . . . helpless? Devlin? She had never before seen him thrown by anything or anyone.

Was it only because Julie was the daughter of an important business associate? Or did Devlin just want to convince Tara that he really did need a fiancée? Tara stared across the room with a frown. Good heavens, she was clutching at straws. Not even Devlin would be that devious, and besides, what would be the point? There was no earthly reason why he should want her here enough to play that sort of game.

His unusual behavior probably wasn't a mask at all. He was with his family now, and able to shed his all-powerful businessman image. Simple enough. Tara's knowledge of him, after all, was entirely culled from either very public or very private moments. He was bound to act a little differently around his family.

Pushing these thoughts from her mind, Tara left her room, determined to find her way downstairs without having to "stand and scream," as Amanda had advised. She located the staircase after making only one wrong turn, and was silently congratulating herself, when she realized it was the wrong staircase. What a house! she thought ruefully. Backtracking, she finally regained her bearings and discovered the stairs that she hoped would take her back to the entrance hall. They did.

Tara hesitated on the bottom step and looked around warily. Her earlier passage through this hall had left a vague impression of the general layout, but she was becoming confused by the sheer size of the house. Four sets of double doors and two separate hallways opened onto this foyer. The doors were all closed, the halls deserted, and Tara was at a loss to know where to go from here.

With a faint grimace she flipped a mental coin and started down one of the hallways. Some doors along this hall were closed and some were open. Tara glanced into the opened rooms but found no one. One of the rooms, a den, had glass doors that led out to a patio and, beyond that, a pool. The sparkle of blue water looked inviting, and Tara started forward, but a sound caught her attention.

Someone was playing a piano. Curious, she continued down the hall until she discovered a door slightly ajar. Unwilling to intrude, she pushed the door open only far enough to peek inside. The room that met her gaze might have been called the Music Room in another age, and Tara thought that the name fit. Instead of the harp, pianoforte, and other instruments that would have seemed appropriate, the room contained a vast modern stereo system, shelves of record albums, deep chairs of Spanish leather, and low tables. And a baby grand piano.

The soft, gentle sound of a popular song wafted to Tara's ears, but she didn't really hear it. She stared at Devlin's absorbed profile for a startled moment, and then her gaze dropped automatically to his long brown fingers, moving easily over the keys.

Here was yet another discovery about the man she loved, and Tara wondered how many men lived inside that skin called Devlin Bradley. She didn't know him. She didn't know him at all.

Entranced, she listened to the soft music and watched the long brown fingers as if hypnotized. Considering that he didn't have much time to practice, he was pretty good.

The last note died away into silence, and before Tara could announce her presence, Devlin began playing something else, a simple, haunting melody that sounded vaguely familiar. Tara frowned as she tried to place the elusive tune in her memory. It came to her slowly as she watched his brooding profile that there were words to the song, words she should know. And then she remembered.

Of course there were words! She had sung them not three months before, when she'd tried out for the part of Maggie in *Cel-*

ebration! No one knew who had composed the song. It was a simple, beautiful love song. Tara had been deeply moved as she'd sung it, haunted and disturbed by the aching love and bitter regret conveyed in the words and melody.

And now . . . She stared as Devlin played this unpublished piece of music as though he'd written it himself, his face filled with an unreadable expression she'd never seen before. He looked weary and sad and strangely vulnerable, like a man who had cared, did care, deeply about someone . . .

Tara's throat ached with rising emotion. Had the press been right, after all, about Devlin's interest in the blonde model? What had happened between them? She remembered various remarks she'd heard during the past months about a possible marriage, and wondered what had gone wrong. Devlin had mentioned nothing about it, but . . . She studied his face and knew suddenly, instinctively, that the emotions that had compelled him to write the song still existed. He had not forgotten the woman or his love. Jealousy swept over her, but she pushed the emotion fiercely away.

It wouldn't stay away. Because she knew now why Devlin had not mentioned love when he had asked her to marry him three years ago. Even then he had loved someone else. She knew that now. That was what he had been holding back.

The last note of the song died away, leaving an aching silence. Tara swallowed hard before she could make a sound. "That was beautiful," she said huskily.

Devlin swung around on the padded bench, surprise wiping the brooding look from his face. A faint redness crept up beneath his deep tan, and his silvery eyes moved restlessly away from her intent gaze. He rose from the bench, shoving his hands into the pockets of his jeans. "I thought you'd still be resting."

Tara advanced slowly into the room, sliding her own hands into her pockets to hide their trembling. "I wasn't all that tired." She realized that she was seeing him off guard and rattled for the second time that day, but this time she had no desire to laugh. Instead something hurt inside her to see the chinks in his armor and to know that they were real. "They didn't tell me at the studio that you wrote that song," she commented.

Something flickered in his eyes and then was gone. He turned toward a bar set in the corner of the room. "Drink, Tara?"

"I don't drink this early." She watched him splash whiskey into a glass. "You never used to either."

"Things change." He sipped the drink, still avoiding her eyes.

Tara took a deep breath. "It's no use avoiding the subject, you know. Why don't you just admit that you wrote the song?"

"What makes you think I wrote it?"

She waited until he looked at her, then said evenly, "The fact that it's an unpublished song. The fact that there's no sheet music on the piano. The fact that you played it with such . . . feeling."

Devlin looked back down at his glass, swirling the whiskey in what almost seemed a nervous gesture. "Didn't think I had it in me, did you?" he murmured.

"No." She smiled faintly. "It seems that there's a great deal about you I don't know." After a moment's hesitation she added quietly, "It's a beautiful song, Devlin."

He shrugged. "Don't read more into it than there is. It's just a song."

Tara's throat tightened. Was he warning her that the song had been written for another woman? "I'm reading nothing into it," she told him flatly.

Devlin turned to stare at her, his gaze intent and a bit puzzled. "I only meant—"

"I know what you meant." Tara heard the shrillness in her voice and made a determined effort to calm down. Summoning up all her acting ability, she went on easily, "You meant that I should mind my own business."

He continued to gaze steadily at her, as though he were trying to probe her innermost secrets, then shrugged again. "Have it your own way." Without waiting for a response, he went on casually, "Rick and Jake are getting cleaned up. Mother took off somewhere with Ah Poo. We'll all meet in the den in about an hour."

Perversely, Tara was irritated with him for changing the subject. She wandered over to the piano and tapped a couple of keys, relieved to see that her hands were now steady. "I didn't even know you played."

He remained silent for a moment, then said dryly, "We all have secrets, don't we?"

"What's that supposed to mean?" She turned to stare at him.

"Nothing sinister." His voice was mocking.

So . . . they were back to *that* Devlin. The mocking, sardonic Devlin who could cut down an opponent without raising his voice or losing his smile. Her nemesis of the past three years, the enemy she felt fairly safe with because she was too busy yelling at him to remember that she loved him.

Once again Tara retreated behind her shield of anger. "This is not going to work. You know that, don't you? We aren't going to fool anyone with the stupid charade of yours. I was seven different kinds of an idiot to let you talk me into this."

"I didn't talk you into anything, Tara." He walked calmly around the far side of the piano, and she turned to keep facing him. "All I did was offer you a deal." He set his whiskey glass down on the piano and came to stand before her. "It isn't my fault if you're too afraid to go through with it."

"Afraid! Why, you—"

"Hush!" He glanced over her shoulder at the door, which was behind her now. "Mother's coming. Make it good, now."

Before Tara could react, she found herself in Devlin's arms, being kissed ruthlessly. From a distance it probably looked like a kiss of burning passion, but for Tara it was no such thing. Devlin meant to punish her. His lips were hard, insistent. His embrace was like a steel cage.

Tara was torn between anger and bewilderment. What was she being punished for? But, despite her confused emotions, a restless ache was forming deep inside her, and she hated herself for responding to him no matter what his mood.

Her role in this masquerade forgotten, Tara pushed against his chest with both hands, desperate to escape from an embrace that was killing her by inches, destroying her ability to resist him. She tried to twist away, but he held her with his mouth and with his hands, and she was helpless under his persistent grip. The heat of passion swept through her veins, choking off the desire to escape. Slowly the hands against his chest curled into his shirt to pull him even closer.

His kiss deepened, probing and relentless, as if he intended to take everything she had to offer. As if he wanted more than she had to give. One hand slid down to her hip, drawing her even closer, and she felt the evidence of his aroused desire.

And then—quite suddenly—she was free. Devlin stepped back, his face pale, his eyes a dark and stormy gray. "You see, honey," he said very softly, "I didn't need to force you."

Tara clung to the edge of the piano and stared at him, her heart beating wildly against her ribs, trying vainly to control her ragged breathing. She glanced over her shoulder to find the doorway empty, and knew without a doubt that she'd been tricked. "Damn you!" she exclaimed, "You rotten, no-good—"

"Bastard?" he suggested, lifting a mocking brow. "Cad? Devil?"

Tara struggled, without success, to come up with a searing insult, but the best she could do was, "Opportunist!" She turned on her heel, hearing his laughter and hating him for it. But his voice stopped her at the door.

"Sure you don't want a drink, Tara?"

She half turned to give him a quelling look. Making no effort to keep her voice down, she retorted, "Only if it's in a barrel—then I can drown you in it!"

She slammed the door behind her with vicious satisfaction—and halted abruptly three steps away from Amanda, who was smiling serenely. Flushing deeply, Tara managed a weak smile. "Hi."

"You're looking better, my dear." Amanda nodded toward the closed door. "There's an old proverb about marriage, you know. Begin as you mean to go on, or something like that. I'd say you were wise not to let Devlin have everything his own way. He takes after his father—the pride of the devil and the soul of a dreamer. Tame the devil, my dear, and you'll have a marriage filled with love and laughter. Destroy the dreamer . . . and you'll never forgive yourself. Ah Poo's swimming in the pool, if you want him."

Feeling a bit off balance, the way she always felt around Amanda, Tara watched as the older woman headed toward the staircase. She considered the other woman's words carefully, and found a nugget of truth in them. Devlin certainly had the pride of the devil. But the soul of a dreamer? She shrugged the thought away and went in search of her feline water-baby.

Not until later did she remember the haunting song, and the woman in Devlin's past. She wondered again what had happened to part them. And, despite the way Devlin had treated her, she wondered why some women didn't realize when they'd struck gold . . .

While Amanda had come as a surprise to Tara, Rick Lawton exactly fit her image of a Texas rancher. He was tall and lanky, with sun-lightened brown hair and a deeply tanned face. Laugh lines fanned out from the corners of his mild eyes, and his smile was gentle. He had a soft, drawling voice, was obviously fond of his stepson, and adored his wife.

Seated in the den with the rest of them, Tara couldn't help but smile as she watched Amanda and Rick. Their love was not dramatic, but soft and warm and obviously very deep. They were sitting on the sofa together, across from Tara's chair, both smiling at her.

Tara returned their smiles and forced herself to lean back, although the movement put her in closer proximity to Devlin, who was leaning against the back of her chair. She took a hasty sip of coffee and sent a guarded glance toward Jake Holman, who was standing by the fireplace. Her gaze met cold green eyes, and she wondered again at the man's hostility. Devlin must have been right when he'd told her in the hospital that Holman wanted Julie married to him.

Julie, of course, wasn't in the room.

"Have you two decided where you're going to live?" Amanda asked in her gentle voice.

Tara's coffee nearly went down the wrong way, but Devlin replied casually, "Not really. Tara usually works on the West Coast, and most of my work is there as well."

"You plan to keep working, Miss Collins?"

Holman's tone was cynical, and Tara felt Devlin stiffen behind her. Before he could say anything, she looked squarely at Holman and answered coolly, "Of course, Mr. Holman. I love my work."

"In my day a woman's work was her husband."

Tara smiled sweetly. "That day is long past, Mr. Holman, or haven't you noticed?"

Devlin chuckled, easing the tense atmosphere. "You can't fight progress, Jake. Women aren't second-class citizens anymore."

Tara was surprised that Devlin would defend her desire to work, but she was relieved when Rick said something to Holman, drawing his attention away from her. Knowing that Devlin would hear her, she murmured softly, "Sorry about that."

He leaned toward her. "Sorry about what?"

"Snapping at Holman. I know his goodwill is important to you. I'll try to be nice to him."

He was silent before saying quietly, "It's not that important, Tara."

She tilted her head back, surprised to find his face so near. "Not important? I thought that was why you were here."

"One of the reasons." He kissed her lightly. "Mother's watching."

Tara gave her bogus fiancé a sweet smile and hissed softly, "I repeat, you're an opportunist."

He smiled tenderly down at her. "Sneaky, too."

"I should be getting combat pay for this."

"Oh, is it such a hardship?" His silvery eyes gleamed down at her mockingly. "Funny, I didn't think so."

"You wouldn't." He laughed softly as she turned her gaze back to the others. Amanda was smiling across the room at her, and Tara returned the smile weakly, wondering just how long she was going to be able to cope with Devlin's loving attitude. How did she get herself into messes like this, anyway?

By the end of the evening Tara was convinced that the fates were punishing her for something. Devlin grew more loving and attentive by the moment, using every excuse to touch or kiss her. He had never been a particularly reticent man, and he voiced his emotions and expressed his affection no matter who happened to be present. If he was angry or humorous, it was obvious to everyone.

Apparently it was also obvious if he happened to be in love.

Aware of Amanda's shrewd, amused gaze throughout the evening, Tara was forced to go along with Devlin's determined lovemaking. He made certain that they were never alone together. She had no opportunity to relieve her feelings with a burst of temper.

Besides, no matter how much she tried to deny it to herself, she found bittersweet pleasure in pretending that he was in love . . . with her. She was wryly aware that she would have a sleepless night. Her body had always responded instantly to Devlin, and believing that he was still in love with another woman did nothing to change that. Their encounter in the music room had left her senses clamoring for satisfaction, and he wasn't, she thought angrily, helping things one damn bit!

It only got worse, of course. Julie finally made an appearance for dinner. Though she wasn't wearing war paint, she was obviously there to fight.

"I've seen some of your movies, Miss Collins," she told Tara in an innocent tone as they sat down at the table. "It's strange, though—you looked so much younger on film."

Tara couldn't help but smile at the blatant insult, but she responded cheerfully, "Yes, it's amazing what they can do with makeup these days." From the corner of her eye she saw Amanda hide a smile.

For a moment Julie looked nonplussed, but she recovered quickly. Wide-eyed, she said innocently, "I've heard so much about the wolves in Hollywood. Are those stories true? I read a newspaper article a while back that said an actress had to be willing to sleep around in order to get good parts. Is that true?"

"Julie!" The reprimand came from Holman and wasn't very strong. Julie ignored it.

"Well, is it true?" she insisted.

The topic was a sore spot with Tara, but she resisted an impulse to treat Julie like a spiteful rival rather than a teenager suffering the pangs of first love. "Only if the actress isn't talented," she replied easily, sipping her wine. "And really it usually isn't necessary," she went on, deliberately outrageous in an attempt to silence Julie. "With the new freedom and the women's movement and all, most of the men in the industry aren't that desperate."

Devlin choked slightly, but Tara ignored him and continued to smile across the table at Julie.

Maintaining her composure, the younger woman asked, "Then it isn't true what the papers wrote about you and that producer?"

"What producer?" Tara asked calmly.

"The one you went to England with last year," Julie supplied with a smug expression.

"Oh, that one." Tara shrugged indifferently. "I went to England, and he *was* with me. But then, so were a couple of dozen other people. We stayed in a terrific old castle and had to huddle together at night to keep warm. Women in one room and men in another, you know. The producer's wife was the warmest, though. She'd brought her hot-water bottle from home, and made her husband get up three times to build up the fire."

Everyone at the table laughed, and Julie looked frustrated. Descending from the heights of character assassination to the depths of childish insult, she interrupted the laughter to ask snidely, "Do you change your hair color for every film? You were a blonde in the movie you did a few months ago."

Sighing, Tara replied calmly, "No, I was wearing a wig. I was born a redhead, and a redhead I'll remain."

"You mean that's your natural color?" Julie asked with feigned surprise, as if Tara's hair were a hideous shade of purple.

"I'm afraid so," Tara murmured, honestly amused. "It *is* red, though, isn't it? My mother must have been frightened by a bottle of red ink while she was carrying me."

Julie apparently decided to give up. It was obvious she wasn't going to get a rise out of her rival. Concentrating on her dinner, she fell silent, sending Tara occasional sullen looks and glancing longingly at Devlin from time to time.

Tara sincerely wanted to make friends with the girl, but she had no opportunity to try after dinner. Devlin demanded most of her attention. He stayed as close to Tara as the hand on the end of her arm, and if he had to go farther away than that, he took her with him. He followed Tara's earlier advice to the letter, mooning over her with tender smiles and loving touches, and practically ignoring everyone else.

By ten o'clock that evening his attentions to his fiancée had approached idolatry. Amanda and Rick were amused, Holman was irritated, and Julie remained silent. Tara had a splitting headache.

Pleading her discomfort as an excuse, she headed for her room. If she heard one more "darling" from Devlin or had to utter one herself, she knew she'd wreak havoc on somebody. Probably him. A pleasant possibility to contemplate.

Devlin followed her from the room, expressing tender concern over her headache. Halfway up the stairs, and out of earshot of the others, she turned to confront him. Since she was one step ahead of him, she faced him eye to eye.

"I can tuck myself into bed alone, thank you," she told him.

His lips twitched. "Just taking a wild guess I'd say that you were mad at me."

"Bingo." She glared at him.

"I was just following your advice," he said innocently.

Tara started to tell him what he could do with her advice, then changed her mind. "Well, I've got another bit of advice for you. Watch out for dark hallways and alleys. And don't look behind you. Something may be gaining on you."

He grinned. "You, huh? With a knife?"

"With anything I can get my hands on," she replied from between clenched teeth. "If I manage to live through this—this farcical situation of yours, Devlin Bradley, I'll make the last three years seem like a tea party."

Devlin leaned against the banister and folded his arms across his chest, smiling wickedly. "Well, I've always enjoyed a good fight. And you've never disappointed me, honey."

Tara itched to throw something at him. "Damn you, quit calling me that!"

For a moment his features hardened. Then he was smiling again. "Just practicing."

"You don't need any practice," she told him flatly. "You were born to this role, Devlin. Everyone in that room would have to have been blind, deaf, and stupid not to believe that you worship the ground I walk on. So you're a success." She heard the bitterness in her voice and ignored it. "A rousing success. If you ever need a job, you won't have to knock on many doors in Hollywood."

Again his expression grew harsh, and again the mocking smile returned. "I convinced everyone but you, huh?"

"I know the truth, don't I?"

"Do you?"

She searched his face, puzzled, and found only mockery. "What's that supposed to mean?"

For a moment he seemed almost indecisive, as if he were trying to make up his mind about something. Finally he shrugged. "Nothing. Go to bed, Tara. We're both tired, and neither of us is making much sense. See you in the morning."

She turned silently and continued up the stairs, feeling his eyes on her until she reached the second-floor landing and rounded the corner. Once in her room she automatically undressed and put on the blue nightgown, reflecting absently that she was going to have to visit her trailer in the morning and find something a little warmer to wear. With the air conditioning it was cool in the room.

With effort she put the disturbing conversation with Devlin from her mind. She *was* tired—too tired to understand cryptic comments or unreadable expressions. Turning out her bedside lamp, she slid between the covers and resolutely closed her eyes, trying to ignore the ache of unfulfilled longing.

Three hours later she turned the lamp on and stared irritably at the travel alarm dock on the nightstand. 1:00 A.M. Terrific. She'd look like a hag in the morning, and wouldn't Julie have a field day with *that*. Swearing silently, she flung back the covers and got out of bed. Ah Poo, curled up on a chair in the corner of the room, blinked at her sleepily, and Tara smiled at him as she headed for her dresser. "Sorry, cat. I think I'll go for a swim."

She dressed rapidly in the yellow bikini and then found a huge towel in her bathroom. Sliding her feet into a pair of thongs, she left the room with the lamp still burning. The hallway was dimly lit, and she had no trouble this time finding her way downstairs.

The lower floor was dark except for the hallways, but there was enough light to locate the den and the glass doors.

Submerged lights gave the pool a blue glow and left the patio in shadow. The air was hot and still, and Tara cast a wary glance up at the sky, relieved to see stars still shining clearly. There was no sign of a storm. Dropping her towel on one of the lounges at the edge of the pool, she stepped out of her thongs and went around to where shallow steps led into the water.

The water was cool and refreshing, and she swam to the center of the pool, keeping her head above the surface, not wanting to get her hair wet.

"What the hell are you doing swimming alone at this time of night?"

Tara gasped in surprise and nearly went under. She stared toward a darkened corner of the patio from which a familiar shape emerged. "Good God! You scared the life out of me!"

"That doesn't answer my question." Devlin dove in and swam toward her, his grim face visible now and his anger obvious. "You little fool."

She glared back at him. "That's the second time you've called me a little fool. For the second time, I'm not a fool. And I'm obviously not alone."

"But you would have been if I hadn't been here." He stopped an arm's length away and began to tread water. "It's dangerous to swim alone, and you know it."

Having just noticed that the only thing he was wearing was his too-attractive skin, Tara struggled to keep her face expressionless and her voice even. "And I suppose *you* have a pact with the devil to keep you safe?"

"I'm a better swimmer than you are."

"To hear you tell it, you're better at everything than I am," she muttered irritably.

"Not quite." He grinned. "I wouldn't fill out that bikini nearly as well as you do."

Tara stared at him in exasperation. "You're maddening. Do you know that? Absolutely maddening. And just what are *you* doing out here at this time of night?" A part of her wished he'd say he couldn't sleep for thinking of her.

"I couldn't sleep. I was up until after midnight talking to Holman," he replied, "and rather than soak *his* head, I decided to soak mine."

Deflated, Tara was nevertheless perversely glad that the evening hadn't been comfortable for him either.

"Well I could have told you that the man wasn't happy with you. You should have waited a couple of days before trying to talk business."

"Did I say we were talking business?"

"I assumed you weren't talking politics."

"As a matter of fact, we were." Devlin shook his head. "That man will talk about anything to avoid a business discussion."

"He doesn't sound like a reliable partner."

"I'm beginning to agree with you." He moved a bit closer. "Couldn't you sleep either?"

Caught off guard by the change of subject, Tara felt her stomach tighten nervously at his nearness. "I wanted a swim. Is that a crime?"

"You didn't answer my question."

"My sleeping habits are none of your business."

"Oh, no?" He reached out suddenly and pushed her completely beneath the water.

Tara came up sputtering. "Damn it—look what you've done! I didn't want to get my hair wet!"

Devlin was laughing. "You look like a furious little girl! Sorry, honey—it was an irresistible impulse."

Acting on an impulse of her own, she grabbed a handful of his hair and ducked him before he could prepare himself. This time he was the one to come up sputtering—though he was still laughing.

Tara started to swim away, but he reached out and caught her. He held her firmly against him, letting her feel the strength of his muscled body as he kept them both effortlessly afloat. Tara's legs tangled with his, and sudden heat spread through her body like wildfire. She was abruptly conscious of the late hour and the fact that they were utterly alone.

The laughter disappeared from Devlin's eyes as he stared at her. Both the droplets of water on his skin and the blue glow from the submerged floodlights gave him an alien look. A stark beauty she had never noticed before held Tara's fascinated gaze as her eyes moved slowly over his face. How odd, she mused. She had never really looked at him before.

"Tara . . ."

She barely heard the unsteady timbre of his voice, the rough note of longing, and then his mouth was on hers, his arms crushing her painfully close.

Tara resisted the kiss for a timeless moment. Warning bells went off in her head. Then her restraint became instead a fierce response, and the irritating clamor died away. Her lips parted willingly beneath his, and she slid her arms around his neck, realizing vaguely that he was steering them toward the shallow end of the pool. As their feet touched bottom and his kiss deepened, all coherent thought ceased.

Devlin pulled her even closer, one hand tangling in her damp curls, the other at the small of her back. His mouth moved hungrily on hers, eagerly, as though he had held himself in check for far too long. The probing exploration of his tongue became an act of possession, pure and simple.

Tara felt her last ties to reality slip away. Her senses reeled. The familiar ache in her loins became an unbearable agony. She wasn't even aware when he removed her bikini, top and bottom. As his lips left hers to blaze a trail down her throat, she opened her eyes to see two scraps of yellow material floating toward the edge of the pool. By then Devlin's lips were on the creamy swell of her breast, and she wouldn't have protested if the entire population of Texas had been grouped around the pool with popcorn, soft drinks, and spotlights.

"You're so beautiful," he muttered hoarsely. One hand slid down over her hips, lifting her slightly, while the other cupped a breast with trembling fingers. His lips gently teased a hardening nipple. "So beautiful . . . so sweet. Tell me you want me, Tara."

She had been half listening, on fire from his touch and bemused by his words, but his last command caught her full and undivided attention. Suddenly aware of her own actions, she untangled her fingers from his hair and pushed fiercely against the hard shoulders. "Let go of me!"

To her surprise he obeyed immediately—so quickly, in fact, that she was caught off balance and nearly went under. At the last moment she regained her balance. Painfully aware that the clear lighted water failed completely to hide her nakedness, she managed a baleful glare at the seemingly amused man standing between her and her bikini. Damn him! How could he stay so firmly in control? Could he turn desire off like a switch?

"You're still fighting, honey," he told her softly. "I'm going to have to cure you of that."

She was furious with both him and herself. "I'll fight you to the gates of hell!" she snapped.

He reached out suddenly to cup her chin, and for a moment Tara felt his long fingers bite into her flesh with a fierce anger that didn't show on his face. In that same soft, intense voice, he said, "You'll have to go farther that that, honey. Because I'll walk barefoot through hell itself, fighting every step of the way, if that's what it takes."

When he released her chin, Tara nearly went under again. Carefully edging into deeper water, she stared at him warily. "What are you talking about?" she demanded.

He chuckled and turned toward the edge of the pool. "You'll figure it out someday." Snaring the floating bikini with one hand, he casually climbed the wide, shallow steps.

Tara tried to keep a resentful glare on her face as she watched him drop the bikini on a lounge chair and pick up a towel to dry himself off, but it wasn't easy. It just wasn't fair, she thought indignantly, that a man should look so good without his clothes on! It didn't seem decent somehow. She told herself that her gaze was completely objective and analytical, but that was a lie, and she knew it.

Unabashed by his nudity, Devlin was drying his tanned body thoroughly, and Tara felt a niggling pleasure in just watching him. If Michelangelo had ever seen this man, she thought dizzily, he never would have bothered with David. Almost hypnotized, she followed the towel's motions over uncompromisingly male planes and angles, watching muscles bunch and ripple smoothly beneath the taut flesh.

Abruptly aware of his silence and of her body's response to him, she began treading water so energetically that she bobbed about like a buoy on rough seas. She attempted to mask her discomfort by calling out with sweet unconcern, "Do you have a streak of the exhibitionist in you?"

"You don't have to watch," he returned pleasantly, bending to dry his legs.

Tara bit her lip and glared at him. "Throw my bikini over here, will you?" she asked, trying to keep her voice casual.

Devlin shrugged into his robe and belted it securely, then reached down for the bikini. Holding the scraps of material negligently in two fingers, he turned to smile at her, deviltry gleaming in his eyes. "Come and get it," he invited gently.

She'd been afraid of that. Getting out of the pool would mean having to walk across twelve feet of concrete, with what dignity she could muster, before reaching either the bikini or a towel. Tara wasn't a prude, but she wasn't about to parade around stark naked in front of Devlin if she could help it.

"Please, Devlin!" she pleaded, letting her teeth chatter for effect. She wasn't really cold, but her toes were beginning to look like prunes.

He leaned casually against one of the patio tables and continued to dangle the bikini. And kept smiling.

"Damn it!" she flared. "At least have the common decency to turn your back!"

"Why?"

He uttered that one word in a completely reasonable tone of voice, which took Tara aback for a moment. "Well . . . just because!" she sputtered.

"Typical female response."

"Don't stick labels on me!"

He laughed softly. "Temper, temper. You'll boil all the water away. Come out of there before you catch your death."

"I'd like to catch yours," she muttered. "On a twenty-foot screen. In Technicolor."

"Come out of there."

"No!"

The silence lengthened, and Tara tread water stoically, trying to ignore her mental picture of Devlin fishing an overlarge prune out of the pool at some future hour. Cautiously reaching to test the state of her toes, she finally wailed softly, "I'm getting waterlogged."

"Then come out of there." His voice was filled with laughter, and Tara's temper flared once again.

"What if someone should come along?" she hissed angrily.

"It's nearly two in the morning. The only living beings still awake are us and the owls."

"If you were a gentleman—"

"Well, I'm not, so there's no use telling me what I'd do if that were the case. Come out of there."

Tara sighed with resignation and began moving toward the steps. It wasn't as if he'd never seen her naked, she assured herself, and then immediately clamped a lid on the memories that thought aroused. Gathering together every iota of poise and dignity she possessed, she started up the steps, fixing her eyes on the towel she'd brought. Halfway there, two large hands reached for the towel and slowly began to unfold it.

Startled, her gaze slid up to Devlin's face and locked there, her breath catching in her throat. It was difficult to read his expression in the dim light, but the absorbed intensity of his silvery eyes was plainly apparent as they moved slowly over her naked flesh.

Something about that look—something elemental and primitive and fiercely male—sparked a response deep within Tara. For the first time in her life, she was totally conscious of her own womanhood. Instead of the embarrassment she'd expected, she felt a strange pleasure in the knowledge that he found her beautiful. Keeping her eyes fixed on his face, she covered the remaining distance between them slowly, a sensual heat flooding her and counteracting the chill of the night air on her wet skin.

As she reached him, Devlin swung the large towel behind her and hesitated, his eyes sweeping over her again. Then he slowly pulled the ends of the towel toward him until she stepped closer, and they were separated only by the fabric of his robe. Bending his head, he whispered huskily, "Lady, you are really testing my willpower."

She tilted her head back to look up at him. "It's probably good for your soul," she murmured, feeling a small sense of astonishment both at her teasing words and her continued lack of embarrassment.

"It's not my soul I'm worried about," he returned with a soft laugh.

A part of Tara knew she was playing with fire and bound to get her fingers burned, but she no longer cared. It had been three long years since she'd known the joy of belonging to him, and suddenly she was tired—very, very tired—of fighting him. She'd have the rest of her life to hate herself for the choice she was about to make, but she would face the consequences in the morning.

She remembered a childhood story about the Little Mermaid, and for the first time understood why that tragic creature had traded her tail for feet, even knowing the pain that would come later. What would be the price, Tara wondered, for a night spent in Devlin's arms? Her pride? Her self-respect?

"There are stars in your eyes," he whispered.

"I know." She smiled faintly, sadly, thinking of broken dreams and impossible wishes and prices to be paid. Stars in her eyes and rocks in her head . . . and what did any of it matter?

Devlin's smile died away, and storm clouds scudded across the silvery sheen of his eyes. He made a soft, rough sound deep in his throat and bent his head to kiss her with a gentleness that shattered her last defenses.

Suddenly the night was filled with magic, and Tara gave herself up totally to its spell. Her arms slipped up around Devlin's neck, and she pressed her body against his hard length, feeling his urgent desire and glorying in it. His kiss deepened into a searing passion, his arms locking her in a fierce embrace, the feeling between them exploding with the force of an unleashed fury.

He raised his head at last, breathing roughly, his storm-darkened eyes flickering restlessly over her soft features. "Tara, honey," he muttered thickly, "I need you so much . . . let me stay with you tonight. . . ."

Her eyes answered a silent yes, and with a harshly indrawn breath, he stepped back far enough to wrap the towel around her and swing her up into his arms.

Chapter Seven

Tara kept her face turned into his neck where a pulse pounded beneath his jaw, as he carried her through the dimly-lit lower floor of the house. She wondered faintly if he would go to her room or to his, but it didn't really matter. Three years of pent-up need and loneliness demanded that she spend this night with him.

All at once aware of just how far he was carrying her, she murmured indistinctly, "I'm too heavy."

His arms tightened around her. "You're as light as a feather," he told her with a husky laugh, climbing the stairs with an ease that confirmed his statement.

Content, she sighed softly, her body relaxed and languid. How wonderful he smelled, how clean and tangy and arousingly male. She was trying vaguely to decide just what "male" meant, when she realized that he had stopped.

Raising her head, she discovered that they were in the second-floor hallway at the end opposite her bedroom. She saw immediately why Devlin had halted.

Julie was coming out of a bedroom directly in front of them, a puzzled expression on her face. She was wearing a black negligee that deserved an X-rating, and when she looked up and saw them, an expression of chagrin that was almost comical in the circumstances swept over her face.

"Something I can do for you, Julie?" Devlin asked with only a trace of hoarseness in his voice, and Tara understood then that the bedroom was his.

A deep blush flooded Julie's face as she stared back at them, shock filling her eyes. Tara realized immediately that the younger woman had never even considered the possibility that Devlin's bed would be rather full of his fiancée.

"I . . . I got lost," Julie mumbled. "I was going to fix myself a snack . . ."

Devlin was kind enough to ignore the outfit obviously meant for nighttime seduction. "Down the hall to the stairs," he directed in a casual voice. "At the bottom take the hallway to the right. That will lead directly to the kitchen."

"Th-thanks." Obviously crushed, Julie started in the direction he had indicated, casting another small glance at Tara's towel-clad figure, her eyes still clouded with lingering shock.

Aware that her towel covered her decently only by the most broad-minded standards, Tara watched Julie disappear around the corner and then murmured, "I warned you." When Devlin didn't respond, she raised her gaze to his.

He was staring at her, his dark eyes hesitant, and she realized that he was afraid the encounter with Julie had altered her mood . . . and her decision. "Your place or mine?" he asked lightly, but with a ragged edge to his voice.

Beyond pretense, she whispered, "Which is closer?"

He bent his head to kiss her swiftly and carried her into his bedroom, closing the door behind them with an impatient kick. The room lay in shadow, lit only by his bathroom light. The rumpled covers on the large bed were mute testimony to his inability to sleep.

Devlin set Tara gently on her feet by the bed, his fingers reaching immediately for the towel. Tara responded by untying the sash of his robe. Towel and robe hit the floor together, and, as she went into his arms, Tara thought dreamily that nothing in the whole world felt quite as right as having this man's arms around her. Had it really been only yesterday that she had realized she loved him?

Without being conscious of movement, she felt the soft bed beneath her back and made a kittenlike sound of contentment as his lips were pressed urgently to her throat. She moved her hands over his firm back, her fingers teasing the length of his spine, and with a feeling of pleasure and power heard him groan hoarsely.

"Yes . . . touch me," he muttered thickly. "I need you to touch me, Tara." His own hands moved over her body with unsteady eagerness, his lips hard and hot against her skin.

Memory guided her touch, desire fueled her own eagerness as she explored the bold strength of him. The way the black hair on his chest caressed her breasts and the sensual abrasiveness of his hands touching her aroused an aching familiarity. She caught a glimpse of rare molten fire in his eyes and moaned softly as his mouth captured the hardened tip of her breast.

The long years and the bitter anger between them dissolved in a flood of turbulent need. That carefully hidden, restrained part of Tara's nature surfaced with a ravenous intensity. She was starving for him, desperate to know again the full measure of his possession. The wild hunger aroused by his touch had often shocked her before, but this time she abandoned herself to it totally.

She was a grown woman, and this man knew all of her body's secrets. He had possessed her body and her mind and her heart, and she was helpless but to acknowledge her own need of him. She moved beneath him restlessly, her nails digging unconsciously into his back. And then he moved suddenly, powerfully, and she gasped, her body arching against his instinctively.

For a moment he was still, as though the simple act of possession were enough. A shudder passed through his strong length. And then he began to move in a graceful rhythm as old as mankind.

Tara moved with him, holding him, glorying in the harmony of this timeless moment. Tension spiraled within her, like a tightly coiled spring, and she buried her face in his neck with a muffled cry.

Their lovemaking was not gentle. They were tossed about on the floodwaters of a desire too long denied, storms breaking over them, around them, and within them, until finally they were left, drained and spent, as if on the shore of some distant sea.

Devlin kissed her gently as he lowered his weight beside her onto the bed, drawing her into his arms and murmuring her name softly. Suddenly a ghostly panic she had always felt at such moments swept over Tara. She tried to fight it, moving closer to him as though to seek reassurance. Did every woman have this peculiar feeling of displacement, this fear and loneliness, after making love with a man? . . . It had happened three years before, and it was happening now.

Unwilling to try to explain what she didn't understand herself, she had never confided the feeling to Devlin. But he seemed to know. His hands moved soothingly over her back in a gentle rhythm. He whispered words of comfort, and she gradually relaxed.

Sleepy, she listened to the steady beat of his heart beneath her cheek. How amazing that the hard planes and angles of his body could provide such a comfortable resting place. It was her last clear thought before sleep claimed her.

She woke sometime just before dawn and opened her eyes to see Devlin looking down at her. She read the renewed desire in his storm-darkened gaze and felt her own need flare again. Without a moment's thought or hesitation, she went eagerly into his arms.

With the sharp edge of their hunger dulled, the almost desperate urgency of their lovemaking was gone. This time they savored each touch, each kiss. Tara was deeply moved by Devlin's tenderness and driven nearly wild by the butterfly-soft caresses he lavished over her body. Her fingers and lips teased him as well, drawing shudders from his body and deep groans from his throat.

Perhaps in payment for her teasing, Devlin turned the lovemaking into a game, holding her still beneath him. His lips moved tantalizingly down her throat to her breasts, teasing without taking, inviting yet making it impossible for her to give. Over and over he refused to take what she offered, driving her out of her mind with frustration.

Eventually his own need became too great, and he finally gave in to her murmured pleas, moving to initiate the final embrace. But some tiny witch inside Tara laughed softly and refused to admit him. The witch took over, taunting him with her body, yet refusing him satisfaction. It was a dangerous game, but Tara played it as if she'd been born to the role, her feminine instinct guiding her.

Devlin responded with a soft laugh and a gentle force of his own, taking control of the game once again with a masculine demand she could not resist. She felt a wonderful satisfaction in finally giving in to him. Abandoning the game abruptly, she responded to his passion fiercely, and the tension built between them until it exploded in a shower of golden sparks.

Again the fear swept over her in the aftermath of their lovemaking, and again Devlin soothed her. Cuddled up against the warmth of his body, she wondered faintly if he even knew what she was afraid of, and then exhaustion eased her into sleep.

The sun woke her hours later, and Tara muttered with sleepy irritability as she rolled over to escape its hateful glare. Her outflung arm encountered an empty bed, and for a long moment she lay perfectly still, with her eyes closed, trying to figure out why that didn't feel right. One eye opened slowly and stared blankly at the dented pillow beside her own. And then the events of the night before flooded into her memory, and she sat bolt upright.

Her startled gaze swept the unfamiliar room until she was convinced she was alone. Automatically reaching to pull up the covers that had fallen to her waist, she noticed her yellow robe at the foot of the bed and considered it for a frowning moment before realizing that Devlin must have gotten it for her.

She was in his bedroom. Alone. And God only knew what time it was. There wasn't a clock or a watch anywhere in the room. Judging from the position of the sun, it was still morning—but not by much. And where was Devlin?

Suddenly appalled by the realization that someone could come in at any moment and find her there, Tara scrambled off the bed and put on the robe. If she could only get to her own room without anyone's seeing her, she thought hopefully, then only Devlin would know that she'd made a complete fool of herself last night. It was bad enough, *his* knowing. She had no intention of announcing to the world that she was addicted to the man. . . .

Opening the bedroom door stealthily and seeing no one, she sighed in relief and hurried out of the room. And nearly collided with Amanda. For an eternal moment Tara stood paralyzed. If there was anything more embarrassing than coming out of a man's bedroom after a night of sin and running smack into his mother, Tara didn't know what it was.

Amanda smiled in her usual gentle way. "Good morning, Tara."

Tara pulled the lapels of her robe together, trying to present a dignified front. "Good morning," she responded, smiling brightly.

Amanda held out a casual hand. "I found these by the pool when I went out for a swim earlier. Yours, I think."

Accepting the bundle of yellow bikini and thongs, Tara felt her dignity cracking. "Oh . . . thank you. I went for a swim last night."

"I hope Devlin was with you, my dear. It's very dangerous to swim alone. Is he up, by the way?"

"Devlin? Oh . . . yes, he's . . . up."

"Probably trying out that filly of his, then. Julie's very subdued this morning. Do you happen to know why?"

"Haven't the faintest idea," Tara lied stoutly.

"Oh. Well, perhaps Jake talked to the girl—although I doubt it. He's spoiled her rotten since her mother died. Poor child."

Clutching her bundle guiltily, Tara smiled politely, wondering if only divine intervention would rescue her from this mess.

But she needn't have worried. Amanda didn't ask a single awkward question. She simply smiled again, told Tara that breakfast would be served downstairs for another hour, and strolled off.

Like a robot Tara walked to her room and closed the door behind her. She threw the bundle of yellow bikini and thongs across the room with a great deal of passion and very little accuracy. "Damn you, Devlin Bradley," she hissed into the silent room, "I'll never forgive you for this."

Of course it wasn't all Devlin's fault, Tara acknowledged half an hour later as she was drying off after a shower. He had given her a choice last night—not once, but twice. First by the pool and later in the hall. Either time she could have said no and trotted away to her room alone. But she'd said yes. And gone to his room instead.

For the first time since encountering him in the pool, Tara suddenly remembered the other woman in his life. She plopped down on the foot of her bed and continued toweling her hair dry, her movements slow and preoccupied. Staring at her reflection in the dresser mirror, she wondered why she hadn't thought of the woman last night. Even if she herself weren't afraid of commitment, Devlin could never be hers. Not entirely. He had given his heart long ago to another woman.

In the mirror Tara's lips curled bitterly. Oh, they made a dandy couple all right. She loved him and was afraid to commit herself. He wanted her but loved another woman. The only relationship they could ever have would be based solely on sexual attraction. And Tara knew with dreadful certainty that another affair with Devlin was unthinkable. Last night—what had happened last night—could never happen again. It was the only way she could continue without him. And even then . . . it just might kill her anyway.

Tara understood now why people did crazy things for love. Killed for it. Died for it. Funny—she'd always believed the poems, songs, and movies about lovers were greatly exaggerated. Melodramatic. But they weren't. She couldn't see any possible way of emerging from this tangle intact and unhurt.

Tossing the towel aside, she went to the dresser, opening drawers and pulling out clothing automatically. She dressed in slacks and a western-style blouse, then decided to go down to her trailer and find her jeans.

She straightened at last and stared into the mirror. During the next few weeks she would have to act better than she had ever acted on the screen. She would have to wave her temper like a flag and convince Devlin that she considered last night a mistake. She would have to ignore her own aching need and wear her independence like an impenetrable mask. She would have to play the loving fiancée in public and hide behind a veil of mockery when they were alone.

And in a few months she would simply hand the engagement ring back to him, smile politely, and walk away . . . never letting him see that she was torn and hurt.

The first step, though—the first step was facing him today. And she wasn't certain she could do it. Haunted eyes gazed back at her as she picked up a brush and ran it through her hair, as she remembered his murmured endearments of the night before. He hadn't said such things three years ago. Had he spoken the caressing words only because he'd thought she wanted to hear them?

She pushed such pointless questions from her mind and resolutely pulled on the mask she would have to wear for as long as this engagement continued. And when she looked into the mirror again, she found her face smiling and her eyes shuttered. You're a better actress than you knew, she told herself bitterly, and watched the face in the mirror lift a mocking brow.

Ten minutes later she walked through the front door, toward her trailer, having elected to skip breakfast. The trailer door was locked, and, remembering that Devlin had the keys, she walked around to the back and fished behind the license plate for a magnet holding a spare set. Once inside, she took ten more minutes to find her jeans and a few other items she might need.

Her arms full, she glanced out the window to see Devlin standing on the porch, an unusually strained look on his face as he stared toward the trailer. Trying to ignore her rapid heartbeat, Tara took a deep breath, pasted a smile on her face, and headed for the house.

She lifted a mocking eyebrow as she passed Devlin. "Afraid I'd escape?" she asked lightly.

He followed her into the house and caught her arm as she reached the first step. "Tara?" Silvery eyes intently searched her politely inquiring face. "Why do I get the feeling that last night never happened?" he finally asked.

"Hold on to that feeling," she advised calmly.

He sighed and, releasing her arm, leaned against the banister. "Okay—What's wrong?"

"Nothing much. By the way, do you know who I happened to run into this morning as I was leaving your room, after having obviously spent the night there?"

"I'll bite. Who?"

"Your mother."

His eyes narrowed sharply. "So that's it. Tara, my mother is not a fool, and she's certainly not straightlaced. As a matter of fact she'd probably be vastly surprised if she discovered we *weren't* sleeping together,"

"Good for her."

"Tara . . ." His features tightened. "You and I are both well over the legal age of consent and presumably know what we're doing. So why am I getting the cold and stony this morning? As I remember," he added evenly, "the lady was willing."

"The lady made a mistake," she replied, just as evenly. "She doesn't intend to repeat it."

Devlin stared at her for a long moment, his face unreadable. Finally he said very quietly, "When are you going to get it through that stubborn, infuriating little mind of yours that we belong together?"

Her heart twisted with anguish, but she managed to reply in the same tone, "On a cold day in hell. Now, if you'll excuse me, I have to put these things away." She continued up the stairs. He didn't follow or call after her, but Tara felt his eyes boring into her back.

During the next three days Tara found plenty to occupy her mind. She swam and sunbathed, talked to Amanda, met Rose, the housekeeper, and Josh, the butler—who turned out to be the prototype of all English butlers and too dignified to weep into anybody's ale, least of all his own. She also met the foreman and half the ranch hands.

A few days later Tara spent an entire afternoon trying to talk Ah Poo down from one of the barn lofts, where he had discovered another cat, of whom he was busily engaged in making an enemy. She and Amanda also spent one morning looking for the mouse Ah Poo had found outside and brought into the house—apparently to replace Churchill.

Tara weathered one midnight thunderstorm by stuffing her ears full of cotton and pulling the covers over her head. It was a childish solution, she knew, but the best she could do.

And she tried to keep up appearances, going out of her way, for the first time in their long and stormy relationship, to avoid giving Devlin any reason to quarrel with her, only to find that he didn't need a reason. He was her public enemy again, his voice harsh and his face cold and withdrawn. If Julie hadn't been so wrapped up in her misery, she would have noticed that her rival was less of a threat these days.

Tara was well aware of the reason for Devlin's anger, but she was a bit puzzled by its intensity. It seemed out of character for him to be so upset over her refusal to share a bed with him. And she was unwilling to try to patch things up between them, because she was afraid that if he began teasing her again, she'd have a hard time keeping her promise to stay away from him.

But by the middle of the second week Tara was so miserable that she was seriously considering packing up her belongings and clearing out. She knew it was a cowardly thought, but she wasn't feeling very brave. Only the knowledge that Devlin was perfectly capable of coming after her if she broke their agreement kept her from running like a thief.

Sitting beneath an umbrella by the pool, she toyed absently with the straw in her glass of iced tea and stared out across the water. She heard a step and glanced up to see Amanda coming toward her. Immediately she pulled on a cheerful mask.

"Don't do that, Tara." Amanda sat down beside her at the table and smiled pleadingly. "Don't pretend."

Tara's smile faltered, and she looked away. "I'm supposed to be an actress," she managed with a shaky laugh.

"And you're a very good one. But it's very difficult for one woman to hide something from another. Especially when one of the women is a mother." An unusual look of worry creased Amanda's lovely face. "My dear, forgive a mother's prying, but I hate to see you and Devlin so unhappy."

Tara stirred uncomfortably. "We had a—little disagreement."

"Little?" Amanda shook her head. "I haven't seen Devlin so upset in years. And it's plain how troubled you are, too. One of you has to end it, Tara."

Tara smiled ruefully. "Meaning me?"

"I'm afraid so." Amanda laughed softly. "I warned you about his pride. He'll go on, day after day, snapping at you and everyone else, being an absolute bear. You'll either have to swallow your own pride or buy a bulletproof vest."

Tara laughed in spite of herself. "I hope you realize how well you named him. Fierce valor. Although I think devil would have done just as well. He's reminded me more than once of Lucifer himself."

"Ah . . ." Amanda smiled. "But even Lucifer was considered to be very charming before his fall from grace. So which does Devlin remind you of—Lucifer before or after the fall?"

"I'm not sure," Tara admitted helplessly. "I think it's six of one and half a dozen of the other."

Amanda laughed, then became serious. Leaning forward, she said softly, "I know you love my son, Tara. I saw that in your eyes the first day he brought you here."

Tara's gaze dropped to her clasped hands. "I didn't realize it was so obvious," she murmured.

"Of course it was . . . and is. Devlin's the type of man who'll love only once in his life, and very deeply," she went on, unknowingly driving a stake through Tara's heart. "I'm very glad that he found you, my dear."

Everything inside Tara wanted to scream: But I'm not the one he loves! Swallowing hard, she murmured, "Thank you for being so kind to me. I'm more grateful than I can say."

"You're a member of the family . . . or as good as one." Amanda leaned back with a smile. "Go and talk to him, Tara. Find a neutral subject. Ask him about the ranch he bought. I'm probably spoiling his surprise, but I'm sure he'll forgive me if discussing it helps the two of you to make up."

"Ranch?" Tara asked hesitantly. "I didn't know he had one."

"Yes. It adjoins this one. He bought it several years ago but put an army of workmen in the house only a couple of weeks ago to start remodeling. The work should be at the point now where someone will have to make decisions about carpeting, paint, paper, and the like. He'll want you to choose, of course."

Tara started to say that *her* opinion would be the last one he'd ask for, but she choked back the words and rose to her feet. "Do you know where he is now?" she asked with a defeated smile.

"Probably in the training ring. He was planning to work with that filly of his."

Tara nodded and headed in that direction, holding onto her courage as if with both hands. She waved at a couple of ranch hands who rode by, her eyes searching the sprawling complex of stables, paddocks, and connecting lanes. Finally she located the training ring, which looked exactly like three others to her, where Devlin sat astride a beautiful black horse.

Leaning against the white fence, Tara watched him easily handling the spirited horse, his hands gentle and firm on the reins, his voice calm and soothing as he spoke. As he finally dismounted, the filly tossed her head playfully and nuzzled him gently, and Tara wondered ruefully if there was a single female creature on earth he couldn't charm.

"Is there anything you can't do?" she called out as he approached, then held up a pleading hand as his brows drew together in an angry frown. "I come in peace," she called in a lighter tone.

Halting on the other side of the fence, he stared at her for a moment before his lips twitched. "I haven't been that bad, surely," he murmured.

"Worse." She watched as he turned to loosen the horse's girth. "An absolute bear. And those are your mother's words."

"I seem to remember that something provoked my anger."

Tara sighed. "Couldn't we just forget about that? Start over, so to speak?" She grimaced slightly as he gazed at her steadily. "Your mother's worried," she added. "I don't like to see her that way."

"Is that your only reason for coming out here?" he asked evenly.

Tara shoved her hands into her jeans pockets and stared at him across the top rail of the fence. "What do you want me to say, Devlin? That I'm miserable? All right, I'm miserable! I don't like it when you snap at me the way you've been doing. I don't like pretending to your mother that we're a normal couple but just too stubborn to make up after a little spat."

"But you still won't admit that we belong together?" His voice was hard.

She dropped her eyes, suddenly very tired and bewildered. "I don't want to fight with you, Devlin," she whispered. "Please don't make me fight with you."

He reached across the top rail to gently turn up her face. "I'm not going to give up, you know," he said softly. "I'm going to get you to admit that we belong together."

"But *why?*" she demanded, hearing the note of desperation in her voice. "There's no future for us. There never has been!"

"There's a future if we want one."

She jerked away from Devlin. "Not the kind of future I want." Tara stared at him, knowing that the only future they could possibly have would consist of a brief affair shadowed by the ghost of another woman.

"You know," he said slowly, "one of these days I'm going to figure out what makes you tick. You're the most baffling woman I've ever met in my life. Just what do you want, Tara? Do you even know?"

Meeting his eyes steadily, she said quietly, "I know what I don't want."

Some of the color seemed to leave his face. "Well, thanks." He turned his back on her and began unsaddling the patient filly, the set of his shoulders clear evidence of his anger.

Tara bit her lip, knowing that she'd offended him but unwilling to call back her words. She reached across the fence to pat the filly's nose. "Beautiful horse," she murmured.

"Don't think you can go riding," Devlin said instantly without turning around. "The horses are off limits for you."

Tara's first impulse was to find a horse and immediately ride off, but she quickly squashed the childish thought. "I know," she murmured. "The doctor said no riding for a while."

"My, but we're meek today, aren't we?" he commented sardonically.

She watched him swing the saddle over the fence. "Don't be nasty, Devlin," she said, tired.

He pulled the bridle off the horse and watched as the animal trotted off. Then he turned to Tara. "My mother really got to you, didn't she?" he said in a softer voice.

Tara shrugged and avoided his eyes. "Your mother's a nice person. I like her. I don't want to see her worried."

"So you'll make peace with me to keep her happy?"

Tara was too honest to agree completely. "And to keep myself happy." She summoned up a small smile. "I haven't been sleeping well lately."

An answering smile lightened his expression for the first time. "Could be that lonely bed," he suggested gravely.

"I doubt it." She kept her voice light with effort. "I've been sleeping alone most of my life."

Still smiling, he murmured, "The problem won't go away just because you ignore it, honey."

Tara's heart skipped a beat at the endearment. She'd never expected to hear him call her that again. "Problem? What problem?" she asked, hoping to avoid it.

"Us. And there is an 'us' whether you admit it or not."

Not wanting to discuss *that* subject again, she said hastily, "Tell me about your ranch."

"Ranch?" Devlin lifted a brow and grimaced. "Mother."

Tara nodded. "She suggested it as a neutral topic. And since we seem to be a bit short on those . . ."

He stared at her for a moment, then laughed suddenly. "Okay, honey. You win this round. But I haven't thrown in the towel yet."

Aware that they'd shelved the argument rather than settled it, Tara was nonetheless relieved. "Will you show me the ranch?"

Devlin climbed easily over the fence and reached for the saddle. "Let me put this away first."

Tara nodded happily and watched him stride away toward one of the barns. Sooner or later they'd have another fight, she knew—and probably about the same thing. But she'd worry about that when it happened. Right now it felt wonderful to be on good terms with Devlin again.

Five minutes later they were seated in one of the ranch jeeps heading out across the pasture. "It's quicker this way," Devlin explained casually when Tara shot him a questioning look.

She scanned the flat green pastureland and sighed softly, sounding wistful. "Why did you buy a ranch here? Most of your work is in New York and L.A."

He shrugged. "I like the country here. As for my work, I've about decided to sell out of the New York end."

Tara half turned on the bucket seat to stare at him curiously. "But why? I thought you loved your work."

Devlin smiled with an odd expression. "What I love is the challenge. But I've found something that will probably keep me on my toes for the rest of my life. If it doesn't drive me insane, that is."

"What's that?"

He hesitated, the fingers of his right hand drumming almost nervously on the wheel. Then he answered, very softly. "You, Tara."

For an eternal moment she thought he was joking. But the determined set of his jaw swiftly convinced her he was entirely serious. "What are you talking about?" she almost whispered.

"I've been doing a lot of thinking these last few days," he answered casually. "I've decided you need someone to watch over you. And I've decided I need a wife and a home—a settled home. So sometime during the next few months I mean to convince you to marry me, Tara."

"Are you out of your mind?"

Devlin chuckled softly, not looking at her. "That almost sounds like what you said the last time I asked you to marry me."

Cold panic gripped Tara, but she tried to fight it. She wanted to marry Devlin. Even with the ghost of another woman standing between them, she wanted desperately to be his wife. But she couldn't! She was afraid . . . and she didn't know why.

Swallowing hard, she stared at the calm man by her side and said with strained calm, "I don't want to get married."

"I know. But I'll change your mind, honey. We belong together. Your body knows that even if your mind doesn't. Tell me that the night we spent together didn't mean anything to you. Tell me that all those nights more than three years ago didn't mean anything to you."

Tara twisted the "Bradley luck" around and around on her finger. "You can't base a marriage on sex."

"We're compatible in other areas as well," Devlin replied, for all the world as though he were discussing the weather. "We're both intelligent. We share the same tastes in books and music. We even agree on major political issues. We both have a sense of humor and a temper."

"We fight all the time," Tara interrupted desperately. "What kind of marriage would that be?"

"An interesting one." He sounded amused.

Tara searched desperately for excuses. "My career—I couldn't give it up."

"I didn't ask you to give up your career." His lips twisted wryly. "Not this time."

"Then you wouldn't have a settled home. Don't you see, Devlin? Being married to an actress—"

"Tara," he interrupted calmly, "you can go on finding reasons against our marriage until doomsday, but it won't do any good. I've made up my mind."

She laughed in spite of herself. "You make it sound like an act of God!"

He grinned. "I thought your meekness was too good to last."

Ignoring his comment, Tara rubbed her forehead fretfully. "I can't decide whether you're serious or joking," she murmured incredulously.

"Entirely serious, I assure you. In fact, I have the game plan all worked out." Stopping the jeep, he turned off the engine and gestured in front of them. "Step one: the bribe."

Realizing abruptly that they had reached Devlin's ranch, Tara looked beyond a maze of wooden white fences to a cluster of barns and outbuildings. Beyond them stood a house.

Even at this distance Tara could see that it was heart-stoppingly beautiful. Surrounded by several large trees, it had been built from a combination of stone and cedar shingles, with broad expanses of tinted glass for windows. It seemed almost out of place on the flat Texas landscape . . . and yet oddly right as well.

Her eyes wide, Tara stared at the house for a long moment. Finally she turned to meet Devlin's intent gaze. "But . . . that's my house," she whispered.

Chapter Eight

He nodded, smiling slightly. *When she continued to stare at him uncomprehendingly,* he said quietly, "We were at your apartment one night, and you had to run down to your agent's house for a script. You wouldn't let me come with you, so while you were gone I glanced through a couple of your scrapbooks. Among the newspaper clippings, reviews, and photographs was a picture of a house, cut out of a magazine." He reached out to touch her cheek in a tender gesture. "It was your dream house, wasn't it?"

"How did you know?" she murmured.

Devlin shrugged. "I just knew."

Trying to get a grip on her churning emotions, Tara conjured up a flash of spirit. "I wish you'd stop these mindreading acts of yours. They're very disconcerting."

"If I could read your mind," he told her dryly, "I wouldn't have to resort to bribery to get you to the altar. I'd just look into that stubborn mind of yours and find out why you're so determined not to marry me."

Resolutely Tara got out of the jeep. "I'm just not going to marry you. And that's final."

Devlin got out and came around the jeep to catch her hand. Leading her to the nearest fence, he said cheerfully, "You *are* going to marry me. And *that's* final." He lifted her easily onto the fence. "Sit tight."

"I'm not helpless, you know," she muttered. "I can get down by my—" She gasped as Devlin, who had vaulted over the fence, lifted her down on the other side.

His hands still on her waist, he glanced toward the house. "The place is full of workmen, and there's probably a ton of plaster dust floating around, but at least you'll get an idea of what it'll look like. And I see the decorator's car, so you can talk to him about paint and wallpaper."

He put a possessive arm around her shoulders and started leading Tara toward the house. "Paint and wallpaper?" she repeated blankly. "Devlin, I'm not going to decorate your house."

"*Our* house. And of course you will."

"Listen to me!" Tara tried to stop, but he pulled her along relentlessly. "Devlin, I'm not going to marry you! It's a beautiful house, but—Are you listening to me?"

He wasn't. Ignoring her muttering, he led her into the house, where he introduced her to the decorator and the foreman. He then asked both men to wait for them downstairs while he took Tara upstairs to see the bedrooms.

Torn between amusement and consternation, Tara listened as he recited characteristics of each bedroom like a salesman until they reached a smaller bedroom that had already been painted a bright, sunny yellow. Leaning against the doorjamb, Devlin abandoned his sales talk to remark blandly, "The nursery."

Tara gave him a startled look. "You do plan ahead, don't you?" she muttered.

"You told my mother you wanted a houseful of kids," he said innocently.

Tara sat down on the low sill of one of the windows and stared at him. "Less than an hour ago," she began in a carefully expressionless voice, "a man bearing a faint resemblance to you glared across a fence at me, as mad as hell. Do you always change moods so quickly, or just with me? I need a scorecard to keep up with you!"

Devlin smiled at her. "You're pretty good at changing moods yourself."

Proving the truth of this observation, she snapped, "I'm *not* going to marry you, I'm *not* going to help you decorate your house, and I'm *certainly* not going to help fill up this nursery!"

"You will, in fact, do all three."

His calm statement infuriated Tara. "Moses had less confidence when he parted the Red Sea," she remarked acidly.

"Moses needed help. I don't," Devlin responded gravely.

Tara bit her lip. "Damn it, why do you do that?" she demanded in a voice that trembled in spite of her efforts to control it.

"Do what?"

Gazing at his glinting smile, she choked back another giggle. "You know very well what! Every time I get angry at you, you make me want to laugh."

Chuckling, he confessed wryly, "You have the same effect on me. Don't you see, Tara—that's why we're good for each other."

"But I'm not going to marry you!"

"Yes, you are. But first you're going to come downstairs with me and tell the decorator that he's chosen the wrong color for the breakfast nook."

Curious in spite of herself, Tara let him lead her from the room. "What's wrong with the color he chose?"

Devlin glanced over his shoulder as they started down the stairs. "It's absolutely hideous."

"Then tell *him* that," Tara suggested.

"You might like it." He draped a casual arm around her waist as they reached the bottom of the stairs, and led her toward the back of the house. "But I give you fair warning. If you *do* like the color, I'm going to demand breakfast in bed for as long as the paint lasts."

"I'm not going to marry you, you know."

"Of course you are. Although why I want to hitch my fate to a redheaded spitfire is a matter I'll have to take up with my analyst."

"I'm serious!" she wailed softly.

"We'll talk about it later—on our twenty-fifth anniversary." He dropped a distinctly husbandly kiss on her forehead and ushered her into the breakfast nook.

Tara had no intention of disputing the decorator's choice of color. Until she saw it, that is. She had an instinctive eye for color, and couldn't help exclaiming, "Oh, no—that won't do at all!"

Immediately the man brought forth samples and swatches, and Tara joined him in a huddle before realizing what she was doing. Frantically appealed to, Devlin only smiled gently and said the choice was hers. Tara was sorely tempted to borrow a hammer from one of the workmen and hit him with it.

Two hours later they exchanged compliments all around, and Tara left the house with the dim realization that she'd chosen the color scheme for practically every room in the house . . . and entirely against her will, too. Remaining silent, she allowed Devlin to help her over the fence again and into the jeep. It wasn't until he'd turned the vehicle around that she remarked dryly, "One of these days you'll have to tell me what your secret is."

"Secret?" He shot her an innocent look.

"Yes, secret! I didn't have the slightest intention of choosing colors for your house—"

"Our house."

"—but I did it anyway. Just when did you develop this knack of making me do something completely against my will?"

"I don't know, but it bodes well for my plans to get you to the altar, doesn't it?" Before she could respond to that loaded question, he added casually, "While we're at it, we might as well drive into Amarillo and pick out the furniture."

"We'll do no such thing!" she gasped.

He grinned. "I won't press my luck. Anyway, it'll be another couple of weeks before the house is ready to furnish."

Tara sighed. "You're insane."

"Was that meant as an insult or just a general observation?" he asked with interest.

"It's the truth. Take it any way you like." She looked at him with a wry expression. "I'll probably hate myself for asking this, but if the house was step one of your little plan, what's step two?"

"Oh, that's easy," he responded cheerfully. "You're going to admit that you want me."

"I beg your pardon?"

"You heard me. You've never actually admitted it, you know. But you will. I don't suppose you'd care to admit it now?"

Out of sheer perversity, Tara snapped, "I want you like I want a migraine!"

Undaunted, he went on easily, "I want you, and very badly, too. However, since you've made it clear you don't want to share my bed yet, I won't press you on that point."

"You won't?" Tara examined him suspiciously.

He gave her an absurdly guilty look. "Well, not much, anyway. I do have to argue my case, after all."

"I'm not going to marry you. . . ."

A week later Tara was repeating the same statement, with increasing desperation. She'd decided that the easiest and least painful way of dealing with Devlin's determination to marry her would be to treat the whole matter lightly. Unfortunately that attitude didn't seem to have any effect on him.

Around the others he played the loving fiancé with the same

talent he'd displayed that first day, showering Tara with adoring looks and tender touches. Alone with her he was cheerful, teasing, and totally deaf to her repeated refusals to marry him. He made certain they spent nearly every moment of the day together, meeting her at her bedroom door in the morning and escorting her back every evening. With excuses that his mother was watching, or the moon was full, or it was the second Thursday of the month, he held her and kissed her.

And it was killing Tara.

Each evening she escaped to her room to sit for long moments watching her hands shake. Her dreams were disturbed by scenes in which she held gray-eyed babies in her arms, and by conflicting images of weddings at which, as the minister asked if anyone could show just cause why the marriage should not take place, a ghostly woman stood up in the back of the church and extended an accusing finger. Tara woke up frightened and uneasy, because the woman had been her.

Slowly it dawned on her just what Devlin was accomplishing by not "pressing" her to share his bed. He was slowly driving her out of her mind! Not only was she tormented by thoughts of the night they'd spent together here, but his lovemaking had also broken through the wall she'd built around the memories of their earlier relationship. And her body, having tasted the pleasures of being in his arms, gave her no peace.

As long as he'd been angry at her she'd been able to fight her desire. But, chameleonlike, he had become a lover instead. He courted her the way any woman would love to be courted, with soft words and tender kisses.

When Tara finally relieved her feelings in a burst of anger, he only laughed and egged her on, until she was laughing too. He was the only man she had ever known who actually seemed delighted by her temper.

The house party went on for a third week and then a month.

Tara found herself at loose ends during the third and fourth weeks, since Devlin was spending a great deal of time helping Rick on the ranch. She was delighted when Amanda asked for her help.

Gazing at the older woman a bit apprehensively, Tara murmured, "I'd love to help, Amanda, but I've never been to a ranch party and I don't know much about kids. What's the party for?"

"It's a back-to-school party," Amanda explained, her gray eyes gleaming with laughter. "It's for the children of the ranch hands. They all work pretty hard during the summer, but they still hate going back to school. The party seems to help a bit. Their mothers drop them off in the morning, and we keep them for the entire day. It'll take a good week to get ready for them—we'll do a lot of cooking and baking—and at *least* a week to recover!"

Tara laughed. "It sounds daunting. Where are the men while all this is going on? Hiding?"

"More or less." Amanda smiled ruefully. "Rick's already decided it's time to round up the foals and call out the vet to check them over. Would you like to bet on which day he chooses?"

Tara smiled, but she soon discovered that Amanda was right. The men avoided the house while the frantic preparations were going on, showing up for meals and not much else. Tara helped with the baking and cooking which, to her surprise, she was good at and enjoyed. She also helped in the day-to-day running of the ranch house.

At first she was surprised by the amount of work Amanda did on a regular basis. Devlin's mother was a rich man's wife, but she was far from just that. She loved people, and, what with caring for the ranch hands, their families, and local people, as well as doing community work, Amanda was a very busy lady. Tara helped with everything, finding herself at a local bazaar one day and driving into town for decorations the next. She even helped answer the phone and mail.

For the first time in her life she was happy doing something other than acting, and she was grateful to Amanda for giving her the opportunity to discover this unexpected side of herself. She was very pleased to find out that she *could* do other things.

She was in the kitchen early on the morning of the party, up to her elbows in the last batch of cookies, when Amanda came in.

"Tara, you have to see this. Come with me," she said with a smile.

Puzzled, Tara followed her through the house to the entrance hall, and burst out laughing at the sight of Ah Poo dashing about decorated with gaily colored bits of ribbon and tissue paper. "Oh, no! Where did he find that stuff?"

Amanda bent down to look under one of the tables. "Here's the box you put the leftover decorations in. He must have—What's he after now? Tara, is that . . . ?"

"It looks like—Amanda, it's that mouse again! We have to catch it before the kids get here. Ah Poo! I *told* you to leave him outside, you dratted cat! Oh, catch him, Amanda, he's heading for the stairs!"

Amazingly enough, the party came off as planned. Although she'd been nervous about dealing with the children, Tara found that her acting ability was a godsend when it came to telling stories and making up games. She had never acted before a more satisfying audience than a group of three-to-eight-year-olds, who sat in wide-eyed, breathless silence as Tara acted out a favorite fairy tale, taking all the parts herself.

By the time she carried a sleepy toddler out to the mother's car late that afternoon, Tara was actually sorry the party was over.

Still the house party continued. In fact, no one showed any signs of leaving. Occasionally Devlin talked to Jake Holman about his business deal, but he seemed in no hurry to sign a contract. One evening he drove Tara into Amarillo for a gourmet dinner and seductive dancing and treated her like a precious piece of porcelain, only to leave her at her bedroom door with a light kiss and a cheerful smile.

Tara lay awake for hours that night, contemplating several methods of committing murder and getting away with it. She spent another sleepless hour aching for Devlin's touch, her heart yearning for his love.

It wasn't possible, though, and she knew it. Devlin was still in love with that other woman—the one Tara was afraid to ask him about. He hid it well most of the time, behaving as if he were perfectly content in Tara's company. But occasionally she would turn unexpectedly to find him staring at her as though he were seeing someone else, and his eyes would be haunted.

Her heart would catch at such moments, and she would wonder with desperate pain why he was so determined to marry her. To exorcise the ghost of a love that was—whatever he believed—very much alive? Was he so willing to settle for second best?

Fearing what his answers would be, she never asked him those questions. And she never asked herself why she was so afraid of making a commitment, why the thought of marriage made her feel lost and alone . . . and very, very frightened.

So day followed day without change, their relationship filled with undercurrents of emotion that neither acknowledged openly. And then something happened that, Tara realized later, caused yet another turning point in their relationship and sounded the first real shot in her battle to understand herself.

It was such a simple thing, really. A common, ordinary event peculiar to the hot summer months. A thunderstorm announced its presence with distant angry rumbles. . . .

Tara had been tense and restless all day, instinctively knowing that the storm was coming. She excused herself early that night, deliberately taking advantage of Devlin's brief preoccupation with a phone call to slip from the den. She went up to her room and took a long hot shower, then spent a few more minutes drying her hair and filing her nails. She let Ah Poo into the room and talked to him nervously for half an hour, until he decided to go out again. She ruined one of her newly-filed nails by chewing on it and tried three times to read the first chapter of a paperback mystery.

By then the storm was approaching rapidly, and it was after midnight. Finally giving in to her fear, Tara stripped off her robe and got into bed, her flesh covered with goose bumps beneath the silky material of her long-sleeved, floor-length nightgown. Turning off the lamp on the nightstand, she lay back and listened to the sound of rain spattering fiercely against the windowpanes.

The first loud crash of thunder caught her unawares, as it always did, and she flinched. Huddled beneath the covers, she shivered violently, hating herself for her childish fear, but unable to control it. Thunder rolled across the night sky, lightning flashed with wicked fury, and Tara trembled even more. She had never understood her fear, never conquered it. In the company of others she could hide it, but alone at night, the smothering blanket of darkness lifted only by jagged lightning, fear gripped her in its steely talons and refused to be shaken loose.

Only one person knew of her terror. He had never laughed at the weakness or scoffed at it, and she had been vaguely surprised that Devlin, who displayed no fear of anything or anyone, should have understood her irrational panic. But he had. On more than one stormy night his comforting presence had made the ordeal bearable.

Tara wanted to run to Devlin now. She wanted to lie in his arms and listen to the soothing, steady beat of his heart. She wanted him, not out of sexual desire but out of a simple, instinctive need for his physical nearness. But she couldn't go to him. Her pride would not allow it. Yet as each eternal moment passed, the need to be with him grew stronger and stronger.

Another crack of thunder interrupted her thoughts, and Tara

drew the covers up around her neck with a faint moan. Oh, God—he was so near, and the temptation was so hard to resist.

"Tara."

She jerked around, her wide blue eyes peering over the blankets in search of the source of the quiet voice. For one giddy moment she wondered if the storm was calling to her. And then she saw Devlin standing by her bed, his starkly masculine outline etched for her in a brilliant flash of lightning. Wearing only pajama bottoms, his silvery eyes glittering catlike in the blue light, he looked like a primitive, pagan figure. To Tara's fear-clouded mind he seemed the devil himself, spawned out of the violent night storm.

Then another flash of lightning lit the room, and she saw that Devlin was smiling gently, reassuringly. The devil image disappeared, and he was once again the safe, comforting presence she craved.

"Would you like me to stay with you for a while?" he asked softly. When she hesitated, he promised gently, "No strings, Tara."

Immediately, silently, she reached over to toss back the covers on the side of the bed nearest to him. He slid in beside her and drew her into his arms, pulling the blankets up around them to create a cocoon of warmth and safety.

Tara snuggled up to his hard male body, silently acknowledging to herself that she would have welcomed him into her bed even if there had been strings attached to his offer.

Devlin's hands moved gently over her back, and he murmured soothingly as she shivered with each crash of thunder. "You're so strong in some ways, honey," he said lightly, "and so unsure of yourself in others. I've seen you force arrogant actors and belligerent producers to back down with only a sweet smile, and you've faced a group of hostile reporters without a blink. Yet you're terrified of thunderstorms. What are you afraid of, sweetheart?"

"I—I don't know," she murmured. "The noise . . . the lightning. It just scares me."

"Have you always been afraid of storms? All your life?"

"Yes—no." She frowned as she thought back. "I think I loved storms when I was very small."

He was silent for a moment, then said on a questioning note, "Your parents were killed when you were very small, weren't they?"

"Yes."

"How were they killed, Tara?"

Puzzled by his question, she momentarily forgot the storm. "It—it was a car crash," she answered tensely.

"Tell me about it."

She stirred uneasily. "There isn't anything to tell. They were in a car and it crashed, that's all."

His lips moved gently against her temple and he murmured quietly, "There was a storm, wasn't there?"

Tara felt her mind rushing back in time to that horrible night and closed her eyes tightly. "Yes," she whispered.

"You weren't with them?"

"No, I—I'd spent the night with a friend." Thunder crashed again, and she started violently. Suddenly the words started pouring out of her mouth, as if she had no conscious ability to stop them.

"The storm woke me up, and I was lying in bed listening to the thunder. The door opened and my friend's mother came in and—and told me what—had happened. She kept telling me it was all right to cry, but I couldn't. I couldn't cry. It was like a bad dream, a nightmare, and I told myself I'd wake up soon . . . but I never did."

Devlin's arms tightened around her. "And you've been afraid of storms ever since," he pointed out gently.

Why hadn't she realized that before? Her parents had been killed on a stormy night, and a ten-year-old child had suddenly developed a fear of storms. Such a simple answer! She lifted her head to stare at him. "I never realized . . ."

How many other fears, she wondered vaguely, did she owe to her unsettled childhood? Had it been responsible for her determination to remain independent all these years? Her fear of leaning on someone else, of trusting anyone but herself? And what of her fear of marriage? She felt somehow that if she could only discover the answer to one of those questions, she would understand it all. But the answer eluded her.

Devlin smiled at her in the dim room and ran a finger down her nose. "You've stopped trembling."

"I have, haven't I?" Tara struggled to come to terms with this new knowledge of herself. She smiled at him tremulously. "You should hang out a shingle. You'd make a pretty good psychologist."

"You see what a handy husband I'd be?"

Tara wanted to tell him about the fear *that* statement elicited, in the hope that he would find a solution just as simple, but the words wouldn't come. She could only shake her head silently.

"You're stubborn. It must be that red hair. Will our children have red hair, do you think?"

"Your mother has auburn hair, so it's likely that—" Tara broke off abruptly, appalled by what she had said, and glared at him. "Why do I let you do that to me?"

"Do what?"

"Drag me into conversations I have absolutely no interest in!" she exclaimed heatedly, if not truthfully.

"I love children. Don't you?"

"Well, yes, but . . ."

"I hope the first one's a girl." His hands were moving in a disturbing pattern over her back. "What shall we name her? Something Irish. I like Irish names."

"My name's Irish," she murmured in spite of herself.

"I know. Tara—the ancient capital of the Irish kings. How many kids shall we have?"

Tara gasped as his probing fingers discovered a sensitive spot on her lower back. She tried to think straight. "We—we aren't going to have any children."

"Of course we will. At least four. Unless you have scruples about bringing children into such a crazy world?"

"There *is* that." Thunder boomed suddenly overhead, but Tara flinched only slightly, almost completely occupied by the restless ache building up inside her body. "Um . . . four? Did you say *four*?"

"Would you rather try for an even half dozen?" he asked calmly.

Tara dropped her forehead against his shoulder with a faint moan. "Oh, God, why do you *do* this to me?"

"Was that a prayer, or a question directed at me?"

"I'm not sure." She watched her fingers trace an intricate path among the dark hairs on his chest. "You should be locked up. You know that, don't you?"

"Only if they lock you up with me."

Tara opened her mouth to reply, but the room swung crazily and she found herself flat on her back, staring up at him. She barely noticed that the storm was increasing in intensity, before his lips were on hers demandingly.

Like an addict deprived too long of a particular drug, Tara was helpless to fight the rush of passion singing through her veins. Her fingers found their way into his hair and locked there. Her lips parted immediately beneath the forceful pressure of his mouth. His arms strained her close, his heart thudding unevenly against her own.

For Tara the moment had a curious unreality, a dreamlike quality of storms without and within. She felt as though she were being carried on a tidal wave, rushing faster and faster. Her eyes tightly closed, she bit her lip as Devlin's mouth moved hotly down her throat. She moaned softly as his hand found the softness of her breast through the silky gown. He pushed aside the low neckline, his lips replacing his hand, and Tara's senses reeled.

She had no thought of refusing him, would have been incapable of refusing him. She'd been crazy to think she could give this up! But gradually she began to realize that Devlin had no intention of allowing their lovemaking to progress any further.

When her hands began to wander, he caught them firmly and folded them gently over her stomach. Butterfly-light kisses covered her closed eyelids as he drew the neck of her gown closed. Tara kept her eyes shut, his breathing coming as ragged as her own in the dim room. Then she felt the bed shift and was horrified to realize that he was leaving her.

Her eyes snapped open. "Devlin?" The question she couldn't put into words was in her voice.

"Shhh . . ." He bent over to pull the blankets up around her neck and kissed her forehead tenderly, then stood up straight.

"Are—are you leaving?" she asked huskily.

"I promised no strings, honey," he replied hoarsely. "And I mean to keep my word. I'll teach you to trust me if it's the last thing I ever do."

Tara tried to tell him that trust was the last thing on her mind just then, but the words wouldn't come. She could only watch with dazed eyes as he went to the door. He turned to look across the shadowy room at her, one hand on the knob.

"You'll come to *me*, Tara," he told her softly.

"What?" Her voice was blank.

"You'll come to me next time. You'll finally admit that you want me . . . and then you'll come to me." He smiled broadly, deviltry gleaming in his eyes. "Step two." And he walked through the door, closing it behind him.

Seconds later, shrieking like an enraged kitten, Tara threw a pillow across the room.

For a good three days Tara told herself fiercely that she'd be *damned* if she'd give him the satisfaction of knowing he was right.

One A.M. on the third night found her pacing the floor of her bedroom with a vengeance.

An hour before, Devlin had left her at her door with a chaste kiss. Now she was trying mightily to think up a way to punish him for what he was doing to her. Oddly enough her fanciful plotting always ended with him in her power for the rest of his life—and in her bed. She wanted to hate him, to despise him for using her physical desire against her, but all she felt was a need and longing so strong that it almost frightened her.

How *could* he do this to her? What power did he have over her? And why could she give him her heart and her body, yet shy fearfully away from any permanent tie?

She stood in the center of her room for a long time, staring almost blindly at the door. Part of her wanted Devlin to win his little game, wanted desperately to marry him. But a frightened little gremlin still cowered in the back of her mind with stubborn resistance. Oh, what was wrong with her?

Tara looked at her lonely bed, and her pride suddenly gave way. It didn't matter. Not her own fear, not Devlin's ghostly love. She needed him. And she had the right, didn't she? Shouldn't every woman have the right to love her man? Even if he wasn't really hers? Even if . . .

With a soft curse Tara pushed the questions aside. She looked down at her peach nightgown and grimaced, knowing it was no more suitable for prowling about the house than Julie's seductive outfit of a few weeks ago had been. But then, Tara didn't have far to prowl.

The hall was dimly lit, as always, and Tara's footsteps led her unerringly to Devlin's door. She hesitated for a tense moment, her stomach filled with butterflies, then took a deep breath and went inside the bedroom. Moonlight spilled across the large bed, and her eyes followed it to where Devlin stood looking out the window.

He was wearing a robe, and his profile had a bleak, lonely look to it. He seemed a thousand miles away, but reacted immediately when the door clicked softly behind Tara. Swinging around, he stared across the room at her, and she could have sworn that his eyes lit up.

"Tara."

Her heart seemed to jump into her throat and hang there, beating madly. His voice was deep, husky, barely above a whisper. It was odd how much could be contained in a single word, she mused vaguely. The delicate scent of a wild rose. The feel of a warm spring breeze. The muted roar of a distant ocean. Magic. And filled with promise.

She walked steadily across to him, knowing instinctively that he would wait for her to say the words. He had been honest about his desire. She would find the courage to be the same.

Reaching him, she halted and looked up to search his guarded, intent expression. She gave him a teasing smile. "I couldn't sleep," she murmured.

An answering smile shone faintly in his eyes. "Why not?" he asked softly.

"Because I wanted you and you weren't there," she whispered. "Make love to me, Devlin. Please."

He drew in a deep, shuddering breath, and then caught her swiftly in his arms, burying his face in her neck. "Thank God," he muttered hoarsely. "I was beginning to think I would give in before you did."

In spite of her raging desire, Tara laughed softly. "Getting desperate, were you?" she mocked as he lifted his head to look down at her.

"Insane is the word," he murmured. "You've been driving me slowly out of my mind for weeks." Urgent fingers smoothed aside the lacy straps of her gown, and the silky garment dropped to the floor. Unsteadily he added, "But I've got you now."

Their lovemaking was different this time. It was shattering gentleness and burning passion, desperate need and teasing playfulness. It was as if they had only this night to belong to each other, and each wanted to make the most of it. Time and again they soared to the very edge of the precipice, only to retreat, postponing the final ecstasy. And when at last they went over the brink, Tara understood why this miraculous moment was called "the little death." She felt as if she were dying, being consumed by fire....

And then her fear returned. Disturbed, she trembled as Devlin held her gently. "I'm sorry . . . I don't know what's wrong with me," she whispered.

He turned her face up, his silvery eyes searching hers intently. "You really don't know, do you?"

She shook her head, and he smiled. "There's a little girl inside you," he told her tenderly. "She doesn't show her face very often, but sometimes she comes out. When we've just made love, she realizes she's lost something of herself to me. And that frightens her."

Puzzled and disturbed by what he was saying, Tara moved restlessly against him and started to speak. But Devlin laid a gentle finger over her lips and continued in a whimsical voice. "She's afraid of giving up anything of herself, afraid of being hurt. So she shows that stubborn, defiant, frightened little face and fights the woman in you."

Tara rested her cheek against his shoulder and thought about what he had said. Then in a very small voice she murmured, "That—that makes me sound emotionally retarded."

He laughed softly. "No, just confused. All we have to do is find out why that little girl is so afraid."

"We?" she inquired uneasily.

"You're going to marry me."

"No, I—"

"And I'll keep you barefoot and pregnant, and that little girl won't have *time* to be afraid." His voice contained a hint of laughter. "She'll be too busy."

"Devlin!" Tara tried to lift her head, but he held it firmly against his shoulder. "Barefoot and pregnant!" she exclaimed.

"Of course. And we'll live happily ever after."

Tara giggled in spite of herself and gave up her useless attempts to raise her head. *Why* did he always make her laugh just when she should have been angry or offended? "That sounds like a line from a very bad movie," she told him severely.

"I'm just a romantic at heart," he responded sadly.

"I won't marry you. And you *won't* keep me barefoot and pregnant."

"Just pregnant, then."

"Oh, for God's sake," she muttered helplessly. "Are you deaf? Or just plain out of your mind?"

"Right now I'm just plain freezing. What did you do with the covers, you shameless wench?"

Tara bit back another giggle and wondered wildly if she was going insane. "I didn't do anything with them. *You* kicked them away. I remember that distinctly."

"I did no such thing."

"You did, too."

"That's character assassination. Be a good girl and pull the covers back up." He sighed comfortably. "I may never move again."

"Some people would call that lazy," she commented.

"Not if they'd just spent a delightful hour with a wildcat. Are you going to get the covers?"

"After that remark, get them yourself!" Tara could feel herself flushing vividly.

He chuckled. "I'll have to be careful when I go in swimming, because if Mother sees the scratches on my back, she's going to wonder what I've gotten myself engaged to."

"Devlin!"

His chuckle became a rich, delighted laugh. "I don't believe it. You're blushing! I thought that was a lost art."

"Well, it isn't!"

"I meant it as a compliment, honey." He patted her hip and complained, "It's like the fringes of the Arctic in here. Are you going to get the covers?"

"I can't. Someone has a hammerlock on my neck."

"Well, I beg your pardon, I'm sure."

Biting her lip at his offended tone, she sat up and rummaged for the covers, then yelped as he swatted her. "Damn it! If you do that one more time—"

"You sound like a wife already," he interrupted.

"What am I going to do with you?" she wailed softly as he pulled her back down beside him and arranged the covers neatly over them.

"You're going to marry me."

"Insane people are barred from marriage. I read it somewhere."

"Don't believe everything you read." He rested his chin on top of her head. "You cuddle up to me just like a kitten."

Sleep was tugging at her mind, "I'm not going to marry you, you know," Tara murmured drowsily.

"Of course you are. . . ."

The sun was shining with irritating brightness when Tara opened her eyes, and she wondered sleepily what had awakened her. She was lying on her back, close beside Devlin, with the heavy weight of his arm across her waist and his face nuzzling her neck. She yawned and came wide awake as a soft knock sounded on the door—the sound that must have awakened her. Before she could gather her wits and poke Devlin, the door opened.

Amanda laughed softly. "Oh, don't look so horrified, my dear. I'm sorry to intrude, but there's a phone call for Devlin. Long distance and important, so the man said."

Tara was mortified. "All right," she murmured. "I'll tell him."

Amanda smiled again and withdrew, and Tara began to laugh helplessly. She reached over to shake Devlin's shoulder gently. He muttered something indistinguishable and tightened his arm across her middle.

"Devlin? *Devlin*, you have to get up!" She shook him again.

He finally woke up enough to raise himself on one elbow and stare down at her groggily. "Oh, hello," he murmured, for all the world as if she were a chance acquaintance he'd just met on the street.

Tara bit back a giggle. "I know you're not at your best in the mornings, but do try to concentrate. You have to get up."

He blinked a couple of times. "What time is it? It feels like the crack of dawn."

"I don't know what time it is, but you're probably right."

"Then why should I get up? I'm much too comfortable." He dropped his head back onto the pillow and nuzzled his face into her neck again.

Tara sighed. "You have to get up because there's a phone call for you. Long distance. And important."

"Damn it, I'm supposed to be on vacation," he muttered, then sighed heavily and rolled away from her. "It'd better be important, or I'll fire whoever dragged me away from you."

"What if he doesn't work for you?"

"Then I'll have him killed."

She giggled again and watched him fight his way out of the tangled covers, then reached to reclaim her share. "Tell me something," she requested. "Why can't you ever get out of a bed without leaving it looking like a war zone?"

"Only my wife has the right to ask me that," he replied with sleepy dignity.

"I withdraw the question."

"Stubborn to the end," he murmured, bending to pick up his robe. As he shrugged into it, realization sank in, and he stared at her. "How do you know there's a phone call for me?"

"Attaboy, champ," she murmured teasingly, reaching behind her head to plump up her pillow. "I knew you'd get there eventually."

He grinned faintly, looking absurdly endearing even with his morning stubble. "Okay, so I'm a little slow in the morning. But I'm awake now, so tell me—how did you know?"

"Amanda came in to tell me."

Devlin's eyes gleamed with unholy amusement. Sinking down on the foot of the bed, he started laughing. "You really don't have much luck maintaining your dignity around Mother, do you?"

"Not much, no. And it isn't at all funny!" But she felt her own lips twitch uncontrollably.

Still grinning, he rose to his feet and belted the robe around his lean form. "You'll have to marry me now, you know. I've been shamelessly compromised!"

"Isn't the shoe on the other foot?"

"Okay, I'll make an honest woman of you, then."

"No, thank you."

He shook his head sadly. "My mother's going to think you're a scarlet woman. You know that, don't you?"

"Go answer the phone!" she said desperately.

Chapter Nine

Half an hour later Tara was fully dressed and back in her own room when Devlin stuck his head in the door to say briefly that he'd have to fly to New York immediately because of a business crisis. She barely had time to nod her understanding before he was gone.

Deep in thought, Tara went downstairs. It was only a little after 7:00 A.M., and since she usually got more than five hours of sleep, she felt a bit woozy. Her stomach was churning in a strange way, and she couldn't decide whether it was because of lack of sleep or because Devlin was leaving so abruptly.

Meeting Amanda in the dining room dressed casually in slacks and a print blouse, Tara smiled as she went to the sideboard to pour herself a cup of coffee.

"Did Devlin tell you, my dear?" Amanda asked, sipping her own coffee.

"About having to fly to New York?" Tara nodded as she carried her cup to the table and sat down across from the older woman. "But will he be able to get a reservation on such short notice?"

Devlin's mother looked faintly surprised. "His manager sent the company jet. It should have landed in Amarillo by now."

"Oh." Tara stared down at her coffee with a wry smile. She had never known anyone who owned a jet. "Are the others up?" she asked a moment later.

"Jake drove into Amarillo about an hour ago with Rick to attend a cattle auction. Rick wants to add to the herd. Julie's still in bed. You were wise not to go with Devlin, Tara."

Tara blinked. "Oh. Well, he'll be busy . . ." she murmured, not wanting to admit that he hadn't asked her to go.

Amanda glanced at her watch and shook her head. "He'd better hurry. Richard sounded almost frantic. He manages the company office in New York," she added as an afterthought.

Having only a vague idea of how the corporate empire was run, Tara could only nod blankly. "It must be serious, for Richard to send the jet after Devlin."

Amanda agreed with a rueful smile. "It has to be serious. I've met Richard, and he is *not* a man to make mountains out of mole-hills. If anything, he's prone to understate trouble. So if he says there's trouble, it's probably nothing short of disaster."

Tara frowned down at her coffee. Had business worries been responsible for Devlin's earlier preoccupation? She wondered. Was he worried that his business was taking a nose dive after more than ten years of success? She glanced down at the ring glittering on her finger and felt a superstitious chill creep up her spine. Was it only coincidence that Devlin should run into trouble just after announcing his intention of marrying a woman he didn't love?

"Tara?" Amanda sounded concerned. "Are you all right? You're a little pale."

Tara drew her gaze away from the glittering diamond with effort. "No, I'm fine. I—I'll just miss Devlin, that's all," she murmured, saying the first thing that came to mind.

"Will you? That's nice to hear," said a calm voice behind her.

Startled, Tara glanced over her shoulder to find Devlin, looking very much a businessman, dressed in a formal suit and tie. He was handsome, formidable, and very distant. Tara couldn't read his hooded gaze and expressionless face. He carried a briefcase in one hand and was obviously on the point of leaving.

"I should be gone three or four days," he told them. "Mother, make sure Tara doesn't kidnap one of the horses and ride off into the sunset while I'm gone."

Barely hearing Amanda's amused assent, Tara stared into Devlin's eyes and found a question there. Only dimly realizing that she was taking the first step toward commitment, she answered his question with a smile. "I'll be here," she promised quietly, and felt rewarded when some of the tension left his face.

"Good," he responded in a suddenly husky voice as he bent to kiss her lightly. "Take care of yourself, sweetheart." For her ears alone, he whispered, "Try to miss me."

Tara felt the sting of tears as she watched him kiss his mother good-bye and walk out the door. For a long moment his whispered plea echoed in her mind. Did he love her after all? At least a little bit? He was willing to give her his name and his children, but was he also offering a part of his heart?

Tara excused herself, conscious of Amanda's sympathetic, understanding eyes, and went out to sit by the pool. It was already hot and hazy, but Tara didn't notice either the sweltering heat or the humidity. She was trying to figure out just what Devlin's love might mean to her. Would it give her the courage to face the fears inside herself?

Could she trust him with her own love? Could she give him her heart without being afraid that he would throw it carelessly aside one day? Or would she end up just like her mother had, trapped in a hate-filled marriage from which she found no escape? . . .

Tara gasped and buried her face in her hands, pain and fear slicing through her. Memories washed over her like acid, eating away at the barrier she had built around that frightened inner part of herself, battering at her facade of self-confidence. She wanted to stop the hateful flood, but after sixteen years the memories pushed their way relentlessly toward the surface.

Even at the age of ten Tara had known that her parents disliked each other, that hate and resentment lay just beneath the surface of their outward lives. With a child's clearsighted wisdom, she had known, too, that her father was mostly to blame. He'd been a charming, handsome man, with eyes as blue as the sea and shoulders wide and strong to carry his adoring daughter. In another age he might have been called a rake, and mothers would have warned their daughters to beware of him.

But no one had warned Tara's mother, Kathleen. She fell head over heels in love with the charming man ten years older than herself who had drifted into the small midwestern town where she lived. She'd even dropped out of school, at sixteen years old, to marry him.

Tara was born less than a year later, in another small town. Her earliest memories were of the family pulling up stakes in the dead of night and moving on—because her father had lost another job and owed someone money or had gotten into a fistfight. She sat drowsily between her parents in their shabby car and listened to them fight, exchanging ugly, hurting words. And then there was always another small town and another school and more new friends. Until they moved once again.

Tara never became accustomed to waking up to the sound of harsh voices and shrill accusations. Adoring her father, she blamed her mother at first. But more and more often her father's goodnight kisses reeked of whiskey, and the stale scent of cheap perfume clung to him like an indictment. She knew then. And she no longer pleaded to be carried on his shoulder.

She became a silent child around her parents and temperamental with others. At school she was belligerent and fiercely independent, scorning the dolls and dresses of other little girls for her scruffy jeans and tomboyish ways.

And then her parents died in a car crash, and her ten-year-old heart was torn between the fear of being alone and a confused sense of guilt that somehow she'd been responsible for her parents' deaths.

With no relatives to claim her, she began living in a long succession of foster homes. Sullen, difficult, she never remained long in any one place. Again and again she ran away, learning to take care of herself and escaping harm only by the grace of God. The authorities always found her and placed her in yet another home. She learned to swear early and took savage delight in using shocking language. Most of all, she trusted no one.

And then, seven years after the deaths of her parents, she met a very special man. A retired professor, he had been acting as dramatic coach to a small group of community players in Tara's town. Because someone dared her to do it, Tara tried out for a part in the play *The Taming of the Shrew*, and to her astonishment, she was cast as Kate.

She found that James Ellis—or "the Professor," as the students called him—was a demanding man who expected the very best from his students. For the first time in her life Tara gave her all. She was fascinated by acting and intrigued by her own talent.

The Professor pushed and prodded her, accepting no excuses for shoddy performances or temper tantrums. He talked to her about acting and his philosophy of life. And sometime during that year she became a woman—a strong-minded, independent woman, who controlled her temper more often than not and knew exactly what she wanted out of life. She wanted to be an actress . . . a good one.

And she had. But only by burying the painful memories of her childhood, relying on independence and fierce determination to get her through the tough times. No one would ever hurt her. Not ever. She wouldn't let them. She was determined to lean on no one, depend on no one but herself.

Tara returned to an awareness of her present surroundings with a jolt, suddenly aware of the intense heat, of bright light reflected off the glassy surface of the pool. She was two people, she realized dimly—woman and child. The child in her was terrified of commitment, the child who had lain trembling in a darkened bedroom, listening to two people hurl angry accusations. The child who had faced a cold and hostile world with a chip on her shoulder and a spark of temper in her eyes—and terrible fear in her heart. The child who was afraid of learning to depend on people, only to reach out one day and find them gone.

And the woman in her? The woman, she understood at last, loved Devlin Bradley and trusted him. The woman in Tara could take daily knocks with a wry smile and laugh at herself. She was intelligent and humorous and a bit cynical. And Devlin Bradley had seen and understood both sides of her all along.

Tara stared out across the water, the wonder of this new understanding shining in her eyes. The chains of her memories seemed to be snapping away from her, one by one. She was letting go of childish promises, letting go of the stubborn, defiant little girl who had clung fearfully to her separate identity. The child began to merge at last with the woman who was strong enough to give herself to the man she loved.

It was only a first step, she knew, but a big one. She would probably catch herself at odd moments wondering if Devlin would grow tired of her. Knowing that he had loved before, and deeply, she would have to learn to accept the ghost of his lost love. But she was willing to try now. For the sake of that lonely, frightened little girl, and the sake of the woman who loved so desperately, she had to try.

"Tara?"

She blinked and looked around, to find Julie standing by the patio table. The younger woman looked every inch a teenager this morning, her hair tied back with a bright ribbon, with no makeup on her face, and a very skimpy bikini on her body that was scandalous and completely in fashion. Julie looked worried.

"Are you all right? You look a little—odd." The younger woman flushed suddenly. "I'm sorry—I should have said 'Miss Collins.' "

Tara laughed heartily. "For heaven's sake, call me Tara. You're putting me ahead a generation by being so formal. And I'm fine, Julie. Really fine."

Julie set her softly playing transistor radio on the table and smiled uncertainly. "I was going to swim, but if it'll bother you . . ."

Realizing that Julie was well on her way to getting over her crush on Devlin, Tara gave her a friendly smile. "I don't mind at all."

Julie walked over toward the edge of the pool and turned suddenly. "You—you really love him, don't you?"

"I really do," Tara answered gently.

Julie nodded briefly. "I knew, right from the first," she murmured, "but I kept thinking . . . Well, I've been a witch, haven't I?"

Tara grinned. "Julie, falling in love is never easy, and when we pick the wrong person it's sheer hell. As for being nasty—well, we all have our moments."

"You're nice." Julie returned Tara's smile. "I didn't think you would be, but you are."

"Well, thank you! You're not so bad yourself."

"Thanks." Julie hesitated before mumbling, "Daddy and I are leaving in a few days, and . . . I was wondering if you could—would . . ."

"Would what?" Tara asked curiously.

Lifting her chin, Julie finished defiantly, "I was wondering if you'd give me your autograph. So that I can show the kids at school. Otherwise they'll never believe I met you."

Startled, Tara began to laugh. "Of course I will. But I hope you and your father will stay for the wedding." She was taking a chance, because she wasn't completely certain a wedding would ever take place. She wondered vaguely if Devlin would become bored when the quarry he was chasing doubled back and grabbed him.

"Will it be soon?" Julie asked shyly.

"I'm not sure." Tara smiled. "A lot depends on Devlin's business trip, but I think the wedding will be fairly soon."

Julie nodded. "I'd love to be here for it. I'll ask Daddy if we can stay."

"Please do." Reaching absently across the table to turn up Julie's radio, Tara watched as the younger woman dove into the pool. She was shocked to realize that Devlin had already been gone nearly two hours. Her thoughts returned to her childhood. Why had she suddenly faced her childhood fears?

Tara wasn't certain, but maybe what had happened the night before had something to do with it. For the first time she had admitted she wanted Devlin, realized that she needed him in a way she still didn't fully understand. But more than anything else Devlin's uncanny understanding of her had jarred a door long closed and locked within her.

More at peace with herself than she'd been in a long time, Tara sat back and listened to the popular music, wondering if Devlin really wanted her love. So far he'd just said he wanted a home and a wife—and children.

But a man didn't have to be in love to father a child, and perhaps eventually he'd feel burdened by her love. Would he be satisfied with what he thought he wanted? Would he be content with her companionship, her humor, and the desire she could offer? Or would he wake up in the night wishing that the woman beside him were someone else?

Tara pushed the painful questions aside. She *would* marry him. If he wanted her love, she would give it gladly. And if he didn't want her love, she'd try not to burden him with it. She would have his name and his children and his companionship. They would be enough. They would *have* to be enough. He was embedded deeply in her heart.

Content at last with her decision, Tara sat back and contemplated the future with a smile. Should she give up her career? Devlin had pointedly denied any intention of asking her . . . *this* time. But did he *want* her to give it up? He'd said he wanted to live here in Texas and raise horses. Would he be happy with a wife who was forever flying off somewhere to make a film? And did she really want to do that anyway?

The timid child inside Tara suggested urgently that she keep an iron in the fire just in case marriage didn't work out, but the woman inside Tara shoved the thought away. No. She would never again base an important decision on a fear of rejection. So . . . did she *want* to go on with her career? Did she want to be separated from the man she loved, and later from their children, because of her career? Did she really *need* that form of self-expression, that outlet for her creative energies?

Tara smothered a giggle as she realized she was rapidly talking herself out of any desire to work. Her career obviously wasn't as important to her as she'd always believed. Or perhaps Devlin was just more important. She was committed to do at least one more film. After that . . . well, she'd just wait and see.

Tara watched Julie splash around in the pool and was just about to get into her suit and join her when she suddenly froze to her chair, icy-cold shock sweeping through her body. Her eyes fixed with painful intensity on the radio, she listened in horror as the announcer reported that a jet aircraft belonging to a private corporation had crashed shortly after take-off from Amarillo, en route to New York. It was not known whether there were any survivors.

No. Tara repeated the silent plea over and over again. *No!* It couldn't be Devlin, it just couldn't be!

As the announcer said he'd report further information as it came in, Tara bit back an agonized cry of protest. She looked around, dazed, knowing she should go in and tell Amanda, do *something*, but her mind wasn't working very well. Pictures of Devlin flitted through her thoughts—Devlin smiling, angry, laughing, tender, passionate, teasing. Devlin in a business suit, astride a spirited black filly, naked beside a shadowy pool. She saw him making love to her and laughing at her and swearing at her. She saw him playing a piano superbly and brooding over the memory of a love gone wrong. She saw him whimsically talking of children and cheerfully proclaiming that she was going to marry him.

And then, horribly, her imagination conjured up an image of a broken, bleeding body, and Tara closed her eyes with a ragged moan.

"Tara!" Amanda was coming toward her, her lovely face taut with the effort to control herself, her eyes gray pools of pain.

Tara was barely conscious of Julie climbing out of the pool with a puzzled, anxious expression. She looked up as Amanda reached the table. "I just heard."

Amanda sat down across from her and reached to grip Tara's hands strongly. "There's a chance that it wasn't his plane, Tara," she told her evenly. "*Two* private jets took off for New York this morning, only a few minutes apart. The airport officials either don't know or won't say which plane went down. Rick and Jake are on their way to the airport now—I managed to reach them at the auction—and they'll let us know as soon as possible what's happened."

"It can't be him," Tara whispered. "I—I've only just found him . . . I can't lose him now."

Julie sat down beside Tara, her concerned expression indicating that she had realized what had happened. "He'll be all right, Tara," she said hoarsely. "I just know he will!"

After a long silent moment Amanda said quietly, "Let's go into the house, my dear. You look like a ghost. I think we both need a drink." Amanda murmured more soothing words as she and Julie led Tara inside to a sofa in the den. As if by magic Josh appeared with a tray of drinks. Tara looked at him with wide, blank eyes.

"Why were you weeping into your ale, Josh?" she asked clearly.

The butler cast a startled glance at Amanda and then, apparently realizing that Tara wasn't quite herself, replied, "I'd had a bit of trouble, that's all, Miss Tara."

Tara dropped her unseeing gaze to the ring on her finger. "No," she murmured, "it was more than just a bit of trouble. People don't cry that easily. I don't. I haven't cried . . . in a very long while. Not since I was a child. Oh, I cried when the director said to cry. But that wasn't real. That wasn't me. It was someone else."

"Drink this, Tara," Amanda ordered gently, placing a glass in her hand and guiding it firmly toward her lips.

Tara drank automatically and choked as the fiery spirit tore its way down her throat. Her eyes watering, she looked up to find the others regarding her in concern and managed a faint smile. "I'm sorry. I don't usually fall apart like this," she murmured. "Josh, forgive me, please. I had no business asking you such a personal question."

"I quite understand, Miss Tara." The middle-aged man smiled suddenly. "To be perfectly truthful I don't remember why I was weeping. I'd lost my job and had one too many, I suppose."

Tara smiled as he left the room and then looked up at Amanda. "It's not knowing," she murmured, her smile fading. "That's what I can't stand. Not knowing."

"Yes," Amanda agreed, sitting down beside her and patting her hand. Julie sat down on Tara's other side, still dressed in her bikini. The three women remained silent for a time, before Amanda began to talk. She chatted about the ranch, the new foals, a comical character she'd met in Amarillo one day. She talked in her usual gentle, disjointed fashion, and Tara began to grow calm.

Julie went away for a time and returned wearing slacks and a blouse. She and Tara listened silently as Amanda continued to talk casually and easily.

All three of them jumped when the phone rang.

Betraying her anxiety for the first time, Amanda leaped to her feet and rushed to answer it. "Hello? Rick, what—" An expression of heartfelt relief spread over her face. "You're sure? Oh, thank God! Yes, I'm fine. And—and the other plane? I see. No, we'll be all right. Yes. Good-bye, darling." She turned to give Tara and Julie a shaky smile. "It wasn't Devlin's plane."

Making careful movements, Tara raised her glass to her lips and downed the rest of the whiskey, scarcely gasping. "From now on," she said calmly, "he can ride the filly to New York. It may take longer, but at least he'll be closer to the ground."

They all laughed, giddy from the sudden release of tension, and all at once Tara realized it was a beautiful day. "What about the other plane?" she asked hesitantly.

Amanda smiled. "The pilot was slightly injured, that's all. He'll be fine."

The phone rang again just then, and Amanda turned to answer it. "Devlin! Yes, we heard. Had a nasty scare there for a while. Yes. No, Rick called from the airport just a minute ago. Yes, she's here. Just a moment." She held the phone out to Tara. "He wants to talk to you, my dear."

Setting her glass down on the coffee table, Tara rose to her feet and moved to take the phone, faintly surprised that her legs were able to support her. "Devlin?"

"Mother said you'd had a scare," he said huskily. "Are you all right now?"

His voice had never sounded so utterly wonderful to her, and Tara shut her eyes as a flood of warm emotions washed over her. "Yes . . . yes, I'm fine. But it was so frightening. We didn't know which plane had gone down."

Devlin sighed. "We didn't hear anything about it until we landed here in New York. I'm sorry you were worried, honey."

Tara bit her lip. "Hurry home . . . please."

"I wish I could believe you'd say that even if my mother wasn't in the room," he murmured huskily. "I'll be home in a few days. Good-bye, darling."

"Good-bye," she whispered, and slowly replaced the receiver. She turned to Amanda and Julie and announced starkly, "Just as soon as I can drag him to the altar, I'm going to marry that man."

Then she walked carefully back to the sofa, sat down, and burst into tears, crying for the first time in years. . . .

During the next four days Amanda threw herself wholeheartedly into the task of arranging a large wedding. She ignored Tara's laughing protests, insisting that she and Devlin would be married from the ranch, with proper pomp and splendor.

Tara, who had visualized a swift flight to Vegas and a simple chapel ceremony, was both startled and amused by Amanda's plans. Her future mother-in-law began calling relatives immediately, stressing the need for secrecy, to avoid undue publicity, and naming a date barely two weeks away. Tara pointed out that the groom was woefully ignorant of these proceedings and hadn't even been consulted about a date, for heaven's sake, but Amanda brushed aside these considerations as unimportant.

Abandoning herself to fate, as she generally did around Amanda, Tara stopped protesting. She was deeply touched that Amanda wanted to give her the kind of wedding mothers generally give their daughters, and she grew closer to the older woman day by day. She even got up the courage to ask Amanda to be her matron of honor and to ask Rick to give her away. She was delighted when both accepted happily.

Even Jake Holman unbent toward her, perhaps because of his

daughter's changed attitude, and started talking casually about accepting Devlin's business deal. Since Devlin had mentioned his intention of selling out in New York, Tara didn't know whether the deal was still part of his plans, but she said nothing to discourage Jake.

See? Already she was learning to be a business wife, she assured herself happily.

By the fourth day plans for the wedding were almost complete, and Tara had already had one fitting for her gown. Although she was still arguing with Amanda that she herself should pay for the dress, she was already resigned to losing. At least now she knew why she never seemed able to win an argument with Devlin—he'd inherited his talent for convincing her from his mother.

Since Devlin was due back that day, Tara found it difficult to concentrate on anything—including what kind of flowers she should carry. Excusing herself to an understanding Amanda, she went for a walk, determined to quiet the butterflies in her stomach.

She toyed with the idea of saddling a horse and going for a ride, but talked herself out of it. She wasn't obeying Devlin, she insisted silently; she just didn't really feel like riding. She climbed over a fence into a deserted paddock, heading toward a pasture in the distance where a group of mares and foals grazed quietly. Then she heard the thud of hooves and realized with a start that the paddock wasn't deserted after all.

She turned swiftly to see an unfriendly looking bay horse bearing down on her, his ears pinned to his head and every tooth gleaming. It was the stallion Devlin had warned her about—the one with a peculiar hatred of women.

Tara had enough sense not to turn and run, but she took an instinctive step backward . . . and tripped. The next few seconds were a confused blur, with the horse approaching angrily and Tara too far from the fence and flat on her back besides. And then she heard a sharp whistle and sat up hastily to see that the horse had abandoned his charge and was trotting docilely back to the stable.

Devlin waved the horse inside the stable and closed the bottom half of the Dutch door, then turned to stare across at Tara. His hands on his hips, he glared at her. "You," he shouted to her with awful patience, "need a keeper."

A giddy sense of relief at his safe return swept over Tara, and she forgot all about the horse's near-attack. Jumping to her feet, she dusted off the seat of her jeans and asked lightly, "Are you applying for the job?"

Something flickered in his eyes, and he stared at her for a long moment. "Before I make a fool of myself by leaping at your offer," he said dryly, "I'd better be sure exactly what you have in mind."

Tara walked over to stand before him. "Will you marry me?" she asked gravely.

"Well, I'll be damned," he muttered blankly.

"Probably," she agreed cheerfully.

Gripping her shoulders, he gave her a gentle shake, his silvery eyes searching her expression with an eagerness that made Tara's heart leap into her heart. "I've been proposing to you for weeks—no, damn it, *years!*—and now suddenly you're proposing to me? Have you been drinking?" he demanded suspiciously.

"Nope." She smiled up at him. "I didn't hit my head when I fell, either."

"Well, thank God!" he exclaimed unsteadily, lifting her completely off her feet and delightedly swinging her around in a circle. Setting her on her feet at last, he gazed down at her flushed face with bright eyes. "What changed your mind?" he demanded huskily.

"I nearly lost you, you know," she responded a little breathlessly. Determined to keep a light tone, she went on, "After all, who would I have to fight with if you weren't around? I decided to stake my claim before you got away."

He chuckled softly, still devouring her with his eyes. "Maybe I'll almost crash more often if it takes the fight out of you this way. Whenever you're too stubborn to give in to me, I'll just plan a near-accident—"

"Oh, no, you won't!" she interrupted fiercely. "The next time you go up in a plane, I'm going with you. Besides," she went on in a mocking tone, "it wasn't really that. I just got so tired of saying no." She yelped when he swatted her lightly, and complained. "Don't bruise the bride! What would your mother say?"

"Probably that you deserved it."

"Oh, no, she wouldn't. She's planning a huge wedding, and she'll be very disappointed if I'm black and blue with bruises when all your distinguished relations see me for the first time."

"A huge wedding? Oh, no!" he groaned.

"Now's your chance to back out," she advised calmly.

"Not a chance!" he replied with reassuring promptness. He bent his head to give her a brief, hard kiss, then grabbed her hand and began leading her toward the house. "Come hell or high water, you're going to marry me. I only hope Mother hasn't invited Aunt Mary. She's deaf as a stone."

"Is she the one who lives in Baltimore? Amanda was talking to someone in Baltimore, this morning . . ."

"Oh, no!"

Chapter Ten

"What I want to know," Devlin demanded as they climbed out of the car in front of their ranch two weeks later, "is how my mother wound up being your matron of honor."

"I asked her," Tara replied absently, shaking her head to rid herself of the last few grains of rice. She stared at the once-gleaming Mercedes, which had been slathered with shaving cream, toothpaste, and soap, and asked, "Who decorated the car?"

"Jim." Devlin grimaced as he came to stand beside her. "Didn't you see his expression during the reception?"

"No. I was busy explaining to Aunt Mary why we weren't having a honeymoon."

He studied her carefully. "There's still time to pack up and fly off somewhere . . ."

Tara shook her head firmly. "A honeymoon isn't a place, it's a state of mind—and I want our marriage to start in this house. It'll be a good omen."

"You think we'll need all the help we can get, huh?"

"I just believe in hedging my bets," she replied calmly. "By the way, whose car is that? I've never seen it before."

"Yours. A wedding present."

Tara stared up at him. "Mine? It—it's beautiful. But you didn't have to do that, Devlin."

"I know." He lifted her easily into his arms. "I wanted to. And now, Mrs. Bradley, shall we go see how the new furniture looks?"

Trying to fight the breathless feeling that being in his arms always gave her, she confided seriously, "I'm a little worried about that Oriental dining room."

"Well, you're the one who fell in love with those fat little vases," he teased her.

Tara frowned at him as he carried her toward the house. "They weren't all little and fat. And if you didn't like them, why didn't you say something instead of just standing there smiling like an idiot?"

"Honey, after two weeks in my lonely bed," Devlin replied, chuckling, "I wouldn't have said a word if you'd decorated the house with items from the Spanish Inquisition." He bent to let her open the door and then stepped over the threshold.

"Look," Tara said conversationally, "for the past two weeks every room between yours and mine has been stuffed with *your* relatives. I wasn't about to do any nighttime prowling. And you weren't exactly breaking down any doors to get to me, either."

"I had visions of Aunt Mary wandering into the hallway and asking what I was doing there," he confessed wryly.

Tara giggled as he set her gently on her feet, then asked a bit breathlessly, "Um . . . shouldn't you wash that stuff off the car?"

He looked injured. "On my wedding day? Besides, it's not my car." Laughing at her expression, he reached behind her to shut the door. "Don't worry, honey. Mother whispered to me just before we left that she'd send someone to pick up the car and have it washed. I only hope she tells him not to disturb us."

"She will." Tara smiled up at him. "Your mother thinks of everything. She even sent her cook over here yesterday to stock the pantry and freezer with easy-to-fix meals. In case we decide to eat, she said. Wasn't that nice of her?"

"Very nice." He bent his head to nuzzle the soft scented flesh behind her ear. "I don't suppose you're hungry?" he whispered.

"Starving," Tara said innocently.

Devlin lifted his head and sighed. "You're determined to drive me out of my mind, aren't you?" he accused ruefully.

"Could I do that?" Tara slipped from his arms with a laugh and started across the foyer. "Come and see the dining room—and this time tell me what you really think!"

For the next hour they explored the entire house, ending up in the kitchen. Like children they rummaged in the pantry and freezer, settling at last on cold chicken and salads and opening a bottle of wine. They talked casually as they ate—about how the new furniture looked, about Devlin's successful business trip, about when they should fly to L.A. to clean out their respective apartments. They talked about everything except what was on both their minds.

Surprising Tara, Devlin offered to clean up the kitchen. She warned him not to break anything, then laughed at his offended expression and left him.

In their lovely gold-and-rust bedroom Tara spent a few moments wandering around with a bemused smile. She'd done it—she'd actually married him! And, except for an uncertain moment at the very beginning of the ceremony, not a qualm had disturbed her.

It was amazing, she thought, how quickly that little girl inside her had learned to handle her fears. The possibility of losing him had done it. Life without him had seemed horrifyingly blank and empty, and that fear had been stronger than the little girl's fears of rejection.

So now she was Mrs. Devlin Bradley. And she still didn't know how her husband really felt about her. More than once during the past two weeks she had seen a watchful, brooding expression on his face, a curiously guarded wariness in his eyes when he looked at her. Though she didn't know why, it hurt to have him gaze at her that way. She was afraid the ghost of his past love was troubling him, and she didn't know what to do about it. How could she fight a ghost?

Brushing such painful thoughts away, Tara glanced out the wide windows, to see that darkness had fallen, and smiled as she went to the dresser to find the negligee that had been a present from Amanda. The day before, she and her new mother-in-law had brought over from the Lawton ranch all of Devlin's and her clothing. They would have to fly to L.A. soon to get the rest of their belongings.

Tara took a shower and put on the negligee, feeling unexpectedly nervous. She turned on a dim light on the nightstand and turned back the covers of the huge bed, then frowned as she went over to pick up her watch from the dresser. Over an hour . . . and the bridegroom remained conspicuously absent.

Another bride might well have ruined her manicure and pulled out her hair, wondering what was wrong. Not being a typical bride, Tara went looking for her husband. She found him in the den downstairs, standing before the window and staring out into the darkness.

And his eyes were haunted.

Tara came slowly into the room, aware that he was too lost in thought—or in memories—to be aware of her presence. What was she going to do? Ignore the problem and hope she could somehow teach him to love her? No, she had ignored too many problems for far too long. She had to face him.

And that meant . . .

Taking a deep breath, Tara said quietly, "It might help if you told me about her, Devlin."

Startled, he turned quickly, the brooding look vanishing as though it had never existed, to be replaced by a guarded expression. He frowned slightly. "Tell you about who?"

Tara held onto her courage and answered steadily, "The woman you can't forget. The one you think about all the time. The one you wrote that song for." Her voice broke a little as she went on painfully, "I have to know, Devlin. I have to *know*."

He took a hasty step toward her and then stopped, astonishment warring with some other unreadable emotion on his face. "*You*, Tara!" he exclaimed softly, fiercely.

For an eternal moment she thought that she had heard only what she'd wanted to hear. A thousand thoughts flitted through her mind. He . . . loved her? *She* was the woman he was haunted by? "You—you love me?" she whispered.

He gave a short laugh, as if the sound were forced from him. "God in heaven, woman—why do you think I wanted to marry you?"

"You wanted a home," she murmured dazedly.

"A home with you!"

"You—you never mentioned love."

Devlin stared at her. "Because you would have run like hell," he said hoarsely. "Even though I didn't understand that maddening mind of yours, I knew you were afraid to commit yourself." His strained features softened for a moment, giving her a glimpse of something she could hardly believe. "So I gambled . . . rushed you into marriage, hoping that you wouldn't wake up one morning and decide you'd made a mistake. Even now . . . I don't know why you married me, Tara."

His words were a plea, and as she gazed at him, Tara saw the wary look she had come to dread, an expression of half-angry vulnerability in his remarkable eyes. A sudden rush of almost painful love and tenderness swept over her, and she knew she would do anything—anything in her power—to wipe away that look on his face. She just couldn't bear to see exposed the chinks in her proud Devlin's armor. It was enough to know they were there.

Taking another giant step away from that frightened, defiant child who had ruled her emotions for so long, Tara said very quietly, "I love you, Devlin. I always have."

"You . . ." He seemed stunned, incapable of taking it in, his silvery eyes filling with a sudden glowing light that lit up all the remaining dark spots in Tara's heart.

She went to stand before him, no longer afraid, dimly aware that an aching wound inside her had finally healed. She was whole at last, the confession of her love binding woman and child together. She had never felt so alive. He could hurt her badly, she knew, send her scurrying back into the dark well she had only just climbed out of. But for this moment she didn't care. She was a woman, taking the same risk women down through the ages had always taken by loving a man, by placing her heart in his hands and her dreams at his feet.

"Tara, honey . . ." Suddenly, she was in his arms, being held as though he would never let her go, as if he would fight demons from hell to keep her. "I love you, sweetheart!" Rough hands turned her face up, stormy eyes glowed down at her just before his lips touched hers with an almost desperate need.

Tara met the kiss fiercely, glorying in her freedom, eager to show him how much she loved and needed him. Her arms slipped around his lean waist, her body molding itself to his hard, demanding length. Like a spark to dry kindling, she took fire in his arms.

Devlin drew away at last, but only far enough to rest his forehead against hers. "Good lord, you're combustible," he muttered hoarsely, half groaning and half laughing.

"You're not exactly a bucket of water yourself," she returned breathlessly.

He laughed unsteadily, molten fire still raging deep in his eyes.

"You and I have a few things to discuss, Mrs. Bradley," he told her with mock sternness, "and I think we'd better talk now. I have a feeling we'll find better things to do with our time in the next few days."

"Days?" She widened her eyes innocently.

"Weeks. Years!" Laughing, he swept her up in his arms and carried her over to a chair, sitting down with her in his lap. In the gentle glow from a nearby lamp he smiled tenderly down at her. "Why didn't you tell me?" he asked softly.

"Tell *you*?" She traced a loving ringer along his jaw. "I didn't even tell myself, at first. And then when I realized—"

"When?" he interrupted, catching her wandering fingers and carrying them briefly to his lips.

Tara smiled a little sheepishly. "It was . . . in Las Vegas, the day you came back from New York."

"That long ago?" His eyes flashed with a fleeting anger. "Damn it, why didn't you tell me sooner?"

She leaned forward to kiss him quickly, taking peculiar satisfaction in the fact that he could still get angry at her. "I was afraid to. I thought I was fighting for my life."

Devlin frowned. "I knew you were fighting something," he murmured, almost to himself. "All along you were fighting. At first I thought it was me. But we were so good together, I couldn't understand that. Then I thought you were fighting for your independence. It only dawned on me slowly that there was more to it than that."

"Much more." She smiled a little sadly and then quietly told him all about her childhood and what her parents' relationship had done to her. She made herself completely vulnerable to him, as she'd never done before.

When her voice trailed away at last, Devlin cupped her cheek in one large warm hand. "It was tragic that your parents had a bad marriage, and even more tragic that you had to suffer through it with them. And then to be shunted from one foster home to another . . ." He shook his head. "No wonder you were scared, afraid to trust."

Tara sighed softly. "I didn't understand myself. And I didn't know how you felt, which made everything worse."

"I'm surprised you didn't guess how I felt." He grimaced. "Everyone else did."

"I thought it was just an act! And you set me up so nicely with that fake engagement."

"There was no fake engagement."

"Would you repeat that?"

Devlin wound one of her bright curls around his finger and stared at it as though fascinated. "No fake engagement," he murmured almost absently. "It was completely real. Once I got my ring on your finger, I had every intention of keeping it there." His eyes slid sideways, filled with laughter and a hint of pleading. "I'm afraid you've been the victim of a plot, my love."

Tara's mouth fell open. "You mean—all along?"

"All along. I made up my mind to marry you, long before you collapsed."

Thinking back to all the fights and arguments they had had, she protested, "But you were always so angry at me. I thought it was hurt pride—because I'd refused to marry you."

"I know what you thought," Devlin told her dryly. "It was obvious from the first. But I've got news for you, love. A man doesn't seek out a woman for three years, *knowing* he's going to get a verbal slap in the face, just because she hurt his pride once upon a time."

Tara stared at him. "But what made you so determined then? Was it because I collapsed?"

"In a way." Devlin smiled. "After three years of fighting, I was afraid I just didn't have what it took to break through your barriers. But then, while you were sleeping so deeply in the hospital, you became very restless if I left the room. You'd cry out as if you were having nightmares. I was the only one who could quiet you. I knew then that I *had* broken through that wall. Something inside you needed me, trusted me."

"I can't believe you've loved me for so long," she whispered.

"Longer than you know. All along, in fact."

"You mean—?"

"I mean all along." He smiled crookedly. "I fell in love with you more than three and a half years ago. The night we met."

Astonished, Tara murmured, "I never guessed."

"It was a premiere party like any other," Devlin said quietly. "The same people, the same empty talk. I was bored stiff." His smile turned rueful. "And then lightning struck. Like a scene from a bad movie, the crowd parted and there you stood . . . a goddess."

Tara was half flattered, half amused. "You didn't think that!"

"I promise you I did." He grinned. "The most insane thoughts went through my mind. Helen of Troy. Diana. Lorelei. Venus. You were standing perfectly still, wearing a black gown, and you were different from every other woman in the room." His voice changed, deepened. "You looked so calm, so completely indifferent to the noise and the glamour and the famous actor who was talking to you. Like a statue carved from my dreams, so still and beautiful. Only the fire was missing."

Tara listened, half hypnotized by the quiet intensity of his voice, her heart thumping against her ribs.

"My view of you was blocked for a few seconds, and I was angry with all those faceless people for coming between us. And then I saw you again. The actor had said something to make you angry, and all of a sudden the fire was there. Your eyes were glittering, shooting sparks. Your face came to life. You turned on that actor with a sweet smile and maybe half a dozen words."

Tara's eyes widened as she recalled the moment. The actor had been talking for nearly an hour, name-dropping and using unsubtle lines older than he was. Tara had finally gotten fed up. Though she didn't remember her exact words, she had the distinct impression that her language had been less than ladylike.

Devlin was smiling. "I don't know what you said to him, but I've never seen a man deflate so quickly! Even with most of my attention on you, I saw him just melt away with an unnerved expression on his face. That's when I knew," he finished simply.

Feeling a bit unnerved herself, Tara managed a slight smile. "I'm surprised you didn't melt away like the actor," she murmured. "My temper—"

Devlin placed a gentle finger across her lips. "Your temper doesn't frighten me, honey," he said softly. "It never has. If anything, it delights me. It breathes fire into you, makes you real. As soon as I saw that, I was hooked."

Tara was suddenly, overwhelmingly aware that she must have hurt Devlin very badly by violently rejecting his first proposal. Holding his hand tightly, she said painfully, "And when you proposed . . . oh, darling, I'm so sorry! What you must have felt!"

Devlin smiled, his wry expression not quite hiding the pain in his eyes. "It wasn't . . . pleasant," he confessed quietly. "I was too angry to feel much of anything else for a while. Then I went out and got drunk—and stayed drunk for three days. I spent a lot of time staring at that damned ring and wondering what had gone wrong. And the hell of it was that I knew you wanted me."

He ran a gentle finger down her slightly flushed cheek. "That was something you could never hide from me," he murmured. "And in a lot of ways it was the worst part. I wanted more than just a lovely, passionate body in my bed. I wanted you—all of you—and it was hell, knowing that I could have your body but not your heart or your mind."

Devlin sighed. "I wrote that song about a month later. I thought it would help to get you out of my system . . . but it didn't. Nothing helped, really. I told myself to forget you, and that resolution lasted until I saw you again at some party. After that I found my-self scheming like a besotted fool to be with you whenever I could. In a twisted sort of way, fighting with you was almost like making love to you."

"I wish I'd known," she whispered.

"I'm glad you didn't know," he told her ruefully. "That was the only thing that kept me sane—the fact that you didn't know how I felt about you. Sometimes we'd be arguing, and the sheer necessity of telling you how I felt would almost choke me."

Tara threw her arms around his neck and buried her face against his throat. "I've been such a fool," she said shakily. "Such a blind, stupid fool!"

He laughed unsteadily, his arms holding her tightly. "No, not a fool. Just confused and frightened. If I'd known that, it would have made things a lot easier. As it was, I just had to play it by ear. I got my ring on your finger and used every trick I could think of to make you aware of me, to make you need me."

Troubled, she murmured, "That night at Jim's apartment—you were so angry at me."

Devlin kissed her forehead gently. "Because you'd given me such a simple explanation of why we'd broken up. I couldn't believe you could have rejected me only because you thought I'd interfered in your career. I was angry . . . and hurt. And bitter, I suppose."

Tara lifted her head to stare at him gravely. "I thought I'd made you hate me after that."

"You could never do that. By the next morning I'd realized there had to be more to it than that. And I knew I had my work cut out for me. So I changed my attitude completely, determined to keep you off guard and off balance. I thought if I could just get you to the altar, we'd work all the bugs out later."

Tara smiled at the phrase. "Were you hoping that the Bradley 'luck' would help too?"

Devlin lifted her hand and gazed at the glittering diamond beside the plain gold wedding band. "Jim said he'd told you the story," he murmured. "I've been wondering why you haven't asked me why I was marrying you."

"I've asked you several times why you were so determined to marry me," she said indignantly, "why you were so convinced that we belonged together. You always dodged my questions."

He grinned. "You didn't ask about the ring, though. Didn't you wonder why I'd take a chance and give that ring to a woman for any reason other than love?"

Tara sighed. "The thought did cross my mind. But your sneaky tricks worked so often that I was usually too off balance to think clearly about anything. *Would* you have given the ring to a woman you didn't love?" she asked curiously.

"No. But not because of the legend connected with that ring." Devlin smiled crookedly. "I've never intended to marry for any reason except love. And I never felt any desire to marry at all—until I met you."

She smiled at him, and then the smile died away. "You were so awful to me after that first night."

"Well, what did you expect?" He grimaced wryly. "We had just spent the night together—an experience, I might add, that I considered to be something dreams were made of—and you told me you'd made a mistake and didn't intend to repeat it! Was I supposed to cheerfully accept that and pretend not to be both hurt and angry?"

She touched his cheek in silent apology and felt her senses flare when he turned to kiss the soft inner flesh of her wrist. Trying to think clearly, she murmured, "You changed so quickly when I came out to the training ring that day. Why?"

"You didn't want to fight with me."

Tara looked blank. "And that meant . . . ?"

He chuckled. "Honey, when you refuse to fight with me, I *know* I'm getting somewhere!"

She stared at him. "Oh. So you decided the time was right for your bribe."

"Exactly. I knew you wouldn't be influenced by material things, but I hoped you'd eventually realize that a man doesn't present his woman with her dream house unless he cares very deeply."

"His woman?" Her voice was innocent.

"Of course." Devlin's eyes sparkled, "Since that very first night, we've belonged to each other."

"I'm glad you made that mutual. I'd hate to think I was just a possession."

Devlin surrounded her face with his large hands. "You are," he said very quietly, "my mind, my heart, and my soul. You're everything I ever wanted in a woman, everything I ever needed. With you beside me I feel . . . better than I am. I want nothing more than to spend the rest of my life with you."

Tara swallowed hard, her eyes filling with tears. "I love you, Devlin," she whispered.

He bent forward to kiss her tenderly. "I love you too, sweetheart," he murmured. "More than I'll ever be able to tell you."

"You're doing just fine," she said, hiccupping and laughing at the same time.

Devlin sat back, his hands sliding down to cup her throat warmly. "There's something I think I'd better confess," he murmured ruefully.

"What? More sneaky tricks?" she teased.

"No. At least, since it hasn't happened, it can't be called a trick." He sighed, then said baldly, "I hoped you'd get pregnant."

Tara's eyes widened, and she started to laugh in spite of herself. "You were going to trap me!"

Devlin smiled sheepishly. "Well, I wasn't counting on it, but I was hoping. I knew damn well you didn't want anything to interfere with your career, but—"

"My career," she murmured, interrupting him. "I've been

meaning to talk to you about that. I'm committed to do *Celebration!* but after that . . . well, I'm not too old to change careers."

"What would you rather do?" he asked in an unsteady voice.

"Be with you," she said softly. "Every minute of every day and night. I want to raise children and horses. I want to go to sleep in your arms and wake up in your arms."

His throat moved in an almost convulsive swallow. "Are you sure, honey? I don't want you to regret anything," he said huskily.

"Very sure. By the way, are we going to sit down here talking all night? I thought we had better things to do with our time."

Devlin rose immediately to his feet with heart-stopping ease, still holding her in his arms. "I thought you'd never ask," he told her, striding toward the stairs.

Tara had thought there could be no surprises in their lovemaking, that it couldn't get better. But that night she discovered how wrong she could be—how wonderfully wrong.

Even if Devlin had mentioned no word of love, Tara would still have felt the love in him that night. For the first time they did not hold back or try to hide their feelings. Murmuring words of love and pleasure, they lost themselves in a world of magic.

As Devlin's lips moved hungrily toward the hardened tip of one breast, Tara wondered dizzily if she'd ever get used to this pleasure. And then his mouth captured her nipple, and she forgot everything but the spiraling tension inside of her. She returned his caresses eagerly, her fingers searching out all the secret places of pleasure. His husky groan spurred her on, and she continued her exploration, desperate to know every inch of his strong body, frantic to imprint the uncompromisingly male form in her mind and heart for all time. Like the wildcat he'd once humorously compared her to, she became a primitive creature in his arms.

For a while Devlin encouraged her fierce attempts to dominate their passionate struggle in the ages-old confrontation between man and woman. Switching roles with the ease of a man comfortable with and certain of his own masculinity, he allowed her the role of master, rolling over on his back and leaving himself vulnerable to her.

Dimly aware that she could control their lovemaking only because he allowed her to, Tara concentrated a certain power of her own into taking his breath away. She rained kisses on his face and neck, her hands moving teasingly over the hair-roughened chest, the flat stomach, and beyond. Exulting in his hoarse groans, she nibbled passionately on his ears and sank her teeth gently into the tanned flesh of his shoulders.

Their eyes clashed as she lifted her head, and Tara saw the molten flame in his gaze, telling her of limits reached and games done. He pulled her completely down on him, his hands guiding her body to fit his own, claiming her with gentle insistence and driving need. He controlled their heated movements with powerful ease, tension building between them until they reached the trembling peak together in a moment like the slow shattering of glass. And then the room became quiet and still.

Devlin's eyes searched Tara's intently as he pulled her down into the crook of his arm. Reading the question there, she smiled contentedly and snuggled up to him. She'd been a little worried herself that the nervous child inside of her might have surfaced again in the aftermath of their lovemaking, but that hadn't happened. Apparently woman and child were really one now. Tara had never felt so happy.

Falling asleep in his arms, she woke abruptly, late the next morning, sitting bolt upright in bed, her eyes snapping open. Her dreams flooded into her mind, and automatically she gazed down at Devlin's sleeping figure, stirring restlessly now that the warmth of her body had left his side.

She turned her gaze back to the sunlit room and frowned as a faint wave of nausea passed quickly. Her eyes widened suddenly as certain symptoms of the last few weeks began to add up. She held up one hand and carefully counted on her fingers, then stared across the room, a silly grin on her face.

Well, for goodness' sake! A grown woman, and she hadn't even realized what had happened!

Half turning, she stared down at Devlin's sleeping face, allowing herself a few moments just to look at him. Then, very deliberately, she picked up her pillow and hit him with it—not very hard, but it certainly woke him up. Before he could open his eyes, Tara mustered all her acting talents and produced a very creditable frown. "I've been wanting to hit you for years," she announced, glaring into his puzzled expression, "and I've finally thought of a good reason to!"

Pushing the pillow away, Devlin raised himself on one elbow and stared at her. "What *are* you talking about, witch?" he demanded, smothering a yawn with one hand.

"You and your plots." She sniffed disdainfully.

He fell back on his pillow with a faint groan and closed his eyes. "My dear wife," he murmured, "I have had an exhausting night and was short on sleep to start with." He peered at her out of one eye. "I have to admit, though, that the sight of your delightfully bared assets is doing wonderful things to my energy level."

Tara glanced down to discover that the blankets had fallen to her waist. Frowning at him, she pulled them hastily back up. "Stop changing the subject!" she told him severely.

He opened the other eye. "The only subject I have on my mind right now is you. Your punishment for hitting me with that pillow is going to be very involved and will probably cost me the rest of my strength. Come here, you thorn in my flesh."

Tara evaded his seeking arms, keeping a death grip on the blankets. "No. I want to talk to you, and it isn't going to do you a bit of good to try to distract me." When he tugged at the blankets playfully, she tried to scoot away from him. "I mean it! You're not going to—*Devlin!*"

"I'm not going to what?" he asked with interest.

Flat on her back, Tara stared up at him. "That's not fair. You're bigger than I am!" she complained.

Devlin loomed over her, grinning cheerfully and neatly disposing of the blankets. "Something I intend to take shameless advantage of, darling," he told her softly, his fingers threading through her red curls. "I am an opportunist, after all."

"You certainly are," she managed breathlessly, trying to ignore the lips moving slowly down her throat. "Oh, lord—if this is the way you plan to end all our arguments, I'm licked before I start!"

He lifted his head, his silvery eyes grown dark and stormy. "Were we having an argument?" he murmured. "I can't seem to remember."

"I think we were going to," she replied weakly, and then muttered, "Oh, hell . . ." and pulled his mouth back down to hers.

The sun had climbed higher in the sky when Tara finally stirred again. Her husband's arms drew her even closer, and she smiled faintly. "You always get what you want, don't you, Devlin Bradley?" she asked in a wry tone.

"Always," he agreed complacently. "Some things just take longer, that's all. But I'm a patient man."

"Shameless. You are absolutely shameless." She rolled over, resting her chin on the hands folded atop his chest. "Between your plotting and the infamous Bradley luck, you had things pretty well sewn up, didn't you?"

He ran a gentle finger down her nose. "You gave me a few uncertain moments," he said dryly. "I was determined to win, though."

"Well, I hope you knew what you wanted," she told him calmly, "because you got it all."

Devlin stared at her. "I get the feeling," he commented, "that you're leading up to something."

"I always knew you were smart."

He reached down to swat her lightly. "Stop being sassy and tell me the reason for that very unnerving gleam in your eyes!"

Tara laughed delightedly. "Is it unnerving? Wonderful! I'd hate to think you were utterly sure of yourself."

"Tara, my love," he said carefully, "if you don't tell me what's on that maddening mind—" He broke off abruptly and frowned. "Why did you hit me with that pillow, anyway?"

She gave him a serene smile. "Because it suddenly occurred to me that all your plotting and scheming couldn't have worked out better—for you—if the whole thing had been a chess game with me as the pawn." Tracing a finger over his chin, she went on conversationally, "You remember that scene in *Celebration!* where Maggie sings your song?"

He nodded. "I remember."

Tara's smile widened. "Well, if you'll remember, Maggie is pregnant in that scene. We'll have to film that scene first . . . and I won't need a pillow."

Devlin went very still, his darkened eyes searching her face. "Tara?" he breathed questioningly.

No longer able to contain the happiness bubbling up inside her, she pulled herself forward to kiss him. "I think you said you wanted a girl," she murmured huskily. "And wanted to name her something Irish."

"Something Irish," he repeated, dazed. "Tara, honey, are you sure? And—you don't regret it's happening so soon?"

"As sure as I can be without going to a doctor. And I'm not the least bit sorry. Are you?"

"My God, don't even ask!" he rasped huskily, drawing her even closer. "It's what I've wanted all along—you and our children. I love you, sweetheart . . ."

"My darling Devlin . . ."

Quite a while later Tara finally roused herself enough to murmur, "Um . . . there's something I'd better tell you. I don't have any living relations, but, well . . . both my parents were twins. And you know what they say about twins skipping a generation."

"You mean—?"

"I mean it's something to think about." She cuddled closer to him. "With the Bradley luck sitting in your corner . . . and you said you wanted at least four kids . . . don't you think we'd better consider enlarging the nursery, just in case?"